Praise for Louise Phillips

'A gripping suspenseful story peopled with well-drawn characters'
Irish Independent

'Chilling, mesmerising. Gets under your skin and stays with you'
Niamh O'Connor

'A real page-turner ... [*The Doll's House*] is laced with tension
and gradually builds to a thrilling finale'
Irish Post

'Fans of Sophie Hannah and SJ Watson will devour *The Doll's House*'
writing.ie

'If you enjoy the psychological thrillers of writers in
the same vein as Sophie Hannah, Erin Kelly, et al,
The Doll's House sits very comfortably'
Raven Crime Reads

'A cracker of a novel, highly recommended, a phenomenal debut'
Arlene Hunt

'*Red Ribbons* is an absolutely brilliant book ... spine-tingling with
loads of twists and turns. A debut novel from a great writer who will
soon be up there with the likes of Patricia Cornwell'
Stafford FM

'Dark, spooky, but believable'
Irish Examiner

'*Red Ribbons* has been getting rave reviews, especially for the insight
it offers into the emotions of a mother who has lost her child'
Irish *Mail on Sunday*

'The pace of this book is spot on, revealing information from the
killer's past bit by bit to keep the reader turning the pages'
Novelicious

Born in Dublin, Louise Phillips returned to writing in 2006, after raising her family. That year, she was selected by Dermot Bolger as an emerging talent in the county. Louise's work has been published as part of many anthologies, including *County Lines* from New Island, and various literary journals. In 2009, she won the Jonathan Swift Award for her short story *Last Kiss*, and in 2011 she was a winner in the Irish Writers' Centre Lonely Voice platform. She has also been short-listed for the Molly Keane Memorial Award, Bridport UK, and long-listed twice for the RTÉ Guide/Penguin Short Story Competition.

In 2012, she was awarded an Arts Bursary for Literature from South Dublin County Council. Her debut novel, *Red Ribbons*, was shortlisted for a BGE Irish Book Award (2012). *The Doll's House* is Louise's second book and won the Crime Fiction Book of the Year award at the 2013 BGE Irish Book Awards.

Also by Louise Phillips
Red Ribbons

www.louise-phillips.com
@LouiseMPhillips
www.facebook.com/LouisePhillips

LOUISE PHILLIPS
THE DOLL'S HOUSE

HACHETTE
BOOKS
IRELAND

First published in Ireland in 2013 by HACHETTE BOOKS IRELAND
First published in paperback in 2014

Cataloguing in Publication Data is available from the British Library.

ISBN 978 1444 743 067

Typeset in AGaramond and Bodoni by Bookends Publishing Services.
Printed and bound in Great Britain by Clays Ltd, St Ives.

Hachette Books Ireland policy is to use papers that are natural, renewable
and recyclable products and made from wood grown in sustainable forests.
The logging and manufacturing processes are expected to conform to the
environmental regulations of the country of origin.

Hachette Books Ireland
8 Castlecourt Centre, Castleknock, Dublin 15, Ireland

A division of Hachette UK Ltd
338 Euston Road, London NW1 3BH

www.hachette.ie

For Jennifer, Lorraine and Graham

The tide is coming in; familiar sights and sounds seem strange to me. My seven-year-old legs wobble, feet sinking into the sand, seaweed between my toes. In my arms I hold a doll, with curly blonde hair and sea-blue eyes. It is neither night nor day; the light is white, sparse, as if, like memory, it can be whisked away. A cold breeze batters my face, exploding into my ears. Against the sea and the sky he stands, trouser legs rolled up, chalk-white skin. He is smiling at me, the centre of my canvas. I wonder about his voice. I try to hear him, even a whisper, but I hear nothing. I scream, the wind cutting out the sound, swallowing my sobs. I'm not alone. Someone stands beside me. The man with the smiling face turns away, looking into the ocean. He has his back to me as the ice-cold water eats his feet. The further he walks away, the smaller he becomes, just like a figure from my doll's house.

Ocean House, the Quays, Dublin

Kate scanned the crime-scene photographs for the umpteenth time. The bruised body of Rachel Mooney lost none of its horror the more she studied them. Her jaw had been smashed, her nose broken in two places, and she'd lost both front teeth. All of her injuries were imprints of her attacker's rage. It was a miracle that she had survived. Anger in rape wasn't unusual, some men having developed a hatred of women, or a type of woman, which made their victims little more than targets for their pent-up aggression. But in Rachel Mooney's case, the more Kate connected the pieces, the more her concentration shifted from the level of violence and assault to the demonstration of power her attacker had shown his victim.

The DNA evidence taken had matched two similar offences in Dublin, but still the police hadn't a suspect. The earlier victims had been attacked outdoors. Rachel Mooney had been attacked inside her home. As a criminal psychologist, Kate knew that every change in pattern meant something, whether it was based on an escalating desire in the attacker, a willingness to take greater risks or simple opportunity. She also knew that the significance of the victim to the offender took on a different perspective when dealing with sexual assaults. Sexual gratification wasn't always the primary motivation. It was more complicated than that. Rachel's attacker wanted to demonstrate his power through control and violence. The sexual act was merely an extension of this need, his victim becoming little more than the facilitator.

The three women had similar profiles: all had been successful career professionals enjoying what seemed happy lives. Unlike the previous two victims, Rachel Mooney had been married. In Rachel's case, the offender had certainly had opportunity: Rachel had left the front door of her house open while her two children played in the garden. However, both children had been inside when the attack had taken place. The attacker had pulled Rachel's blouse over her face, wrapped a tie tightly around her eyes, then secured her hands behind her back. When he had instructed her to walk upstairs, she had done so without fuss, not wanting to scare her children in the downstairs living room, unaware of her plight.

The similarity in victim profile meant that none of the women had been chosen at random. His level of control prior to the violent attacks, and subsequent sexual assaults, conveyed that power was paramount to him. But with Rachel, the attacker had moved on. He had invaded her home. It was too early to tell whether this had been opportunistic or was connected to Rachel being the first married victim.

Since she had worked with DI O'Connor on the Devine and Spain murders, Kate had become more involved with the Dublin police force in profiling offenders. The perpetrator in this crime hadn't arrived overnight: he'd offended before, including physical assault, breaking and entering. This was a well-travelled path for him. If he wasn't on the Irish PULSE database, he would come up somewhere else.

Locking the photographs of Rachel Mooney in her desk, Kate checked the time on the wall clock. Ten minutes to two. Her appointment with Imogen Willis was for two o'clock.

Although police investigations took up more and more of her time, Kate's work was still primarily based in Ocean House, working within the Counselling and Reintegration Programme. Over the last few months, through weekly counselling sessions, she had developed a strong relationship with Imogen, a teenager who very much needed her help and with whom Kate had every intention of following through on.

Harcourt Street Police Station

Officially, O'Connor's dark shadows and baggy eyes would be put down to the previous months of operating nights. They say working outside the daily routine of other fellow mortals alienates you from reality. That wasn't so with O'Connor. To him, doing the ghost shift had brought him far too close to reality: his own.

Harcourt Street station was the hub of the Dublin police force, but to O'Connor it felt like a bigger version of the suburban Rathfarnham station where he had worked for the previous six years. In other ways, Harcourt Street was a whole different ballgame. It got you closer to the stench of the city, the bigger players and the lowlife who performed their menial tasks. Most of the bums were barely out of nappies, destined for two things: crime and a very short life.

Unofficially, a couple of people close to O'Connor had taken him aside, told him to go easy on the sauce and the late nights. Most had put his recent heavy drinking down as par for the course. You had to let the job seep out of your skin somehow, and booze was legal.

He cursed to hell when he pulled the empty box of painkillers from the bottom drawer of his desk. If he didn't get rid of his thumping headache, he'd be no use to anyone. Grabbing his heavy woollen coat off the stand, he barely grunted to his colleague, Mark Lynch, as he marched out of the door, heading to the corner shop for paracetamol and juice.

Outside, he felt a little less pressured. If he got the head on him sorted, he'd be fine. No one would be any the wiser, except himself, of course. He waited until he was outside the newsagent's to pop three tablets into his mouth, swallowing them with a full carton of orange juice. The morning painkillers hadn't worked, and it would take another while before these had a chance to do their bit. It was nearly twelve hours since he'd emptied the last of the whiskey bottle, but this time the painkillers should take effect. Once they had, he'd be grand, at least until the end of the shift when the same demons that had fucked up his head in the first place would pay another night call.

Ocean House, the Quays

Kate smiled as Imogen sat down in front of her. Over the previous few months Kate had learned to let Imogen initiate the proceedings. The teenager had tried to starve herself to death. At least, that was the way everyone viewed it, including her own family.

Severe cases of anorexia nervosa were not uncommon, and since Kate had begun working at Ocean House, it was a condition she had become all too familiar with. In Imogen's case, Kate was convinced that the girl's severe and progressive self-harming was connected to some earlier trauma.

Imogen was a cutter too, a condition she had managed to conceal for a long time. That was the thing about cutters: they became expert at hiding the very thing their subconscious mind was doing its best to get noticed. She was an observant girl. Kate had figured that out during their early sessions: her noticing the slightest change Kate made either to herself or the environment.

The previous week Imogen had been completely withdrawn, closed down. But, as with other patients, the intricacies of her mind were complex. At any moment everything could change.

At seventeen, Imogen looked tiny in her pale pink hoody and faded jeans, the heavy sweat top giving her eighty-six-pound body extra bulk – an improvement of ten pounds on her weight after her discharge from hospital. A few months earlier, her heart had nearly stopped, no longer able to pump blood efficiently: her body had turned to her internal organs for its protein needs.

'You seem in good spirits today, Imogen.'

'Do I?'

'Yes, you do.' Kate smiled again.

Instead of improving Imogen's form, Kate's compliment did the opposite, as if she'd been caught out in being happy. Kate let the moment pass, keeping her eyes firmly locked on the girl. Imogen's eyes had made an irrevocable first impression on her. They held a story: one which Kate believed was her job to unravel.

Imogen had enormous memory gaps. She was unable to remember the names of any of her teachers in National School. She had no recollection of making her first Holy Communion, other than how she had looked in an old photograph. She found it difficult to piece together a cognitive stream of events from childhood, apart from the day her grandmother had died when she was six years old. Unlike her other childhood memories, Imogen could take Kate step by step through the events that had happened, not only on the day of her grandmother's death but on the days that had followed, from her mother's initial screams at finding her dead, to the gleam from the brass handles of the coffin being lowered into the ground.

Imogen's keen observation skills, coupled with the memory gaps, pointed Kate in one direction: disassociation. Opting out of certain times in your life, especially at critical moments, is not uncommon. It is a basic human technique we're all equipped with, especially for those events when emotion may get in the way of survival. In Imogen's case, her inability to remember the commonest details, even from a relatively short time back, illustrated that her disassociation was more than a one-off reaction to a particular event. It had progressed, and done so for the most part without Imogen being consciously aware of it.

Kate watched Imogen tuck her hair behind her ears, closing her lips tightly. She waited, sensing that today the girl had something to say.

Imogen sat upright. 'That thing you were telling me about last week, about how the mind doesn't always store things in straight lines.'

'In fragments, you mean?'

'Yeah, that.' Again Imogen fiddled with her hair. 'You said the bits get divided up, then can be put together differently from how they might have happened.'

'That's right, Imogen – it's something we all do. Our minds don't operate in an unbroken line of consciousness, rather a stream of discontinuous fragments. It can make recalling certain events tricky, which is why memory can't always be relied on.'

'I remembered something. It mightn't mean anything.'

'Tell me anyway.'

'I could have imagined it.'

'Go on, Imogen. It's good to talk these things out.'

'I'm not sure. But once I thought about it, I couldn't get it out of my mind.'

'Thought about what?'

'A smell.'

'What kind of smell?'

'Of a wet dog.'

'A wet dog?' Kate was intrigued.

'We used to have a dog when I was younger. I don't remember him, but my sister, Jilly, she does. His name was Busker, a Jack Russell. Jilly says he was snappy. You know, kind of aggressive when he got excited.'

'And you remember his smell.'

'I don't know if it was his smell, but last week at my friend Alicia's house, her dog came in from the rain. He came over to me, licking my hand like, and that's when I got it – the stench.'

Imogen turned away, looking out of the only window in Kate's office, as if the October sun held answers to this confusing chink in memory. 'It was so strong. It wasn't only the smell of the wet dog. It was more than that.'

'What else?'

'I thought I remembered Busker. I remembered noises too – doors slamming – and then I must have leaned in closer, because in the memory, the smell became stronger. I could feel Busker's heart when I put my hands on his body. It was jerking in and out really fast. It was then I realised I'd never remembered him before. Do you think I imagined it, Kate?'

'I'm not sure. You could have – but the recall, the feeling, it seems important to you.'

'Yeah. Like it shouldn't have meant anything at all when Alicia's dog licked me, but it felt familiar somehow. Then it was gone, without me knowing why.'

'That's not unusual.'

'Isn't it?'

'Not really. As we discussed, the mind often cuts things up, hides them. As one part of your brain is opening a memory, another part could be shutting it down.'

'So you think it's important?'

'What else did you remember?'

'Right then, nothing. It was like I'd caught hold of something, only for it to go away again. Later, when I got home, I went to my room. I tried to push myself, to think really hard about it. It felt like an opening.'

'Go on.'

'I thought if I tried hard enough, more would come back – but I drew a blank. Then I felt exhausted again, as if I needed sleep. I went to bed. At four o'clock in the afternoon, I curled up under the covers and slept.'

Kate believed Imogen's intermittent bouts of exhaustion were another side effect of her condition, but she continued to encourage her. 'And then what? How did you feel when you woke up?'

'I couldn't remember my dream, but the dog, the one with his heart thumping inside his chest, the one I thought was Busker – I remembered something else.'

Kate waited.

'His breathing stopped. I rubbed his coat, and there was that smell again, but he didn't move.'

'Did you ask your sister, or your parents, about what had happened?'

'Not straight away – I wanted to get my thoughts right – but, yeah, I did.'

'And what did they say?'

'They said it couldn't have happened that way because I was at school when Busker was knocked down.'

'But you felt sure that you'd been there when he died?'

'Completely, and that was the thing. It wasn't a happy memory, I knew that, but it felt real. As I said, I stayed in my bedroom for ages, getting more bits, feelings, smells, dragging pieces from my mind, until I felt sure I had it right.'

'So what happened then?'

Kate saw tears in Imogen's eyes.

'When Mum and Jilly told me it wasn't true, that I must have imagined it, I felt awful.'

'Because you thought the memory was wrong.'

'No, that wasn't it.'

'What was it, then?'

'The worst bit wasn't thinking I'd got the memory mixed up. The worst bit, Kate, was that I didn't believe either of them.'

Clodagh

My mother was always fond of a good Merlot. She had very specific tastes. She would have liked Hubert's, our swanky restaurant for this evening's dinner, recommended by Valerie's tennis-club friends. My sister-in-law has 'in-the-know' social connections. The candles on each of the small tables remind me of Mum too – attractive on the outside, but capable of inflicting pain if you got too close. We're all trying hard to act normal, except for Martin. He likes to act the arsehole. He has a degree in it.

Our attentive waiter with his tight black hair and Mediterranean skin stands back from our table of four, waiting for Martin to taste the wine. My charming husband winks at me before lifting the glass, as if we're a pair, and the two of us are in some kind of secret game together. Val, always quick to pick up on things, gives Dominic a fleeting glance, a code to my brother that this could blow up at any moment.

'Beautiful restaurant,' Val says to no one in particular.

Martin tilts the glass, and the blood-red wine stops halfway up. His sharp, narrow nose reminds me of an overzealous badger as he sniffs the aroma, his eyes closed for an irritatingly long time. The waiter, like Val, Dominic and I, waits for Martin to give his approval.

Lifting his head back, he swirls the wine inside his mouth, then swallows it, before looking at me again. No wink this time.

Dominic is the next to break the ice, another alcoholic connection. They're bloody everywhere. 'Well, Martin,' my brother raises his eyebrows, 'what do you think?' He's hoping his facial expression will speed things up.

'Fine. Perfect, actually.' Martin barely turns to the waiter as he says, 'Ladies first,' gesturing to Val. She smiles in that polite, stiff way.

I already know my glass is the next target. 'Bastard,' I mutter, below my breath. They all pretend not to hear me, including the young waiter who catches my eye. I can see he's balancing Martin's instruction against my obvious hostility. It's not the waiter's fault. I give him a reassuring look, covering the top of my glass with my hand, saying, 'Not for me, thanks.'

Martin smiles again. He's enjoying himself now. 'Let me,' he says, reaching for the water jug at the centre of the table. The ice cubes tumble into my glass. I look away.

With everyone's glass full, Martin lifts his towards Dominic. 'To Lavinia,' he says. Val shifts awkwardly in her chair, raising her glass alongside my brother's. Our four glasses clink above the flickering candlelight.

'Cheers to Lavinia,' I say, with more than a hint of sarcasm. They all look at me.

'"Cheers" is hardly appropriate, darling.' Martin's voice is smooth and patronising.

'I don't see why the hell not. No point in being miserable.' Inside I'm thinking, I don't feel like his darling or anyone else's for that matter.

Dominic gives me the dagger eyes. Then, to Martin, he says, 'Let it go.' This is new for Dominic, the role of peacemaker. There was a time when he would have given Martin a dig just for the hell of it.

'I don't see why you're taking his side.' I can hear the hurt in my voice, even if the others don't.

'Christ, can't we have a civilised meal out without picking on one another ...' Val gulps some more wine '... even for Lavinia's sake?'

She wasn't your mother, I want to say. You can't know. But instead I let it go.

'It's not about taking sides, Clodagh. There's been enough crap, that's all.' My brother eases the conversation.

'Your sister's bloody-minded, Dominic. She likes to stir things up.' Martin's tone is measured, like he's some kind of expert. 'She was the same when she was younger, just like Ruby is now.'

'Leave Ruby out of this, Martin,' I snap, but I know he's on a roll.

He directs his next comment at Val. 'You and Dominic are so lucky not having any children.'

Once, I would have kicked my husband for saying something like that. But what's the point? They both know what he's like.

Val shifts in her chair again. Martin takes the silence as an invitation. 'There was a time when our daughter looked up to her parents. Not any more.'

'Ruby's fine,' I say. 'She's like any other teenager.' They're all probably thinking she's like me at that age, only perhaps not quite so bad. But then again, I know only the half of it.

'Ask a teenager now while they still know everything. That's what they say, isn't it, darling?' Martin laughs.

I wish he'd quit the 'darling' crap. We all know each other too well for that. 'I'm not sure, *darling*. You seem to be the expert here.'

Martin smirks. 'Clodagh was the same, wasn't she, Dominic? Always headstrong.'

'We were all headstrong, Martin. It comes from being young and foolish.' My brother isn't ready to give Martin free rein.

Val smiles at the waiter as he delivers our starters, maintaining a civilised overture to our family meal out. That is, until the young man is out of earshot. 'Don't start bringing up the good-old bad-old days. Lavinia's death is still raw. And I'm sure Ruby misses her as much as we all do.'

'You're right, Val.' Martin's speaking again like he's the one in charge. 'Considering everything Ruby's been through, a little rebellion is understandable.'

That last dig is meant for me. Throw the guilt at the alcoholic mother. I swallow some water. 'Four months today,' I say, swirling the ice cubes in the glass. There's that sarcastic tone again.

Martin ignores me. 'How are things at work, Dominic?'

'Busy.'

Val moves uncomfortably in her chair. 'He's pushing himself too hard.'

'Life has to get back to normal, Val.' Martin sticks a fork into his wild mushroom starter. 'Lavinia would want Dominic to fire himself into things.'

I could almost scream at Martin. Ever since Mum's death, he's talked about her as if they were close, when neither of them could stand the other. 'Let's change the subject, shall we?' Suddenly I feel weary.

Martin fills Val's glass this time. As an alcoholic, I notice every movement involving booze. How much everyone is drinking, how much wine is left in the bottle. I stare at the candles, remembering how Mum used to light them in the evening. Not when we were small, but later, when Dominic and I had moved out. Four months since her death. It feels like a lifetime. Four months since that awful row between Dominic and me.

'There's no point in walking on eggshells,' says Martin. 'Death will happen to us all.'

'I need some air,' says Val, 'and a cigarette.' She stands up. The waiter hands her her coat with the fur-lined collar. She looks like an escapee rushing out.

It's just the three of us at the table now, Dominic looking after Val as if she's abandoned him. And, for the first time since we arrived, I realise my brother looks like a man who could do with a good night's sleep. 'Dominic, are you okay?' I ask, not allowing Martin to dominate the conversation.

'Sure,' he says. 'Why wouldn't I be?'

'Sisterly love, what?' That stupid grin is back on Martin's face, and I wonder if any of us has moved on one iota from where we left off as children.

Neary's Pub, Mount Street

Neary's had one of those throwback-to-the-olden-days front bars with framed images of men carrying Guinness barrels on their backs, and toucans with protruding yellow beaks, each object, picture or oddity giving punters the sense of stepping back into another time. A large mahogany mirror stretched the full length of the black wooden counter, multiplying the crowd, creating the impression that everyone was somehow at the centre of something exciting.

By the time Stevie McDaid arrived, the buzz had already started rising, and the only thing missing was a lighted match to ignite the mix of alcohol and bodies moving closer together. He made his way past the front bar, the throng of regulars looking disgruntled that their hideaway was being taken over on a Friday night – the nightclub at the back was getting into full swing.

Pushing open the double doors into the club, Stevie could hear the music of the Black Eyed Peas, bellowing, and, like the old pro he was, he moved instinctively to the beat as he walked in past the two oversized bouncers. To his left, a group of yummy mummies he had chatted up the previous week waved at him. Proper eager for it, they were. But Stevie was already getting off on the buzz of someone new or exciting coming along.

There were mirrors everywhere, behind the bar, over the bar, on large pillars dividing the dance floor. Large glass chandeliers hung low, glistening in the changing waves of light – blue, red, purple, and an electric mix of black and gold. He spotted a pair of lovebirds stuck into one another at the back wall, the guy's hand on the girl's breast.

Not yet midnight, and the vibe was already pumping through the roof. Neary's was the kind of place where you left your hang-ups and crappy life behind you at the door. It was all about the beat, a rapid shift of mood from bloody boring to full-on pulsing escapism. The nightclub, like the front bar, kept you always wanting more, with its mix of locals, wannabes and newbies, all smiling at one another, like prisoners who'd been granted a few hours out of jail.

Stevie wasn't the kind to hang his baggage at the door, but he'd learned enough over the years to keep it to himself, unless things dictated otherwise. 'Leave the women guessing' was his motto. Different strokes for different folks. Most of them only wanted a bit of proper attention. If Neary's had given out Oscars for insincerity, Stevie would have smiled himself to the front of the line. Not long back, the place would have been packed with cleaned-up construction workers and their fat pockets on a Friday night. Not now. That day was long gone. Still, there were a few survivors huddled at the bar, watching the girls dancing from the mirror angled above them, holding their pints in one hand and ambition in the other. The numbers of well-dressed guys had shrunk too, hanging out somewhere in Negative Equity Land. But Neary's had an appeal that swelled, despite the changes in who had what money in their pockets. Even in a recession, people needed escape.

Mick and Jason behind the bar, wearing black shirts and pants, were good-looking guys, but not so pretty that they couldn't drift into the background. Mick gave Stevie a wave, and once he'd received the nod, he pulled Stevie's pint as another track started up – faster, darker, feeling infinitely more dangerous. Stevie never sat down in Neary's, not at the bar, not anywhere. Sitting was for the settled, and Stevie made a point of never being settled. He might be in his early forties, but he'd no intention of looking or acting it.

Below one of the high glass tables he spotted long, smooth, tanned legs with silver stiletto sandals. Stevie had a personal fondness for ankles. Good legs and ankles made a woman. It didn't take his eyes long to travel up to where the hemline of her skirt offered better prospects. He could hear the giggles from some young girls behind him. Stevie had taken them in too, even before he'd placed his order with Mick. Big wavy hair, barely out of their school uniforms, with their pink and purple mobiles, blackened eyes and skinny bodies with big boobs. More hormones than sense, just the way he liked them. He smirked when he thought about young Ruby. They had yet to get fully acquainted, but he had a feeling their time would come soon enough.

Some guys with money were already hovering around them, exchanging looks with each other, perfect smiles at the ready. But they had competition tonight, young testosterone bods – college boys, no doubt with rich parents filling their pockets.

Stevie could never get enough of the place, the music bouncing, flashing lights, loud conversations, laughter, clinks of glasses, some eejit or another shouting or thinking he was the next big thing. Everyone in Neary's wanted something, and once inside, the gravitational pull of the earth wouldn't take you the hell out of it. Just as Stevie was thinking about the giggling skirts behind him, figuring they might have to wait for another night on account of Silver Stilettoes, he heard his name called.

'Hiya, Stevie, my man.'

'Ah, hiya, how's it going?' Stevie had no intention of sticking around for the answer from the fool. He simply smiled, turning as if he was looking to meet someone else.

The guy was one of those eejits who came into the garage: mouth, money and all too fuckin' clean and pretty for Stevie's liking. Not one of them understood anything about cars, except how glossy and cool the latest models looked. Stevie had no problem dealing with those suckers in work. They were easy fodder, easily screwed. But here, in his domain, the association wasn't to be encouraged. He had done the guy out of a fortune last week, told him the suspension was gone in his car. Set the rich eejit back a right packet. It had been like putting a duck into water.

'Jesus, Stevie, can you not do better than that?' he'd asked.

'Like what?'

'Christ, I thought you were a pal.'

'Ah, sure there's only so much I can do – it's the boss who sets the prices, the one who's never here.'

'Exactly, Stevie, so surely we can sort something out.'

'It'll mean jigging the paperwork – you'll have to fix me up direct, cash only, no cheques or any jumpy credit cards.'

'Sure, Stevie, you know there's never a problem there.'

As Stevie had walked away from him, he'd muttered, 'Wanker,' below his breath, then turned back. 'Don't forget to mention me to your mates,' he'd said, his perfect smile pasted all over his lovely face.

'As always, Stevie, my friend.'

Tonight wasn't for eejits. Tonight was a million miles away from work, and even further away from the fuck-up of a week he'd just had. When Stevie looked back at Silver Stilettoes, she'd been joined by her mates, none as classy as her. No point heading over yet. Best to give them time to settle. Nothing like a few drinks to loosen things up. He'd downed his first pint and it was time for another. He'd been gagging all day for a few scoops and the first couple of drinks were always special, the taste hitting his mouth like old friends getting back together.

He spotted Joe and Kev at the far end of the bar and waved to them, all the while keeping his eyes on his mark in the stilettoes. He liked how she crossed her legs, how, when she bent forward, he could see her breasts and the outline of a black bra, the imprint of her red lipstick on the glass. Her expression, too, was a pull. Confident – you don't look that hot without bleeding knowing it, he thought. She wasn't cheap either. Apart from the shocking red lipstick and high heels, she had the makings of so much more, and no doubt proper good at it. Her long black hair was tied sideways off her neck, falling down in soft curls, touching her bare shoulders. She was putting it out there all right, with just enough class to say, 'Only if you dare, mate, only if you dare.'

'What does a guy have to do to buy a girl like you a drink?'

Although there were five of them, each girl knew who Green Eyes was talking to. Stevie gave them one of his captivating smiles, the kind that said he was the guy all of them wanted to fuck.

'Just ask – vodka and Coke, no ice.'

'Gen.' A warning shot from one of her female fan club.

'He's just being friendly, aren't you?'

'Steve, Steve McDaid, or Stevie to my friends.'

'Thanks, Steve … Stevie.'

'Cool.' Stevie was pleased she planned on being a no-nonsense type from the start. And with that, he shouted over to Mick, 'Vodka and Coke, no ice, and another pint … Are you girls sticking around for long?'

'We'll be here for a while,' said the oldest and ugliest one, giving Stevie the I-fucking-hate-blokes-like-you look. The ugly girls always had the biggest mouths, a sort of compensation for lack of other qualities.

Stevie placed the vodka and Coke on the table with a fresh beer mat. Women loved attention to detail. 'For you, Princess. I didn't catch your name.'

'Gen, as in Genevieve.' Her body moved a little as she lifted the glass.

'The naked beauty.'

'That's me.' She laughed, even though she'd probably heard the same line a thousand times before.

Stevie laughed too. 'Catch you later, Gen.' He smiled with his pearly whites again. There was no point in having a major asset if you didn't use it. Holy crap, he thought. Sometimes it was so fucking easy.

Pint number three was slower. Why mess up the night when it was proving promising? As Joe and Kev ranted on about the usual suspects, soccer, cars, and women, Stevie kept a watchful eye on Gen, sending the odd nod, letting her know he wasn't forgetting about her.

Timing was everything. Let her get a few more vodkas into her, ease out some of the rough edges. Soon enough the girlie groups always disintegrated. Give it another hour and they'd divide, turning outwards instead of in. It was just a question of waiting.

∞

The arsehole from the garage and his slick cronies were well gone by the time the night hit fever pitch. And as Stevie decided he'd had about enough of Kev talking about his failed marriage, and Joe acting like he was Ireland's answer to Dr Phil, it became time for a change of company. Looking back at the table behind him, he was full sure Silver Stilettoes would still be waiting for him. But Mick was already picking up their glasses from the table. Maybe they'd gone to the jacks. Fucking hell, why do women always go to the toilet in groups? Clearing the table wasn't a good sign. He shouldn't have listened to Kev for so long. Fuck, fuck, fuck and fuck again, he thought.

When he heard a girl laugh behind him, he turned expecting to see Gen. Instead he saw one of the young ones separated from her pals. She was small, fake tan, orange hands, and straightened long brown hair. Her pretty face said underage for sure. A prick of a suit was mauling her. Stevie could tell she was pissed. Asking for it, she was. The gang of guys hovering around her all looked married, each of them smirking, egging on their pals. She was out of her depth and the guys knew it.

Stevie wasn't long in making up his mind. Better him than those arseholes. He overheard one say, 'Be nice to little Susie now,' laughing as the mauler stuck his tongue so far down her throat that Stevie wondered if it would ever come back out. With no sign of Gen, Stevie hung back and waited. Soon little Susie was holding up a wall on the way back from the toilets.

'Come on, Susie,' he whispered. 'Time to go home.' It was like picking candy from an opened bag.

Mervin Road

It had been a long week. Kate was already regretting staying up late. There would be an early start in the morning, with Charlie, her five-year-old son, who was now asleep in his bedroom, wearing his new Power Ranger T-shirt. The one sent over by his dad in Birmingham. In some ways Kate was relieved Declan was still working away from home. She had thought she would miss him more than she did. Four weeks of his three-month stint setting up a company division in Birmingham had already gone by, and from a distance there had been less opportunity for them to snipe at one another – when he was at home, they bickered constantly. The only one missing Declan was Charlie. He had started to wet the bed again, and none of Kate's efforts to help him feel more secure had made a blind bit of difference. Tomorrow he was due to spend time with his friend, Shane. Perhaps that would take his mind off his dad.

Kate was still thinking about her earlier conversation with Imogen Willis. Imogen found it hard to trust people. Recalling what she thought had happened to the family dog had unearthed far more than the perceived memory. It had highlighted some of the reasons for her current distress. If Kate was correct, and Imogen had previously disassociated from events because of trauma, she was a girl who could no longer trust her memory, or people in her life, even those closest to her. Whenever others contradicted her fragmented recalls, they became untrustworthy. In essence, she was being forced to decide whom to trust, herself or them, and instinct told her everyone else was lying.

Switching off the lamps in the living room, Kate thought how lonely Imogen must feel to be somewhere that trust was no longer an option, where her mind kept contradicting the truth. But what if the information Imogen remembered had been correct? Even people with prolonged patterns of disassociation could recall factual events a long time afterwards. There had been only one family session with Imogen's closest relatives, her mother, father, and sister. Perhaps it was time for Kate to set up another.

Witnessing Imogen's vulnerability today had brought up Kate's own memories. She had thought again about the murdered schoolgirls, Caroline Devine and Amelia Spain, the last investigation in which she had teamed up with DI O'Connor. Her years spent in the UK working in criminal psychology had taught her a great deal about the way the mind functioned, and the many different directions it could operate from. She had not expected the double murder to prompt her own childhood memories to surface, but it had, and in so doing, it had complicated the investigation, bringing things far too close to home. Kate was determined that wouldn't happen again.

Off Mount Street

In the alleyway, the only sound Stevie heard was that of his breathing as he thrust himself forward, shoving himself further inside young Susie. She was completely out of it. He pulled her legs apart, holding her up against the wall. The girl's head sagged, flopping forward as if her neck was partially severed, like a rag doll. She was tiny, light. With his jeans and boxers halfway down his legs, he jerked forward again. Minor moans from Susie, begging him to stop, were a waste of time. He yanked her head back against the wall, grabbing her hair, her eyes bulging from their sockets. She gave him that look – stretched eyes, strained as if they might somehow push him away. He had seen it before. The look of fear, the look telling him that whatever control they'd thought they had was well gone. He shouted, 'Fuck,' into her ear as he came off inside her.

Afterwards, the alley was quiet. Like a television set with the sound turned down. Straightening his clothes, Stevie noticed the empty beer cans and cigarette butts around his feet. Urine stains of some other fucker's piss drained in tiny streams down the wall. Stevie used the girl's skirt to wipe himself. He thought he saw tears. It was time to get out of there. Susie was a crumpled mess, motionless and silent, her heavy black mascara and eyeliner trailing down her cheeks. The light from the streetlamp at the top of the alley stretched out, like a giant tongue. He caught a glimpse of someone in the shadows, a guy lighting a cigarette, his puffs of smoke billowing sideways, before he turned away again, minding his own business.

'Fix yourself. Come on, will ya?' was all Stevie said to the girl.

He thought about tossing little Susie out onto the main road, excess baggage and all that, but fuck it, she was only young. Once in the mayhem of the busy streets, with other drunks filling the pavements, there were as many taxis as there were eejits. It was easy to shove Susie into one. No doubt tomorrow morning everything would be a blur to her. If not, then maybe she'd pick up a dose of the morning-after pill. He didn't give a fuck either way.

Stevie could have gone back to Neary's. The bouncers would have let him in. But right then he was glad of the long walk back to his flat, giving his head time to clear. He could hear the waves bashing onto the shoreline along Sandymount strand. The road was empty except for him and one other important night-walker.

He would have recognised Clodagh Hamilton anywhere. Stevie had seen her before, but had kept his distance. Tonight he did so again. In Dublin, familiar faces had a habit of reappearing, especially when their owners lived in close proximity to one another.

She had felt like a ghost from his past, with her wild ginger hair. Tonight, her hair was partly tucked beneath her coat collar. As she sheltered herself from the chill, the full moon of a clear sky looked down on the two of them, hovering like a large white ball.

The Grand Canal

It's just me and him now in our own personal cocoon, two lone men. And somehow I can't shake the notion that I always knew this moment would come. A glimpse of destiny set in the darkness of your mind, taking hold long before you quantify its existence. He was always a slimy bastard, deep down or any other way you'd think about him. A leopard can't change its spots, or can't be bothered. I'll leave that judgement to others. I made up my own mind a long time ago. There are some things you know in the gut from the very beginning. It wasn't only that false smile of his, plastered across his face, like a George Clooney lookalike, or his inclination to talk too much. It was more the way he managed to win people over, those who should have known better, and those without the wherewithal to see past the veneer. Until, that is, they became one of the unlucky ones, and saw him for the mother-fucker he really was.

The wild grasses on the canal bank are wavering, and so too is my train of thought, wild and unknowing. As if this whole thing is bigger than me now and, like the tall grasses, I'm trying to make sense of it within some erroneous dance. My mood keeps changing, a swinging pendulum, sharp at the edge, cutting away at me. At times it all seems crystal clear. At other times things get mixed up. Until the anger takes hold.

There isn't a sinner out walking now. I roll down the car window, gasping at the chill outside. A mist has built up on the glass, and I see my younger self silently fingering the word 'scream' on a fogged bathroom mirror. The cold air cuts into my thoughts, cold and crisp, like an awakening. It's moved faster than I thought, swift, clear, sometimes without doubt, and now almost too easy.

His head is bent in the passenger seat. I can no longer see his eyes, but the blood is oozing from his chest. He lost consciousness with the final thrust of the knife. Perhaps better that way. The fucker always talked too much.

It's time, and every part of me knows it.

I stare at the windows of homes dotted along either side of the canal. They, too, are closed off, just like me and my silent passenger. Without thinking, I look up at the sky. I imagine driving off a cliff edge, ending it all. But that would be too easy. That would be the action of a coward. I'm a lot of things, but I'm not a coward. I have a job to do, a clear, definitive pathway of unfinished business, a stain that cannot be removed until every part and everyone involved, including dearest Clodagh, is history.

I feel my mind drift again, taking in this oasis of calm within the madness. Some of the stars are now fading, holding on for their last moments before going into hiding again. People in this city seldom look up at the sky. They see the streets as the beginning and end of everything. But the stars are there for a reason, and I'm not talking rubbish about guiding us. I'm talking the whole bloody universe out there, far bigger than we know, and right about now I'm also thinking, I hope someone bigger than me knows that what I'm about to do should have been done a long time back. It was destined from the moment I first saw that gleaming set of pearly whites.

A couple of hours ago, I had stood watching him. Part of me wondered why he didn't know what I was about to do. Why nobody knew. The thought had felt huge, pressing. Surely people should know these things.

I had felt the adrenalin rise, my heart beating fast, remembering the swift movement of the panther – his silent shadow as he stalks his prey. My eyes locked in that same fixed stare, as my blood curled, knife in hand and foot to ground, an ancient soundless lethal shift, the call of the wild, moved me closer as I waited for my time to pounce.

Mervin Road

Kate said nothing about having to change the sheets on Charlie's bed, as he reluctantly allowed her to remove the Power Ranger T-shirt he'd worn the night before. Neither did she mention cleaning up the mess in the kitchen – a large pool of milk and cereal on the table and the floor. For now, the only important thing was Charlie feeling okay. She had had a broken night. Rising at dawn, she had already spent a couple of hours in her study at the back of the apartment, setting out her plans for the following week.

Once the mess was tidied up, Kate called to Charlie who, as on most other Saturday mornings, was watching cartoons in the living room. 'Come on, Charlie. Shane and his mum will be here any minute.'

'I don't know where my clothes are.' He didn't take his eyes off the television.

'They're on the bed. Hop to it.' Kate switched off the cartoons using the remote control.

'Ah, Mum, don't.'

'I just did, Buster. Now, go before I get cross.' She'd kept her tone gentle.

'Bold Mum,' Charlie snapped back, his lower lip stuck out.

'Less of that, Charlie Cassidy.'

Kate hadn't changed her surname after marrying Declan, but there was never any doubt as to which their son would have. Trying to keep her face straight, she called to him again, 'I can see Shane's mum parking her car – come on, hurry up.'

'Is Shane with her?'

'Of course he is, and they'll be here in a second. Now come on!'

As Kate waved goodbye to Charlie from the front window of the apartment, an unexpected wave of loneliness swept over her. Suddenly the apartment was quiet again, without a living soul to talk to. Kate had made up her mind earlier to use this free time to go for a run, something she hadn't done in ages. It was only as she walked out from the bedroom in her running gear that she noticed the orange flashing light on her answering machine. Tying her long black hair in a ponytail, she pressed the play button.

She had been expecting a call from Declan, knowing he would be upset to have missed Charlie. Instead, she heard police sirens roaring in the background and O'Connor's voice filling the room. His message was blunt: 'Middle-aged male, multiple stab wounds, found drowned in the canal. You have my number. Call me.'

O'Connor wasn't one for social niceties, or unnecessary detail, but after what they had been through together in the Devine and Spain murders, a simple 'Hello, Kate' shouldn't have been too much to ask. As she was thinking this, another thought crossed her mind. If O'Connor wanted her involved, this wasn't going to be any ordinary investigation.

On her first attempt at ringing his mobile phone, she got 'Please leave a message.' Forgetting about her run, she switched on the television to check if anything important had hit the headlines. The story was already up on Sky News and, like all top news stories aimed at whetting the public's appetite, it had the markings of one that would run and run.

According to the news reports, on the previous night the well-known television personality had waved goodbye to a group of downbeat Ireland supporters in Gogan's pub after the soccer team's crashing defeat against Germany. He had made his way to the Caldine Club on Kildare Street in Dublin's city centre. Images posted on Facebook that morning of the last photographs of the TV personality's life formed part of the news coverage. Men and women wearing the green jersey, who had managed to be the last of the many public faces captured with the popular celebrity, had earned their place in the record books, not for what they had thought was Ireland's historic defeat but because, unknown to them, they would be among the last to see the television personality alive.

Neither the popular TV host nor his long-running morning show was a favourite with Kate. Unknowns airing their dirty linen in public, being booed or cheered on by the audience, usually caused her to change channel. People with broken lives, willing to forfeit everything for their desperate few minutes of fame, made her want to cringe rather than empathise. Keith Jenkins was considered a man who pushed out cultural boundaries, asking questions others didn't ask.

The ever-smiling Keith Jenkins could inspire drama in the most mediocre family circumstances – an estranged husband engaged in a love affair with his pigeons, an unmarried mother loving the father of her child despite his denials of parentage, a woman putting drink ahead of her grown-up children, all had danced as players in the nation's most popular car-crash television programme, *Real People, Real Lives*. If the advertising campaigns promoting it were to be believed, it had found its way into the hearts and minds of a nation.

To Kate, he was now a murder victim and, like all murder victims, had a history that had led to the stabbing and dumping of his body in the murky waters of the Grand Canal.

She tried O'Connor again. The phone rang once before his sharp, controlled voice answered.

'Kate.'

'Detective Inspector.'

'You took your time.'

'If you check, O'Connor, you'll see I've already left a message.'

'Glad to hear you're bright-eyed and on the ball. The phone's been a little congested.'

'Popular today, are we?'

'Not really, only you and three million other people – just as well they don't all have my private mobile.'

'I assume Morrison's already at the scene?'

'His Highness arrived over an hour ago. I'm heading back there now. The bloody area is a disaster to cordon off. City traffic is practically at a standstill.'

'Our killer picked a lively place.'

'Yeah, and a lovely victim too.'

'The media will ride this out for all it's worth, O'Connor. Public figure, public place – not exactly low key.'

'Indeed.'

'Any witnesses?'

'A young mother, Grace Power. She was awake with her new-born baby.'

'What exactly did she see?'

'She didn't witness the drowning. According to the 999 call, she heard a car pull up at speed close to where the body was found. It was the sound of one car door opening and closing then another that caused her to look out the window. She saw two males – the victim and presumably the killer.'

'Drowning? So the victim was alive on reaching the canal?'

'So it would seem.'

'Did the witness recognise either of them?'

'No. She only saw them from behind. Her initial thought was that the victim was drunk and he was being taken out of the car to get sick. He was stooped over. The other guy had his arm around him, holding him up. Apparently the victim, although weak, was walking.'

'What else did she see?'

'At that point she looked away, only returning to the window when she heard the car pull off again. That was when she saw Keith Jenkins's body floating in the water.'

'Not a nice memory.'

'Murder is never pretty, Kate.'

'So the body was on the same stretch of the canal as the car pulled in at?'

'That's right. The canal gates at either end were locked. The body wasn't going anywhere fast.'

'What time did the witness ring in?'

'Log states five a.m.'

'You say the victim was weak?'

'Yeah – he'd multiple stab wounds to the chest.'

'Multiple – how many?'

'Too many to say. Morrison will give us an estimated minimum when he's done the autopsy.'

'Any slash wounds?'

'Some on the arms, but it looks like the attacker got his victim under control quickly. According to Morrison, he would have been extremely weak by the time he got to the canal.'

'Which backs up Grace Power's statement.'

'Yeah, but even without it, Morrison figured Jenkins was alive going into the water.'

'Why?'

'You know what that son of a bitch Morrison is like. He's only saying so much until the full autopsy gets under way this afternoon. He loves this bloody stage in the proceedings, gets excited on the whole prospect of what he's about to find out.'

'But he must have said why he believes Jenkins was still alive.'

'A frothy cocktail in the mouth and nostrils, made up of water, mucus and air, apparently.'

'And that's it?'

'He'll know more later. But that's his reading on it for now.'

'And the stab wounds, any more details there?'

'Slash and puncture wounds, as I said. The victim lost a lot of blood. Had it not been for our pal wanting Keith Jenkins to take a swim, most likely he would have bled to death.'

'Did Grace Power have anything else to say?

'She said both guys had dark brown hair. The pal's hair was slightly shorter than the victim's. She was unsure of the height as one of them was severely stooped over, and the other was leaning down trying to hold him up, but she reckons around the five-ten mark, both similar in build, stocky, but not overly so.'

'Pity she didn't stay at the window.'

'Her baby was crying, but it was only a few minutes later that she heard the car door being opened again and slammed shut. The second time, it was just the once. When she walked back to the window, the car was gone.'

'She didn't get a registration plate?'

'No, but she thinks it was a Volvo, black or navy. It was then she saw the body floating and the blood on the road and footpath. That's when she called in.'

'How come she didn't notice the blood earlier?'

'She'd only looked out for a split second. She was pretty shook up.'

'I'd imagine she was.' Kate looked out of the front window of her own apartment down onto the street below, trying to visualise the events. 'Were the stab wounds front or back?'

'Front, just below the ribcage.'

'Then Keith Jenkins saw his killer.'

'Well, he isn't going to be a whole lot of help to us now, is he, Kate?'

'No, but if the victim was still alive when they arrived at the canal, and the killer didn't make any attempt to hide his identity in such a public place, it means something.'

'What? That he panicked?'

'Perhaps he did panic, but it's unlikely that even a panicked killer would choose a public place, unless, of course, he had something else on his mind.'

'Jesus, you're beginning to sound like Morrison. Spit it out, Kate.'

'Maybe the killer not only wanted his victim to see him, but others too. Either that or the risk of being caught was outweighed by other, more important factors. I assume I'm in on this one, O'Connor?'

'You assume right. How are you fixed?'

'A couple of important cases, but I can work around them.'

'Good – I'll see you shortly. We're below Leeson Street Bridge.'

'I know where it is. You've organised the clearance?'

'Don't ask stupid questions, Kate. I don't have the patience for them.'

'Neither do I. I'm on my way.'

'Kate.'

'Yeah?'

'Keith Jenkins's body is already on its way to the morgue.'

'Then I'll need the images taken at the scene.'

'Consider it done.'

As Kate drove away from her apartment in Ranelagh village, the thing uppermost in her mind was not the victim's celebrity status, or the slimy waters where his body had been found, but why the killer hadn't finished off Keith Jenkins with the first attack. Why bring a half-dying man to the canal to drown him, leaving his body where it was easily found?

Clodagh

During the night I awoke because the pipes were gurgling – Martin washing his hands for the umpteenth time. At one point I thought I heard a car turning into the drive, but I must have imagined it. It was the morning seagulls that finally got me up.

I've waited all morning for Val's call. So, when the phone rings I pick it up immediately, recognising her mobile number on the small screen.

'Clodagh, it's Val.' She sounds like she's whispering.

'Do you have the number?' I keep my voice steady. It seems like forever since the dinner party. We finally finished before nine. That wouldn't have happened in my drinking days. Val hadn't expected me to take her aside – we'd never got past first base in our relationship – but when you need to know something, unexpected people become your ally.

'Clodagh, I'm not sure about this.'

'Don't worry. Nothing ventured, nothing gained.' My voice is upbeat.

'That's all very well, Clodagh, but after the therapy and everything …'

'It's precisely because of the therapy that I'm doing this.' I sound more assured than I feel. There's no point in making her nervy.

'Well, he does come highly recommended.'

'I'm sure he does.'

'Does Martin know about this, Clodagh?'

'What do you think?' Her silence answers her question. 'Val, hold on while I get a pen and paper.' I place the handset on the hall table, pulling out the small drawer underneath. Then, with the phone between my ear and shoulder, I write down the name, address and phone number.

'I can drive you there,' she says. 'I don't mind.'

'Thanks, Val. I'm best going on my own.'

'But you're not allowed to drive.'

'There's such a thing as taxis.' Immediately I regret sounding harsh. I soften my voice: 'I don't want to drag you into this, Val. I appreciate your help.'

'Well, if you're sure.'

I think about the night I crashed the car. The road before me was like a runway being chopped up with speed and heavy rain. I was drunk out of my skull. I remember the windscreen wipers flipping back and forth so fast they dazzled me. 'I'm sure, Val, honestly.'

'It's a mercy no one was injured that night, Clodagh.' The first note of disapproval in her voice.

'I know that.'

All the times I drank, I never drove at night. But the argument with Dominic, even days after the funeral, wouldn't go away. I still see the dark trees either side of the road whizzing past me, giving me a false sense of getting away. The faster I drove, the freer I could be of the hurt.

Martin had said it was the last straw. I couldn't be putting myself and others at risk. At first, waking up on the hard bed in the police cell, all I remembered was the flashing lights of the squad cars hurting my eyes from the night before. Martin collected me. He said little more, but he organised everything. Eight weeks of rehab to sort me out. A twelve-month driving ban wasn't a high price to pay.

'Val, you won't say a word to Martin or Dominic, will you?' I need her reassurance.

'You're not drinking again, Clodagh, are you?'

'No. I'm done running away from things.'

'Glad to hear it.'

'Listen, Val, I've got to go. There's another call coming in. I think it's Ruby.'

'Okay, then. Give her my love.'

'Thanks.'

Before picking up the second call, I think about what an arsehole Martin was last night. Val might be highly strung, but she and Dominic would have made better parents than Martin and I.

'Ruby,' I maintain the upbeat tone.

'Hello, Mum.'

I can hear her hostility. She's being standoffish. I can't blame her. 'Thanks for calling me back.'

'No problem, what's up?' Again her words are tight, but I let it go. I was two years older than Ruby when I'd left home, at the brave age of nineteen with my big job in the bank. 'I just wanted to know how you were.' I want to tell her I miss her, but I don't.

'I'm fine, Mum. Is Dad there?'

I don't know what time Martin left this morning. Since Ruby moved out in September, I've slept in her old bedroom. Something else Martin has turned a blind eye to. 'No, sweetheart, he had to go into work.'

'But it's Saturday?'

I pause. 'Ruby, I know he gave you a hard time the other night. He wants the best for you. We both do.'

'Mum, I don't give a shit.'

'Well, I do.'

She doesn't answer me, the sound of nothing loud and clear telling me it's too late to play the supportive, protective parent. I bite my lip. Ruby misses my mother. I know that too. It makes the pain worse.

'Ruby, I'm hoping to see someone soon, someone who'll help

me.' I sound like I'm looking for her sympathy. I sound like a pitiful idiot. My mum hadn't cried when I left home. She told me she had no intention of being one of those silly mothers who couldn't bear to let their children move on.

'How's college, Ruby? Have you made any new friends?'

'A few.'

'That's good. It would be nice to meet them – when you're ready, of course.'

'Listen, Mum, I'm going to be late if I don't go soon.'

She's giving me the brush-off.

'But it's Saturday, you don't have lectures …'

'I've promised to see someone. Look, Mum, I need to go.'

'Well, you mind yourself.'

'Whatever,' delivered with as much couldn't-care-less as possible.

'I love you, sweetheart …' But Ruby doesn't hear me. The call ended before I started my last sentence.

I guess nobody, including Ruby, was one bit surprised when I hit the bottle again. An alcoholic likes to feel insular. I check the time. Martin will be ringing soon to check up on me. You don't realise what you do to others when you drink. But after a while you learn to live with the fact that they can never quite trust you any more. Ever.

I ring the number Val gave me. I expect his secretary to answer, before correcting myself. People like Gerard Hayden don't have secretaries.

'Hello,' I say. I can hear my own nervousness. 'My name is Clodagh Hamilton.' And I've no idea why I'm using my maiden name. 'I got your number from my sister-in-law, Valerie Hamilton.'

'Hello, Clodagh. Good to hear from you.' He sounds confident. 'I've been expecting your call.'

Leeson Street Bridge

Approaching Leeson Street Bridge, Kate could see more television crews setting up on the south side, a reasonable distance back from where the body had been discovered. It was a great vantage point. Close enough to ensure those viewing the broadcasts would feel part of the action. The nearer the reporters managed to get to the murder location, the better the news coverage would be received.

It hadn't taken Kate long to decide to abandon the car. Now, walking past the stream of photographers and television crew without attracting too much attention, she saw O'Connor before he saw her. From a distance, she watched him giving instructions to everyone around him, picking up his mobile phone every few seconds to take another call. His short but unruly auburn hair and beard stubble gave him the look of a guy who didn't get hung up on the small stuff, but his profile within the force had risen since his investigation of the Devine and Spain case. His recent promotion – he was now heading up a team at Harcourt Street – and the expectation of high media interest yet again made him the obvious choice for senior investigation officer in this case.

On seeing Kate, O'Connor began the walk over, a young male following in his wake. Mark Lynch had been in the élite National Detective Unit attached to Harcourt Street for over a year. Kate hadn't met him before, but she took an instant liking to the lanky young detective, with his heavy dark-rimmed glasses and cropped curly black hair.

'Mark, I want you to take Kate through absolutely everything we have so far. Every detail, no matter how small or irrelevant it might seem.'

'Not a problem, sir.'

'Kate, Mark will be working closely with you on this investigation. He's your contact. You can take it that everything you hear from him is also coming from me. Is that okay with you?'

'Of course.' She nodded. She'd assumed she would be working directly with O'Connor, but he had clearly decided otherwise. Within moments of their initial introduction, O'Connor turned on his heels, leaving her and Lynch to get acquainted.

'How long have you worked with O'Connor?'

'The last few months. Before that I covered the Sweetman case. O'Connor was part of the final review squad before we handed the file over to the DPP.'

'The young model who committed suicide?'

'That's the one. Gloria Sweetman.'

Lynch had obviously earned his stripes, and if he was working closely with O'Connor, he was a detective to depend on. There was something sharp about him, a quiet confidence that Kate liked. Sensing Lynch wanted to move the conversation on, she obliged. 'So, what do we have here, Mark?'

Flicking open his notebook, he began: 'Victim was found floating face up in the water. No effort had been made to hide the body, nothing attached to it to weigh it down, or any form of covering over it.'

'Perhaps the killer was short on time?'

Lynch took her question as rhetorical, looking up briefly from his notebook before continuing as if she hadn't spoken. 'The grassed area running alongside the canal bank has recently been cut, so the grass was tight. Some bagged and tagged items have been taken from the immediate vicinity. Surface litter mainly, including a receipt for a hotel.'

'Which one?'

'Maldon House – it's in Blessington.'

Kate knew it might be nothing – the receipt could have belonged to anyone – but it wouldn't be the first time a killer had made a slip-up of such magnitude. She turned away from Lynch to where Hanley and the rest of the techies had set up shop. 'And the blood markings, there must be plenty?'

'Examination of blood characteristics is currently being carried out on the grassed area, footpath, roadway, and the canal ledge.' Lynch also looked over to where the techies and their large white van were parked.

'Anything concrete in yet?'

'Not to me, but it's early days.'

'Apart from believing the victim was alive going into the water, what else did Morrison have to say?'

'He's confirmed that the stab wounds were to the lower chest. The details of angle, estimated type and length of blade will form part of his autopsy report.'

'Mark, you can call me Kate.'

'Kate.' For the first time he looked slightly wrong-footed.

'Did Morrison say if the attack was frenzied?'

'There were multiple stab wounds. The slash mark on the victim's right arm means he put up some kind of initial fight, but Morrison is not saying any more than that. I'm no expert, but from what I could see, the killer did a lot of damage.'

'You're the most expert person I have right now.' She hoped her smile would put the detective at ease.

Returning to his notebook, Lynch continued: 'House-to-house

enquiries are under way. Harry Robinson is in charge of those. Witness statements from the last known sightings of the victim in Gogan's pub and the Caldine Club on Kildare Street are also being taken. They'll be ready for the briefing at midday. Hanley, as you can see, is in charge of the tech team. He and the guys will be here for a while.'

'Where have you set up the incident room?'

'We're operating from Harcourt Street.'

'Is Mick Butler still the chief super there?' Kate watched for Lynch's reaction. If he had any negative opinion of his line boss, he was keeping it to himself, nodding in confirmation and continuing.

'CCTV footage is currently being pieced together. We're running through our own cameras in Temple Bar. As for the rest, we're dependent on footage from businesses or personal premises. As you know, these are erected for the protection of the premises only, so any shots we get of public areas or roads sighting the victim will be pure luck.'

'I see, and the same with the canal.'

'Indeed.' Lynch paused to allow the last piece of information to sink in before continuing. 'The victim was on foot leaving Gogan's, and also when he left the club on Kildare Street. Based on the eye-witness statement, we believe Keith Jenkins was taken here by car. Clothing on the victim was the same as he was last seen wearing, apart from a scarf, which he could have mislaid at any point after he left the Kildare Street club.'

'Lynch filling you in?' Kate hadn't noticed O'Connor walking up behind them.

'Yes, he is.' Turning back to Lynch, Kate noted he had taken the arrival of his superior as his cue to stop talking.

'Lynch?'

'Yes, sir.'

'The techies have some details on possible tyre markings. Get what you can down before the briefing and I'll fill Kate in.'

As Lynch left them, Kate waited until he was some distance away before saying, 'He's a good guy, O'Connor.'

'The force is full of them, Kate, but, yes, I agree. I think young Lynch has great possibilities.'

'Does he remind you of yourself? When you were young and enthusiastic?' Kate couldn't help but allow some friendly banter into her voice.

'I'm always enthusiastic, Kate. I've just learned to hide it a little better, that's all.'

Was it her imagination or had O'Connor changed? He was always a workhorse. A cop with a strong moral base who probably cared too little about promotion and too much about solving crimes than was likely to be good for him. She had noticed the dark shadows under his eyes earlier, but it was more than that. His posture, his body language, even the way he spoke to her, had an extra edge to it, as if she had wronged him in some way. But he didn't look like a man in the mood for sharing his inner thoughts with her or anyone else.

'Were you up late last night, Detective Inspector?'

'What?'

'Those black shadows under your eyes.'

'Tired is all, Kate.'

'I see. Well, spread some of your permanent enthusiasm by telling me what Hanley has on the tyre markings.'

O'Connor seemed relieved to switch the attention from him to the investigation. 'Grace Power, in her statement, said she thought the car was speeding when it drove away.'

'Go on.'

'It looks like the car drove through the blood markings on the road. Hanley's photographing what he thinks are pretty good tyre impressions, standard ninety-degree-angle stuff.'

'I'm listening.'

'With the low level of traffic at that time of the morning, and the speed at which the emergency call was acted upon, the tread markings are clean, but it's always a race against time before blood deposits deteriorate.'

'Does Hanley think there's enough to get a match?'

'He thinks so. A good tyre impression will give us tyre size, tread design, even manufacturer, if we're lucky. Of course, there's no guarantee they're the originally fitted tyres.'

'Important if you find the car.'

'My guess is it will turn up burned out, or not at all.'

'Rather pessimistic.'

'I've learned to be that way, Kate. Unlike you, I don't have a degree in criminal psychology, but even without it, some things come naturally.'

Again Kate detected the edge in his voice. 'Glad to hear it.' She wondered if the aggression was the result of work pressure, but she had seen him under that kind of pressure before. This was different. Perhaps the expression on her face gave away her thoughts because he was quick to respond.

'Don't get me wrong, Kate. If Hanley has something, it's a good place to start, and the way this case is shaping up, a start is at least somewhere.'

'I hear you have a hotel receipt.'

'We do. Too early to determine the relevance, but I'll have answers soon.' O'Connor stared straight ahead of him. 'You know, Kate, there are enough possible motives in this case to cover half a dozen homicides – a crazed fan, a hate crime based on that damn stupid show of his, even a disgruntled ex-lover. The guy was a known player, not to mention his well-aired bloody opinions, and God knows there was no end of those. But for what it's worth, it doesn't seem like the motive was money – at least, not instant money. Every one of the victim's credit cards, along with a substantial amount of cash, was left on him.'

'You say he was a ladies' man?'

'So it would seem. Not that I go in for all that celebrity gossip, but those in the know have already said as much. Officially, at this point, everything is on the table.'

Turning away from O'Connor, Kate took in the surroundings once more. 'Well, even ignoring why the killer chose drowning over stabbing to finish off the victim, the location is always important.'

'Tell me something I don't know.'

'Statistically most offenders live close to the scene of their crime. When a vehicle is involved, the offender is likely to have travelled six times on average further than those on foot.'

'You're really cheering me up. This case is a bloody resource nightmare.'

'Still, O'Connor, drowning a near-dead victim in a public place puts some interesting slants on the reasons behind the killing.'

'You've already formed possible scenarios, then?'

'Like everything else at this early stage, it's too soon for absolutes, but the way the victim was killed, and the location chosen, suggests that avoiding being caught wasn't uppermost in the killer's mind. Perhaps the stabbing was simply a means of weakening the victim. Keith Jenkins was well built. He wouldn't have been an easy man to drown – assuming drowning was the preferred means of killing. I'll need those images from earlier. The ones taken before the body was removed.'

'You'll get them by courier. I've a full squad briefing at midday.'

'I don't have to tell you, O'Connor, our victim's celebrity status means this will spread wide and, as you say, in plenty of different directions. Right now, the late Keith Jenkins has to be my starting point. I'll need whatever information you can get me on him, sooner rather than later.'

'You'll have it, Kate, I promise you that.'

Clodagh

Arranging to meet Gerard Hayden has somehow cemented my focus. I've begun and that's important. If I've learned nothing else from rehab, it's that you can't move forward without looking back.

I check the time again, conscious that I need to get Martin's call out of the way before I leave. He's late, and that's not like him. When he does call, his form is damn awful but, thankfully, for once, he's brief.

It's shortly after midday when I reach the strand. I have the keys for Seacrest, our old house in Sandymount, in my bag. I had them last night too. Martin was furious with me for wanting to go out again, especially as we had only just come home from dinner. 'You're crazy,' he said. 'It's only a house.' Maybe he's right about that. Either way, I didn't go inside, deciding to wait until daylight.

Inside, the house feels cold and empty. I think of years ago when it was filled with noise. When Dominic and I chased each other, or fought over which television programme we wanted to watch. I stare at the empty coat hooks where we hung our coats. The place is like an empty shell. For an instant, the oblong mirror in the hallway catches my eye. The last witness to my mother's face before she went out, checking her makeup, her ginger hair neat in a low bun.

She had changed the interior after Dominic and I left. 'A whole new look,' she had said, one that was more reflective of her modern taste. The house changed purpose for her, became something different. It was no longer a family home. Not any more.

For a split second I see the rooms as they used to be, when there was flowery carpet on the stairs and the kitchen had a large wooden table, the one Dominic and I did our homework on, not the high-gloss counter with its tall high-gloss red-backed chairs.

I had offered to help her with the redesign. I hadn't done a bad job on our house, the one Martin and I brought back from near collapse. That feels like a lifetime ago, Martin and I happily married. He was a different person when I married him, before all his new-found charm slipped away.

'I like to be independent, Clodagh,' she had said. 'There's no point relying on others when you can do things yourself.' She was giving me the cold shoulder again.

Walking upstairs, the wood below the new taupe-coloured carpet creaks. My hand glides along the mahogany rail, the one Dominic and I wrapped the Christmas garland around every December, and I held tightly when loud voices from downstairs scared me. I touch the walls. They're cold, smooth – flawless. Standing on the landing, it's as if every corner, nook and cranny holds layers of my past.

Of the three bedrooms upstairs, it's my mother's I enter first. Dad is so long gone now that when I think of him in this room it's like a different life, one belonged to the little girl I used to be.

Since her funeral, I've thought about him a lot. How he always seemed in a hurry to leave the house. I remember his navy pinstripe suit, and him kissing my forehead before grabbing his briefcase and rushing out of the door. It was a time when the little girl in the photographs smiled. It was a time when Dominic smiled too, when he was less serious, warmer. At least, that's how I remember it.

Dominic doesn't understand me wanting to keep the house either. He and Martin have been so eager to get rid of it. Crossing the landing, walking across the floorboards where the two of us once ran, I think about him again, wondering how both of us had come from the same mother, the same womb.

Most things in the house have been removed. A clear-out done when we knew the cancer wouldn't let her home. Dominic had looked after that. All I'd asked of him was that he should leave the contents of her bedroom and mine as they were. None of the other stuff mattered.

There is very little daylight. I switch on the centre ceiling light.

Her bedroom, like downstairs, looks like something out of a design magazine, but seems larger without her in it. I feel like an intruder. My mobile vibrates inside my pocket. I pull it out. 'Hi, Dominic,' I say, in my upbeat voice.

'Where are you? I called to the house and didn't get an answer.' His tone is sharp.

'I'm not a prisoner.' My voice immediately matches his.

'I didn't say you were.'

'What do you want?'

'That's a lovely way to greet your brother. I just wanted to talk.'

'I'm in Mum's bedroom.'

'I see,' he says. Like I've told him someone has died.

'Dominic?'

'Yeah?'

'Do you think she was lonely here?'

'How the hell should I know?'

'Was losing Dad the ruination of her life?'

'For fuck sake, Clodagh, that was forever ago.'

'But it matters, it all matters. I learned that in rehab.'

I hear him sigh.

'Dominic, can I ask you something?'

'What's that?'

I look around my mother's bedroom, a kind of foreboding crawling over me, like a snake easing its way inside me. I spit it out before I think better of it: 'Dominic. Why did she stop loving me?'

'She did love you.' He's trying hard, I know that.

'I wanted to drive her to the doctor that morning, the morning she got sick, but she shut me out.' I'm sounding hysterical. 'Ever since her death I've tried to think of the two of us having a proper conversation. Normal stuff, the kind most daughters and mothers have.'

'Calm down, Clodagh. You both talked all the time.'

'Talked about nonsense, you mean. Where we went on holidays, or what each of us wanted for Christmas. None of it was important. And then at the hospital—'

'I thought we were putting that behind us.'

'I can't, Dominic. I tried to, but I can't.'

'Suit yourself.' The anger is back in his voice.

'Dominic, do you know what I'm just thinking?'

'What?'

'This is the first time since Dad died that I've been in her bedroom on my own.'

'It can't be. Before the funeral—'

'You and Val collected her stuff. I was in Gaga Land, remember.'

'Clodagh, no one blames you for that, not now.'

'Yes, they do,' and then I say it: 'She always loved you more. Mum was different with you.'

'I'm not listening to this rubbish.'

'Why not, Dominic? Because it's the truth? Is that it?' I'm shouting at him.

'Jesus Christ, Clodagh.'

I can't hold back my anger. 'Two peas in a pod, you and her together. I was always the outsider.'

'One day soon,' he's roaring back at me, 'you're going to have to stop feeling sorry for yourself, Clodagh, and forget about all that shite. Did they not teach you that in rehab?'

'It wasn't a fucking school, Dominic.'

'Well, I wouldn't know, seeing as how I never had the luxury.'

My hand is shaking as I press the disconnect button on the phone. I turn to the photograph of my mother on the bedside locker. 'Happy now?' I say, with as much loathing as I can muster.

Leeson Street Bridge

Kate took photographs of the surrounding area, beginning with the houses at either side of the canal, including the one from which the witness had made the vital 999 call. They were Victorian, most converted to offices. Others looked divided, like Kate's building on Mervin Road, into separate apartments. By now there was plenty of activity along the terrace, but in the early hours of the morning, it would have been a different story.

Turning towards the canal, Kate saw the long grasses swaying in the water with the October breeze. She photographed the canal bank from different angles, as well as the bridges at either end of it, including the one with the reporters.

Because of Jenkins's celebrity status, huge resources would be pumped into the investigation. Information would arrive like a tsunami, members of the public believing they had been close to the victim. Like the previous investigation Kate had worked on with O'Connor, when the age of the young victims had created such an outcry, the public's attention would be a double-edged sword, feeding the investigation while stretching it to the maximum.

Although Keith Jenkins's body had been removed, the large white tent in which the state pathologist had carried out his initial investigation was still *in situ*. Kate looked down at Hanley and his crew. Hanley had grown a beard since they'd last met. From her current vantage point on the bridge, like the reporters and television crew behind her, she watched the team in their white bodysuits working alongside the various uniformed police officers and detectives, including O'Connor, stationed outside the cordoned-off area, a world within a world. It was almost as if those who were part of the crime scene were under some kind of microscope.

The seagulls that swooned and squawked overhead, seeking leftovers from the previous night, seemed to be waiting for their moment to pounce. Kate thought about what the area would have looked like the night before, after an international soccer match, with unhappy fans falling out of the bars and nightclubs nearby. The canal linked many of the inner suburbs of the city, so a few hours before the sighting by the young mother there could have been any number of people walking up and down it. The 999 call from Grace Power had come in after most of the crowd would have dispersed. Still, the killer had taken a chance in bringing his victim here. The thought was in the forefront of Kate's mind as she watched O'Connor.

It had been nearly a year since she had worked with him, and it wasn't a surprise that he hadn't been in touch. Once an investigation was over, there was no reason for either party to make contact. Speaking to him earlier on the phone, she'd been surprised by her own reaction. Despite the nature of their conversation, she was pleased that they would work together again and had assumed that O'Connor would be too.

Clodagh

Damn Dominic. Not that I give a toss about his idiotic comments regarding rehab. It's all the other stuff that riles me.

After Mum had become ill, I felt numb for a long time. Denial, they called it during therapy. We continued to play our shambles of a game, pretending everything was okay between us, as if we had a normal mother-and-daughter relationship. But all our talking was no more than surface banter, spreading out like candyfloss spun from nothing – and another reason to get that telephone number from Val.

During her last days, when I pressed her about Dad's death, all she would say was 'Not now, Clodagh, please not now.' But it had been different with Dominic. Even at the end she had confided in him.

I clench my hands. They all think it was her death that drove me back to the bottle, but it wasn't. It was her and Dominic's closeness, especially in the weeks coming towards her death, and if Dominic lived for another two hundred years, he would never understand that. Sitting on her bed, my fingers loosen, my hands spreading out across the crisp white embroidered cover.

When I cross the landing and open the door of my old bedroom, the first thing I see is my doll's house in the corner. I told Martin I wanted to take it before the house was cleared out. Like Dominic, Martin doesn't understand my need for these things. I can't remember the last time I opened it, but I know the tiny yellow flowers in the blue vase are still there, with the small china cups and plates. The furniture, the picture frames, the dolls, they're still there too. Even Ben, the brown terrier with his bright red collar, will still be holding the black-and-white-spotted ball in his mouth.

I hear traffic speeding outside on the main road, dulling the sound of the tide breaking on the strand. Looking around my room, I'm relieved that none of the furniture has been removed. The pine wardrobe, the dressing table, my old bed, they are all as they should be. The bedcovers have been changed, of course, and the array of bits and pieces scattered across the top of the dressing table was cleared away a long time back.

I smile, thinking about the dressing table piled with notes from school, nail polish, hairspray, lipsticks, the small photos stuck into the silver clasps on the mirror. For the life of me, I can't remember where the black-and-white photo strip of me and Orla has gone. We were sixteen, a right wild pair. But Orla had known when to stop.

She made contact before the funeral, telling me how sorry she was, and if I ever needed anything, even though she lived in Boston, she was only ever a phone call away. Perhaps in better circumstances our conversation would have felt less forced, but it was still kind of her to call. When you feel lonely, even the actions of someone from the past can relieve the isolation.

In the corner, I kneel down, touching the tiny white sash frames of my doll's house windows, jumping this time when my mobile bleeps – a text from Martin: *Where the hell are you?* The whole world wants to know where I am today. I'd better answer him. If I don't there'll be no peace later. I text him in reply: *I'll be back soon. I'm getting papers from Mum's.* He won't be happy, but I don't care. I'm still angry after my conversation with Dominic. I'd thought about taking a drink earlier on, to say to hell with it, an alcoholic's answer to everything. Drink when you're happy, drink when you're sad, when there's a reason to celebrate, when there's a reason to cry. But there's Ruby. Because of her, until the day I die, I won't forgive myself if I hit the bottle again, but that doesn't mean I feel strong enough not to slip.

When Ruby was younger, she didn't understand my drinking. I learned that in rehab too. Children develop trust issues, the alcohol messing with their parent's emotions, ecstasy one moment, anger and desolation the next. The child never knows what to expect, changing their behaviour to gain your attention, not realising that none of your mood swings are connected to them. The bottle, the alcohol and the beautiful blur call all the shots.

Now it's different. Ruby knows what's going on. Her anger is palpable. I don't blame her. I've let her down. I've let everyone down, but her most of all, and I damn well know that feeling better than anyone.

Mervin Road

Two hours after leaving the crime scene, Kate pinned the images couriered by O'Connor to the wall of her study. The simple act of pinning them up, bringing the victim, his life and death close to her, formed the intimacy that began her task of working out the kind of person who had committed the crime.

Knowing Charlie wouldn't be back for another hour, Kate decided to go for the run she'd promised herself earlier. It would be a good way, she hoped, of digesting the images she'd seen.

Outside there were dark rainclouds, but once she heard the repetitive sound of her feet hitting the footpath, and her breath got into a settled rhythm, it wasn't long before her mind returned to the images.

The first group of photographs were of the body prior to its retrieval from the canal, Keith Jenkins's brown hair floating in the water like a mass of tangled seaweed. His arms and legs were stretched out in perfect alignment, his outer clothing ballooning with water and air. His shirt, covered with blood, had loosened, revealing the lower part of his upper torso. It looked a mess. The froth O'Connor had referred to was also visible, oozing from his mouth and nostrils. The short time the corpse had been in the water meant there hadn't been any bloating, although the skin had the faded colour of death.

O'Connor had confirmed the victim's wallet and other personal possessions were intact, yet although Jenkins had been married, Kate noted there was no wedding ring on his left hand. Perhaps he didn't wear one, or he'd removed it prior to going out that evening. He had a reputation for being a bit of a ladies' man. But as a well-known figure, he would have gained little from hiding his marital status, unless the ring had been removed by someone else. If it had, there were very different implications.

Depending on what Morrison came up with on the stabbing, if this turned out to be a crime of passion, the ripples might reach close to Jenkins's home life.

Alleyway off Mount Street

I'm not altogether sure why I've come here, back to where I spotted good old Stevie McDaid. Watching him in the alleyway brought back something sordid. Nonetheless, at least here I can be on my own and do some straight thinking. It hasn't ended with Keith Jenkins. If I doubted it before, I don't doubt it now. There's satisfaction in knowing he's gone. Like any other piece of lowlife, best forgotten. He didn't go too easy, and not before he'd pushed that final nerve before going under. The thin strands of the spider's web move further out. At times the links feel faint, almost transparent, but at the core, Keith Jenkins was the beginning of it all.

I could have taken Stevie out as well. Beaten the crap out of him for good measure. He was always one step closer to shithead than most other scumbags. I have enough anger in me to do it. But now the thought of killing feels more measured, and that's important. Bet he would have laughed in my face, jerked around even if his head was near done in. His kind is made like that. Part of their survival mechanism. Brought up that way from the time their mothers and everyone else decided they were worth shit.

Maybe that's why Stevie always wanted to smell of roses, pretending to be the furthest thing from scumbag that his small intelligence imagined he might be. Either way, makes no difference now. Like Jenkins, he wouldn't be of the mind for changing. The only thing that would change Stevie McDaid is a bullet in the head. It would have to be a perfect shot. Miss the target by a millimetre and Stevie would laugh in your face, wearing the hole like some kind of bloody medal.

It made me sick watching him with that girl, pushing himself inside her like she was some kind of dead thing he'd found discarded but worth dragging into an alleyway for a fuck. That was what he shouted in her ear as he came off inside her. He was already too far gone for me to do anything for her. A couple of minutes earlier, I might have pulled the lowlife off her. The bastard even used her skirt to wipe himself, standing back, smirking at her.

I got one decent look at her, sixteen at the most. I think she was crying. Out of habit, I flicked my lighter, lit a cigarette, not thinking. He looked my way, aware of an uninvited stranger. 'Fix yourself. Come on, will ya?' I heard him say. It gave the night an aftermath of something rotten. At least this time the girl was a stranger.

I turned away from the alley, leaving the jerked-off Stevie McDaid behind me, knowing I had a long path ahead. That wouldn't include good old Stevie. For now, at least.

Mervin Road

When Kate got back to the apartment after her run, she put on Sky News, deciding to grab a sandwich before Charlie came home. In less than fifteen minutes the first full police briefing would be under way in Harcourt Street. Lynch had agreed to give her an update afterwards.

Each bulletin posted on Sky News glossed the reports as if they were offering something new about the murder. Various psychologists had been lined up and interviewed about the downside of celebrity culture – subjecting your professional and personal life to public consumption. The merits, or otherwise, of reality television, where ordinary people hung out their dirty linen in public for their fifteen minutes of fame, were well thrashed out on account of Keith Jenkins being the latest addition to the fallen stars.

Kate wondered how many people, including Imogen Willis, looked up to these celebrities, aspiring to copy them, not for any particular skill but for their status. The world might think they knew Keith Jenkins, but his television persona was most likely very different from reality.

Keith Jenkins may have been known to many, but behind the makeup and the flashy lifestyle there was simply a man. Even if this killing was random, the psychological inner map of Keith Jenkins and the killer was part of the reason why their paths had crossed. The voice inside the killer's head, formed through life experience, was the route to his identity, and the map that had led him to the murder of another.

There was no doubting, even in the early hours of the morning, that it was an open and exposed location. Why had the killer driven there? Why had he chosen drowning over stabbing, and why had he risked killing in the open with no attempt to hide his identity?

Monica Bramble from Sky News began interviewing ex-contributors to Keith Jenkins's television show. According to his fans, Keith Jenkins made them feel he was their friend, a good mate to have in your corner. Of course, not everyone got the same treatment. Some participants in *Real People, Real Lives* received the sharp end of Keith Jenkins's tongue. Monica Bramble might not be interviewing those participants on live television, but Kate was fairly sure the detectives investigating the murder would.

Clodagh

Walking back along the strand, I feel like a thief. I have my mum's old papers and photographs hidden in my bag. If she was alive, I wouldn't have dared take them. I had planned on removing just one photograph, the one with Dominic and me standing on the strand, with the twin red-and-white chimneys of Sandymount behind us. In the photograph, our arms are wrapped around each other, me with my wild ginger hair blowing across my face, him wearing a pair of flashy black sunglasses. I was five, and he was ten. We both look happy.

I pass row after row of houses overlooking the sea. When I was younger, if the tide was out, I used to look back at them in the distance. Their different-coloured doors reminded me of toy houses. Even now, all these years on, there is something about the sound of water that conjures up my father. If I try hard enough, I can imagine his voice floating in the rhythm of the waves, his words soft, calling me, saying things will be okay. During my eight weeks of rehab at Rosses Bay, I thought about a great many things, including how everything changed once he was gone.

At the house, the drawer in my mother's dressing table had resisted when I first tried to pull it open. I needed to give it a good tug. It was filled with papers, chequebook stubs and old bills. The contents, unlike the rest of the house, were a mishmash of everything – an old television licence, bills, bank statements, and a diary from 1967, the year Dominic was born. It was full of handwritten notes about childhood injections, when both of us had measles and other illnesses. I took the diary with their marriage certificate, Dad's death certificate and a clutter of old photographs stuffed into a large brown envelope, including the one with me and Dominic on the strand. I don't recognise that little girl in the photograph. She doesn't seem real to me, but real or not, I'm not ready to let her go just yet.

That was another thing I realised in rehab. For all the parts of my childhood that I can remember, huge chunks are completely lost to me, gaping black holes, especially around Dad's death, and also Emmaline's. I'm ashamed of being jealous of her. She was only a baby. Five days old. Cot deaths are tragic. I can't imagine losing Ruby. I was seven when Emmaline died, shortly before Dad, but I remember little of it. Sometimes it feels like things were much easier when I was drinking. At least back then I could choose to opt out for a while.

As I round the corner onto our road, I see Martin's car pulling into his side of the double garage, my own car permanently parked in the other. The thought of facing him concentrates my mind. Martin is so bloody moody these days. He is another part of my life that I need to work out.

I turn the key in the front door, knowing I don't want to face him. Suddenly I feel drained again. Perhaps he won't stay long. Grab a bite of lunch and go. The house seems so quiet since Ruby left for college. At first I worried about her, she being only seventeen. She seemed far too young to be away from home. Yet at that age I'd thought I could change the world. I worry about her more than Martin does. I know the trouble she can get herself into.

∞

We have lunch together, Martin and I. Not that 'together' exactly covers it. He doesn't mention my trip to Mum's house last night, or this morning, and neither do I. We're like mechanical clones that happen to live together. As I clear away lunch dishes, he says, 'I never checked the postbox last night.'

'Really,' I say. I couldn't care less.

He is still cool with me when he returns to the kitchen, putting the letters into his briefcase. Then, for no good reason, his mood changes, as if he's a different person. He kisses my cheek and says, 'All I want for you, Clodagh, is the best, and that you're safe.' He has been keeping the mail from me lately. I can't even be trusted with that. Right now I'm not bothered what game he's playing. I ignore his words and the kiss.

As Martin closes the front door behind him, I wonder if seeing Gerard Hayden will give me the answers I need. I'm not sure I can trust anyone now. At times, I don't even trust myself. Last night, walking back along the strand, I hadn't felt safe. Listening to the tide coming in, I had a sense of foreboding, convinced someone was following me. I looked behind me briefly. He reminded me of a guy I used to know. I kept walking but faster until, thankfully, I couldn't hear him any more.

I pull the piece of paper with Gerard Hayden's address out of my purse, checking it again. As if looking at it will make some kind of difference. There is no denying I feel apprehensive. But I'm not running away. As I told Val, I'm done with that.

Incident Room, Harcourt Street

O'Connor mulled over his meeting with Kate as he approached Harcourt Street station. He hadn't liked her reference to his late nights. The last thing he needed was Kate putting him under some kind of emotional microscope. Nor did he want to allow any personal feelings towards her to get in the way. Professional and personal lives shouldn't cross. He had made that mistake a few months back, and he had no plans to speed down that road again. It made sense to bring Kate into the investigation, but any ideas he might have about their relationship going anywhere were off limits. She was married for one thing.

Passing the corner shop, he was relieved that, with the newspapers going to print before the killing the previous night, Keith Jenkins's face wasn't plastered all over them. O'Connor had enough painkillers in him to ease the tension of a horse but, headache or no headache, he loved this point in an investigation. The pace of information flooding in, facts, rumours, data from witnesses, possible sightings, the team moving at top speed to find out everything and anything people might know about the victim and how they managed to end up dead: each segment was raw, fresh and full of potential.

Detectives Quigley and Patterson had pulled in a pal called Johnny Keegan. They had already set up shop in one of the interview rooms at the back, the video cameras hanging high in the corners of the room, recording every word, movement and change of expression. One of the lads would be sitting opposite Keegan, the other moving around. Keegan might keep them company for a while, but he wouldn't be the only invited guest. Plenty would follow in his footsteps.

Pushing open the double doors to the side of the building, O'Connor waved to the two uniformed officers stationed outside. Both wore their full Garda apparel, including luminous yellow-striped jackets and navy cloth hats. Striding through the corridors of Harcourt Street, the closer O'Connor got to the incident room, the more he felt he was being sucked into the centre of things. In perfect synchronicity, O'Connor and Chief Superintendent Mick Butler met outside the door.

Butler had only a couple of months to go in the force. After fewer than half a dozen meetings with pension advisers and accountants, he'd made the decision to take the current early-retirement package, before those cowboys of politicians in Leinster House decided to cut his well-deserved salary even more. O'Connor heard Butler had set himself up with some media contacts. Rumour ran that he had a nice juicy income organised with one of the Irish tabloids for post-retirement. But there were two things O'Connor was sure of. Even with Butler's imminent retirement, he would maintain his status, and with an unsolved murder from ten years ago still blighting his glorious career, he wasn't about to add a second. That would be considered sloppy. The killer of Keith Jenkins was the highest thing on Butler's agenda right now, so O'Connor and everyone else had better deliver.

'O'Connor, fill me in on what's happening.'

'Quigley and Patterson have pulled in a Johnny Keegan, an ex-participant in Jenkins's TV show. The two of them have history.'

'What about the autopsy?'

'Morrison will begin it this afternoon. That's my next destination after here. Hopefully we'll have a full update from the guys on the

CCTV footage later as well. The briefing will cover whatever witness statements we have in so far, but I understand there's a canary at the club in Kildare Street. It's always good to have a talker.'

'Go on.'

'Mick French has been allocated as family liaison officer. He's out in Malahide now.'

'He'll need help. The fucking media will be everywhere on this one.'

O'Connor didn't mention Butler's prospective change of career. 'I've put two crews operating around the clock at the victim's residence.'

'Matthews is the bookman on this one.'

'Good choice.' When it came to interactions in the incident room, the right bookman, O'Connor knew, was critical. He was the one person who saw everything worth seeing, and in allocating tasks, and shifting through material, could turn an investigation.

'Your approval as the senior investigation officer pleases me,' Butler's tone loaded with sarcasm, 'so make sure you keep it that way.'

'I've every intention of it.' O'Connor smiled at the puffed red face of his superior. Butler would want to watch that weight of his when he retired, or his heart, if it existed, might decide to stop beating.

'Anything else, O'Connor, before we go in?'

'We have a hotel receipt.'

'Brilliant. I can't wait to hear all about it.' And with that he pushed open the incident-room door.

All heads turned as the men walked towards the top table, and the sound of multiple voices lowered, as if the room had its own audio control button.

The chief superintendent cleared his throat, then bellowed,

'I'll let you kick start the proceedings, Matthews. Let's hear what everyone has to say.'

Sitting beside Chief Superintendent Butler, Matthews's frame looked like a matchstick. His strong Cork accent was very much still in place despite more than thirty years in Dublin. It had a harsh, no-nonsense sound to it.

'I see you there at the back, Quigley. Is the interview over? Is Mr Keegan talking?'

'Patterson's getting his girlfriend Suzanne Clarke in for a chat. Keegan's adamant he was with her all night.'

'And your take?'

'There's a history of domestic abuse there. She'll say whatever he wants her to say. We'll put the squeeze on both of them. Chances are she'll be the first to crack.'

Matthews, checking the next job number in the file, turned to O'Connor sitting directly to the left of Butler. 'O'Connor, fill us in on Morrison.'

'Post-autopsy, he's hoping tests will confirm substantial amounts of liquid in the lungs. If the heart was still beating when Jenkins was plunged into the water, then the pathology reports should confirm diatoms travelling from the bloodstream into the kidneys, brain, and perhaps even the bone marrow.'

Butler interrupted, 'If Jenkins has some of the killer on him, under his fingernails or anywhere else, O'Connor, tell Morrison we need that information ASAP.'

'The trace evidence has been coded top priority.'

Matthews continued, his next question to Sarah Walsh, Hanley's assistant. 'What have you techie guys got from the scene?'

Standing by the side wall, Sarah Walsh answered, 'A bonanza of items. Enough blood samples to keep everyone busy for a while.

Hanley is still there, but we have some visuals.' Pointing to the projector, she asked, 'Will I load them?'

'Go right ahead, Sarah.' Matthews gave the nod to two male officers at the back to close down the blinds.

The opening images were of blood deposits found on the interior ledge of the canal wall. Sarah Walsh's voice held everyone's attention as she flicked through the slides. 'These blood deposits were in close proximity to where the body was found floating. They are also in line with the eye-witness statement regarding positioning of both men after they exited the car. The angle of blood splatters is relevant. When large drops of blood fall on a hard surface, in this case a concrete ledge, how the splatters form defines the angle of blood loss. Here,' Sarah Walsh pointed towards the image, 'when the blood hit the surface, small secondary droplets developed, surrounding the original circular stains formed from the larger ones. Because the smaller droplets hit the surface at angles of less than ninety degrees, these secondary stains are elongated and the tails are clearly visible.' She paused, allowing everyone to take in the information. 'These tails indicate the relationship of the body to the surface being somewhere between a thirty-five- or forty-five-degree angle. Meaning the victim was practically lying on the ledge before he was plunged into the canal.'

'If what you're saying is true, Sarah,' O'Connor observed, standing up and walking over to her, 'the killer used the ledge to support the victim before drowning him, positioning himself on it, making it easier to hold Jenkins under water.'

'Probably — we'll be running fibre tests. If the killer knelt on the ledge, we should be able to pull something from it, no matter how minute.'

Butler turned to O'Connor. 'I'll want to know what that profiler of yours has to say about this. What's her name again?'

'Kate Pearson.'

'We'll need her report as of now. Allocate that to O'Connor, will you, Matthews? And, for God's sake, will someone open those bloody blinds? We might be still in the dark, but we don't have to make it a permanent state of affairs. Right, O'Connor, get back up here and tell everyone what else you have.'

O'Connor didn't like being summoned like some unruly teenager, but he did as he was told. The line of command within the force was never questioned, even if the chief super, at times, was the biggest gobshite going.

'All items of value belonging to the victim were intact from what we can see – cash, credit cards, an expensive watch. Everything was left on the victim, with the exception of his wedding ring, a plain gold band. According to Morrison, the indentation on his finger meant it was worn on a consistent basis.' O'Connor sat down, but continued talking: 'We're getting an image of the ring from the insurers. We've also picked up a hotel receipt. The receipt is eight months old. Higgins and Clarke are driving to the hotel now. The receipt belonged to a couple signing in under the name of Salmon. The car-registration details given were false, so the name could be as well. The account was paid in cash, unusual enough in this day and age.' He cleared his throat. 'All the CCTV footage is currently being compiled. By the next briefing we'll have most of what's out there on Jenkins's last movements.'

Matthews looked around the room for Harry Robinson. 'Harry, what have you in on witness statements?'

'We've statements from a couple of a dozen people at Gogan's pub, and a number from the Caldine on Kildare Street. Nothing major coming out of the Gogan's statements, but the hotel manager in Kildare Street, a Mr Devoy, seems to have a lot of information on the late Keith Jenkins. I've filled DI O'Connor in, but I'll get a typed copy of everything to you within the hour.'

O'Connor turned to Matthews. 'I'll be talking to Mr Devoy. If he likes to talk, I'll help him by listening. If what the grapevine says about Jenkins's extra-marital affairs is true, my guess is Mr Devoy will know who the latest models are. The hotel receipt might belong to anyone, but whoever got close to Keith Jenkins in the romance department might give us more information than the family.'

'When are you talking to the family?' Butler's tone carried a hint of warning.

'French has been with them from early this morning. He's covered the preliminaries, but there's nothing jumping out as yet. It's still early days.'

Butler sounded rattled: 'Keep it nice and easy with them. They have connections everywhere.'

O'Connor continued, 'That's about it for now, except for you, Lynch.'

The young detective looked up at his superior.

'I'll need you to fill Kate Pearson in on what we have from here. The rest of you, get out there and get some answers. This unit has a reputation. The word "élite" isn't simply a label, it's bloody hard earned.'

If nothing else, Butler allowed O'Connor to have the last word.

Clodagh

I tell the taxi driver to let me out at the end of the street. I have no idea what to expect from Gerard Hayden and, walking towards his house, neither do I know what the house of a hypnotist should look like.

The road itself is narrow, with barely enough space for cars to park on either side. There are small red-brick cottages on both sides, with equally small front gardens. Some look well kept, others are the way I feel: in need of repair. I know the number of the house without having to look at the piece of paper, but I take it out of my bag all the same.

I hesitate at the low garden gate before entering, standing close enough to read his qualifications on the brass plaque to the side of the panelled black door. It confirms his registration as a hypnotist in Ireland, whatever kind of guarantee that gives me.

I'm early. If I was still driving I could have sat in the car. Now I regret coming so close to his house: it makes the possibility of changing my mind more difficult. Not wanting to look a complete fool standing there, I reach down to open the gate. It's not too late. I could still turn and walk away, but the same hand that opened the gate is now pressing the brass bell button.

I hear carpeted footsteps, the creaking of floorboards, before the door opens and I see Gerard Hayden for the first time.

Like the house, he is small, and older than I'd expected him to be, with short, dishevelled grey hair. He is wearing a navy tartan waistcoat, and I immediately think of the Mad Hatter's Tea Party.

His voice, as before, sounds confident, but he speaks softly, and somehow that is reassuring. He stands back, holding the door ajar as I go inside. He leads the way, both of us walking along the dark carpeted hallway, with an occasional creak from the floorboards, to a back room with the word 'Office' in black stickers on a faded cream door. Once inside, I smell candle wax.

There is something about his voice that I find calming. I hear myself talking, telling him about my estranged relationship with my mother, how we never seemed to get past the barrier that existed between us. Gerard Hayden listens, not saying a word, nodding, tilting his head sideways every now and then. He waits until I run out of words.

I think he will comment on my anxieties, try to analyse my fears, but instead he says, 'Good. Thank you for that, Clodagh.'

Standing up, he turns down the wooden blinds on both windows in his office, talking with his back to me. 'Clodagh, regression is used for many purposes. It is not something you should either be afraid of or nervous about. At all times you will feel safe and be safe.'

I think again of Martin's words. He wants me to be safe. After eighteen years of marriage, he doesn't make me feel so, not any more and not for a very long time. It was Val who reintroduced us. She hadn't realised that I'd known Martin from childhood. As a kid, he was a bit of a nerd, but his appearance changed with his charm. Gerard Hayden is sitting opposite me now, his conversation continuing.

'There are many interesting aspects to how our minds work, Clodagh, but for now, we'll concentrate on the relationship between the conscious and subconscious mind. Try to imagine an iceberg. Our conscious brain is at the tip, the point visible above the waterline.'

I visualise the iceberg, wondering about the vast expanse beneath.

'When you regress, Clodagh, and you go back to childhood, you won't be there alone.'

'How do you mean?'

'Your adult self will be with you.'

I wonder how useful that adult self will be.

'Regression is particularly helpful for people with certain conditions, such as an inclination to blush, or a phobia towards spiders, or even a stammer. If we're lucky, it is possible to trace the first memory, the one permanently held in the subconscious, the frightening event that caused a particular problem to occur. What is interesting, Clodagh, is that, as I explained, the adult self also forms part of the regression process. He or she is capable of recognising that the circumstances or events which the child perceived as frightening may be something else entirely.'

'I see.'

'It's very possible, Clodagh, that your conscious mind is preventing you from remembering. It can block your subconscious, the part that stores all your memories perfectly intact, from connecting to those memories. Even if you could, for the briefest of moments, gain access to a particular event, your conscious brain would respond far too quickly for you to realise, or recall, your attempt at trying. You might be left with a sense of unease, without any explanation as to why.'

I must look nervous, because he explains again about how, when I regress to my younger self, my older self will be present.

'Memory, Clodagh, is rather suspect in our conscious mind. People think they store memories in a particular way, that they don't change, but we're constantly updating our memory, or perception of it, creating layers, obscuring the original, until what we actually believe happened can differ dramatically from the truth.'

'Gerard, I haven't been completely honest with you.'

'How do you mean?'

'As I've already said, I had an estranged relationship with my mother for years. It wasn't always like that, at least I don't think so, but there is something else.'

'Clodagh, you don't need to tell me everything. Once you trust me, we can work through whatever comes up together.'

'I feel there are secrets in my past …'

'There usually are, Clodagh.'

'There are things that others, including my mother, kept from me.'

'Clodagh, if it's okay with you, I believe the best way to begin your regression is for you to visit a happy memory. I hope you're comfortable with that idea. We need to tread carefully. Understandably, people can feel apprehensive about being hypnotised. The process isn't one to be rushed. It's always better to start somewhere that you feel at ease.'

I recognise the scent from the lighted candles as vanilla, and the walls of Gerard Hayden's office, which at first were white and sparse, feel warm in the muted light. Apart from the two comfy chairs we sit on, and his desk, there is little other furniture. By the two windows, there is a bed, like in a doctor's surgery, and beside it, a low wooden chair, which I assume he will soon sit on. He gestures me towards the bed, the candlelight flickering on the closed blinds, saying, 'Clodagh, have you any more questions before we begin?'

'No, I don't think so.'

'Okay, we're going to bring you back to a happier time. While you're relaxing, I'll ask you to remember a time when you were older than a baby, but younger than the Clodagh you remember with sadness, or with whatever barrier existed between you and your mother. All the time you will be the one in control.'

'What if I can't remember? What if I don't have those memories?'

'You will, but don't worry. I'll be with you every step of the way. We'll take it gently. My hope is that today you'll simply experience regression, become familiar and relaxed with the process. You've waited a long time to reach this point, Clodagh. I see little benefit in rushing things now.'

Lying on the bed, I stare up at the ceiling. I hear Gerard's voice asking me to breathe in and out, counting backwards from ten. 'Ten, breathe out, relax, nine, breathe out, relax.' He tells me that during this time, if I hear sounds, cars driving by, people out on the street, any noise from outside, my mind will not be disturbed. This exercise is to relax my body. Soon he will ask me to count backwards from two hundred. I should say the numbers inside my head, breathing out between each one. When I can no longer keep track of the numbers, I should raise the index finger of my right hand.

I can feel the numbers slowing in my brain, but I can still hear his voice, talking about visualising a garden, somewhere I feel safe. I smell flowers. I think it's spring. I see daffodils and snowdrops. I'm still counting, but the counting is more difficult. I want to touch the flowers in the garden, feel their soft petals. I hear his voice again, asking me what I see, and how I feel. The numbers are nearly gone now and, as instructed, I raise my index finger.

'Okay, Clodagh, I'm going to take you down deeper. I want you to imagine a set of stairs that will lead you out of the garden. As you walk down them, we will count backwards from two hundred. When the numbers get muddled, you can raise your index finger again.'

He counts, the numbers gently bringing me down a staircase. At the bottom, again his voice is soft, reassuring.

'Clodagh, I want you to imagine your eyelids are stuck down, as if with glue, glue so strong you can no longer open them.'

I remember him mentioning this beforehand, explaining that when this happens, it is his way of testing the intensity of my trance.

'Now, Clodagh, if you can, I want you to try to open your eyelids.'

I keep listening to his voice, doing as he asks, but my eyes won't open.

'Good,' I hear him say. 'Now, Clodagh, at the count of three, you will be able to open your eyes once more. One, two, three ...'

I feel loose, unburdened.

'Clodagh, can you hear me?'

'Yes.'

'Where are you?'

'I'm in a corridor.'

'What do you see?'

'Doors.'

'What is on the doors?'

'Numbers.'

'Clodagh, look at the doors, look at the numbers.'

'Yes.'

'I want you to go to the door with the number five on it. Open the door and walk through to the other side.'

I hear sounds. There is laughter, little-girl laughter. I know it's me. My curly ginger-red hair is falling across my face. I'm searching for something in the wardrobe, down at the bottom.

'Where are you, Clodagh?'

'I'm in my parents' room.'

'What age are you?'

'Five.'

'What do you see?'

'I see shoes, high shoes, sandals, shiny gold sandals.'

'Can you hear anything?'

'I'm giggling. I'm pulling out the gold sandals, putting them on my feet. When I stand up, I feel tall, wobbly. Dominic is downstairs with someone, a friend. They don't want me playing with them. Girls are silly, they say.'

'Dominic?'

'My brother.'

'Does this upset you?'

'No. They're boring, wanting to play their stupid boy games.'

'What are you doing now?'

'I'm sitting at my mum's dressing table. It's full of perfumes, lipsticks. There is a golden lipstick case with a pretty rose design in the middle. I touch it. It feels cool, and I like the colour, rose pink like Sandy wears.'

'Who is Sandy?'

'She's one of my dolls.'

'Where is your doll, Clodagh? The one called Sandy?'

'I've left her in my bedroom, sitting by the doll's house. My mother's lipstick smells sweet. It's sticky on my lips.'

'What do you feel?'

'I can hear footsteps – clickety-click, clickety-click.' My voice is more excited.

'Do you recognise the footsteps?'

'They're my mother's. We're going out. We're going to a party at my friend's house.'

'What do you see now, Clodagh?'

'I see my mother. She's smiling at me. I'm still giggling. She's holding a dress in her hands. It's purple taffeta, with silver beads on the collar. It's my party dress.'

Again he asks, 'What do you feel?'

'I feel happy. I want to go to the party.'

'And your mother?'

'She's happy too. She's laughing as she cleans my face. The wet cloth makes me giggle even more. My dress feels nice against my skin. My mother is brushing out my curls – putting a purple hairband with a tiny silver rose in my hair. I don't want to take off the high sandals. I want to wear them to the party. My mother laughs again.'

'What's happening now?'

'She's picking me up, putting me on her lap. She kisses my face. She wriggles off the gold high heels. My new shoes are flat, shiny black patent. They have silver buckles. They're nice, but not as nice as the high sandals.'

'Is it just the two of you in the room?'

'Yes, and the sun is shining. I think it could be summer.'

'Why do you think that?'

'Soon I'll be starting big school. I've never been there before. Mum tells me I'll love it, but I don't think she's telling me the truth. Dominic goes to school, and when he comes home, he never looks happy.'

'What do you feel now? What does the adult Clodagh feel?'

'I don't know. I'm looking down at the two of them, my little-girl self sitting on my mother's lap.'

'Do you know what the little girl is feeling?'

'She's still smiling, so she must be happy, but there's something else.'

'What is that, Clodagh?'

'I think … No, I'm nearly sure of it.'

'You're nearly sure of what, Clodagh?'

'The little girl …'

'What about her?'

'I think she feels loved.'

'How do you know?'

'I just do …' My voice trails away.

'Are you ready to come back, Clodagh?'

'Yes, I think so.'

'I want you to close your eyes again. Start counting forward. As the numbers change, you will leave the room, and walk out through the door, the one you opened with the number five on it.'

I keep counting forward, one, two, three …

'Down the corridor, Clodagh, you will see a staircase. I want you to begin walking up the stairs. Are you walking up the stairs?'

'Yes.'

The counting is continuing inside my head, but I can still hear his voice.

'Soon you will be near the garden again. Do you remember the garden, and how good it made you feel?'

'Yes.'

'I want you to keep breathing in and out, slowly, deeply, counting upwards. Are you in the garden, Clodagh?'

'I'm in the garden.'

'Now look for the staircase that will lead you out. Can you see it?'

'Yes.'

'Count forward again, from one to ten.'

I feel different, but I'm still relaxed.

'As you count, Clodagh, you will climb the stairs. When you reach the top, you will be aware that you are back in this room. You will hear sounds from outside the window. You will hear my voice easing you back to the present. When I tell you, Clodagh, you will be able to open your eyes and I want you to keep your breathing steady.'

'Okay.'

'Now open your eyes. Stay resting on the bed. Keep relaxed. Whenever you're ready, you can sit up.'

I smell the vanilla-scented candles. I hear cars driving past. Gerard Hayden is sitting on the chair waiting for me to wake. I feel as if something has changed, although I'm not sure what.

'Are you okay?'

'Yes, I think so.'

'You did very well.'

'How long was I out for?'

He looks at his watch. 'About an hour.'

'Really? It felt like minutes.'

'Do you remember anything?'

'Yes.'

'What do you remember, Clodagh?'

'I was a little girl. I was going to a party. I was happy.'

'Anything else?'

'My mother.'

'What about your mother?'

'She … ' But the words won't come out.

'It's okay, Clodagh. Take your time.'

I know the words. They hang inside my brain for the longest time, as if they're imagined or they belong to someone else, but then I say them, almost in a whisper, 'She loved me.'

Gerard says nothing. Despite a sense of disbelief, the recall has brought up something I least expected: a feeling of loss. For the first time since my mother's death, with the noise of traffic coming in from outside and the strong smell of vanilla candle wax, I cry, loud, uncontrollable sobs, while Gerard Hayden remains seated on the chair, looking as if he has experienced this scene many times before.

38C Seville Place, Ringsend

Stevie McDaid wasn't one for being overly energetic on a Sunday morning, unless he had someone nice in the bed beside him. But Keith Jenkins's murder had spiked his interest. Seeing Clodagh the other night had got him thinking too. He had stopped following her once she'd turned away from the strand. He already knew where she lived, her and good old Martin – a guy not to be underestimated. Even as a kid, the bastard had had another side to him. It's been a while since Stevie's thought about the old gang, Martin, Dominic and himself. After that baby died, everything had changed. The whole lot of them had such high and mighty ideas about themselves. Yet none of them ever moved from Sandymount. Laughable, if it wasn't so fucking predictable.

Looking around his flat, he smirked. That had probably been predictable too: 38C Seville Place was the latest in a very long line of fuck-ups in his accommodation choices. Spending money on women, and generally having a good time, cost a guy. Something had to give. His priorities were hot water and a comfy bed, but 38C Seville Place was bang in the middle of flats supported by welfare. He hadn't known it moving in, thinking, with the flat being in Ringsend and close enough to Sandymount, he would avoid most of the scumbags. The landlord knew people in high places, people who'd got him on the approved-landlord list, a list that guaranteed him a thousand smackers a month for his shit boxes.

Stevie's shit box had a bedroom with a double bed, a fitted wardrobe without doors, a kitchen the size of a small lift, and a sitting room with a view of the backyard. It housed a black leather couch, a lamp without a shade, cream-painted woodchip wallpaper, only surpassed by the barred windows and a cracked mirror above the fireplace – one that, hopefully, had given all the bad luck to the previous tenant. Stevie could hear everything through the walls: crying babies, couples shagging, toilets flushing. It wasn't until he realised he lived near to Clodagh Hamilton that he began to look on the shit box as some warped twist of Fate. But it was the wayward daughter who had first attracted his attention. Her, and the old man crawling all over pretty Ruby. Another face Stevie wouldn't forget in a hurry.

Crappy accommodation was nothing new to him. He had lived in it from childhood. At first he hadn't known it was crappy. He'd thought it was the way things were. People living in shacks in Africa didn't dream about living in semi-detached houses. They dreamed of having food, and not bleedin' dying. It was only ever him and his ma. She used to tell him that, with the absence of a father, they were like the Immaculate Conception. It was their private joke. If anyone else mentioned it, it wasn't funny.

The array of boyfriends was an education too. There was one arsehole in particular, one of those 'new age, save the planet' types, dressed in his neat jumper and jeans. It was the backpack that really got Stevie going, green and pink, like the bit of pink said something about the arsehole breaking down stereotypical gender bias. Once Stevie knew the guy's cover, well, he was there for the taking. He was only ten at the time, and his ma told him to behave, but she was a softie. He knew how far he could push her before he'd get a clip around the ear.

'You do much hiking with that backpack of yours, Mister?'

'Sure do. Maybe we could do some hiking together, Stevie.'

'Stevie would love that, wouldn't you, Stevie?' his ma had piped up.

'I ain't going up no poxy hill with him.'

'Stevie, watch your language.' His ma had given him the evils. Stevie's ma could give the evils better than Marlon Brando in The Godfather, and Stevie knew this guy was getting the whole nine yards when it came to his ma wanting to make a good impression. Mr Save the World had lasted longer than most. He wasn't even put off when Stevie asked him how he thought the Pope did a piss with all those bleedin' clothes on. But he lost interest in the end. His type always did, just like the bloody Hamiltons.

Stevie's ma never went to Mass, and she didn't send him to a religious school either. He'd figured out a long time back that she and the clergy had crossed swords more than once, and his ma wasn't in the mind of forgiving them. But she still made him go, and it was at Mass that he met the people who didn't live in crappy houses. He would see a girl he liked and follow her home. Every one of the good ones lived in big fancy houses to go with their silky hair and pretty faces.

Back then he didn't have the charisma he has now. That was something he'd had to develop. If any of them smelt a hint of crappiness off him, they'd bloody leg it. The accent was the hardest to shift, but the telly was great for that, movies especially. Some people used to think he was from the States. He took to calling streets 'blocks' and presses 'cupboards'. But it was better than school learning. School learning was all right as far as it went, but real life required something a whole lot different. It was all about judging your mark. If he had a rich punter in the garage, he would lean on the Dublin accent, helping the eejit think they were more intelligent. Being thought stupid had its advantages, once you knew things were the other way around.

Girls, they were different. They liked the Sandymount accent, or every now and again, he would pretend to be American, but never to an American: that would have been plain stupid. Seeing Clodagh Hamilton had brought back the old days, like the grime he'd felt under his skin when he was younger. The kind no showering ever washed off. Clodagh and Dominic Hamilton might as well have lived on a different planet, with their big house and nice clothes. Neither of them knew anything about shit. Born into Cosy Land, and a bit like Stevie not knowing he lived a life of crap, they didn't know they lived a life of luxury either.

Following Clodagh last night had brought back some of the old resentment. Stevie was smart. As a kid, he'd known more about the world than Dominic, Clodagh and even Martin McKay rolled into one. When you started off with nothing, you learned to fight for what you wanted. It was the only battleground that put you one step ahead of the likes of them.

That idiot Jenkins turning up dead meant something, but Stevie had no intention of meddling with the bigger fish first. Better to rattle Ruby McKay's cage. You can get so much more out of the mouths of babes.

Mervin Road

When the phone rang at lunchtime on Sunday, Kate thought it would be Declan, but she was wrong. Charlie had asked to go to Shane's again, and she hadn't the heart to say no. She didn't know whether to be relieved or disappointed when she heard Miriam's voice.

'Hi, Kate.'

Kate could hear both boys playing in the background. 'Is everything okay, Miriam?'

'Oh, yes. Perfect. The boys are in great form. They want to stay together for another while. I'm hearing "sleepover" but I'll see how they go. You know what they're like when they get overtired. You don't mind, do you, Kate? If you drop Charlie's stuff over later, I can take them both to school in the morning.'

'Miriam, you're very kind, but I'd prefer if Charlie didn't stay overnight.' Kate knew Miriam wouldn't be happy. Her refusal indicated a lack of trust. But she wasn't going to share information about Charlie's bedwetting, fearing Miriam would say something out of turn in front of Shane, and Charlie would end up the butt end of it. 'He's overtired already and his dad will be phoning him tonight.'

'Well, if you're sure. It's no bother.'

'No, honestly, you're too kind. Let me know when I'm to pick him up, and phone me if World War Three breaks out beforehand.' Kate let out a short laugh, hoping to lighten things.

'No problem. You can pick him up at five, and don't worry, I'll call you if they get too hot to handle.' It was her turn to laugh.

'Great. You have my mobile?'

'Sure, sure. Got to go. They're roaring for food.'

'Good luck.' Again Kate laughed.

'Let's hope I don't need it.' And with that Miriam hung up.

Kate decided to play the disk sent over by Mark Lynch, of Keith Jenkins's show, *Real People, Real Lives*. Lynch had put a note in the box, advising that Johnny Keegan, one of the people on the show, had been taken in for questioning.

The first thing Kate noted about Johnny Keegan was that, physically, he fitted the description given by Grace Power of the man holding up the weakened Keith Jenkins. On the second viewing, Kate rewound the tape to before Johnny Keegan sat beside his girlfriend, Suzanne Clarke, who also happened to be the mother of his child.

Keith Jenkins is positively energised by the time the lame Johnny Keegan walks onto the set, attacking Johnny verbally even before he's sat down. 'Do you know what always amazes me, my friend? It's how guys like you, with the ability to destroy people's lives, walk out here all downbeat, with their eyes looking to the floor, as if they're all sorry and humble.' Johnny sits up straight in the chair, not looking at his girlfriend. Kate noted the controlled rage in Keith Jenkins's voice when he turns to the audience, as if to get them on his side, then asks, 'What have you to say for yourself? What have you to say to the mother of your child? Go on. Look at her. Have a good look at the woman you like to beat around the place, like she's your personal punchbag.'

'Nothin'. I've nothin' to say.' Then, looking at his feet, 'I'm disgusted with myself. I can't explain it. I don't know what gets into me.'

'Don't know? Don't know? That's a nice easy answer.' Then, like the seasoned professional he was, Keith Jenkins turns back to the audience, keeping the camera in view, bringing the home and studio audience with him, and continues his attack on the now shrinking Johnny Keegan. 'Yeah, well, men like you, you're always disgusted afterwards. Did you feel disgusted when you hit her? Did you feel disgusted then?'

'I was drunk.'

'That's a reason for it, is it?' Jenkins points to Johnny's girlfriend. 'Suzanne here, she's scared of you. Do you know that?'

'I don't want her to be scared. I love her.'

'What's that? You love her? You've a pretty funny way of showing it, mate.'

'Doesn't mean it's not true.' His tone was quiet, but harsh.

'Will I tell you something, mate? She might be scared of you, but I'm not, far from it.'

'I know dat.' Johnny sits upright again, legs stretched out and apart, shoulders back.

'Do you know what, Johnny? Do you know what else? When I think about women, girls like little Suzanne here, I have to ask myself a question. Why can't they see what I can see? Do you know what I see?'

'No.'

'I see a selfish idiot who gets his kicks from beating up defenceless women. Someone more interested in pouring alcohol down his throat than doing something to help the woman he says he's in love with.'

'That's not true.'

'Isn't it? Well, mate, tell that to your girlfriend here. Tell that to your baby son. Let's see if he gives a damn about you when he's older, because that, my friend, is very questionable.'

'I told her I was sorry.'

Suzanne, who has remained silent throughout the whole

interview, finally speaks: 'But you gotta change, Johnny, for me and the baby.'

'Do you hear her, Johnny? Are you listening? Why don't you use some of the time you spend drinking to look after your son instead? You do remember him?'

'I'm nervous.' Again the young Johnny Keegan looks down to his feet.

'Nervous? Nervous of what? Is this another handy excuse? What are you saying? That because you drink you can't be trusted to mind him, to care for him, to do all the things fathers should do? Is that what you're saying?'

'In a way, yeah.' This time he locks eyes with Keith Jenkins.

'So, because you can't be trusted, you don't take any responsibility. That is convenient, isn't it?'

'You don't know anythin'.'

'Don't I? I know you, my son, your sort, too busy beating up women to take on a real man.'

And with that, Johnny Keegan's had enough, leaping out of the chair, attempting to land a blow on Keith Jenkins's face, before being pulled back by two mules dressed from head to toe in black.

As they drag Johnny Keegan off the set, Keith Jenkins kneels beside the now distraught Suzanne Clarke, putting his arms around her shoulders for a number of seconds, before standing up again. Turning to the television camera, he fixes his tie back neatly into the collar of his shirt, saying, 'We'll take an interval here, folks, but don't go anywhere – Keith Jenkins, *Real People, Real Lives.*'

Kate watched the final ten minutes of the recording, covering an interview with a woman who had had numerous extra-marital affairs, an interaction that reaffirmed some solid views that were forming in her mind about Keith Jenkins. He was no shrinking violet, and if he lived aspects of his life in a similar manner to his screen persona, then he must have picked up a lot of enemies along the way. If the rumours about him and women were true, then judging by how he'd attacked the last victim on the show, *vis-à-vis* her extra-marital affairs, then the old adage that people who live in glass houses shouldn't throw stones was not a concept the late celebrity had lived by.

The media would be jumping all over his family soon enough, not initially to dish any dirt – it was still a little early for that – but to empathise with the wife and kids left without their model husband and father. When it came to dissecting these stories for entertainment value, it was to be expected that the media would operate like a circus, one act following another. But one thing was for certain. Once the initial hype and sadness were over, the media would ultimately turn, and every single negative aspect of Keith Jenkins's life would be there for the taking.

Clodagh

Yesterday I had decided against taking a taxi home. It was a long walk, but I reached the strand faster than I expected. With the tide out, the beach stretched for miles. Instead of turning away from the strand and heading home, I kept walking towards the red-and-white chimneys of Sandymount. The calmness I'd felt with Gerard Hayden was gone. I knew something had changed inside me. There were questions to be answered.

In Mum's final hours she was delirious with morphine, but she still had moments of lucidity. 'Don't blame your dad,' she'd whispered to Dominic.

He'd thought I couldn't hear her, but I had grown accustomed to the low voice. 'I don't,' he whispered, the two of them holding hands like lovers.

To hell with them both, fuck them and their little secrets. Dominic shut me out, like he's always done, telling me it wasn't important. I felt like the outsider, and I hated her more than him for that.

Under the hypnosis, I'd talked about my old doll, Sandy. I have a fleeting memory of holding her in my arms, sitting with my back against my bedroom door, trying to keep it shut. Since Mum's death, other memories have seeped through. Images, smells and feelings I had forgotten. The smell of nicotine in my bedroom when my father came in to say goodnight; sitting at the top of the stairs with Dominic, his arms wrapped around me, telling me everything will be okay. I can't place the time, or work out why I'm crying, but for some reason I keep seeing my mother fixing her face in the hall mirror, lifting her right hand up to settle her hair, a turn, an extra-long glance towards me, then walking away without saying goodbye, as if she hated me. I want to catch her image before the mirror wipes it clear, before the woman who used to smile disappears all over again.

For the briefest moment, I wonder should I tell Martin about Gerard Hayden. I haven't told him about the row between Dominic and me either. The one after Mum died. Or how during my time in rehab I became more and more convinced that there was some darkness in my past, something I needed to face up to. He'll think I'm making excuses for being an alcoholic, dismiss me as nuts, or both. And maybe he'd be right.

Gerard Hayden told me my subconscious mind would protect me. It wouldn't bring me to a place of harm. I've made another appointment for tomorrow. Next time the regression will be different. Next time I'll be going back to that gaping hole in my memory. Gerard says all memory is kept intact by our subconscious. I hope he's right, and that my years of drinking haven't messed the whole bloody thing up.

While on the strand, I'd wondered why Dominic and I had both chosen to live in houses only a stone's throw from Seacrest. Martin wouldn't hear of living anywhere but Sandymount. 'Better an area you know than one you don't.' Maybe fucked-up familiar was strangely safe for us all.

Mervin Road

Mark Lynch phoned Kate after the Sunday-afternoon briefing. Morrison wouldn't have any test results from the lab until Monday at the earliest, but it was something he said about the blood deposits on the canal ledge that caused Kate to pause.

'Hold on a second, Mark. I want to take another look at the photographs in my study.'

'Okay.'

She looked at the images from the wider viewpoint. 'Mark, the low concrete wall running the length of the canal on either side, it links the two bridges together. You say Sarah Walsh picked up the blood deposits on the inner ledge. From here it looks about six foot long.'

'That's right.'

'Long enough to rest a body.'

'That's the theory. He used the ledge to assist the drowning.'

'We can assume the ledge formed part of the original canal structure.'

'I suppose.'

'But I can only see one ledge, and I'm looking at a full view from one bridge to the next.'

'So?'

'The ledge is parallel to where the tyre markings were found. The killer knew the exact point he wanted to stop at. He picked the location beforehand, even before the stabbing. The canal was his final destination.'

'Meaning?'

'That from the outset he wanted Keith Jenkins to die by drowning.'

'Kate, they're all screaming for your preliminary report.'

'You'll have it after I get the autopsy results. Tell O'Connor he should know better than to think these things can be rushed.'

'It's not only O'Connor.'

'Well, he's my link.'

'I'll pass on the message.'

'And the missing wedding ring. Did Morrison confirm his earlier views that the finger indentation meant it was routinely worn?'

'He did.'

Hanging up, Kate heard the Rathmines town-hall clock chime. She wondered again about Declan not being in touch. Maybe he was waiting for her to make the first call. Checking the signal on her mobile phone, she pressed 'contacts' and rang his number. As she did, it struck her that she hadn't thought about what to say to him. They would probably talk about Charlie, keeping it nice and civil. She would ask him about work, and he would do the same, both of them pretending that everything was fine. It was easier to bury your head in the sand from a distance. But what they weren't saying to each other was far more important than what they were. Judging by their last conversation, neither of them was prepared to move past simple pleasantries, keeping everything on safe ground.

Kate allowed the phone ring six times before hanging up. It wasn't like Declan not to be in touch, so instead of leaving a message, she texted two words, *Ring me*, her mind turning back to Keith Jenkins's murder.

The risk of the killer being seen was high, although his use of the ledge to facilitate the murder also meant he'd wanted to get in and out of the area quickly. The images from the study wall were still in her head: Keith Jenkins's floating body, his brown hair, the dark shade of a female blackbird, swaying like seaweed in the icy waters. As a child, she had picked up a near-dead female blackbird from the side of the road. Her mother had said it was cruel to let the bird suffer. The beady eyes had stared at Kate, one female to another. She never found out what had happened to it. Her father had probably dealt with it. Even now, passing that spot on the road, she thinks about the blackbird, the worn-out eyes, beating chest, and the feel of bloodied feathers in her hands as she carried it home to what had been certain death. Thinking about the murder location, she knew place was always important. People and places come together for a reason. If the canal was chosen, could that particular stretch be of significance to the killer? And what was the thinking behind Keith Jenkins dying in that way?

Murder was full of secrets. Why had it happened? Who knew about it? Were there crimes within the crime? Nothing operates in isolation. Everything had connections, small or large.

Kate went back into the study, staring again at the images on the wall. She thought about how often the answers were not in what you saw but in what you couldn't see. The wedding band: it being missing was significant, but was anything else missing? According to O'Connor, everything else was intact. None of the victim's clothing, other than his scarf, which could have been lost anywhere, had been removed. Even his shoes had remained on his feet. Kate nearly missed hearing her mobile phone ringing in the other room, but she got to it in time to catch O'Connor, knocking her leg off the side of the couch in her effort to get there fast. Ever since their meeting at the canal, with Mark Lynch appointed as the official go-between, she had figured her contact with O'Connor would be less direct. On answering the call, she registered the sharpness in her own voice, which was less about her throbbing leg and more about their new communication set-up.

'You sound frazzled, Kate.'

'Me? No, I'm fine.'

'I hear the killer's objective from the start was to drown Keith Jenkins.'

'It's looking like that.' Kate sat down, rubbing the side of her shin to ease the pain.

'What's your theory on why the killer chose the canal? He could have drowned the bastard in a bath – no witnesses. It would have saved him a whole lot of bother.'

'I've been thinking about that. People, events, they're not straightforward, as well you know. There could be any number of reasons for the canal being chosen. Ease of distance from where the killer lived. Maybe he doesn't live alone, eliminating his place as a location for murder. The canal waters are significant, but so is the choice of drowning. He wanted Keith Jenkins to die in that way. Perhaps the icy waters meant something to the killer and the victim. And there's also the timing. The lack of people on the streets. It all made sense to the killer. Right now that's all we can be sure of.'

'I'm planning a trip to the Caldine Club on Kildare Street, the one where Keith Jenkins was last seen being friendly. I have the glossy brochure in front of me. It says it embodies the heart of the city.'

'Do I detect a note of disbelief, O'Connor?'

'If people want to see the heart of the city, they can take a lift in one of our squad cars on a Friday or Saturday night.'

'I don't think you'd get too many volunteers.'

'Probably not, Kate. Somehow I think the queue for the Caldine could be longer.'

'Selective membership, I assume.'

'From what I hear there are only three ways of gaining access.'

'And what are they?'

'If you're God Almighty, if you're rich and famous ...' O'Connor paused for effect '... or if you strike gold and become part of the team investigating the murder of an ex-member.'

'You got lucky.'

'*We* got lucky. Things have been crazy here today, but I'll be paying them a surprise visit in the morning. It might be a good idea if you're with me.'

'I hear you're also looking for my preliminary report.'

'You know the score, Kate. Everything is needed yesterday. Are you able to meet me tomorrow or not?'

'Fine. I'll let you know if there's any problem.'

And with that the line went dead.

Parnell Road

My pent-up, fucked-up anger seems to have taken a vacation for now. But it will come back. It always does. 'Rich man, poor man, beggar man, thief.' I repeat the mantra below my breath, over and over again. It helps my mind to remain centred on the task in hand, to be clear and without hesitation.

Yesterday I passed the reporters and squad cars at Leeson Street Bridge. That place is behind me now. There's a chill blowing in off the canal. The kind that should make me feel more alive, but instead, despite Jenkins's blood being washed away, I feel sullied. Some stains are not for shifting.

I think of Clodagh, shrouded in her veil of ignorance and, for the moment, safe. She is part of all of this, the most important part. But Clodagh isn't going anywhere. You don't run unless you know you're in danger. And right now she doesn't know the game plan. Or even that one exists. It will all be finished business soon enough.

I see the two old lads up ahead – partners in crime. Desperate times dictate desperate bedfellows. I have no plans to make my move now. I'll wait until the two boys settle down for the night, with their charity sleeping-bags, and curled-up memories of what it was like to have a warm bed. If it doesn't happen tonight, I can wait for another.

I have become a man of the streets too. When you're out walking, no one asks the hard questions. You'd think killing someone would change things. It doesn't, not really, 'Rich man, poor man, beggar man, thief. Rich man, poor man, beggar man, thief.'

Clodagh

I've tried to reach Ruby a number of times and got the usual 'The person you are calling is not available at the moment. Please try again later.' No doubt her battery is dead, or her phone hidden under a pile of dirty laundry. Perhaps she's switched it off. There's no landline in her bedsit. At least the place is close to college. Ruby says she loves the buzz of town, away from the boring smugness of suburbia. I thought that too. God, I hate her being on that bloody stuff. She says the coke isn't a problem for her. I've to get off her case. I used the same lines, neither of us fooling anyone.

I switch on the television in the kitchen. The news is full of the murder of that celebrity, Keith Jenkins. I've never watched *Real People, Real Lives*. My life is real enough. But there's something about him that I can't quite put my finger on. It could be Martin's investment business. He's had dealings with people in RTÉ. Martin's always been good with other people's money. But there's something else, I'm sure of it.

I check for messages on the answerphone. None from Ruby, but there's one from Orla. She wants to know if I got her letter – bloody Martin, controlling the post. If Orla sent me a letter, he should have given it to me. More images of Keith Jenkins appear on the screen. Some are recent, showing a handsome man in his late fifties, then others, when he started out in his career. It's when I see the images of the young Keith Jenkins that I realise why I know his face.

I walk out into the hall, pulling the old photographs I took from Seacrest out of my bag. I had not expected to be looking at this one so soon, my father with his friends. It's his graduation year. The year after my parents married, and Dominic was born. Up until now, I didn't know anyone in the photograph other than Dad and Uncle Jimmy. But now I have another name. Keith Jenkins can be added to the list. He looks a lot younger than the others, barely a teenager, but tall. His right arm is resting on Jimmy's shoulder. Maybe they're related. I don't know the fourth man. He stands alone, but there's something familiar about him too.

I hear the sound of the electric gates opening. Martin's car is pulling into the drive. Lately, even Sundays have turned into work days for him. Perhaps he's avoiding me. I tell myself to be calm. If he's taken Orla's letter, it doesn't mean he's read it. Orla addressed it to me. But to Martin, information is power.

His key turns in the front door, and right away I can sense his mood isn't good. It's the small things, the sharp twist of the lock, extra force brought to bear on the door, the way he slams it shut, fires his keys onto the hall table. They're all signs. I brace myself for a row, steadying my nerves. He drops his briefcase with a thud on the floor, taking a couple of steps closer to me. He goes to kiss my cheek, but I turn away. He looks down at the photograph in my hand, surprise on his face. He's quick to get his dig in. 'Taking another trip down Memory Lane?'

'Do you have Orla's letter, Martin?'

'And how are you, my darling?'

'Do you have it, yes or no?'

'Yes, I do, actually.'

'Why didn't you give it to me?'

'I didn't want to bother you. Lately your mind has been all over the place.' He looks at the photograph again.

'Stop treating me as if I'm a child.'

'Then stop behaving like one.'

'Have you read it, Martin?'

'Should I have? You and Orla used to be as thick as thieves.'

'That was a long time ago, and you know it.'

'I never liked her,' he says, with disgust in his voice.

'The feeling was mutual. You've read it, haven't you?'

'Do you think I've sunk that low? That I've taken to reading other people's mail? Now why would *I* do that? Why would *I* do such a thing?' He emphasises *I*, as if making an accusation against me. He moves closer again, so close that, if I wanted to, I could reach out and touch him. I need to keep my nerve.

'Martin, why have you been keeping the mail from me?'

He walks past me, into the living room. 'Do you mind, darling? I'd prefer to sit inside.'

I follow him. 'It's a free country,' I say.

'Is it, Clodagh? Maybe for some people it is.' He sounds angry. 'I can see what's happening here. Suddenly I'm the bad guy. I guess working hard, paying the bills, being here to support my alcoholic wife counts for nothing. Maybe Orla thinks you can do better. Be with someone less boring.'

'Don't be ridiculous.'

He doesn't respond.

'Just give me the letter, Martin.'

'Polite people use the word "please".'

'Please give me the letter.'

'See how easy that was, Clodagh?' He walks back out to the hall, and returns with his briefcase, slamming it onto the low coffee table. When he lifts the lid, I can see Orla's letter sitting on the top. He hands it to me. 'You look tired, darling. Maybe you should lie down. Your mother's death is still very fresh.'

I don't answer him, but I can already see that the letter has been interfered with. There is a small tear on one side, and the line of adhesive is bubbled. I think about not passing any comment, but instead I say, 'You've opened it.'

'Have I?'

'Martin, what's going on?'

'What do you mean?'

'Why are you keeping the mail from me? Is something wrong?'

'I'm not keeping the mail from you. Most, if not all of it, is addressed to me.'

'But you opened my letter. I can see it's been opened.'

'Is that the case for the prosecution? You're an expert on letter-opening, are you?'

'Don't be flippant.'

'Flippant? Seems to me I'm not the one being flippant. It seems to me, I'm the innocent party here.'

'I can tell you opened it.'

'Can you? How do you know it was me?' His face is mocking.

'Martin, stop twisting things.'

He walks into the kitchen. Again I follow him. He takes down a bottle of Beaujolais from the wine rack. I wait while he pops the cork.

'Clodagh, I'm not the person with the problem here. You are.' He looks at the photograph in my hand again. 'I didn't open your precious letter for one very good reason. It wasn't addressed to me. I thought about it, yes, but I have standards. I know where to draw the line.'

'You're lying.' He's an expert liar.

He puts the glass to his lips, swallows some wine. I can tell he's trying to restrain himself. Instead of letting it go, I push further, a part of me wondering if I haven't learned anything over the years.

'Liar,' I say, my voice shaking.

'What's that?'

'You heard me. You're lying,' I roar at him. 'You opened it. I know you did.'

He puts his glass down. It has been a while since his last outburst, but I recognise the way he looks at me, and know what will happen next.

The back of his right hand hits my left cheek. His aim: determined, solid. I fall back, but remain upright. I won't be upright for long. The next belt hits my jaw, the photograph falling to the floor. It's almost a relief, the physical pain, like I'm getting punished for all the mistakes I've made. Martin has played on this before, my need to blame myself.

Once he starts, there is no going back. Afterwards, he will say, 'Sorry.' He will tell me he has been under pressure. He will say how much he loves me. How much he loves Ruby. That he loves us more than anything, that we mean the whole world to him. Then he will twist and turn things, until everything is the gospel according to Martin.

Harcourt Street

On Monday morning after Kate had dropped Charlie to school, she headed to Harcourt Street, instead of driving to Ocean House, parking as close as she could to the station. She was keen to see the private members club on Kildare Street. The victim's lifestyle was important, whether it was directly connected with his death or not. Patterns of behaviour, where and with whom the victim came into contact, often formed the opportunity for a crime. Did Keith Jenkins's lifestyle make him particularly vulnerable, or the very opposite? Was it a lifestyle shared by his killer? The Caldine Club was the last place Keith Jenkins had been seen alive, and it was as good a place as any to begin the journey backwards into the dead man's life.

∞

Kate rang O'Connor as soon as she entered the station. The Special Detective Unit at the heart of the building felt very different from your standard police station, where people could walk in off the street. The further into this building Kate went, the more the outside world seemed to be left behind.

She already knew O'Connor would be a couple of minutes late. As she waited inside a long corridor without windows, lit by fluorescent lights, she couldn't help noticing a teenage girl with her head down, sitting on one of the black plastic chairs against the wall. The girl's light frame reminded her of Imogen Willis. But it was more than her slightness. It was the crumpled look of her body. The girl's hands were locked together. Sitting beside her, an older woman was holding her by the shoulders. Before Kate could take in any more, a female police officer poked her head out of a side door. 'Susie, we're ready for you now.' The girl looked sideways at the older woman and, as if reading her mind, the female officer added, 'It's okay, Susie. You can bring your mother with you.'

Kate didn't have to wait much longer for O'Connor.

'Are you ready for our excursion, Kate?' His manner was upbeat as he joined her in the corridor.

'What?'

'Our trip into how the other half lives.'

'Oh, sorry, yeah. I got distracted there for a minute.' Standing up to follow him through the double doors, she said, 'O'Connor?'

'Yeah?'

'There was a young girl here a minute ago, Susie, I think her name was.'

'What about her?'

'Do you know why she's here?'

'Suspected rape – Hennessy's looking after it.' His voice turned sharp: 'It's his area of expertise.'

Kate knew the drill, and it wasn't easy. A nurse would do the initial examination, including inspection of genitalia for evidence of trauma, bruises or abrasions. The girl's fingernails would be checked, scrapings collected, any stains swabbed, samples taken from her clothing, everything collated, right down to the combing of her pubic hair. It was an ordeal for sure, but a lot had changed in how victims were treated. Nothing would be done without explanation, the consent of the victim and, depending on her age, her parent. The most important thing for her was the sense that she was back in control. Rape victims experienced far more than the assault. It was nothing like a punch in the face or other kinds of physical attack. It carried emotional and social damage that few other crimes came close to. Despite her ordeal, this was Susie's first step to recovery. As well as receiving medical treatment for any injuries, and prevention against infection, her mental well-being would be monitored.

As Kate followed O'Connor out onto the street, she remembered for the zillionth time how close she had come to being another Susie.

'O'Connor?'

'Yeah?'

'I'd like to talk to Hennessy about the girl.'

'Kate, focus on the case in hand. There's no point trying to save the bloody world. Besides, Hennessy and I aren't exactly on the best of terms.'

'So?'

'So drop it. I've got news from Morrison.'

Off South Circular Road

It had been a while since Stevie had called in a Monday-morning sickie, so he felt relaxed enough sitting in his car watching a pair of lovebirds kissing. This area was student flatland. The girl was playing coy, but she was probably different in the sack. Had he not noticed Ruby McKay's ginger hair from the corner of his eye, he might have missed her altogether. Like Mummy dearest, she had that clear porcelain skin, but instead of beautiful curls, Ruby's hair was cropped tight. She had the high forehead too, but with her small pert nose and pretty lips, she had more the look of Lavinia Hamilton than Clodagh.

There were six of them in the group. Stevie could tell Ruby was playing the boys off against one other, the other two girls barely getting a look in. The guys wanted her, the girls wanted to be like her. Anyone within a five-mile radius could see that.

None of them took any heed of him, far too caught up in their own conversations to be bothering with anyone else. Stevie didn't believe in gangs, not any more. Gangs required allegiances, and he wasn't an allegiance kind of guy.

They chatted among themselves for as long as it took Stevie to smoke two cigarettes, laughing like hyenas at each other's jokes, finding the whole bloody world hilarious.

Ruby hadn't looked quite so happy puking her guts up outside Neary's when her friend had to call her a taxi home. Stevie was glad he'd noted the address off the South Circular. She hadn't looked happy the night he'd seen her in the window of that fancy restaurant either, living it up with a man three times her age.

Perhaps it was the smile growing on Stevie's face that had caused

Ruby to notice him for the first time. She'd given him a look all right. He had seen it a couple of times before, the who-gave-you-permission-to-enter-my-magical-kingdom look. He smiled right back at her, and the testosterone-fuelled idiot beside her must have sensed something was wrong because he looked across at Stevie, asking, 'Are ya all right there, bro?'

Fucking bro, thought Stevie. The one thing he sure wasn't was this guy's brother. 'Ah, yeah, cool. Waiting for someone. You don't mind, do you?' It wasn't a question Stevie expected an answer to. 'Pretend I'm not here.' He shot them another smile.

'Let's go,' Ruby said to the others, continuing to stare back at Stevie. And as they walked away, the thought uppermost in Stevie's mind was that he had managed to rattle the little princess. There had been something in the flicker of those eyes. She hadn't liked seeing him there, convincing Stevie that his hunch was right. The girl was hiding something.

He drove on past the group, slowing down to register the exact address. The place was a bit of a hovel, a far cry from her home in Sandymount, which was a three-storey number with wrought-iron gates and a gravelled drive. He had heard through the grapevine that Martin McKay, despite driving a top-of-the-range black Mercedes, was feeling the pinch moneywise. Maybe Ruby wasn't the only family member keeping secrets.

Thinking about the old house on Sandymount Strand, it irked him that, as a boy, he had imagined being part of it, not just some unwanted visitor. Ruby wasn't his type. She was too much like the grandmother. Clodagh was special, though, the gorgeous feel of her hair, and how the rain frizzed it into a wonderful mass of tiny curls. He remembered her as a kid too, how she was always talking to those bloody dolls of hers. As if they knew the answer to everything.

Harcourt Street

Striding up Harcourt Street heading towards the Kildare Street club, Kate had to pull O'Connor back. 'Will you slow down and fill me in on what Morrison had to say?'

'Oh, yeah, right. Sorry, Kate.' Then, pointing to a small coffee shop near the top of the street, he said, 'Let's grab a coffee. Mr Devoy can wait for a bit.'

It was far too cold to be sitting outside, but Kate didn't object when O'Connor waved to the small iron tables at the front of the café. Once a copper, always a copper: less chance of being overheard outside than in. When O'Connor appeared back with a tray and two tiny cups of coffee, she smiled, but he kept his face serious.

'Blasted cups wouldn't last two seconds in the station. Places like this have no idea what the size of a proper mug should be.' He lit a cigarette.

'I thought you'd quit.'

'Yeah, well, that was then.'

Kate let it go. 'You were going to tell me about Morrison.'

O'Connor took a long drag. 'He's got some early results. The liquid in Jenkins's lungs confirmed diatoms in his system. Morrison is a happy man – the bastard loves it when he's right.'

'Diatoms?'

'Yeah – minute organisms scurrying around in the water. It's the final confirmation that Jenkins was alive before taking the dip. Morrison also took swabs from under the fingernails. Weak or not, Keith Jenkins put up a fight, so let's hope our pal has history.'

'When will I have the autopsy report?'

'Whenever I get it. I've only got verbals from Morrison.'

'So let's hear them.'

'Half a dozen puncture wounds, all within the same location on the body, below the ribcage. The width, thickness and depth implied severe thrusting into the torso. A double-sided blade was used. It wasn't a large weapon. The attacker could have hidden it on his person before the assault.'

'And the dimensions of the blade?'

'Approximately an inch in width. It sank into the body seven inches. Allowing for the area below the handle, it could have been an eight-inch knife. Morrison thinks it might be a domestic kitchen knife.'

'And the sequence?'

'All but one puncture wound happened directly after one another. There was a final, deeper thrust, probably seconds after the first attack. The last wound did the most damage. After that, the victim would have been like putty.'

'So it was a frenzied attack initially, then a last deciding penetration.'

'That's what the master says.' O'Connor lit another cigarette. 'So, what do you think?'

'I think we need to look on the knife attack and the drowning as separate entities. The stabbing is primarily expressive violence, but the drowning was undoubtedly instrumental violence.'

'Meaning what, Kate?'

'The first tells us more about the emotional feeling involved. It was aggressive, frenzied, and the sequence is also interesting.'

'Go on.'

'The drowning brings a different dimension. When I say, "instrumental", it represents a means to an end.'

'He wanted him dead.'

'Yes, and this was his chosen way of achieving it.' Finishing her coffee, Kate looked at O'Connor, waiting for the signal to move. But he didn't seem in any hurry. If she hadn't known better, she'd have said he was stalling.

'So how are things with you, Kate, and young Charlie? What age is he now? Four?'

'Five. He's finding some things difficult – you know, school and all.'

'Five! God Almighty, that's old.' O'Connor managed a laugh. 'You'll be worrying about his college points so.'

O'Connor didn't have any children, nor was he married, which meant he lived in a separate universe as far as Kate was concerned.

'Come on, O'Connor. I don't know about you, but I'm freezing.' She stood up. O'Connor did the same. Then, both of them walking towards Kildare Street, Kate asked, 'What's the final upshot with Johnny Keegan?'

'He'll probably walk. Right now it looks like the girlfriend is backing him up. But you can be darn sure that whatever Morrison got from beneath those fingernails, we'll be looking to play snap when the test results come in.'

'What about the CCTV footage?'

'We've pieced a lot of it together. There's a sighting of Jenkins shortly after he left the club, heading down Hatch Street, then another at a late-night shop near Charlemont Street.'

'Very close to the canal.'

'Yes, but two hours earlier on.'

'Have you any idea why Jenkins was out walking? He could have got a taxi home to Malahide.'

'The current girlfriend lives in town, a Siobhan King. Maybe he was planning to spend the night with her.'

'What does she do?'

'PR stuff mostly.'

'But why walk, O'Connor?'

'Perhaps he needed some air.'

'He was alone, I assume.'

'Yeah, for the most part.'

'For the most part?'

'A guy standing outside a late-night shop was picked up on the footage. The two of them had a chat. They both lit cigarettes.'

'So they knew each other.'

'Not necessarily, Kate. Strangers often ask each other for a light.'

'But whoever it was, they would have recognised him?'

'Maybe. The press office put out a request on the lunchtime bulletin, asking the guy to come forward, but nothing yet.'

'And after Charlemont Street? Anything after that?'

'Not so far.'

Looking up at the building on Kildare Street, O'Connor asked, 'Are you ready to see how the other half lives?

'Sure, why not?'

'Good. Let's start disturbing these lovely people.'

'Careful, O'Connor,' she chided.

'You know me, Kate. I'm full of sensitivity.'

Clodagh

The skin on my face is still throbbing. It will bruise more, but there's no blood. I've no intention of leaving Ruby's room until Martin has gone to work. Orla's letter is still downstairs on the coffee table.

Opening my compact, I check the damage, twisting to get a better view in the small, round mirror. My face looks like it's been split down the middle. One side normal, the other side puffed up like an oversized black mushroom fermenting in the dark. It has been a while since Martin hit out. The last time it was because he had been taken for a fool in some property investment deal. They say you always take it out on the ones you love. Well, he showed his love that time all right. I was drinking then. I let it go. Now it's different. Now it's more a question of time.

If I wasn't a battered wife, I might ask why women stay with such men. They're seen as monsters, best written out of your life. But outsiders don't understand. Perhaps I'm a coward – yet another label to stamp on my forehead. Martin has his own demons. I'm not the only one carrying hang-ups from childhood. I'm merely the punchbag. What most people see when they meet Martin is an illusion. He can even trick himself, setting himself up as the guy who likes to put things straight, show what a great man he is.

Martin is still moving around downstairs. His next meeting must be late morning. He's listening to the news on the radio. He drank the bottle of Beaujolais last night, before going out again. Martin isn't really a drinker. He took it to spite me. I hear the radio being switched off. He'll leave soon. I wait until he pulls the front door behind him, giving it a few seconds before I open the door of Ruby's bedroom.

I catch a glimpse of my face in the hall mirror downstairs, and think about my old doll, Emma. The one we put in the attic in the box for broken toys. I had forgotten about that box too. Emma had a white porcelain face, cold and smooth when you touched it, except for her eyelashes, which were long and frail, as delicate as a spider's web. Her face split in two one summer after a fall. Mum and Dad had had a huge fight. Both Dominic and I were sent upstairs. Dominic was dragging me up by the arm, but I didn't want to leave. I didn't want to be sent upstairs. It was a Sunday. I hated Sundays. Dominic was hurting me, and I was telling him to stop. That was when I dropped her. An ugly jagged crack went from the top of her forehead into her neck. The rest of her body was soft so it wasn't damaged. Even her eyelashes remained intact. Every bit of Emma's face was still there; not one piece of the porcelain had fallen out. It had just cracked in two, leaving a gaping black slash where once there had been a beautiful face. I remember looking into the crack, trying to find out what was behind it, wondering if the line was something bad, like the cracks in the pavement I used to skip over as a child so I wouldn't go to Hell. But all I saw was emptiness.

When she fell, she became a different doll, her insides exposed. I thought there was a change in her expression, a kind of sadness to her eyes, knowing everyone would see her differently from then on.

'Once broken, it can't be fixed.' That was what Dominic had said. 'You can't fix her, so throw her away.' He was being mean. He wasn't usually mean, but he was upset too. He didn't want to go upstairs either. He would get like that sometimes. It was the same when I wanted to play with him, Stevie and Martin, and he would tell me I couldn't be in their gang because I was a girl. But I didn't throw Emma away. A part of her is still here, living inside me.

Caldine Club, Kildare Street

Kate waited beside an open fire on the upper terrace. The place was the ultimate in chic, with rectangular stone tables, blue-and-white-striped couches on one side, pale-yellow-cushioned armchairs on the other. Each chair and couch had its own charcoal blanket with the emblem 'CC' embroidered in silver-grey thread.

She took in the two fifty-something females, with their designer bags, and the men in business suits at the far end. All of them sent only a fleeting glance towards her and O'Connor, then returned to their private conversations, except for the attractive waitress, who'd brought O'Connor downstairs to find the manager, Mr Devoy.

Under her arm Kate had the glossy brochure O'Connor had given to her. Flicking through the pages, she read the section on the upper terrace where she was standing – 'an exceptional delight, superb dining under the Dublin skyline, with glorious music. A place where friends can meet and beautiful memories can be formed.' Looking down on the street below, at the rough and tumble of the city, Kate was reminded of *Gulliver's Travels*, and how from on high, Gulliver looked down on the little people of Lilliput.

It wasn't long before O'Connor reappeared, gesturing to her to follow him. Inside, the building was as impressive as the terrace, reflecting sophistication and history, a place for the rich élite. James Devoy brought Kate and O'Connor into a second dining room. This time it was an empty one.

Devoy was a small man, no more than five foot two, and looked even smaller alongside O'Connor. He had dark Italian features, and Kate figured him to be in his late thirties. The second dining room was elaborate, its dark solid wood panels carved with floral designs. Again the tables were dressed in a combination of blue and complementary shades. This time the pale yellow was replaced by dark navy, contrasting with white candles and napkins.

'Mr Devoy.' O'Connor's voice sounded strangely out of place.

'James, Detective Inspector, call me James.' Kate could tell the manager was already too friendly for O'Connor's liking.

'James,' O'Connor replied, not offering the same instruction back, 'my colleague tells me you were on duty the night of Keith Jenkins's murder.'

'Yes, that's right.' Devoy looked uncomfortable with the word 'murder'. 'I started my shift at eight, and continued until three the following morning. I have already given your colleague a list of those who attended the club.'

'Was there anything unusual about Keith Jenkins's behaviour, or anyone he came into contact with?'

'We had a full house, Detective Inspector. Mr Jenkins, Keith, drank in the private members bar.' His voice weakened as he mentioned Keith Jenkins's name, as if he'd lost someone close to him.

'So it was a busy night? The drink flowing, was it?'

'It was a long night, Detective Inspector.'

'How would you describe Mr Jenkins's mental state during the evening?'

'He was his usual cheery, chatty self.'

'Was there anyone in particular he spent time with?'

'Only Pete.'

'Pete?'

'Pete Moore, the DJ.'

'Buddies, were they?'

'You could say that. I think Pete wanted more out of their friendship, if you get my drift.'

'Really?' O'Connor made no attempt to hide his curiosity.

'Don't get me wrong, Detective Inspector, all our gents behave with discretion. It's something we pride ourselves on at the club.'

'Well, in my book, Mr Devoy, the avoidance of discretion usually gets to the truth faster.'

'All I'm saying is, they were good friends.'

'I see Siobhan King wasn't on the list of visitors that night.'

'No, Keith tended to enjoy certain nights with the boys. She hasn't been here for a while. The last time must have been over two weeks ago.'

'And how was their mood on that occasion?'

'Good. They had dinner downstairs, the public section.'

'And did they stay for long?'

'No. They left in rather a hurry, quite surprising.'

'So what spooked them, James?'

'"Spooked" might be a bit dramatic, Detective Inspector, but I will admit Keith's demeanour changed rather quickly.'

'Maybe a friend of his wife saw the two of them. It's never good when the *little wife* catches you out.'

'Perhaps you're right, Detective Inspector,' a degree of hostility had come into his voice, 'but it's not like their relationship was secret. Either way, if they wished to remain, we could have brought them to dine upstairs. There's always a private table for special members of the club.'

Kate, who had taken a back seat up until this point, decided to take it gently with the club manager. 'Mr Devoy?'

'James, please.' He turned his attention from O'Connor to Kate.

'You seem to imply that Keith Jenkins felt uncomfortable in the public restaurant. Otherwise, why suggest the private one upstairs?'

'Well, when he asked for the bill early, I asked him if there was anything wrong.'

'And what did he say?' Kate kept direct eye contact with James Devoy, knowing O'Connor was also waiting to hear the answer.

'I thought it strange at the time, but then I forgot about it.'

O'Connor stood forward. 'Forgot about what, Mr Devoy?'

'Keith said everything was fine, then muttered something about old friends best forgotten. It was a strange thing to say, but you get used to hearing a lot of strange things around here. You learn not to bat an eyelid, one way or another.'

O'Connor, who had been taking everything down, turned another page in his notebook. 'The diners in the public restaurant that night, you would have a list of them, Mr Devoy?'

'Oh, yes. We're very careful when it comes to taking bookings from non-members. I'll get it for you.'

'Most kind of you.'

When Devoy had left, Kate couldn't resist taking a swipe at O'Connor. 'I see you're already getting used to this high life, "most kind of you"!'

'Ah, get off my case. This type of place messes with your head. Ten minutes into it, and I'm already acting like a performing monkey.'

'Would you put Keith Jenkins into that category?'

'I don't know, Kate. Like me, apparently, he came from humble beginnings. The only difference is, I stayed there.'

'My heart bleeds for you.'

'You know what they say about new money, Kate? It can fuck you up fast.'

'Hardly new, he's been successful for over twenty-five years.'

'About the same age as his latest female companion,' O'Connor retorted, with emphasis.

'Well, apparently men never grow old, O'Connor, if they have enough money.'

'I'm screwed so.'

Kate laughed, and O'Connor smiled, looking more like his old self. 'Kate, I was thinking. Maybe at some point the two of us could meet up for a drink.'

'I'm not sure – it's kind of awkward. Declan's away.'

'It's just an idea, don't worry if you'd prefer not.'

'No, it's fine – perhaps when my case work gets a little less manic.'

'Grand so.'

When Devoy returned, he handed O'Connor the list, looking pleased with his efficiency. 'Anything else I can help you with, Detective Inspector?'

'No, thank you, Mr Devoy. We know where you are, should anything else come up.'

'Great.'

Outside, O'Connor received a call from the station. Kate took it as her opportunity to leave, merely waving goodbye.

Why had O'Connor asked her out for a drink? Her head felt in a mess. And why had Declan bloody well not called? Driving to Ocean House, Kate put the conversation with O'Connor to the back of her mind. She had a long day ahead and plenty on her plate, not only this case but working out a strategy for Imogen Willis. But she couldn't shake the thought that O'Connor wasn't the kind of guy to ask female friends or colleagues out for a quiet drink, unless there was something on his mind.

Parnell Road

I followed the two of them from the temporary shelter in Camden Street last night. It was the final one on the list, and I was hoping it wouldn't have room for Jimmy and his pal. Opportunity will beckon soon enough. I need to control my rage. Clodagh has a habit of knowing which buttons to press. I can't afford to allow silly emotions get in the way.

The first killing was easier than I'd thought it would be, easier than the anger. My mind has slipped all too readily into this half-life. I have held conversations keeping up the pretence. I have even closed my eyes, as if I'm entitled to sleep, as if I remain the same man. And, as night follows day, the next deed will be done.

He's with that tramp called Ozzie Brennan again. It's hard to miss that thick grey curly hair of his, not to mention his drink-ridden face. Calls himself a poet, he does. Well, maybe he is. My gripe isn't with Ozzie. He can write a lament about his friend Jimmy when he's gone.

I light a cigarette, keen to get some nicotine inside me. The two old lads will be together for the rest of the afternoon. They've already picked their special bench, with its folded cardboard layers to keep them snug, and their ringside view of the canal, Ozzie thinking he's Kavanagh, mourning the dead poet, while Jimmy does what he's always done: sweet fuck-all.

Give the two of them enough cans, and the boys will start arguing. Night will come soon too, and if they separate, then Jimmy and I can have our date with Destiny. He won't see it coming. I'll make sure of that.

Mervin Road

At Ocean House, Kate checked if she'd missed a call from Declan – still nothing. Blast him to Hell. If he didn't want to check in on their son, that was his problem. Her next appointment wasn't until later in the afternoon so she contacted Imogen's social worker to set up the family meeting. After that she began her preliminary report on the Jenkins killing.

There were set norms in the psychological investigative cycle, the first stage of which was information-gathering. Every detail was important, no matter how obscure it might seem. In the early stages of an investigation, there were any number of ways could go, but irrespective of this, the facts as presented were the solid blocks from which everything else followed.

Preliminary Report on the Murder of Keith Jenkins
Compiled by Dr Kate Pearson
Crime-scene characteristics
- Primary crime scene
- Middle-aged male victim, age 57
- Well-known public figure
- Public location – Grand Canal (below Leeson Street Bridge)
- Cause of death: drowning
- Other factors: multiple stab wounds to lower chest
- Slash markings on victim's right arm
- Knife attack at secondary location
- Estimated time of death five a.m.

- Last sighting pending CCTV footage: late-night shop, Charlemont Street
- Wedding ring missing
- Scarf missing (based on witness statements from earlier sightings)
- All other valuables left with victim
- Victim semi-conscious: capable of walking while aided prior to death
- Assailant and victim arrived by car
- Assailant similar in build to victim, with dark brown hair
- Death by drowning within moments of arrival at canal
- Large blood pooling and blood splatters at crime scene; blood type that of victim
- Victim put up resistance prior to drowning
- Deposits below victim's nails – test results outstanding
- Secondary evidence found at scene inclusive of hotel receipt: awaiting full police report

Crime Inferences
- Crime scene: semi-organised
- Killer capable of overcoming victim with aid of weapon – small double-edged knife, exact type unknown; could be domestic kitchen knife
- Degree of planning: knowledge and use of canal ledge to facilitate drowning
- Minimal human traffic, reducing potential witnesses at time of killing
- Access to knife, or present on person, during initial stabbing
- Access to transport: car
- Victim: well-built male in good health, capable of defence

- Slash markings on victim's right arm consistent with attempted defence
- Knife attack at secondary location severe; victim would have bled to death if left unaided
- Death does not appear to be financially motivated
- Multiple stabs wounds; frenzied attack, then a final thrusting
- Killer capable of planning next move
- Stabbing, although frenzied and indicative of emotionally driven aggression, inconclusive as to principal motivation
- Location and means of killing: appears planned
- Initial attack: also potentially planned
- Celebrity status of victim opens up wide pool of potential suspects

Conclusions

- Killer: male
- Similar in build to victim; possibly similar in age
- Physically capable of overcoming victim with a weapon (knife)
- Stabbing indicates aggressive mental state
- First assault – knife wounds – 'expressive violent act', resulting from an outburst of emotional feeling
- Second fatal assault – drowning – 'instrumental violence': used as a means to an end
- Killer capable of displaying calmness after initial attack, following through on actions by driving to canal to carry out murder
- Choice of location could be critical
- Cause of death – preferred choice of killer – drowning, could also be critical

- Despite being deserted at time of killing, choice of public place 'high risk': fear of being caught not uppermost in the killer's mind
- If method of killing, location of murder, and timing are not random, choice of victim <u>unlikely to be random</u>.

In many ways, it all pointed to the one question that had played on her mind since she had received the first call from O'Connor. Why bring a dying man to the canal to drown him?

She thought about the images pinned on her study wall at home. If she could turn back the clock, what would the dead Keith Jenkins say to her? Where would he tell her to look? Was it his missing wedding ring, the hotel receipt or something else? Semi-conscious when he arrived at the canal, Keith Jenkins would have seen the face of his killer. He would have been aware that the killer had the power to determine his fate. Had Keith Jenkins called out for mercy or, when he had looked into the eyes of the killer, had he known death would be the only outcome?

Kate hadn't thought about Professor Henry Bloom in a while but they had had many conversations about society's reaction to the killing of another. Socially acceptable in wartime, when the group dynamic shifts its view from the norm, doesn't rest easily on the shoulders of the civilised world when the killing is outside this margin. The very existence of killers, people willing to harm others, threatens us all. Kate also knew from her time with Henry that the line between good and evil is within everyone. Given the right set of circumstances, all of us are capable of doing harm to another.

After the Jenkins report, Kate then forwarded her interim report on the Rachel Mooney rape. As she grabbed a coffee before her Monday-afternoon appointments, her mind again turned to Charlie. The way things had been with Declan lately, the two of them drifting further apart, must be affecting their son.

Opening the window in her office, she instantly felt the cold October wind attack her skin. Wrapping her arms around herself, she felt more alone than ever. The sound of traffic outside was drowned by the ringing of the bells at St Matthew's. Instead of closing the window, she remained staring at the street below, wondering if Declan's silence said more than his words. And as if Declan, for once, had the same thought in his mind, he rang her mobile. Only this time, from his opening words, Kate knew they wouldn't be indulging in polite conversation.

'Kate, it's Declan. I know you're at work, but we need to talk.'

'I'm listening.'

'I don't know how to say this. It's really difficult for me.'

She held the phone close to her ear, turning her back to the passing traffic outside, believing she already knew what he was about to say, for the words 'it's over' were already etched on her mind. Clearing her throat, she spoke as calmly as she could, relieved Declan would be the first to say it. 'It's okay, Declan, go on.'

'I've met someone else.'

Harcourt Street Police Station

O'Connor still hadn't fully worked out why he'd asked Kate out for a drink, almost regretting it the moment the question had popped out of his mouth. He had no doubt what was keeping him awake at night. Sharing it with Kate, no matter how bloody understanding she might be, wasn't going to help matters, and he'd no intention of discussing it with anyone in the force, irrespective of what support mechanisms were in place. He'd made his bed, and now he had better learn to lie in it.

Lynch, who'd been checking the CCTV footage when O'Connor arrived, seemed intent on spending the tail end of the afternoon constantly rewinding the tapes. Rubbing his hands down his face, in an effort to rejuvenate his thoughts, O'Connor was the first to break the silence. 'Lynch, tell me there's a good reason for you constantly rewinding that fucker.'

'I'm looking at the sightings in Hatch Street and at a late-night shop. The quality is suspect in places, but the second sighting is bothering me. It looks like more than a casual conversation to me.'

O'Connor stood behind him.

'Look here.' Lynch stopped the tape as Jenkins exited the shop. 'When Jenkins steps out, he stands there alone, opening the packet of cigarettes he's just purchased. Watch him. He looks up and down the street before lighting the cigarette, almost as if he's expecting someone. It's only when he's about to walk away that the other man appears.'

O'Connor leaned in closer, looking again at the stranger walking out of the shadows. At first the male seemed to be walking in the direction of the shop, but another few rewinds of the tape confirmed he had come at Jenkins from behind, out from a laneway to the right of the shop.

'It's at this point, sir, that they exchange words.'

'How long are they talking? What does the tape say?'

'Four point six five seconds.'

'It could be simple pleasantries, Lynch.'

'Maybe – but look here. Both men stand facing each other. Then Keith Jenkins either stands back or is forced back. It's hard to tell with the split-second gaps in the footage. The second man lights his cigarette, his back to the CCTV camera, while Jenkins is facing it. They're both standing further back than before, as if they've stepped in from the road for more privacy. Do complete strangers stop to have a cigarette together in the shadows? Maybe – but not for as long as it looks here. Look what happens next, when Jenkins walks away, leaving the other guy behind him.'

O'Connor kept looking at the footage. 'The other guy stays put.'

'Only long enough to let Jenkins think he isn't being followed.' Lynch moves the tape on. 'Five seconds later he leaves in the same direction.'

'What are you thinking, Lynch?'

'The interaction is too intimate for complete strangers. Jenkins doesn't look like he was forced back into the shadows, but he certainly went there.'

O'Connor looked at the tape again. 'If this turns out to be the last sighting of the victim, this other guy is critical. Right, Lynch, let's get agreement from the chief super to put the entire footage out there. I want it on every news bulletin going. We may not be able to make out who the mystery man is, but perhaps someone else will.'

'Okay.'

'Also, hassle Morrison on the weapon, and the distance the attacker would have been from the victim when the initial assault happened. If the killer and Keith Jenkins's cigarette companion are one and the same, the killer could have used the earlier incident as a means of getting Jenkins to engage with him again.'

'Sure.'

'Did we get any more on Jenkins's business associates?'

'Mr Jenkins didn't just like upsetting his studio guests.'

'I'm listening.'

'He had his finger in a number of shady dealings, not least of which was a property investment in Portugal. You know the kind of stuff, golf clubs, health spas, designer apartments and villas.'

'So what's shady about it?'

'He didn't put his own lolly in. He managed to convince other investors to put theirs in instead. He used a company set up a number of years back under the name of Hamilton Holdings.'

'It has a nice ring to it, but you still haven't told me why it's shady.' O'Connor sat back behind his desk.

'When the shit fell out of everything here and in Portugal, numbers began plummeting. Some of the regular investors got nervous, especially when their accountants began hitting brick walls on percentage shareholdings and who they were in bed with on the deal. There were rumours about dirty money in there. Either way, Jenkins was playing hardball. It was only a matter of time before the money lawyers started asking awkward questions.'

'Have we the list of the legitimate players?'

'It's proving tricky to unearth. Looks like everyone has gone to ground.'

'We'll need to do some digging. Get the CAB guys in. The

money trail always leads somewhere. If anyone knows where to start, the guys in the Criminal Assets Bureau will.' O'Connor stood up, stretching his arms. 'This bloody haystack keeps getting fucking bigger, Lynch.' Walking over to the wipe board, he looked at the headings from the previous night – missing wedding ring, mystery man and late-night shop, hotel receipt, method of killing, likelihood of another. O'Connor added the incident at the restaurant with Siobhan King to the list.

Turning back to Lynch in a more upbeat manner than he felt, he said, 'Get French on the phone. Let's see if we can get up close and personal with the family. Something tells me this investigation still has a long way to go.'

Clodagh

Orla's letter was filled with the usual pleasantries. If Martin had read it, there was nothing in it for him to pay much heed to.

Once out of the house, my mood is less sombre. I have cash with me, so I think about hailing a taxi. I look across at a bus, pulled in at the stop on the far side of the main road. I wouldn't even know what the fare is now. I remember bus rides with my father and Dominic, the three of us travelling into town, going into the shops for a treat, having lunch with ice-cream in tall glasses. When I talk to Dominic about them, he tells me I'm mixing everything up. That I couldn't possibly remember because I was too small.

I wait for the traffic to clear before I cross the road, and as I do, the bus pulls away. There is a young girl in the bus shelter, sitting alone. She is holding a doll, her arms wrapped around it, rocking it back and forth like it's a baby. I stare at her. She wants me to watch her. She has waves of curly ginger hair. It practically covers her whole face. When she looks up, there are hollows where her eyes should be, and her lips when she smiles are the same colour as my mother's rose pink lipstick – the one in the golden case with the pretty roses in the middle.

∞

Gerard doesn't mention my bruises when I arrive. And, just like two days ago, he asks me to count backwards from two hundred, and soon I'm back in the garden. This time the flowers are different, red fuchsia and trailing white and blue lobelia hanging down from above. The ground is soft, full of wild flowers, pansies, daisies and huge sunflowers, all scattered among the high grasses. I can feel their cushioned carpet beneath my bare feet. It smells of summer. This time I can hear sounds, birdsong falling like the flowers from above. I walk down another flight of stairs, and I am back in the same corridor. I know the room I want to go to. Gerard asks me what age I am, and I tell him I'm seven.

I open the door to my old bedroom. There are toys on the floor, and in the corner is my doll's house. I see Sandy sitting beside it. Sandy has curly blonde hair and sea-blue eyes. Her legs and arms don't have elbow or knee joints, so they can only move in a certain way. Golly sits beside her, with his large yellow bow. His eyes look as if he's about to be knocked down by a truck. That doesn't matter, because his eyes are always like that, as if he's been given the fright of his life.

I hear voices, loud adult voices, coming from below. A man is shouting. I don't know who he is. I must have finished a snack. There is an empty glass on my bedside locker, which looks like it was filled with milk, and a willow-pattern plate with crumbs on it. Debbie, my other doll, is the first to break the silence.

'Ah, go jump in a lake,' she says, as if she doesn't care about the voices coming from downstairs. Debbie always says things like that. Things you have to listen to. Debbie has airs and graces. She thinks she's the most important doll. Unlike Sandy, she has elbow and knee joints. I don't like her, really, but I don't ignore her either. You'd have to be mad to ignore Destructive Debbie. She'd make you pay the price. Debbie and Sandy live inside the doll's house, but Debbie is definitely the one in charge. She often whispers when the voices from downstairs get too loud, as if she wants Sandy and me to listen carefully, but then yells at the top of her voice when others speak low.

Debbie is not impressed today. She is not one bit happy. Debbie has attitude. You need to understand that when you're dealing with her. She has rights on account of being both clever and beautiful. She's telling me about the man, the one without a name. The one she knows likes Mum. I don't think Dad is at home. It's the middle of the day, and he would be at work. I can hear Gerard Hayden's voice. He's asking, 'Who is talking, Clodagh?'

'I am,' I say. And I realise it's me, the little-girl me, although there are no words coming out of her mouth. Debbie is staring. She is sitting in the corner by a spinning top, on top of the box of snakes and ladders.

The adult voices downstairs are quiet. Sandy wants me to put Debbie into her cardboard box, the one under my bed with the lid on it.

'Don't you want to know who the man is?' Debbie laughs.

'No, she doesn't,' says Sandy, right back at her.

'The man loves mummy, the man loves mummy,' Debbie sings, to the music of 'Three Blind Mice' – 'See how they run'.

'Shut up, Debbie,' roars Sandy.

But she doesn't stop: 'I saw him kiss her, I saw him kiss her.' Debbie sticks out her lips, like she's about to kiss someone too. Then she says, sharp and cold, 'Let's all play house.'

'What if we don't want to play house?' asks Sandy, but her face says she has already given in.

My doll's house has three floors and an attic. The front opens when you release the small clip at the top. One panel, the larger one with the front door on it, opens to the left and the other to the right. The roof with the attic room has a flip-back lid, so when you open the house you can see all four levels and look inside every room.

Each of the rooms has different-coloured wallpaper. On the bottom floor, there is a living room to the left of a wooden staircase and a kitchen to the right. Upstairs there are three bedrooms. The largest one is on the second floor with the bathroom. The other bedrooms are on the third, and the attic toy room is at the top. It runs right across the house. Here, people from the doll's house lie flat, like Egyptian mummies, when I want everyone to be asleep.

Today Sebastian is waiting for Sandy and Debbie to join him. He looks happy when the house opens. He doesn't like being left in it with the little ones, Katy and her brother Kim. They are twins. Katy's hair is soft, the same colour as Sandy's. Kim's hair is like Sebastian's, short and brown with a plastic wave.

When Gerard speaks, I feel caught between two worlds. 'Clodagh, who are you talking to?'

'The dolls from my doll's house.' My voice sounds surprised.

'Who else is in the room, Clodagh?'

'Only me and the girl.'

'The girl?'

'Yes,' I say, 'my little-girl self.'

I'm not sure if I should speak to the little girl. If I do, I might frighten her. She might not know that I don't mean her any harm.

'Clodagh, do you think she knows you're there?'

'I don't know. I think I can see what she sees. It feels as if I can.'

'Anything else, Clodagh?'

'She's scared. I'm sure of it.'

'Scared of what?'

'I don't know.'

I watch her move her dolls around, bringing Debbie, Sandy and Sebastian downstairs. She leaves the younger dolls, Kim and Katy, lying on their backs in the attic. I hear her say, 'You two stay there, where it's safe.'

Debbie is shouting again: 'Let's get Jimmy. The game's no good without Jimmy.'

'We don't need Jimmy today,' my little-girl self says back, sounding like she's defying Debbie.

'Yes, we do, Clodagh.' Debbie is smirking now.

'I can tell good stories too, Debbie.' She doesn't sound so sure any more.

'Can I hear a story, Clodagh?' Sandy pleads.

'Suck-up,' Debbie teases.

'You won't be in the story unless you're nice,' says Sandy, sounding like a teacher.

I watch my younger self arrange all three dolls, Debbie, Sebastian and Sandy, placing them in the living room of the doll's house, before bringing in a tray with cups and plates from the tiny kitchen. She lifts the china cups up one at a time to their lips, then puts spoons with pretend food from their plates into their mouths. Sebastian isn't his real name. It's a name Clodagh has made up.

'Drink up and eat up,' she says, like she is all grown-up. Then lying on her tummy, leaning on her elbows, she whispers, 'Once upon a time there was a little girl called Clodagh who loved her dollies very much.'

'Who do you love best?' roars Debbie.

'Shush,' says Sandy.

'Clodagh loves you all the same, because I don't have any favourites.'

'Bet your mum loves the man downstairs more than your daddy. I never see her kissing Daddy when he's here. She doesn't make herself all pretty for him any more.' Debbie looks defiant.

'Debbie, stop it. Clodagh loves us all. Why do you have to be so rotten?' Sebastian sounds like my brother Dominic.

'Blah, blah, blah … Clodagh knows the truth, don't you, Clodagh?' And again Debbie gets the upper hand.

I walk over to the little girl and stroke her hair, wondering if she'll look up. I say to her, 'Dolls can't hurt you.' I don't know if she can hear me, because she doesn't turn.

I hear Gerard Hayden's voice again. He's asking if I'm okay. I tell him I am. Now he's asking me to leave the room. I'm not sure I want to. I look back at the little girl. This time, she turns around. I feel a cold breeze coming in from the corridor, as if it wants to whisk me away. I stand in the doorway, my older self looking back at the little-girl me. I tell her, 'Everything will be okay. I'll come back.'

Walking from the room, I see the stairs at the end of the corridor. Soon I'm back in the garden, and soon after, I hear traffic coming in from the outside. I hear someone opening a gate – it squeaks before the handle clicks shut. I open my eyes, and once more, I can smell the vanilla scent of candle wax.

Gerard Hayden looks concerned. He asks me what I remember, and I recount what happened, as if I've been to see a movie, but instead of watching it, I'm part of it. He says he thinks the dolls could be a way of my subconscious mind protecting me, an extra layer between my perception and actual events. He talks to me about thinking long and hard as to whether or not I want to go back again, telling me I need to be sure. I start to think about my subconscious mind, wondering what it's protecting me from.

Maybe Martin's right. Maybe I'm completely cracked, but the room and the memory felt real, and it's like I'm at a crossroads.

If I hold back now, I might never come here again. Something is changing inside me, even if I'm not completely sure what it is.

Gerard Hayden has been talking for a while, but I haven't been listening, so I say, 'Sorry?' hoping he will repeat what he has just said. Instead, he stands up and walks over to the windows, opening the blinds. He has his back to me. I sit up, feeling a little stupid. I wonder if we've finished for the day. I remember the gate: perhaps it's his next appointment.

'Clodagh, I know you've lost both your parents. Who else could you turn to to ask about the past?'

'Dominic, my brother, I suppose, and my husband, Martin. Martin and Dominic were friends as kids. They used to hang out together.' What an unlikely gang they used to be, the two of them and Stevie McDaid. Dominic was the leader, of course. He picked up the other two as strays. 'Why do you ask, Gerard?'

'I would consider talking to them before we have our next session.'

I realise I don't want to talk to either Martin or Dominic, so instead I say, 'They'll probably tell me I'm crazy.'

'Still, it's worth trying. If your subconscious mind is protecting you, it would be important to establish what we're dealing with before we move on.'

'Not remembering is frightening too.'

'It's your choice, if you wish to continue. I'll respect your decision. But don't worry. You don't have to make your mind up now.'

Sober, everything feels more difficult. Nothing is clear any more; nothing is concrete. The truth is, I'm unsure what I'll do, but I made a promise to that little girl. I told her everything would be okay, and I would go back to her.

Sandymount Strand

It was late Monday evening by the time Stevie sat on the small stone wall, the palm trees and the red-and-white twin chimneys of Sandymount Strand behind him. Staring at the old house, with its high-gated pillars and ivory façade, he thought about the first time he had been inside Seacrest.

He and Dominic had been playing soccer on the strand at Cockle Lake – a large inlet of water at low tide, their target practice. They'd run past the rusted iron gates of the O'Malleys' old house on the corner. Dominic had invited him in. It had felt to Stevie as if he had entered another world. Either that or he had stepped inside a television soap opera, one in which he was playing some big rich guy.

He'd practised his American accent with Dominic. Bleedin' brilliant, it was. Until the mother had come in from the garden, and given him a stare that said she thought he was less than dog shit, something to be left outside, although not on her ladyship's driveway. She was a tough bird, but she'd got her comeuppance in the end, and Dominic had got to play the fucking hero son.

Stevie could have written a book about the goings-on in that house. That's the thing about dog shit: once the smell is covered up, no one sees the shit until it's too late. It seemed to Stevie that, one way or another, his life kept bringing him back into contact with the Hamiltons. It was as if their paths were always meant to cross.

There was no reason other than soccer and a large stretch of beach that two young guys from either end of the social spectrum should meet, but now he was getting himself tied up with that family all over again, including little Ruby. The girl was the spit of the grandmother. She had the same lofty, up-her-own-arse manner, the one that suggested she didn't want to share the same air with the likes of Stevie McDaid. Still, the pretty little thing was taken aback when she'd found him in her flat. The young lover boy hadn't hung around for long. When Ruby came back, she came alone.

It was easy enough for him to break in. She was an untidy young thing, no doubt well used to others picking up her crap for her. Stevie had had a good rummage. He'd even found her secret stash of coke, and the envelope with nearly a thousand smackers in it. He had been tempted to help himself there and then, but had thought better of it. Still, the little find had turned out to be a bit of a trump card when Angel Face returned, even if she'd nearly had a heart attack at seeing him.

'What the fuck?' were her first endearing words.

'Steady now, Princess. Let's not get all panicky.'

'I'm calling the police. Get the hell out of here.'

'Relax, chill out, Ruby, precious. First, I'm not going to let you do that, and second, they might be interested in your little treasure trove over there.' Stevie had pointed to her bedside locker.

'You've been through my stuff?' Her mind was ticking over. 'How the hell do you know my name?'

'Just getting to know you, that's all, getting acquainted.' He pushed her down on the bed.

'How do you know my name?' Ruby attempted to sit back up again.

'Let's just say we have connections together.'

'What do you want? What kind of connections?'

And that was when he saw it. The same stare that the grandmother, Lavinia Hamilton, had given him years before. Stevie had been standing at the bottom of the stairs pretending to be a Yank. Now the look concentrated his mind. He leaned over the girl, holding both her arms above her head, Ruby's lower body fighting him off. 'I have to say, Ruby, you have fight in you. I like girls with a bit of fight. It makes getting to know them all the more interesting.'

'FUCK THE HELL OFF ME,' Ruby spat in his face. Stevie jumped back before her right foot got him where it would hurt most. He laughed at her.

'You haven't answered my question, arsehole, what connections?'

Stevie knew, if he wanted to, he could get the better of her, but decided instead to push her a little, saying, 'What connections?' raising his eyebrows in disbelief. 'You'd think discovering an uninvited stranger in your apartment, a girl like you would be more concerned about what an unknown man might do next, rather than playing Question Time.'

'I don't know who the fuck you are, but you'd better leave.' Her tone was level, calmer, as she stood up from the bed regaining her composure.

'Now, Ruby, I'm not going to leave until I'm good and ready. Still, I appreciate that you're not creating a fuss. I don't like my women screaming.'

'I'm not your woman.' Her face distorted as if she had swallowed something revolting.

'No?' Stevie walked closer to her, all the time wondering whether she would keep her head, and Ruby didn't disappoint. Standing upright, rigid, like some beautiful mannequin in a shop window, she waited to see what the stranger would do next. Rubbing the back of his right hand down her left cheek, he felt her cool porcelain skin, like a doll with a hard smooth skull, capable of being smashed to smithereens.

'I'm not afraid of you. You're that shitbag from Neary's.'

'The name is Stevie. Perhaps, Ruby, you're used to near strangers being in your place.' His smile didn't unnerve her. Again she passed the test. Ruby McKay was going to be a worthy opponent – a pity about her fucking tripping habits.

'What do you want?' She pushed his hand away from her face.

'Just for us to be friends – that isn't such a terrible thing, now, is it?'

'Get the fuck out of here.'

'Now, now, Ruby, that's no way to talk to a friend of your lovely family.'

'Has he sent you? Has he asked you to keep an eye on me?'

'Do you mean Daddy dearest?' Stevie reached out, touching Ruby on the neck this time, then pulling his hand back.

'My dad? Why would he? Stop playing stupid games. Admit it. He sent you, didn't he? You're one of his fucking crawlers, aren't you?'

Stevie wasn't keen on the crawler reference, but she'd ruled Martin out of the equation so the noose was getting smaller. 'Listen, Ruby, you sound like a girl who needs a friend, someone to protect her. Why don't you give me your side of the story, and between the two of us, we can take it from there?'

'Why would you help me? Why the hell should I trust you?'

She was being cagey, but he could tell her nerve was starting to give. Stevie figured she wouldn't say no to a hit.

'Why don't you give yourself a little buzz with some of that charlie over there?' He pointed to the drawer. 'I'm not the fucking Drug Squad.' He didn't want her flaking out, but he needed her to soften. He remained standing all the while Ruby snorted. Stevie could be a patient man when he had to be. It didn't take her long to lose some of her harder edges.

Kneeling in front of her, he said, 'Feeling a bit better now, Ruby, are we?'

She didn't answer him.

'You wanted to know why I would help you.'

'Yeah.' Her voice softer, slower.

'Let's just say I'm an old and close friend of your mother.'

She stared back at him. 'You know my … mother?'

He needed to play it carefully. Ruby was on the ropes, and he had a pretty good idea why. 'Dublin is a small place, Ruby. Keeping bad company gets you noticed.'

'What?'

'Sugar daddies pick on little girls for a reason.' He moved closer to her. 'We both know who we're talking about, don't we?'

'He's a prick.'

'I know he is.'

'Do you know my fucking dad too? You're not going to tell him shit, are ya?'

'Not a word, Ruby.' Then, with as much sincerity as Stevie could muster, 'I know exactly what he's like.'

∞

Stevie's meeting wouldn't be for another quarter of an hour, but he was glad he had decided to get there early, and all the more poignant that they should meet near the old house in Sandymount. Stevie had been a lot younger the last time they had spoken face to face, but some impressions are lifelong ones. His conversation with Ruby McKay had been educational. Fear has a way of concentrating the mind, even for a tough little junkie like Ruby.

At first, he'd thought she had been afraid of him, but the way she'd stood her ground had contradicted that. There was another shark afloat, the one old enough to be her grandfather, and someone who really knew how to scare precious Ruby. If he played his cards right this time, getting embroiled with the Hamiltons could turn out to be a very lucrative move indeed.

Mervin Road

By the time Kate curled up on the couch on Monday night, she was exhausted. Charlie hadn't gone to bed until after ten o'clock, and it was another hour before he'd fallen asleep. Alone, Kate thought back to her phone call with Declan, realising how ill-prepared she'd been for it. Notwithstanding the difficulties in their marriage, she hadn't expected that. The whole conversation had felt alien, as if she'd been transported into someone else's life, and the person at the other end of the phone wasn't her husband any more but this other man. A man she no longer knew.

Within seconds of hearing the words 'I've met someone else', a wall had been built up between them different from anything that had gone before. Declan had wanted to talk to her about this stranger, this woman who had become part of his life. It had felt abhorrent to Kate to listen to even the smallest detail. She hadn't wanted to know any of it. And it wasn't simply thinking she wasn't good enough for him any longer. It went far deeper than that, a throwback from her being an only child, that feeling of detachment from the world around you, and a sense that, ultimately, you would end up alone.

Kate had put her mobile phone on silent, not wanting to talk to anyone, but jumped when it quivered on the armrest. She had lost track of time, and despite it being after one in the morning, she was somewhat relieved to realise it was O'Connor rather than Declan.

'Kate?' His voice was higher and snappier than her current mood.

'What is it, O'Connor?'

'There's been another killing. Same as Jenkins, knife wounds to the lower chest, body floating in the canal.'

Kate wasn't ready to answer.

'Kate, are you still there? Did you hear me? There's been another—'

'I heard you, O'Connor. What part of the canal?'

'Parnell Bridge, five bridges down.'

'I assume the first location is still being monitored.'

'You assume right, Kate.'

'He would have been a fool to go back to the first location.'

'Not unless he was looking for some police volunteers.'

'Another male victim?'

'Yeah, early sixties, maybe more. It's hard to tell at this point.'

'Any connection to Jenkins?'

'They didn't mix in the same social circles.'

'What do you mean?'

'Our victim slept rough, no fixed abode.'

'He was homeless?'

'That's right, with a capital H, and it's something he's been doing for a while.'

'You know him?'

'Yeah, Jimmy and I were old pals. I pulled him in a few years back. He was a small-time con artist. Last time he was taken in, he was minding someone else's credit cards. Jimmy was a bit of a storyteller. When he was cleaned up, and had some money in his pocket, he'd come over as a regular friendly fella. Until, that is, you checked the next morning and discovered he'd taken something you hadn't planned on sharing.'

'How did he pull those cons if he was homeless?'

'Every now and again he'd get himself off the streets. It's thought he had a personal benefactor of late, but nothing definite. Jimmy never stayed off the street for long. My theory is, he would get some money, maybe after lifting a wallet, live it up for a while, building up hotel bills and the like all over the place. He liked the sauce. The money kick-started the pattern – stolen cards and money, hotels, pulling a few more cons, drinking. Then, when the money ran out, he was back on the streets again.'

'You'll be checking the people affected by his scams?'

'For sure, and cross-checking them with what we know about Jenkins and his contacts. So far there's no obvious connection.'

'They might have known each other from years back, even if they didn't mix in the same circles.'

'Lynch is chatting to some of Jimmy's pals now. Jimmy liked to talk to everyone except the bloody police. If there was something going on of late, I'm thinking his friends on the street will know more about it than anyone else. What do you make of it, Kate?'

'You have my preliminary report. I don't think the killing of Jenkins was random. Either the killer knew him or he fitted a particular target preference. A homeless person and a celebrity feel too far apart for it to be going down to type. Either there's some other connection between the two victims, or they knew each other.'

'At least Jimmy's social circle is smaller than Jenkins's.'

'As I say, look backwards, even to school and college records. Being homeless doesn't mean he didn't mix in the same circles as Jenkins at some point. People who sleep on the streets are a microcosm of groupings. They're a wide mix, coming from every social background.'

'Kate?'

'Yeah?'

'Are you okay? You sound a little distant.'

'I was just thinking of the nursery rhyme.'

'Which one?'

'Tinker, tailor, soldier, sailor, rich man, poor man, beggar man, thief ...'

'Why?'

'Keith Jenkins was a rich man. The latest victim was the opposite.'

'Well, let's hope it's not a childhood favourite of our pal, because that, Kate, is a bloody long list.'

'He's upped the stacks of there being more killings, O'Connor, and he's moved relatively fast. The sooner you find out what Jenkins and Jimmy had in common, the better.' Kate paused. 'What's Jimmy's full name?'

'Jimmy Gahan. At least, that's the only name we have – other than Jimmy the Juggler that is.'

'I see. Was Jimmy brought to the canal as well?'

'No, this time it was the main crime scene. Why? What are you thinking, Kate?'

'By stabbing and drowning Jimmy Gahan at a single location, he isn't sticking to a pattern. Perhaps opportunity is playing a role.'

'How do you mean?'

'Jimmy Gahan might have somehow played into his hands. Assuming the killings aren't random, it could also mean the killer was following Jimmy before he died.'

'We'll retrace Jimmy's last movements, see if we can get any witness details.'

'Going back to the first killing, it points to a risk-taker, and a need to kill the victim in a particular manner and a particular place. The way this is going down, the drowning is the constant, and is therefore becoming more paramount. But, despite the risks, he's also calculating the odds. He won't make sloppy mistakes. But I agree retracing Gahan's last movements could unearth something.'

'Anything else?'

'Has Morrison been able to work out the time gap between Jenkins's knife attack and the drowning in the canal?'

'You're talking an hour at most, possibly a little less.'

'Still, O'Connor, there was an interval. It could mean there was a level of hesitancy on the part of the killer, but it looks like he isn't hesitating now.'

'There's no guarantee, Kate, that he has other victims in mind.'

'I know, but the canal and the water connection appear primary. Let's hope killing Jenkins hasn't set him off on some kind of spree.'

'The canal could have been an easy-picking ground for him, especially with a vagrant.' O'Connor's voice was cautious.

'Maybe, but a killer capable of moving this fast will think nothing of acting quickly again.'

'You said you didn't think Jenkins's killing was random.'

'No, I don't. Either, as you say, our guy is working off the canal as a hunting ground or something else is at play.'

'Right, Kate, I'll keep you posted.'

'O'Connor, where is Jimmy Gahan's body now?'

'Here at the canal. Morrison's about to start his preliminaries. The press are going to go ballistic with this bloody story. I can see the headlines now, "Riches to Rags" and all that blah, blah rubbish. Thank God Stapleton's in charge of the media and not me.'

'Two men are dead, O'Connor.'

'Thanks for stating the obvious, Kate. I know two men are bloody dead, and if we don't all get our arses in gear, that number, as you so nicely remarked, might get even bigger.'

'O'Connor, you said Lynch is talking to Jimmy's pals.'

'Yeah.'

'Where's he interviewing them?'

'The great outdoors. The last I heard he was in Camden Street.'

'I have his mobile. I'll give him a call.'

'Listen, Kate, I have to go. Hanley and the guys have just arrived. I'll get Lynch to keep you in the loop.'

'Okay.'

Hanging up, Kate tried to pull together the information she'd just been given by O'Connor. Thinking she heard Charlie, she walked down the hall to her son's bedroom. He was still out for the count. Kate wished she was too, but she rang Lynch all the same. He had just left one of the temporary shelters off Camden Street, and was on his way to look for an Ozzie Brennan, one of Jimmy's old pals. Lynch had already checked some of their usual hangouts, and had a few more to visit.

Walking back into the study, Kate looked again at the images of Keith Jenkins. Two dead men. Those had been her words to O'Connor, two dead men, but only one killer. Who was going to be the next? *Rich man, poor man, beggar man, thief?*

Clodagh

Martin was on edge this morning. He hasn't yet apologised. I don't care one way or the other. Lately, he's been spending more time out than in. This house is beginning to feel like nothing more than a series of connecting rooms. I emailed Orla after he'd left for work. She'd put her email address at the end of her letter. Somehow it felt like taking a step closer to normality. She's married now, with two young boys, twelve and ten. It's hard to think of Orla as a mother. I think of myself as a mother, feeling frustrated that I haven't been able to contact Ruby. I daren't tell Martin she's not answering her phone.

I can't believe it's only Tuesday. It feels like an eternity since I saw Gerard yesterday. I pick up a photograph of my own mother, the one with Ruby in her first year at secondary school. The two of them were so alike. They were close. I assume even closer when I drank. I was jealous of that love too. I think about phoning Dominic, doing what Gerard suggested yesterday, but then I think again.

I can't get that little girl out of my mind. Since the regression sessions, it's as if she's always with me. I'd seen her at that bus stop too, even before I went to see Gerard yesterday. I wonder if my mind's playing tricks with me. But something is pulling me back to her.

Out of impulse, I phone Ruby again. The ringing tone is loud in my ear.

'Hello, Mum.' Her voice sounds impatient, almost patronising, as if I've interrupted her from something more important. I hate it when she sounds like Martin.

'How are you doing, Ruby? I've been trying to get you since the weekend.'

'I'm fine. You don't have to keep tabs on me.'

'I'm not. Ruby, I wish you'd stop shutting me out.'

'Jesus Christ, Mum, it isn't all about you, you know.'

'I didn't say it was.'

'What is it, then?'

'Can't I simply phone you?'

'You just did.'

'Don't be smart, Ruby. It doesn't help matters.' I'm trying to keep calm. 'I hear you're seeing someone.'

'Who told you that?' Her response is both snappy and accusing.

'Does it matter?'

'It matters.'

'It was Dominic, if you must know. He mentioned it over dinner the other night. He saw you in town with a young guy. Dominic said he called to you, but you didn't hear him. Is he a student?'

'He's just a friend, that's all.'

'It would be nice to meet him.'

'Look, I can't be dealing with this.'

'Dealing with what, Ruby? What can't you be dealing with?'

'You bloody playing the caring-parent game.'

'Well, I do care.'

'It's a little late for that, don't you think?'

'I hope not.' My voice pulls back. 'I know you miss your grandmother.'

'It's not about Granny.'

'What is it about, then?'

'I have to go.'

'You're always running away from me, Ruby.'

'That's a bit rich, Mum, coming from you.'

I draw a deep breath. 'I know that, but I'm trying, Ruby. I'm trying hard.' I hear a long silence at the other end of the phone. 'Ruby, are you still there?'

'I'm still here.' Her voice sounds like mine, as if we're both waiting for the right thing to be said.

I want to tell her how much I love her, but instead I say, 'Will you be calling over soon?'

'For another inquisition? I don't know which of you is worse, you or bloody Dad.'

'Ruby, it's just …'

'It's just what, Mum?'

'He doesn't want you ending up like me. He worries about your drinking, and the rest of it. If you need help, Ruby, we can get it for you. I didn't want to go to rehab, but—'

'I don't need fucking help.'

'We all think that.'

'I'm not listening to this shit any more.'

'Ruby, please don't hang up.'

But she does. And I can't hide my anger. I slam down the receiver, my hand still shaking. At first, I'm not sure who I'm more upset with, her or me.

You think you can put back together all of the broken pieces, but you can't. None of this is Ruby's fault. When I think about her being small, the memory is unbearable. All those wasted weekends when I was so hung-over that we never left the house, or the school functions I missed with one excuse after another. It's when children stop asking you to be part of their life that you know things have gone too far. I can't keep blaming my mother for that. The fault is mine. I was the adult, Ruby the child. The one she should have been able to trust, the one who turned her back on her. If I've learned nothing else from my mother, I've learned that. I hope to Christ it's not too late for us. I may be a fuck-up, but I love my daughter more than anything else in this godforsaken world.

Inchicore

When Clodagh left Gerard Hayden's yesterday, she didn't know I'd been following her. She barely turned as she left his house. Her appointment had lasted longer than I'd expected. She was obviously upset. Clodagh is a woman on the edge, someone who doesn't require much pushing to topple. I envy how gullible she is. I stopped being gullible a long time ago. I learned that lesson the hard way. Never judge a book by its cover. Never trust. Never walk easily into a trap, because traps are always hidden. Traps are not meant to be seen.

My conversation with Gerard Hayden hadn't taken long, another communication on a need-to-know basis. He'll continue to play his game for now. Gerard Hayden is no more than a pawn, the weakest piece in the game of chess, moving things forward, shifting the balance of play, but only until the real player ultimately does battle.

Jimmy is history. My next move will need to be handled carefully. It feels like days since I've slept properly, but that doesn't matter. If anything, it adds to the half-dead, half-alive feeling I've carried around with me for so long. And still the anger bubbles below the surface. I know I have so much more to do. Each step is its own means to an end. It won't be long before people start putting two and two together, connecting Jenkins and Gahan. It will bring things closer to home, but no mind. I still have time. If I don't fuck things up.

That's the funny thing about secrets. For some people they feel huge, as if they should be obvious to everyone. For me, they dictate my every move. Either way, once you have them, it's impossible to know who you can trust, or how far you can trust anyone with them.

Darling Clodagh, you looked so fragile yesterday, yet resolute. In a way it makes what I need to do somewhat easier. You're looking for answers and that's understandable. That's what I want you to do. But you have no idea what you're messing with. The answers are never enough. The answers lead to more questions and, ultimately, the truth, and the truth isn't always what it's cracked up to be.

Last night the sky looked bruised, just like your face, Clodagh – a mishmash of faded purple. Gahan, the stupid idiot, died too fast.

As I walk, the trees cast shadows, and again my mind drifts. I pass others, wondering why they don't know what I've done. There is power within this feeling – retribution for past sins, and the feeling that what happened in Seacrest has never really left any of us.

I think about Jenkins again, his last moments on this earth, swallowing the water, gasping for air. How I pushed him in further, my arms stretched, knowing everything had changed. I was the one in control. His eyes had bulged from their sockets, his body losing its resistance as his arms flailed his defence, until even he accepted death was the only outcome.

Ocean House, the Quays

Lynch had no luck in finding Ozzie Brennan, and Kate had finally gone to bed in the early hours of Tuesday morning. After she'd dropped Charlie to school, she felt a sense of relief at being back at Ocean House. Somehow, within the confines of her office routine and the interaction with others, she could put her failed marriage and Charlie's vulnerability temporarily behind her. There was a time when she might have phoned her mother and talked to her about Charlie. That hadn't been an option since her mother's death last year, or for a very long time, the Alzheimer's having stolen her mother's mind long before death finished off the task.

Kate scrolled down her appointments for the day, then contacted the social worker attached to Imogen's case confirming the family appointment for the following morning. If nothing else, after the consultation Imogen's family would have a better understanding of her condition. The girl had enough to deal with without having to educate those around her.

Kate had asked Lynch to let her know as soon as Ozzie Brennan turned up. She received his call shortly before midday. Before leaving her office, she glanced at a framed photograph of her, Declan and Charlie on the desk. It already felt as if what they'd had together was something in the distant past.

Lynch had located Ozzie a couple of quays up from Ocean House. It was easier for Kate to get there on foot than by driving. Dublin, like all major cities, had a serious problem when it came to people living on the streets, with a couple of thousand people putting their heads down every night to sleep in a place none would ever call home. Kate had come into contact with the homeless community as part of her work for Ocean House, and all her previous encounters had told her the same thing: most homeless people had no desire to live on the streets, and the continuing government policy was solving little. With the demise of the Celtic Tiger, and the purse strings getting tighter, any improvements would be extremely low on anyone's agenda. Homeless people didn't vote, so they were about as important to certain elected politicians as the city's ever-growing waste problem.

It was still too early to tell how the murder of Jimmy Gahan reflected on the killing of Keith Jenkins, but there was a connection, Kate was sure of it. She couldn't have left Charlie last night. Visiting crime scenes in the middle of the night was a thing of the past. She would have to depend on the images again, but they were never the same as seeing the scene at first hand. A copycat killing couldn't be ruled out, but assuming otherwise, the location and method were forming part of the killer's signature. On the surface, Keith Jenkins and Jimmy Gahan seemed poles apart. But they were connected. It was simply a question of finding out how. Right now, only the killer knew which way the dots were joined, but both men had been chosen for a reason. Their paths had crossed and, considering everything, she was sure O'Connor would come up with something once he'd dug into their earlier backgrounds.

She wondered if it was some kind of personal vendetta. If so, how many targets were on the killer's list? Again she thought of the location. The second killing had taken place further up the canal, but the killer had taken another risk. Even late at night with low visibility, he could have been seen in such a public place. There was also the time gap with Jenkins. Had the killer stalled? If he had, he had been more focused with Gahan's murder, meaning he had progressed. Differences happened for a reason.

∞

Ozzie Brennan was the embodiment of life on the streets. Like many of the homeless, he wore multi-layered clothing, had weathered skin, and carried his sense of isolation from regular punters as a given. He was tall and broad, his tossed grey hair, thick beard and moustache in stark contrast to his large pink face. Ozzie's high forehead now frowned in anticipation of whatever it might be that Lynch and Kate wanted to get out of him. He sat with his legs crossed and arms folded. There were no office walls or furniture, but as far as Kate and Lynch were concerned, to Ozzie Brennan, they were meeting in the middle of his domain.

Despite his confident demeanour, Kate figured he wasn't very different from many others on the streets. Beneath the surface there would be the same undercurrent of loss, brought about by the lack of somewhere warm, dry and safe to call their own, a proper home. Even if, by and large, most of them kept their feelings hidden.

It was Lynch who started the conversation, filling Ozzie in on how his friend Jimmy Gahan had been killed, how the police were keen to know if there was any connection between his late friend and the celebrity Keith Jenkins. As Lynch continued with the explanation of what had happened, Kate watched Ozzie's glassy eyes and blank stare, figuring he had probably already heard most of the story.

The news of what had been done to Jimmy would have reached Ozzie long before it ever reached Lynch or Kate, but that didn't deter the young detective from going through the motions. He wanted to put Ozzie at his ease, to let him feel the police were keeping him up to speed on things. Lynch told Ozzie about how he had heard that he and Jimmy had been real close, allowing a couple of moments to pass before asking Ozzie if he knew of any relatives they should contact. Looking down towards his toes, Ozzie started to sing, a low, breathless, mournful rendition of 'Row, row, row your boat gently down the stream, merrily, merrily, merrily, merrily, life is but a dream.'

Kate looked down at the man's feet. Despite the chill of the day, all he wore were thick brown sandals, his toes as red as the tip of his nose. Even with his head slightly bowed, she could see the drippings from his nose, which Ozzie Brennan wasn't bothering to wipe away. Unsure if the drips were from the cold or his upset over losing his friend, Kate willed him to lift his face and look at one of them.

By the time Ozzie did look up, she got her answer. The man's eyes might have been bloodshot from the previous night's drinking, but there was no mistaking the tears, none of which poured down his face but rather filled his eyes, refusing to go anywhere.

His voice sounded cracked. 'Jimmy wanted to get himself sorted. He wanted to lie on a nice comfy bed, have a bleedin' flat-screen television and smell nice. Not a lot to ask, really, is it?'

It wasn't a question Ozzie expected either Lynch or Kate to answer. Instead Kate looked at Lynch, then asked Ozzie if she could sit down beside him.

'The bench is free. That's why I'm here.'

'Tell us about Jimmy.'

Just like Lynch, Kate allowed time before expecting the man to answer, but this time Ozzie seemed ready to talk.

'Jimmy always had a story, an idea, a regular entrepreneur he was. He would have given Alan Sugar a run for his money. We'd be queuing up at Merchants Quay for breakfast, and he'd be going on about some bloody crap idea or venture.'

'Do you think he knew Keith Jenkins?' Kate tried to maintain eye contact.

'Jimmy didn't mention names. It's not that he didn't trust me, the very opposite, but names never came into it.'

'I hear Jimmy might have found himself a nice benefactor.' Lynch flicked to a new page in his notebook.

'You can close your bloody book. I'm not planning on giving out autographs today.' Ozzie stared straight ahead of him, as if talking to no one other than himself. 'On the streets, everyone is our fucking benefactor, whether it's an arsehole in a suit, or one of them young girls helping out with the food parcels. They're all our bleeding benefactors. It's shit about Jimmy, but his wasn't the first bodybag to be taken off the streets. That famous guy, the one that got killed the other day, he's the only one you pair are interested in. People like me and Jimmy can go to Hell for all you lot give a fuck.'

Kate put her hand on his shoulder. 'That's not true, Ozzie. Detective Lynch and I want to know who did this to Jimmy. When it comes to murder, all victims are equal in the eyes of the law.'

'Yeah, well, dead is dead. There's nothing going to help Jimmy now.' Ozzie unfolded his arms and legs, then refolded them in the opposite direction, the shift of body position giving more weight to his words. Kate kept her hand on his shoulder.

Lynch, who had remained standing, moved in a little closer, shadowing Ozzie, his voice sounding cold. 'Maybe not, pal, but later on tonight, when you're here on the streets, when your body is rattling with the cold, you might get to thinking about the benefactor who did this to Jimmy.'

Ozzie gave Lynch a look. Clearly he wasn't surprised by the

detective's coldness, at least, not as surprised as Kate had been. 'I'm not your bleedin' pal. I might rattle with the cold tonight, but I'm no snitch, and I won't be worrying about any benefactor either.'

'No?' Kate's tone was softer than Lynch's. 'Why not, Ozzie? I know you cared about Jimmy.'

'I did care about him. Jimmy was my pal. Me and him … Well, let's just say we had a lot in common.'

'Like what?'

'Both good-looking for a start.' Ozzie attempted a laugh but it got stuck in his chest, like a mucus-inflamed cough.

Kate remembered the cocktail Morrison had spoken about after Jenkins was pulled out of the canal, thinking of how the finality of death, no matter how you dressed it up, was the same for rich and poor alike. 'I can see that. The good looks that is.' Kate smiled. 'What else did you and Jimmy have in common?'

'Let's just say we both got fucked over by folk, but we were different as well. Me, I had my way of surviving, and he had his. The odd days, when I'd get a shower and fresh clothes from the shelter, I'd pick up a bit of work, nothing permanent, mind. I used to be a bricklayer, you know, fully qualified. I was never afraid of a bit of lugging around, never afraid of hard work. Well, once I'd get a few bob together, I'd usually pick myself up some cider. Then I'd come back here to my bench or party in some cosy doorway. Jimmy wasn't content with that. He used to be posh, you see, lived the life of Reilly. He wanted more than a few bottles of cider. Jimmy wanted his old life back.'

'And this benefactor, Ozzie, the one Jimmy never mentioned by name, was he a way of him getting that life back?' Kate waited.

'Maybe, Miss. As I said, Jimmy always had some scheme or other on the go. He did have family, though, a sister.'

'A sister?'

'Yeah. I think her name was Deborah, or Debbie.'

'Go on, Ozzie.' Kate rubbed her hands together to keep out the cold.

'She never wanted anything to do with him. As I said, we both got fucked over by folk.'

'Ozzie, when Detective Lynch asked you a minute ago about the name of the benefactor, the guy who could have done this to Jimmy, you seemed very sure that you wouldn't be worrying about him.'

'Did I?'

'That's the impression I got.'

'You're very clever, Miss. Jimmy would have liked you. He always admired intelligence, did our Jimmy.'

'So tell me, Ozzie, why wouldn't you be worrying about that benefactor of his?'

'Because it wasn't his benefactor who did Jimmy in.'

'No? How can you be so sure?'

Instead of looking at Kate, he rearranged the newspapers on his bench. Then, with his voice as flat as a pancake, he said, 'Dead men can't commit murder,' looking coldly up at Lynch, 'nor can murder be blamed on them either.'

Estuary Road, Malahide

With Lynch and Kate interviewing Ozzie Brennan on the quays, O'Connor was irked that things weren't moving fast enough. They had another victim and were no closer to pulling in a suspect. Nothing conclusive had come in from the CCTV footage shown on television the previous night, and the lab results of what was under Jenkins's fingernails had given Johnny Keegan his get-out-of-jail-free card. They had a test sample. What they needed now was a match.

Despite any number of motives and a shitload of information coming in from the public, the only thing mounting up was victims. The last incident-room meeting had felt like a momentous amalgamation of unanswered questions, and with Morrison dissecting another body, the house call O'Connor had planned for the Jenkins residence had been delayed long enough.

Nodding to both sets of police officers stationed outside the Jenkins home, the first car on the public road directly in front of the house, the second at the top of the long gravelled drive, O'Connor was in perfect form for talking to the family. The police presence was deemed to be secure, but low-key. Chief Superintendent Butler didn't want the family upset, but at the same time he wanted his own arse protected should anything go awry.

O'Connor parked his car on the main street beside the unmarked police car and walked up the drive to one very impressive house. He could smell the sea air, and the whiff of seaweed tangled within it. A perfect setting, he thought, for a perfect celebrity home, one which jutted out from the landscape like a millstone wanting to be seen. His head ached, and the dazzling white lime-rendered walls forced him to squint. The house was double-fronted, two-storeys high, with a flat roof linking to another part of the building, almost like a second house, to the rear. Both front and back buildings had apex-shaped roofs, each with a circular window in their top gable, like a large vessel out at sea.

There were several cars at the front. O'Connor leaned down to the driver's window of the police car parked closest to the residence. 'I see there's a big crowd here today, guys.'

'It's been like that from the beginning, sir.' The officer turned to his colleague in the passenger seat, mocking, 'Archie here's been taking notes. Tells me his wife reads all the glossy magazines so he can spot a celebrity from a mile off.'

'Well done, guys.' He gave them a reassuring look. 'Keep your eyes on the others too, the non-celebrities, that is. Killers aren't in the habit of wearing signs.'

O'Connor was surprised to find the front door open, but as he stepped into the hallway, half a dozen heads turned, everyone knowing instantly that he didn't belong. It was the youngest of the group who addressed him first, a well-built teenager, whose voice sounded as if it had just broken. The guy had a mass of blond hair. He was wearing jeans and a black T-shirt with *Cool* written in white across the front. 'Can I help you?'

'Detective Inspector O'Connor.' He reached out to shake his hand. 'And you are?'

'Jay Jenkins.' He had an unexpectedly strong grip for a teenager.

Opening a heavily panelled wooden door behind the main stairway, Jay Jenkins held it ajar as O'Connor walked inside. 'I'll get my grandmother for you. Just a second.' He left the room before O'Connor could clarify that it was the boy's mother, not his grandmother, whom he wanted to see.

'Jaysus Christ,' O'Connor muttered below his breath, 'this investigation is starting to grate on my nerves.'

He didn't have long to wait before Isabel Blennerhasset, Keith Jenkins's mother-in-law, introduced herself in the same courtly manner as her grandson. From the moment she made her entrance, wearing black from head to toe, except for her pearl necklace, O'Connor could tell she was a force to be reckoned with. If she was harbouring any anxiety about being the first to talk to the detective, she kept it well hidden. She entered the room like a woman who had places to go and things to do, but with no particular urgency about any of them.

'So, you want to see my daughter, Detective Inspector?'

It was the crisp business-like manner in which she asked the question that precipitated a less than sympathetic response from O'Connor: 'That was the general idea.'

'You're in charge of this investigation, I understand.' She beckoned him to sit down.

O'Connor obliged. 'That is correct. I'm heading up the team.'

'You're working with Chief Superintendent Butler?' She remained standing.

O'Connor caught the inflection in her tone: she wanted him to know she was well aware of who was ultimately in charge. Isabel Blennerhasset had done her research.

'I'm here to help, Mrs Blennerhasset. It's important for everyone concerned that we try to work out who might have done this wrong to your family.'

'Indeed. Nothing but awful crime these days. Don't you agree, Detective Inspector?'

O'Connor was taken aback by her distant remark. 'Mrs Blennerhasset, no offence, but I came here today to talk with your daughter.'

'And why would that be?'

For a moment O'Connor wondered if the woman was senile. 'Your son-in-law has been murdered, Mrs Blennerhasset. I would consider that a very good reason.'

She gave O'Connor a wry smile. As he glanced from her stiff but focused expression to her walking stick, O'Connor wondered if she was capable of hiring a killer.

'Do you mind if I sit down, Detective Inspector? The old legs aren't what they used to be.'

'Of course not.' O'Connor took out his notebook, unsure how he was going to handle this one.

Sitting down opposite him, she showed the first sign of being human, rubbing what appeared to be an aching shin. 'Don't go feeling sorry for me, Detective Inspector. This is just a temporary affliction – boating accident on the Shannon. A darn table hit it.' O'Connor held his silence while she repositioned herself on the couch, sitting upright like an aged goddess. He could see where her daughter had got her attractive features, and if the daughter was anything like the mother, this was going to be a long afternoon.

'You can call me Isabel, Detective Inspector.'

'Your daughter, Mrs Blennerhasset – I mean Isabel? I was hoping to talk to her.'

'Now, Detective Inspector, I want you to understand something. This is a difficult time for all of us, especially my daughter.'

'I understand that.'

'I doubt that, Detective Inspector, unless you're walking in our shoes, which obviously you are not.'

Looking at her holding her walking stick tightly, as if it was her most important prop, O'Connor decided he was beginning to like the old bag. He admired people with spirit, and, despite her advancing years, she had plenty of that. She oozed the kind of beautiful elegance that not many can. Her perfectly groomed grey hair, cut short, exposed her long neck, and with her shoulders held back, Isabel Blennerhasset's posture had class.

'Mrs Blennerhasset – Isabel, please ...'

'Don't rush me, Detective Inspector, a little respect if you don't mind.'

O'Connor let out a sigh. He checked his watch, deciding to give her five more minutes.

'You see, Detective Inspector, young people, children, they're allowed to be silly. They can hide, get up to mischief, come home covered in muck, and nobody would think it strange. They have their own rules, sulk when they don't get their own way and refuse to do as they're told – although, by and large, they learn ultimately to toe the line. When they enter adulthood, everything changes. But when you get old, like I am now, it's different again. If I were to run like a young girl, not that I can with this stick,' she lifted it like a weapon, 'my bones wouldn't have the same agility. I might look awkward, like a lazy old mule, but I do gain something in old age. At my age, I'm allowed to be silly again. I'm allowed to be eccentric. I can even sulk if I want to. It's all part of the advantage of being elderly. People accept my ill-mannered madness as endearing, humorous, even.'

O'Connor shifted on the couch. *Four minutes.*

'I suppose you're wondering why I'm telling you this, Detective Inspector.'

'Well, Isabel, I'm still hoping to speak to your daughter.'

'In good time – my daughter is vulnerable right now. In spite of everything, she loved the bastard. Of course, she was far too young when she married him. Some men like younger girls. They find them less threatening.'

O'Connor shot her a glance of surprise.

'Don't look so shocked. I may be old but I'm not stupid. I know all about my late son-in-law's reputation. The reason I'm talking frankly with you, Detective Inspector, is so you can gain an understanding of how our family deals with things. We live in a wicked world, and for all the trappings of wealth, which, no doubt, you have already observed, we have our own torments, even if we hide them well.'

'Torments?'

'Yes. Torments. Our world is full of subterfuge. Take this dress, for example.'

'Your dress?'

'Yes, my dress. Detective Inspector, please try to keep up.' If Isabel Blennerhasset heard his next grunt, she paid no heed. 'Just before I came in here, one of them out there,' she pointed to the door to the hall, 'said she loved me in it. Do you know what that means?'

'That she loved you in the dress?'

'No, Detective Inspector. The very opposite. What she meant was that I have worn this dress far too often.'

'I see. At least I think I see.' *Three minutes.*

'What I'm trying to explain to you is that our kind lives by a different language. I know this because I wasn't born into it. People, our people, they talk in riddles. I never trusted Keith Jenkins but, because of my daughter, I tolerated him. Much like my overly worn black dress is tolerated by that gang out there. The house has been full of wannabe celebrities since my late son-in-law's demise.' Isabel made no attempt to hide her bitterness.

'So I take it, Isabel, you're not like them.' O'Connor sat forward. 'You're a straight talker.'

'I'm the queen of straight talkers, Detective Inspector.'

'So if I was to ask you about your son-in-law's business interests or friends you would tell me what you know?'

'I know enough not to trust them. I swear if he's messed things up for my daughter financially, even if he is dead, I'll kill him all over again.'

'Did you know a Jimmy Gahan?'

'The name is familiar. Keith was friends with him from a long time back.'

O'Connor stopped counting the minutes. 'And how do you know that? It doesn't sound as if you and your late son-in-law got on particularly well.'

'I'd be worried about your observational skills if you hadn't picked that one up, Detective Inspector.' Again the wry smile. 'My daughter told me about him. She and Keith met him recently. In Temple Bar, I think.'

'And why did your daughter share this story with you?'

'She was quite taken aback. You don't expect to meet an old friend of your husband and for him to be a vagrant.'

'And you're sure it was Jimmy Gahan?'

'I'm excellent on names. In our world names matter a great deal.'

'You say they knew each other from years back?'

'Jimmy Gahan completed the same business degree at Trinity as Keith. Keith would have been a number of years younger. I think Jimmy got Keith a summer internship at one point.'

O'Connor remembered Kate's remark about older connections. 'Are there any other names you'd like to throw into the hat from back then, Isabel?'

'A couple, but one does come to mind, considering how my son-in-law died.'

'Go on.'

'Adrian Hamilton.'

The name Hamilton spiked O'Connor's interest, the same name as Jenkins's investment company. 'What about Adrian Hamilton?'

'It's of no relevance, really. The man has been dead for at least thirty years.'

'Yet his name is the first that came to your mind?'

'I understand from my daughter that my son-in-law, that Jimmy Gahan fellow and Adrian Hamilton had been good friends at one point. Jimmy and Adrian Hamilton met at Trinity. I understand they were also business partners. I guess my son-in-law thought both of them would be useful to know for future career development. He was right, as it turned out. When Keith's career took a very different direction, it was Adrian Hamilton who got him his first break into television. RTÉ was a very closed shop back then. It still is to some extent. It was all very tragic, really.'

'What was?'

'Adrian Hamilton's death – a dreadful accident.'

'What happened?' O'Connor locked eyes with Isabel Blennerhasset.

'As I said, it was a very long time back. But it's the reason he came instantly to mind. The man drowned. Some said it was suicide, but people say a lot of things. Either way, he left a young wife and two children. I knew Lavinia, Adrian Hamilton's widow. She was a member of the tennis club in Rathmines. My daughter's on the committee. In truth it was a double tragedy.'

'Double?'

'Lavinia lost a baby that year too. A little girl, I understand. She was never the same afterwards, but, like many, she hid it well.'

'You say Adrian Hamilton's death was a possible suicide? Was there an inquest?'

'There was an investigation, but I heard little about it, other than the rumours. They tend to be very loud and far-reaching, Detective Inspector.'

'Thirty years back, you say.'

'Around that time. Now Keith has drowned. You never know what's ahead of you, do you, Detective Inspector?'

'There's been another drowning, Isabel. Jimmy Gahan's body was found yesterday.'

'Oh, dear Lord.'

'It was close to where we found your son-in-law, in the canal.'

'Heavens above.' Isabel Blennerhasset turned her head away from O'Connor, her neck narrow, lined, and looking like a featherless bird.

O'Connor could see that the last piece of information had unsettled her. Lifting herself up from the couch, she leaned heavily on her stick and walked to the French windows, which were filled with a view of the estuary. Despite the cold, she opened them. The breeze swooped in around them, the noise of squawking seagulls sounding like laughter. Isabel Blennerhasset kept her back to him.

'My daughter and son-in-law, Detective Inspector ...'

'What about them?'

'He met her on the rebound, you know. An older woman broke his heart,' she faced O'Connor again, 'not that I ever thought the lowlife had a heart. Wait here, Detective Inspector. I'll get my daughter for you now.'

Clodagh

When I arrive at Gerard Hayden's, he still doesn't mention my bruises, although they're a lot deeper now. I remind myself that he isn't a friend. I'm paying for his services. And even as I think this, I know I've already crossed a line. The two of us are in this together, and for the first time since meeting him, I wonder about his personal life. Gerard Hayden has all the appearance of a man living alone. I've not sensed that anyone else shares this house. There are no photographs on the wall, nothing that might belong to someone else.

Before we start, he questions me again, asking if I've spoken to Dominic or Martin. I tell him that I've decided not to.

'Okay, then, Clodagh, if you're sure,' he says.

I ask him again if my regression is unusual.

'Some people when they regress only hear things, others might simply see things. Not all their senses are realised. But you are slightly different again.'

'Because of the dolls,' I say.

'They definitely complicate things.'

'But you said they might be part of my subconscious protecting me.'

'Yes. Or cutting things up in such a way that you can't really trust what you're remembering.'

'So I shouldn't set much store in what they're saying?'

'That's exactly what's complicated about it, Clodagh. What they're saying could be the very thing you should be listening to.'

'I see. But about the hearing and seeing ...'

'What about it, Clodagh?'

'During my regression, I could hear and see, but I could also smell and touch. More importantly, I felt like I was inside that little girl's head.'

'I know.' He stands up and paces around the room, as if the last piece of information has unsettled him.

'Gerard,' I say, sensing he might be reluctant about bringing me back again, 'I need to go back. I need to know if my subconscious is protecting me, and if so, from what. There are large chunks of my memory missing, and I don't understand why. The missing bits are making me feel stuck. I can't stay in this nothing place forever. Where I am now is not a good place to be.'

'Very well,' he says. 'Let's start.'

This time when I regress, I realise I'm somewhere different. I'm inside the doll's house. Jimmy is there, and so are Kim and Katy. Jimmy is telling them a story about a sailor who travelled the high seas. Debbie and Sandy are there as well. I don't know where Sebastian is.

Debbie says, all smarmy, 'I've invited Mum and Dad to tea. Take out the good china, Clodagh. You know how fussy your mum is, and don't forget the blue vase with the lovely yellow flowers.'

Gerard asks me where I am.

'I'm inside the doll's house.'

'Who else is there?'

'Everyone except Dominic. He's playing football. My doll Sebastian isn't there either.'

'What else can you tell me, Clodagh?'

'Debbie's invited Mum and Dad to tea. My mum has a bump. I think she's pregnant. My little-girl self doesn't know. She thinks

Mum is fat. Sandy wants me to give Mum one of the chairs from the dining room with the tall backs so she can be comfortable.'

'Go on.'

'Mum has her hair tied up because she's hot. Debbie's trying to copy it, putting her hair up in a bun like a tight ball, the way ballerinas wear it. Dad puts his hand on Mum's tummy. She pushes it away. Dad says nothing. He looks angry and hurt at the same time.'

Debbie is whispering in my ear: 'Your mum's keeping another secret from your dad. Your mum has lots of secrets.'

'What are you feeling, Clodagh?'

'I'm sad. My little-girl self is sad. She wants to play happy families. Debbie is laughing, but it isn't a nice laugh. It's one of her evil ones.'

Sandy says, 'If Clodagh wants to play happy families, then I do too. I love that game.'

I hear Gerard saying, 'I'm listening, Clodagh. Remember that at all times you're perfectly safe.'

'Ben, the brown terrier, is barking. He nearly drops his black-and-white ball.'

Dad says, 'Jimmy, it's time to go home. We've had enough of your stories for one day.'

Mum says, 'It's about time you saw sense about that fool.'

'Leave it,' Dad says back.

'Mum and Dad are not talking to one another any more, but neither of them can leave the doll's house. In the doll's house people have to live by the doll's-house rules. Rules are important. I give Mum the pretend powder from the pretty dressing table in the upstairs bedroom, but she's not happy.'

'Powder your nose,' my little-girl self is saying, 'you know you love to powder your nose, Mum.' But she doesn't.

She says, 'I don't want to powder my nose, Clodagh.'

Dad says, 'Leave her alone. It's not Clodagh's fault.'

I take the perfume and the small white hand mirror from the dressing table and ask Mum would she like them instead. She doesn't look up. Sandy is sitting beside me. I love Sandy's curly blonde hair and her blue eyes like the sea.

'Debbie takes the perfume, powder and mirror. "Waste not, want not," she says. "Her loss is my gain." Gollywog looks shocked, but Golly always looks shocked.'

'Keep going, Clodagh.' I hear Gerard Hayden's voice again.

'Dad wants to be alone. He doesn't say it, but I know it. I put him in the attic, lay him down flat. He'll get some peace and quiet there. Mum doesn't say anything once he's gone, but it doesn't feel like peace. It feels the opposite.'

I stop talking, and my face must look worried, because Gerard asks, 'Is something wrong, Clodagh?'

'It's the ringing – I can hear ringing, and it won't stop.'

'Where is the ringing sound coming from?'

'I don't know.'

'What's making the ringing sound, Clodagh?'

'It's like a long buzz in my ear. The way an earache feels. It's not nice. It reminds me of something rotten.'

'Is it still there?'

'Yes. It's like a bluebottle thumping against a window, relentless. But this noise isn't a bluebottle, it's …'

'What is it, Clodagh?'

'It's a doorbell. It's the doorbell on the front door of the doll's house. I'm not sure if I want to open the door.'

It's then I hear Debbie scream, loud and ferocious. 'OPEN THE DAMN DOOR, CLODAGH.'

'What are you doing now, Clodagh?' Gerard asks.

'I'm going to open the door.'

'Who is at the door, Clodagh?' Gerard's voice remains calm.

'I don't know. I'm opening the door, but all I can see is an empty space, black like the night. But something is making a shape. It's a face, I think. The face is the size of the doorframe, but it's blurred, the way mirrors at a funfair make big people small, and small people big.'

Mum says, 'Shut the door, Clodagh, *now.*'

'The blurred image is clearing. It's a man's face, tilted, large, like a giant looking through the small doorframe of my doll's house. I don't want him to see me. I don't want him inside the doll's house. He isn't part of happy families.'

'What do you feel, Clodagh?'

'I want to close the door, but I'm afraid. I reach out and grab the handle. I worry that the man will do something, but he doesn't. His face looks at me blankly.'

'Did you not hear me, Clodagh? Close that bloody door.' My mum is roaring, and Debbie is laughing behind her.

'I shut the door, and the walls of the doll's house start trembling. My little-girl self is crying. She picks up Sandy, telling her, "We don't want to play this game any more." I don't want to play either.'

'Clodagh, can you still hear me?'

'Yes.'

'Clodagh, this is important. Do you know who rang the doorbell?'

'Yes, Gerard. I do.'

Harcourt Street Police Station

A sharp beam of sunlight shot across O'Connor's face with an unexpected break in the clouds. The next full squad meeting would be at three p.m. and, with his shirt sleeves rolled up, O'Connor had been surfing the net since getting back from the Jenkins house in Malahide. Edwina, Isabel Blennerhasset's daughter and Keith Jenkins's widow, had proved to be something of a red herring, but Isabel linking Jimmy Gahan and Keith Jenkins was the first bit of decent luck they'd had. Adrian Hamilton was part of this story. Three men meeting their deaths through drowning was a coincidence too far.

Keith Jenkins had been the only publicly named director of Hamilton Holdings, but the original company had been set up thirty-seven years previously by Adrian Hamilton. O'Connor was keen to find out why Jenkins had been currently running the show.

He checked his watch. Lynch would be back there soon. If what Ozzie Brennan had implied to Kate and Lynch was true, and Jenkins had been Jimmy Gahan's benefactor, the next question was why? What had Gahan on him?

Higgins and Clarke had paid another visit to the hotel, Maldon House, this time with a selection of mug shots. O'Connor hadn't been particularly surprised to discover Jenkins had registered under a pseudonym. What had surprised him was the description of the woman, which Higgins had been quick enough to pick up on. He'd shown the receptionist a number of images, including one of Jenkins's latest girlfriend, Siobhan King, and on a hunch, Gloria Sweetman. The receptionist couldn't be one hundred per cent sure, but she had picked out Gloria Sweetman's face from the bunch as Jenkins's companion.

Jenkins spending the night with a model wasn't a shocker. But Gloria Sweetman was now very much a dead model, and the word 'suicide' attached to the death of Adrian Hamilton and Gloria Sweetman was circling in O'Connor's brain. The hotel receipt had been dropped by either Jenkins or the killer, and O'Connor had his suspicions that it was the latter.

O'Connor's eyes felt as if two large prodding fingers were pressed on top of them. He needed to get his drinking under control. This case was tough enough without him voluntarily putting obstacles in his way. Isabel Blennerhasset had been on the phone to the chief super already, and although Butler was glad the connection had been made between Gahan and Jenkins, he had again warned O'Connor to tread carefully.

Stretching his back, O'Connor then took a gulp from the cold cup of coffee by his computer, before scanning through the files on screen. *The Irish Times* newspaper archive was the only one searchable online. There had been an inquest into Adrian Hamilton's death, and misadventure was the outcome. Hamilton had borrowed a small boat from a business colleague, leaving the estuary at Malahide very early on the morning of his death. The alarm was raised later that evening when he had failed to return the boat as promised. It hadn't taken long to find him and, with calm waters, bad weather was quickly dismissed as the reason for Adrian Hamilton's fully clothed body having ended up in the water. According to the report, large amounts of alcohol had been found in his system. That, coupled with the fact that he hadn't worn a lifejacket, had led to a verdict of misadventure: he had fallen overboard while intoxicated.

If Adrian Hamilton's death was connected with the current case,

O'Connor needed to discover who had owned that boat. He couldn't find any mention of a name anywhere in the archives. He'd have to gain access to the old case notes, an arduous task that he would assign to Lynch. O'Connor stared at the image of Adrian Hamilton on the screen. He'd been a successful businessman. The Irish economy wasn't exactly booming at the time, but it hadn't hit the full deprivation of the late eighties. If Hamilton's death hadn't been an accident but suicide, as Isabel Blennerhasset had said, he needed to talk to the family. Unfortunately Adrian Hamilton's widow, Lavinia, had recently passed away from cancer. There were surviving children, Dominic Hamilton and Clodagh McKay, but they would have been very young at the time of Adrian's death, and probably not a whole lot of use to him. Jimmy Gahan had a surviving sibling, Deborah Gahan, now chairperson of Kenmo International, a thriving export business. She was top of O'Connor's list for the next house call. He'd have to run background checks on the others. He also needed to be careful not to put too many eggs in the one basket.

The next call O'Connor received was from Monroe, a new detective to the squad at Harcourt Street. 'I have that number and address for Deborah Gahan.'

'I assume she's been told about the demise of her late brother?'

'Yeah, she's just identified the body.'

'Right. Does she know I'm looking for her?'

'Not yet, but I can set it up.'

'No, you're fine, Monroe. Just give me the number, and I'll make the contact.'

As O'Connor scrawled the number and address on a yellow Post-it, he remembered Isabel Blennerhasset telling him about how their kind didn't speak in straight lines. O'Connor wasn't in the mood for riddles. Deborah Gahan might have lost her brother but, from the sound of it, they weren't exactly close. If she had information, he'd get it out of her, even if it meant applying extra pressure.

Walking over to the wipe board, he wrote down a number of questions to which he wanted answers. If Adrian Hamilton's death had been suicide, what had lain behind it? If Keith Jenkins had been Jimmy Gahan's benefactor, what had Jimmy on him? Why the hell had an old hotel receipt been left at the scene? Was Gloria Sweetman part of all this? And how the heck had Jenkins become the principal director of Hamilton Holdings?

O'Connor looked at Deborah Gahan's phone number and decided to ring Lynch before he made the call.

'How close are you to the station?'

'We're leaving the quays now. Hold on, sir, I'm putting you on the hands-free set. We had another couple of stragglers to chat with after we spoke to Ozzie Brennan.'

'Any more of interest?'

'Not really, sir. Waste of time, other than the link of Jenkins to Gahan.'

'You said *we*, Lynch. Is Kate still with you?'

'Yes. I'm dropping her back to her office. She's right here beside me.'

'Kate?'

'O'Connor.'

'Your preliminary report.'

'What about it?'

'I have a question for you.'

'Shoot.'

'You used the term "expressive violent act".'

'I did.'

'Well, you infer that the two stages of the attack on Jenkins, the stabbing and the drowning, were motivated by separate driving forces, the initial attack resulting from an outburst of emotional feeling.'

'That's correct. I don't think it was the killer's intention to kill Jenkins during the first attack, but he wanted him to suffer. The level of stab wounds, frequency and sequence of the attack are indicative of high emotions at play, but that isn't the only element. As I said, the killer didn't want Jenkins to die that way. If he had done, he could easily have finished him off, which brings us to the method of killing and the location of the murder. As I stated in the report, if neither of these things was random, then the killer's choice of victims isn't likely to be random. We now know Jimmy knew Keith Jenkins. Jenkins and Gahan are part of some chain.'

'There are a couple more links.'

'What do you mean?'

'You were right on the mark when you suggested old connections. Isabel Blennerhasset has added another name to the mix, an Adrian Hamilton. He and Jimmy Gahan went to college together. Jenkins arrived at Trinity a number of years later, but they knew each other.'

'Go on.'

'Adrian Hamilton died after a boating accident in 1978.'

'Drowned?'

'It was put down as an accident, but rumoured as suicide. As I said, Keith Jenkins would have been the junior of the bunch, but I'm sure this is connected.'

'It's tempting to jump to conclusions, O'Connor. Adrian Hamilton's drowning is significant, but it may not be linked.'

The pain in O'Connor's eyes intensified. 'Well, I'm going to meet someone who'll shed some light on that.'

'Who?'

'Deborah Gahan, Jimmy's sister. She's just identified her brother's body.'

'When are you seeing her?'

'I'm going to ring her now. She lives local to you, Kate – Ranelagh, Benton Avenue. It might make sense if you came along.'

'I need to get back to Ocean House, but I could be there for around four.'

'Perfect. I'll text you the address and time. Any problems get back to me. Also, Lynch, when you drop Kate off, I have a job for you.'

'Not a bother, sir.'

'And some questions for you too. Higgins and Clarke have reported back from Maldon House. Jenkins booked in under a false name with a woman who fits the description of the late Gloria Sweetman.'

'What are you getting at, sir?'

'Did Jenkins's name come up anywhere in that investigation?'

'Of course not, or I'd have said so.' Lynch sounded affronted.

'Just checking, Lynch. Keep your hair on.'

'Sir?'

'What?'

'We never did find out who supplied Gloria Sweetman with the drugs.'

'I know that.'

'Someone gave that shitload to her.'

'Lynch, tell me something I don't know.'

'Well, it was something Ozzie Brennan said.'

'What?'

'He said, "Dead men can't commit murder, nor can murder be blamed on them."'

'So?'

'I didn't get the impression Ozzie was just referring to the murder of Jimmy Gahan.'

'Why? What else do you think he meant?'

'I don't know, just a feeling. It was more the way he paused mid-sentence before saying, "nor can murder be blamed on them".'

'You're thinking Gloria Sweetman.'

'As I said, sir, someone gave her that bag of drugs.'

Mervin Road

O'Connor agreed to meet Deborah Gahan at six o'clock. While Kate waited for the babysitter, Sophie, to arrive, she and Charlie made animal shapes with Play-Doh. The package with the crime-scene photographs from Jimmy Gahan's murder had arrived, but she had decided to spend one-to-one time with her son before she disappeared again.

Every now and then she would notice a silence between them, as if they both had something on their mind. And everywhere she looked, there were fragments of Declan: photos of them together before Charlie was born, two smiling faces; bookshelves filled with their books. She looked at a tiny antique jewellery box that Declan had bought her in Rome, more for decoration than anything else, because she'd fallen in love with the intricate pattern of two doves. She scanned the pieces of furniture in the apartment that they had picked out together, before deciding which piece would finally make it home. Now the question was when Declan would come home. He had another two months in Birmingham, although he'd promised to visit every second weekend. Kate wondered if that would fall by the wayside too.

The man on the phone the other evening had seemed alien, not the one she'd married. The Declan she knew, despite everything, loved her, but now he loved someone else.

She felt torn at having to leave Charlie so soon after arriving home, especially now. It was more than simply the pressure of the murder investigation, or her caseload: she was unwilling to face up to how much their lives were about to change.

It was only as Kate drove to the address O'Connor had texted her that she realised she had forgotten to tell Charlie how long she would be. Picking up her mobile phone, she called home, asking Sophie to put him on. 'I won't be long, Buster. I'll be back a little after seven, if that's okay.'

His voice sounded lower and less confident than normal: 'Okay, Mum. Sophie is helping me make a rocket with the Play-Doh.'

'Be good, honey.'

'I will, Mum.'

'Charlie?'

'Yes, Mum?'

'I love you tons.'

'I love you tons too.'

Clodagh

At home, I check my emails. Seeing Orla's name on the screen feels like another step back into normal life. She wants to know if I use Skype. I haven't done so before, but the laptop has a camera so I download the link. I'm shocked to see my bruises on the screen. Boston is five hours behind. I could try her now, but she might ask me to use the camera.

The last hypnosis session had left me feeling raw. After I'd left Gerard's, other memories crept in. The first was from before Dad died. Martin, Dominic and Stevie McDaid were out playing soccer. I was watching them. We were all sent outside because Emmaline had come home from hospital. I was just seven. Mum was settling her to sleep. Stevie called Dominic a sissy. Martin was laughing his head off. There had been a huge fight. Dominic told me to get the hell inside. I was the only one in the house with Dad and Mum and Emmaline. She was asleep in her cot. I heard the Mr Whippy ice-cream van driving up the strand, playing 'Pop Goes the Weasel'. Then the house went dark. I was crying and Dominic was telling me to shut up. Martin and Stevie were there too, but they weren't talking. Stevie was Dominic's soccer buddy and they both loved Manchester United. Martin was crap at sports, but Dominic pitied him because others at school picked on him. We were all in the attic. We'd done something. I think we were hiding. Dominic had the latch over on the inside of the attic door.

The next memory was Dad's funeral. Dominic was wearing a suit, a shiny grey one. He looked like a miniature big person, as if he could fit inside my doll's house. I was alone on the front steps of Seacrest looking at the sea. Dominic ran by me, flinging his jacket on the ground, hightailing it over to the strand. Uncle Jimmy dragged him back. I'd forgotten Jimmy was one of my dolls. He told us stories, long ones if he was in a good mood. Jimmy made everyone laugh – everyone except Mum. Jimmy was the same age as Dad; he called him Jimmy the Juggler because he kept so many balls in the air.

Back in Gerard's office when I was under hypnosis, Mum was pregnant with Emmaline. She had pushed Dad's hand away, shutting him out, and then that awful sound of a bell ringing, and the man's face at the door.

I wonder should I write all this down, but instead I go to Ruby's room. I lock the door behind me. I press the record button on my mobile phone. I say, 'Testing, one, two, three,' then listen back. My voice sounds strange, but it's loud and clear. I press record again and start.

'I'm on the strand. The sun is beaming down, burning the back of my neck. My neck feels hot, like a furnace, but I don't want to turn around. I'm building sandcastles with my red plastic bucket and yellow spade.'

I stop, press pause and look around the room, checking that I'm alone. I listen for any sounds downstairs. When I hear nothing, I press record again.

'My dolls are with me. Sandy and Debbie are sitting opposite, but Debbie is watching my mum and him. I stand up and walk down to the sea. I wobble back having filled my bucket to the brim with water. It feels heavier than me as I struggle with it, not wanting to spill any. My feet are sinking into the sand. My right arm is stretched and pained. The sun is dazzling. Debbie doesn't take her eyes off the two of them. The closer I get, I catch the smell of his smoke in the breeze.

I can hear my mother laughing. Her legs look long, tanned from our holiday in France. "Today is a treat," she had said. "We don't need the boys, just us two girls down on the beach." But it isn't only the two of us. She looks beautiful, my mother. She always did. I don't want to look at him, but Debbie never lets him out of her sight. Did I know his name back then? I must have done. Perhaps I blocked it out. He stands up, stubbing out his cigarette into the sand. I look at Mum. She's laughing. I see my sandcastles in his sunglasses, the ones blocking out his eyes. He doesn't stand for long. He kneels down, then lies on the far side of my mother. Her head turns away from me to him. I hear whispers, the kind I hear downstairs when Debbie wants to shout. Instead of looking at them, I stare at the cigarette butt, the one he's shoved into the sand. The more people pass, the deeper it gets buried. Soon it will disappear. The blue of the sea is blinding.'

I stop again, noticing the panic in my voice. I need to calm down. I press record again. Now my voice is more measured.

'When he props himself up on his elbows, his head causes a shadow over me. His hair is brown, past his ears. My mother runs her fingers through it. He keeps his eyes on her. It's as if I'm invisible. "Go and get her an ice-cream," my mother says, but he doesn't move, at least not at first. He turns towards me, as if he's waiting for me to ask the question. He's staring at me, and I don't like it. I don't say anything. "Go on," she says, and this time he moves. As he walks away, he gets smaller and smaller, and all the time, my mother is watching him, until she picks up her magazine, holding it with her pink-polished nails, pretending she doesn't care about him now that he's gone. But she does care. She folds the magazine over, fixing her hair, smoothing the sand off her legs.

'When he returns, he puts the cold choc-ice on her tummy. She jumps, then laughs again, before handing it to me. I want to sink like the cigarette butt into the sand. I turn away, my back to them, talking to Sandy and Debbie, feeling the heat of the sun burn the back of my neck , but not caring. I eat the choc-ice. When some of it drops on my legs, melting, I wipe it away, but it feels sticky, the sand hurting my skin, and they both laugh.'

I stop the recording. I press the play button and listen. The first time I met Gerard Hayden, he'd said that after regression some memories might come flooding back. But they feel disjointed. The man with my mother on the beach is the man whose face I saw at the door of my doll's house. I remember he wouldn't put his cigarette butts in the ashtray. Instead he would put them in the bin, or flick the butt into the bushes before entering the house. Dad was never there when the man came in the afternoon, at least not that I remember.

Part of me doesn't want to press the record button again, but if I don't, I might lose it. When I do, I wait a few seconds before I start.

'Our house is filled with people. They're dancing in the front room. The music is loud and fast. I can smell alcohol and smoke. Sometimes the boys would sneak alcohol up to the attic, and they would all stink of it. At first I'm not sure if he's there, the man from the doll's house. I feel small among all the adults, with their tall, tight bodies. Some of their faces smile down at me. I think I'm six or maybe seven. I open the door to the hall, and see the kitchen door is ajar. There's a light coming from behind it. I pass my father before going out into the hall. He's in the corner chatting with Uncle Jimmy and another man. The man's face is in the shadows. I feel I should know who he is, even though I can't see his face. There is something about him that scares me. The lines on my dad's forehead look tight, making that bumpy pattern, the one he used to make when he was worried or angry. None of them notices me. Out in the hall, the loud music becomes muted, and I feel cold. I'm curious about the light from the kitchen. When I push the door open, at first I don't see anyone, but I know somebody's there. I hear voices, mutters. I hear laughter, my mother's, then the man's.

'They don't know I'm there, so I move closer to the sounds. They're in the storage room off the kitchen. The light is off in there. It looks dark, but I can make out their shapes. Mum has her back to me, her arms around his neck. He is leaning into her, kissing her face and then her neck, moving from one to the other, before burying his face in her beautiful ginger hair. It's trailing down her back. Their bodies are tight together, they're engrossed in one another, until he sees me. I freeze, not knowing what to do next. He keeps staring at me, saying nothing, like I'm somebody else's problem, nothing for him to worry about. My mum turns, scooping me up in her arms, moving fast, leaving the man behind her. She brings me upstairs, pretending to be cross because I've got out of bed. She tells me it was all a dream, I should go back to sleep and not leave my bed again, not to come down until morning. She puts my doll Sandy in beside me.'

I stop talking, press the stop button, and again listen back.

I phone Dominic. When I hear his voice, I feel instantly reassured.

'Dominic, it's Clodagh.'

'Are you okay?' His voice is soft.

'Where are you, Dominic?'

'I'm at home.'

'Are you alone?'

'Val's gone out with friends.'

'I was wondering if I could call over. I've been remembering stuff.'

'You sound hassled. Martin hasn't hurt you?'

'No … Well, yes, but that's not it.'

'I'll kill that prick if he's hurt you again.'

'Shut up, Dominic, it doesn't matter.'

'It matters, Clodagh.'

'Dominic, will you stop talking for a minute? I'm not ringing you because of Martin. I need to talk to you about Mum.'

'Clodagh, when are you going to let that go? It's all history.'

'It's not about our argument. It's about her and a guy called Keith Jenkins. Do you remember him? He used to visit Mum in the afternoon when Dad wasn't there. Someone has killed him.'

He doesn't answer. I wonder if Dominic remembers him. He must do. I couldn't have been the only one to know. 'Dominic, I want to talk to you about Keith Jenkins.'

'What about him?'

'I remember the two of them together. Dad didn't know.'

'Are you sober?' His question sounds loaded.

I want to lose it with him, but if I'm going to get anywhere, I need to keep calm. I say, 'I'm perfectly sober. I haven't been drinking, I've been remembering. I'm seeing someone. He's a hypnotist. He's helping me to regress.'

'For God's sake, Clodagh, what the hell are you going to one of those fraudsters for?'

'He's not a fraudster.'

'How do you know?'

The truth is, I don't, but I'm not going to admit that to Dominic.

'Dominic, I need to remember.' I hear another silence at the end of the phone. Before he has a chance to speak, I say, 'Dominic, you know more than you're telling me, don't you?'

'Know what, Clodagh?'

'You knew there was someone else. He used to call in the afternoons, when Dad was at work. I know his name. I know who he was. Dominic, are you still there?'

'Of course I am.' He pauses. 'Clodagh, this isn't going to do anyone any good, least of all you. None of this matters.'

'What do you mean, least of all me?'

'It's not going to help, all this looking back.'

'It's my past, Dominic, not yours. My choice.' I'm screaming at him now. 'If you know something, you'd better tell me.'

'I can't.'

'Why can't you?'

'I promised Mum.'

'Fuck Mum! Tell me.'

'Calm down, Clodagh. If it mattered, I'd tell you.'

I take a deep breath, speaking calmer. 'Dominic, the man I remembered, the one with Mum, he's dead. He was murdered.'

'I know that.'

I don't know why I feel surprised, because then he says, 'I heard about it on the news, same as you, no doubt.'

'Do you remember him, Dominic?'

'Yes, but it's a long time ago.'

'What do you remember?'

'I remember he was a prick.' Dominic isn't even trying to disguise his anger, but then he calms down. 'Clodagh, there's something else, but before I tell you, I want you to promise me you're not going to start going off on any wild tangent.'

'What is it?'

'Promise me, Clodagh.'

'I promise.' Again I attempt to sound calm.

'Jimmy.'

'Uncle Jimmy?'

'He was never our uncle, Clodagh. You know that.'

'What happened?'

'You promised to stay calm.'

'I'm fucking calm.'

'We haven't seen either of them in years.'

'Dominic, will you goddamn tell me?'

'He's dead.'

My silence feels deafening. Dominic continues to talk, but I don't hear him. When I speak, my voice sounds slower, as if it belongs to someone else, someone in control, someone who will be able to take in this information and make sense of it. 'Dominic, tell me how he died.'

'I don't want you to worry.'

'You are worrying me.' My head hurts. 'Dominic, tell me.'

'According to the news, he died the same way as Keith Jenkins.'

'I can't believe what I'm hearing.'

'Clodagh, they're part of the past.'

'Dominic,' my voice is more assured than I feel, 'I want to meet you at the house tomorrow.'

'What house?'

'Seacrest, of course – I need the key to the attic. You still have it, don't you?'

Again he takes his time answering, and while I wait, I can't get the image of the attic out of my mind – Dominic, Martin, Stevie and me hiding up there as kids, as if we'd done something wrong. It feels connected to Emmaline, but I can't work out why.

'But, Clodagh—'

'No buts, Dominic. When can you get time out from work?'

'I'm not in work tomorrow.'

'Good. I'll meet you after Martin's ten o'clock call.'

'Clodagh, I don't think this is a good idea.'

'Dominic, bring the key. I'll see you there at eleven.' I hang up before he can say another word.

27 Benton Avenue, Ranelagh

Kate made good time getting to Benton Avenue, somewhat relieved to arrive before O'Connor. She looked at her face in the rear-view mirror. In the blame game, if she was being honest, she had been part of the problem, but that didn't make the pain of Declan being with someone else any less. She laid her head against the headrest. She felt utterly alone.

Losing her mother, her only surviving parent, had changed things. Something happens when both your parents die. It's like all traces of what went before are abandoned to memory. You can never hear their voices again, see an expression change on their faces or touch them. You think there must be some kind of continuation, but of what?

Had that been why she'd been fooling herself, thinking she and Declan could make things work, a desperate desire for family, to feel normal? Surely she of all people hadn't been that naïve. Charlie was her world now. But if he was, why the hell wasn't she with him, instead of sitting here waiting for O'Connor?

O'Connor didn't need her there. He could have handled the interview with Deborah Gahan alone. Yet she'd agreed to meet him. Would she have agreed if it hadn't been him doing the asking? What the hell was wrong with her? Kate drew a deep breath.

Whatever her reasons for being there, she had to use this time wisely to consider aspects of the case. Was the murder of both men a form of perverted justice on the killer's part? Had either or both known their killer? The connection to the Hamilton drowning could turn out to be important or send them on a wild-goose chase. She looked in the rear-view mirror again. Passion and emotion were playing a role in the attacks. If the killer was on some kind of crusade, who or what was he seeking justice for? Himself or someone else? Kate thought again about the eye-witness statement from Grace Power. She'd described the men as similar. There was nothing obviously different about their dress or appearance, meaning Jenkins's attacker wasn't some thug he'd accidentally stumbled upon. If the killer was middle class, he might not have a previous record. She thought again about the risk. Was it geographical convenience, a form of familiarity?

Adrian Hamilton had met his death in a similar way. Again, it was a long shot, but a connection. All three men had known each other. It was obvious from what Ozzie Brennan had said that there was no love lost between Deborah Gahan and her late brother. Deborah Gahan wasn't the killer, but that didn't mean she wasn't involved.

Kate sat in her car as she watched O'Connor pull in on the opposite side of the road. Soon they would be talking to Jimmy's only surviving sibling.

38C Seville Place, Ringsend

Stevie's meeting yesterday evening hadn't gone according to plan. The smooth bastard had gained in arrogance over the years, becoming a lot more powerful than Stevie had realised. Still, timing was everything. Ruby McKay was only seventeen, and even if she wanted to keep her mouth shut, that didn't mean Stevie had to.

She had opened up completely, once she'd got some coke inside her, believing she had a listening ear, thinking, like most spoilt brats, that it was her way or the highway. Stevie wasn't so green. He'd fed her full of the crap she'd wanted to hear. Once she'd believed he was on her side, it had all come spluttering out, every last rotten bit of it. And anything little Ruby didn't care to share wasn't too difficult to fill in.

He had wondered if their new trust would mean getting more intimately acquainted. But he wasn't on her radar. Nor was he about to start meddling with the bag of candy that might furnish him with a good pay-off. If the situation had been different, he would have given her one for sure.

Stevie had thought long and hard, waiting for his mark to arrive. The guy had had plenty of accusations levelled against him – suspected fraud, corruption, back-handers – but nothing had stuck, and the recent spate of government tribunals hadn't bothered him either. Everything could be easily forgiven if not forgotten. Most people turned a blind eye if it suited them. But messing with someone as young as Ruby McKay was something else entirely, especially when your socialite wife was chasing one bleeding good cause after another, opening gala events all over the damn city.

Stevie had underestimated his opponent. The two heavies who had come along with him for the 'welcome meeting' had certainly made their point. Normally, getting the shit kicked out of him wouldn't have made any odds to Stevie. But the heavies were ex-Provos. They were a whole different ballgame.

He wasn't sure how far he could push things with those bleeding fanatical heavies in tow. He had no real desire to spill the beans on the fucker either, but you couldn't blame a guy for wanting to make some money out of it. Even the fat, smarmy bastard could see that.

None of this was about making waves. Once both parties knew they were talking the same language, it should have made things easier – that was, once Stevie agreed to play ball.

He'd get his money all right, but first he had to earn it. It was all part of the same old fucking game. Stevie would need to get his fingers dirty, gain back the guy's trust, as if he had been the one to fuck things up in the first place. 'Insurance' was what the slimy fucker had called it. He would get half his money now, the other half later. Stevie wasn't particularly keen, but considering everything, he had no plans to mess about with that fucking crowd. Not unless he wanted to end up dead.

He needed to rest for a while, get himself on the mend. Grabbing a cold beer from the fridge, he put on the television. With all his visits over the last couple of days, he hadn't seen much of the news. He didn't feel a whole lot better when he saw Jimmy Gahan had taken a swim in the canal. His gut told him it was linked. His head told him not to ask too many questions. Sometimes in life the less you knew, the better, and the safer it would be for everyone, especially Stevie.

27 Benton Avenue, Ranelagh

If either Kate or O'Connor had had any illusions that they were about to meet Jimmy Gahan's grieving sibling, they would have been disappointed. Deborah Gahan was one well-groomed lady, with the kind of grooming that didn't happen in a couple of hours. Her face was locked with so much Botox that her heavy makeup gave the impression of holding up something that should have collapsed a long time ago. But behind the forced facial façade, there was no denying that this unnatural blonde had once been a very attractive woman.

Kate and O'Connor took their seats opposite the late Jimmy Gahan's sister, in her opulent living room with its original Victorian features and an overdose of cream and gold. Behind her scarlet lipstick and powder pink skin, Deborah Gahan looked more than ready for them.

The contrast between how Jimmy Gahan must have lived and the lifestyle his sister obviously enjoyed was nearly as blatant as the distance Deborah Gahan wanted to put between her and her latest visitors.

'I fail to see how I can be of any use to you, Detective Inspector O'Connor. Jimmy and I were not close. We lived completely different lives, and I'm not going to pretend any belated sorrow at his loss.'

'Fair enough.' O'Connor was sitting on the edge of the antique sofa. 'I appreciate your honesty, Ms Gahan, but there are a few things you might be able to help us with.' His use of 'us' caused Deborah Gahan to look directly at Kate, sitting to O'Connor's left. As if picking up on the question in the woman's mind, O'Connor continued, 'My apologies, Ms Gahan, this is Dr Kate Pearson. Her field is forensic psychology.' Kate rose to shake Deborah Gahan's hand and although she returned the handshake, it wasn't with enthusiasm.

'Two men have been murdered, including your late brother, and I understand you knew both of them.'

'A lot of people knew Keith Jenkins, Detective Inspector.'

'I'm aware of that, Ms Gahan, but I understand your brother had been friends with him since college.'

'Keith was a few years younger than Jimmy.' She shifted in her seat. 'They met in Jimmy's final year, and I wouldn't exactly call them friends. But, yes, Detective Inspector, I did know of him, and of their acquaintance with each other.'

'And Adrian Hamilton, you knew him too?'

'Yes. As far as I remember, he was in the same year as Jimmy.'

'He died in a boating accident, Ms Gahan.'

'That is correct.' She faced Kate again. 'I understand he had the same fondness for the bottle as my late brother.'

O'Connor stood up from the sofa, moving around the room, while Deborah Gahan's eyes followed him. 'What can you tell us about Adrian Hamilton?'

'Really, Detective Inspector, I don't see how that could be of any use.'

'Humour me.' O'Connor stood still and stared at Deborah Gahan, who looked far from the humouring kind.

Kate watched them both. O'Connor was on well-rehearsed territory: encouraging others to share information with him was something he did extremely well. Deborah Gahan wasn't exactly an obliging informant, but she reluctantly recited her knowledge of Adrian Hamilton as if she was answering questions on *Mastermind*.

'Adrian Hamilton was a dreamer. Successful in business, yes, but it takes more than dreams of success to be successful. He got lucky, as far as I understand it, invested in stocks and shares when many other people were risk averse, a little like now, really.'

'Go on.' O'Connor was already writing in his notebook.

'He set up his own business – Hamilton Holdings, I think it was called.'

'And what kind of business was that?'

'Anything that would make money. Investments primarily … venture capital for new ideas, property, you know the kind of thing.'

'And it was successful you say?'

'For a time, Detective Inspector, but at some point Adrian's luck ran out.'

'How do you mean?'

'Every dog on the street knew he had big money worries. That was partly why suicide was suspected the moment his body turned up in the water.'

'Do you know what happened to the company, Hamilton Holdings, after his death?'

'And why would I know that, Detective Inspector?' Deborah Gahan's voice chilled.

'You're a successful businesswoman, Deborah.' O'Connor smiled, hoping his charm might do him some good. 'You strike me as someone who would know these things.'

Kate couldn't help but admire how O'Connor got information out of people. He figured out fast which buttons to press, and using Deborah Gahan's first name, while alluding to her business acumen, loosened the tight rein ever so slightly.

'It was sold, as far as I know. Quite early on, actually, long before an official receiver could be appointed.'

'When?'

'It was soon after the inquest, Detective Inspector. A generous benefactor, I understand.'

'Generous?' O'Connor waited again.

'It was believed that whoever acquired it paid a heavy price to Adrian Hamilton's widow. She was the sole beneficiary of Adrian's estate. There was the life-assurance policy, of course, but that alone wouldn't have been enough.'

'You seem to know a lot about the Hamiltons' life?' It was the first question Kate had asked Deborah Gahan, and it wasn't one she expected to be received well.

Deborah Gahan cleared her throat, as if contemplating her response. 'Dr Pearson, people with money tend to know a lot about each other's lives, especially when they fall down on their luck.' Her tone was harsh.

Kate knew she had to tread carefully. 'Ms Gahan, whoever killed your brother most likely also killed Keith Jenkins. Everything indicates a single offender, and we can't rule out the possibility of him acting again. If you know anything, anything at all, it's important you share that knowledge.'

'And do you have any idea, Dr Pearson, of the type of man who would do this? After all, that is your field of expertise.' Deborah Gahan was fishing, and Kate knew it, but she needed to gain the woman's trust if they had any chance of getting some concrete information out of her.

'We know from witness statements that we're looking for a male, someone similar in build to the late Keith Jenkins and possibly similar in age. Both crimes strongly suggest someone within a mature age grouping, and someone capable of keeping his cool. On each occasion, the killer was able to control the proceedings long enough to maximise his chances of success, especially as the murders happened in public places. I'm pretty sure this man knows exactly why he has carried out his actions, and is quite specific in how and what he wants to achieve. We can't be one hundred per cent sure that he knew either your brother or Keith Jenkins before they met their deaths, but all the indicators point to that being the case. Until we know *why* your brother and Keith Jenkins were killed, we have no idea who else is at risk.'

Kate let the last piece of information sink in, hoping it would be enough to shift Deborah Gahan's attitude to them. O'Connor sat down beside Kate and waited.

'My brother wasn't a particularly nice man,' Deborah Gahan responded, 'and I'm not talking about his fall from society. He was a schemer, always looking for the next scam he could pull. I'm not sure how involved he was with Adrian Hamilton's financial collapse, but if he was part of it, it wouldn't surprise me in the least.' She looked from Kate to O'Connor. 'I can't be completely sure but I believe it was Keith Jenkins who put the money up for Adrian Hamilton's widow.'

O'Connor asked the next question: 'And what makes you think that, Deborah?'

'He was a single guy and flash with his money – expensive cars, designer clothes, living it up. He was only starting to make a name for himself in television, so it wasn't from there that he got his money but he had plenty of it all the same.'

'So why would he help Adrian Hamilton's widow?' This time Kate did the asking.

For the first time since they had arrived, Deborah Gahan smiled, but it was more like a smirk than any positive change in her mood. 'For the same stupid reason that most men do what they do, Dr Pearson.'

'You're saying Keith Jenkins and Lavinia Hamilton were involved with each other?'

'It was only rumoured but, a bit like how Adrian Hamilton's money worries surfaced once his dead body turned up in the water, everyone started asking questions. Answers soon rose to the surface. Keith Jenkins and Lavinia Hamilton might have been discreet, although it wouldn't have mattered too much if they hadn't. That is, of course, if Adrian Hamilton didn't know about it.'

Kate sat forward. 'You don't think Adrian's death was an accident. You think he killed himself.'

'Dr Pearson, whether he ended up in the water intentionally or the alcohol put him there doesn't really matter. He was losing his business, and was probably about to lose his wife. Either or both of those things might have been enough for some people to take matters into their own hands.'

Kate felt Deborah Gahan was still holding back. 'Was there something else?'

'It was a long time ago, Dr Pearson.'

O'Connor had no intention of letting Kate's last question go unanswered. 'Deborah, if you know something else, you'd better tell us.'

'The wife – Adrian's wife – she lost a baby the year her husband died. A girl, I understand.'

Kate asked another question, one to which she suspected she knew the answer. 'Ms Gahan, you said Adrian's wife, Lavinia Hamilton, lost her baby. You didn't include Adrian Hamilton in that loss.'

'Oh, he was part of it all right, but perhaps not in the way he wanted. I can't be sure, no one can, but the parentage was in some doubt. Keith Jenkins's name was floated as the possible father. I understand after the baby died Lavinia Hamilton started to unravel.'

'Mentally, you mean?' Kate kept eye contact with Deborah Gahan.

'Post-natal depression, call it what you will, but either way, she became a mess and it's thought Adrian finally put two and two together.'

'Who told you all this?' O'Connor was standing up again.

Deborah Gahan turned from Kate to O'Connor. 'Jimmy, if you must know. He was very close to the family back then.'

'What about the two children?'

'What about them?' She turned back to Kate.

'How did they cope with it all?'

'They were children. How do you think they coped? They got on with things.' Deborah Gahan took a deep breath, then stood up to face O'Connor. 'Now, Detective Inspector, if you don't mind, I can't be any more help to you.'

'Just one more thing, Ms Gahan.' Kate stood up too. 'If Keith Jenkins was the father, he would have been a number of years younger than Lavinia.'

'So?'

'I was just wondering how they got together in the first place.'

'Jimmy introduced Keith to the Hamiltons.'

'And how did Jimmy and Keith meet originally?' O'Connor, like Kate, was reluctant to let Deborah Gahan off the hook.

'They were both at Trinity, but attended at different times.'

'Really, Detective, it was a long time ago.'

'Try, Deborah. It's important.'

'I guess in the same way Jimmy met everyone else, in some bar ...'

'Go on.' O'Connor still not prepared to let go.

'Keith would have been seriously underage at the time, but that wouldn't have bothered Jimmy. Keith seemed to look up to him ...' She paused. 'Jimmy liked the attention. Even as a teenager Keith Jenkins had charisma.'

'Are you saying Jimmy—'

'I'm not saying anything of the sort. My brother was a weak man, Detective Inspector. He had an ego, and liked it when others bolstered it. You asked me how they all met, and I've told you.' Deborah Gahan was digging her heels in. 'It was all a long time ago.'

'What about lately, Deborah? Were they still friendly?'

'I doubt it, Detective Inspector. Keith Jenkins moved on from the likes of my brother a long time ago.'

'Rumour has it they were still in touch.'

'I wouldn't know about that.'

'Someone killed your brother, Deborah,'

'I'm aware of that, Detective Inspector. Now, I think I've spoken to you both for long enough.'

The Mansion House, Dawson Street

The breeze made the voice at the other end of the phone difficult to hear. After his conversation with Stevie McDaid the previous evening, he knew he needed to put more pressure on Martin. His brief interlude with Ruby McKay hadn't been the wisest decision on his part, but he had every intention of keeping his cool. The heavies had served to keep McDaid somewhat in check. That pretty-boy face of his hadn't aged too badly, but he hadn't looked too pretty after the lads were finished with him.

He pulled up the collar of his heavy cashmere coat, bringing it tight around his neck. His leather-gloved hand held the mobile phone close to his ear, watching his breathing make smoke signals in the chill of the afternoon. In a low but determined voice he said, 'Martin, it's good to talk to you again.'

'What do you want?'

'We have another fish out for a swim.'

'Who?'

'Stevie McDaid. You do remember him? You two were quite friendly once, if my memory serves me right.'

'What does he want?'

'What does his kind ever fucking want, Martin?'

'Money?'

'Of course bloody money. He has no idea how dangerous his meddling could be for him.'

'What are you saying?'

'You're not going all nervous on me now, are you?'

There was silence at the other end of the phone, Martin taking his time answering. 'I'm no bloody coward. I'm a lot of things, but I'm not that.'

'Glad to hear it, Martin.'

'What does McDaid have on you?'

'Never mind. There's no need for you to worry about McDaid for now. I've sent him on a little errand.'

'So what do you want me to do?'

'Just warning you to be careful. Sit tight, stay fucking calm, and keep your mouth shut.'

'I'm good with secrets. You know that too.'

'Well, keep it that way, Martin.'

'What do the cops know about the killings?'

'They've connected Gahan with Jenkins, nothing a rookie out of training college wouldn't be able to do.'

'And that's it?'

'They're doing some digging. Don't worry about that either. I'll keep you posted. That's not why I rang you.'

'What is it, then?'

'Make sure you're still keeping a good eye on that wife of yours.'

'She's getting shakier by the day.'

'Is she hitting the booze again?'

'Not yet.'

'Well, keep close to her.'

'I have it under control.'

'Good to hear it. Keep it that way.'

Hanging up, he took a long look at the historic building in front of him, before sprinting up the stone steps. He may have been in his sixties, but he wasn't a man to let age, or anything else, get in his way.

27 Benton Avenue, Ranelagh

Once outside, O'Connor lit a cigarette, dragging on it like it was a much-needed fix. 'So what did you make of her, Kate?'

'I think Deborah Gahan was telling us as much truth as she was prepared for us to hear. You don't become a successful businesswoman like her without knowing how to play your cards close to your chest.'

'So you think she's still hiding something?'

'She knew an awful lot, O'Connor, to not get how Keith Jenkins fits into all this of late.'

'I agree.' When his mobile phone rang, he kept his gaze on Kate while he answered it. 'What? He's sure?' O'Connor's expression was changing from agitation to stern determination, a look he often displayed when something in the investigation had shifted.

'What is it, O'Connor?'

'That was Lynch. It turns out Jimmy Gahan was dead going into the water. Heart attack, brought on by the shock of the stabbing.'

'What exactly did Morrison tell Lynch?'

'Well, apparently with drowning it's often a diagnosis of exclusion, meaning Morrison began by determining what didn't happen. Unlike Jenkins, there was no evidence of diatoms in the bloodstream. Nor did he find any sign of pressure trauma on the sinuses or the lungs. He would have expected to find haemorrhaging in the sinuses and airways …' O'Connor hesitated as if he was still trying to take the information in.

'Go on.'

'Morrison also checked for water debris, which Jimmy Gahan

would have sucked in, attempting to breathe. Again he came up blank. Once drowning was ruled out as the cause of death, Morrison looked elsewhere. Jimmy Gahan suffered severe heart failure, and was a dead man before taking his plunge.'

'But the killer still put him in the canal?' This time it was Kate's turn to ponder.

'What are you thinking, Kate?'

'We're back to the water connection, and it could also explain something else.'

'What?'

'Did Morrison say if there was any time delay from when death occurred to the victim being immersed in the water?'

'I'm not sure. What are you getting at?'

'Jenkins was taken by car to the canal. We know there was a time interval from the last sighting of him until he turned up dead. We also know he was alive when he was brought to the canal.'

'So?'

'So, it gave the killer time with the victim before death.'

'I'm still not getting you, Kate.'

'What if the killer was looking for information from the victim? As I said in the report, with Jenkins, the initial attack was an expressive violent act, resulting from an outburst of emotional feeling and pent-up aggression. The second element of the attack, the drowning, was a means to an end. If Jimmy Gahan's heart gave up as a result of the stabbing, it took away the killer's opportunity to converse with his victim afterwards but, perhaps more importantly, it meant when Gahan ended up in the water, it wasn't for any instrumental reason. He was already dead.'

'Go on.'

'If the killer put a dead Jimmy Gahan in the canal, then the water is confirmed as the constant. No matter how the killing goes down, he wants his victims there, which could bring us back to Adrian Hamilton's death, although there's no denying the extended gap in time.'

The alarm on her phone rang out – six fifty. She'd promised Charlie she'd be back a little after seven.

Kate silenced her mobile. 'You'll have my report on the Gahan killing tomorrow evening. Let's see what that throws up. There may even be a religious or ritualistic connection.'

'Go on.'

'In some religions, water is used as a symbol of soul cleansing.'

'What the hell?'

'I'm only pointing out a possibility, O'Connor. Don't shoot the messenger. The killer wanted his victims to feel pain, and with Jimmy Gahan, assuming the killer knew Jimmy was dead going into the water, he carried out the same ritual. It establishes drowning as important beyond the act of actual killing.'

'Kate, let's assume Gahan had something on Jenkins. Otherwise why be his benefactor? The late Keith Jenkins doesn't come across as the naturally benevolent type.'

'No, he doesn't. Look, O'Connor, I need to head back.'

'Just a second, hear me out. Lynch thinks there could be a link with Gloria Sweetman. The hotel receipt ties them together. And, as Lynch said, someone gave that killer mix to her.'

'Perhaps he's right, but who gave Gahan the information? There are more pieces to this jigsaw than we're seeing.'

'What are you getting at, Kate?'

'I'm not sure yet, but there are other influences afoot – the missing ring for a start.'

'That's been bothering me too.'

'O'Connor, if this is some kind of personal vendetta, and the killer took the ring, it could be a form of moral judgement on his part, not thinking Jenkins good enough to wear it. It might tie into what Deborah Gahan said about Jenkins and Lavinia Hamilton although, again, we're talking ancient history. Jenkins would have had other affairs in the intervening period.'

'So what do you think is really motivating our guy, Kate?'

'We're dealing with multiple deaths at this point. Not quite spree killings, but close. Although the victims aren't random, research has shown in similar cases that the killer tends to be male, angry and probably with a history of either social failure or perceived personal failure.'

'You mean like Jimmy Gahan?'

'Not really. Our guy feels isolated and, as I said, is carrying a sense of failure. Often there is a trigger event or events, marital difficulties, for example, or financial problems, anything which has the potential to put him under a heightened level of stress, increasing his anxieties to the point of tipping over.'

O'Connor leaned against his car. 'Keep talking.'

She checked the time on her phone again. O'Connor was getting another five minutes max. 'Depending on how much pressure he's under, the trigger or triggers have the power to make his mind contract, becoming utterly focused. It could be some kind of revenge. But what's particularly important about perpetrators in these types of crimes is that they no longer see people as people but, rather, as targets.'

'Sort of like a soldier in a war scenario.'

'Not quite. We all have basic needs, fundamentals by which we achieve social integration, including physiological needs, sleep, hunger, thirst et cetera, but there are also the needs of personal security – feeling safe, affection, love, self-esteem. The lack of any of these basics can inhibit positive personal development.'

'But our guy isn't some young kid, we know that. He's been around the block, and possibly living a somewhat normal life up until now.'

'Many people carrying pent-up anger or aggression do so under the radar. When they surface, it's not unusual for others to say things like they would never have thought them capable of such an act. But someone capable of this level of violence will have displayed certain traits – egocentrism, impulsivity, paranoia, aggressiveness. The aggression may have raised its head already, through domestic violence or in other forms, and many cases of domestic violence are never reported and therefore go unnoticed.'

'We've eradicated Johnny Keegan from our enquiries, but we can drag him back in again.'

'It's not him, O'Connor. He doesn't fit. Our killer has much more than aggressive outbursts on his mind. He has an agenda.'

'Great. Butler will love to hear that.'

'I'm sorry I can't be more specific. I need time. There are no shortcuts, O'Connor. In a way, it's a bit like Morrison working out the cause of death, first establishing what didn't cause it. Our man hasn't arrived here overnight. There will have been tell-tale signs, but perhaps those signs are only apparent to those closest to him. On what we have so far, his *modus operandi*, the drowning, looks likely to be linked to the motivation. It's giving him something, a form of payback, possibly feeding into his need to feel superior, in control of people and events, or it could be a form of compensation.'

'Compensation for what?'

'Loss, rejection, betrayal. Within a sense of failure, the list is endless. But he does have a plan. To him all this makes complete sense. He is utterly focused, determined, his mind contracted, and he won't be deterred, unless, of course, he has already achieved what he wants.'

'And if he hasn't?'

'He'll keep going, doing whatever it takes. My guess is there's more than one motivation at play here, O'Connor, and if our man was looking for information from Jimmy Gahan and didn't get it, his sudden heart attack interfering with things, he'll keep on looking.'

'So what next, Kate?'

'I don't know, and neither can we be sure that other crimes aren't going on.'

'I don't get you.'

'The hotel receipt.'

'What about it?'

'It's all too convenient. It links Jenkins to Gloria Sweetman. The killer could have wanted us to find it.'

'I was thinking that too. I'm always suspicious of anything that comes easy.'

'If Gahan was blackmailing Jenkins and it was connected to the model's death, then Jenkins wouldn't have been carrying the hotel receipt around in his pocket. He would have got rid of it a long time back.'

'You're thinking our guy is up to more than murder?'

'There might even be more than one player involved. Someone else could be in the driving seat. The crime scenes are only part of the picture.'

'What do you mean?'

'It's a bit like how I break down my analysis of a crime scene for profiling purposes. Many think of the concept of a crime scene as a single location, but that's not the case. There can be a variety of other locations, unknown or otherwise. There's the first encounter, or subsequent encounter, with the victim, the assault, which in Jenkins's case was the initial knife attack, and the location where the murder took place, and sometimes where the body is finally found. All four can be in separate locations. If we move our thinking out beyond simply murder, and as you know, we've already suspected blackmail, plus alleged financial wrongdoings, and who knows what else, we're looking at any number of potential crime scenes and interconnecting events. Have you found out any more on Hamilton Holdings?'

O'Connor, let out an exhausted sigh. 'Not so far, but the criminal-assets boys are on board. We should have something soon.'

'All I'm saying, O'Connor, is that this case is stacking up to be more about what we don't see than what we do.'

'For a moment, let's keep this simple. How is our killer operating?'

'I told you, O'Connor, I have to go. I'll put all of this in my report.'

'I don't have time to wait for it. You mentioned spree killings. How's he seeking out his victims?'

'There are four basic hunting typologies – hunter, poacher, troller and trapper.'

'For less educated souls like me, Kate, what's the difference?'

'I'm not sure it's going to help.'

'Let me be the judge of that.'

'A troller is someone involved in a non-predatory activity, who opportunistically encounters his victim, while a hunter will specifically set out to meet them. A trapper assumes a position facilitating his encounter with the victim, but a poacher will travel to find them.'

'Our man has transport, so he could be a poacher?'

'Maybe, but wherever he's operating from, he's not choosing on type. Nor is he accidentally encountering his victims.'

'Meaning he's displaying hunter and trapper type qualities.'

'That's correct.'

'If Gahan was putting the squeeze on Jenkins, as you say, someone gave him the information. We need to find out who, and how the hell they're connected to all this.'

'There is one other thing, O'Connor.'

'What's that?'

'There's no guarantee our killer's motivation is gender specific. I'd keep an eye on Deborah Gahan, if I was you. If she's holding something back, she could be in danger, even if she isn't our favourite person in the world.'

'More bloody police resources. Butler will be thrilled.'

'As I said before, don't shoot the messenger. Now, I have to go. You'll have my report tomorrow.'

'Grand, but shooting the messenger happens to be one of Chief Superintendent Butler's favourite personality traits.'

'Tomorrow, O'Connor.'

Macquay's Bridge, Grand Canal Street

It's nearly midnight. I feel lost inside my own mind. Almost as if everything that's happening is happening to someone else.

The canal has become a second home for me. It holds my secrets. I watch the moon shine on the water as it pours ferociously through the locks, a sharp wind wrapping my face – cold and fierce, the way I killed the two of them.

Did they ever imagine my face would be the last one they would see? I try to visualise Jenkins and Jimmy Gahan being dragged out of the water, like rubbish.

Time is a funny thing. It can jump years. But the past lingers all your life. No matter what kind of shine Keith Jenkins put on things when he gained celebrity status, or whatever new deal Jimmy Gahan ventured on, their past stayed with them. It's my past too. Now I'm taking ownership of it, and with that, I've regained my sense of power and control.

The future is somewhat trickier. It requires a steady hand. Too much haste and I could fuck it up. I have no intention of letting that happen. Once Jimmy's body was discovered, seeing the police at Deborah Gahan's house hadn't surprised me. I knew it wouldn't take them long to call on her. She's a shrewd nut. Always was. If anyone could send the police on a merry dance, she could.

I think about paying her a visit tonight, but think again – far too risky.

Clodagh's different. It won't take a lot for her to hit the sauce again. I need to keep her close. The hypnosis is opening doors for her. She's gaining confidence, I can tell. But confidence can be shattered. The more Clodagh meddles, the worse it will be.

Soon she won't have to worry any more. Soon there will be no need for answers, because very soon, there will be no more questions.

Ocean House, the Quays

Imogen Willis looked nervous during the Wednesday-morning family meeting. Kate had met the family once before, when Imogen was initially referred to her. Imogen's mother had a kind face, with short bobbed black hair, the obvious donor of Imogen's large eyes. Imogen's sister, Jilly, took after their father, both with pale skin, stockier build and wispy blond hair. They all looked to Kate, waiting for her to start things off.

'It's great to see you today, and I'm sure you're delighted with Imogen's progress.'

Imogen's mother, Mary Louise, was the first to answer. 'We are, Kate. Imogen is a changed girl. Isn't she, Harry?'

'Happier, much happier.' Harry looked at his daughter, but Imogen didn't turn to him.

'What about you, Jilly? Have you noticed any change in Imogen since coming here?'

'Yeah, she's making real progress.'

Imogen smiled at her sister.

'Good, that's great.' Kate paused, giving Imogen a reassuring look. 'I suppose you're all wondering why I've asked you here today.'

'There isn't anything wrong, is there, Kate?' Mary Louise, unable to hide her anxiety.

'No, no. Actually, it's quite the contrary.' Kate looked at her audience of four, wondering which of them seemed the most nervous. 'I think this is an opportune time to chat a little about what's been happening with Imogen. That is still okay with you, Imogen, isn't it?'

'Sure.'

'Great. You all know that Imogen has begun to remember some things. Not everything that she remembers is making complete sense. At least, it isn't right now.'

'You mean about Busker dying?' Again, Mary Louise was doing the talking.

'Yes, that's right. Imogen and I have spoken at length about her large gaps in memory, and her recollections, which is partly why I wanted to explain how disassociation works.'

'This disassociation, can it be cured?' Harry sat upright in his chair.

Kate spoke as gently as she could: 'Harry, we all have the ability to disassociate. It's part of our survival mechanism as human beings. Disassociation allows us to disconnect from our feelings. It's not unusual for a person who has experienced the trauma of a car crash to say that they almost felt someone else was going through it. But it doesn't have to be something traumatic for us to disassociate.' Kate looked to the others. 'I'm sure you all watch movies on television.' They each nodded. 'Well, disassociation can happen there too. What was the last movie you saw, Mary Louise?'

'*Taken* – the one with Liam Neeson.'

'Where his daughter goes missing?'

'That's right.'

'Mary Louise, that's a great example. Can I ask you a couple of questions about it?'

They stared at Kate as if she had gone temporarily insane, but Mary Louise gave a tentative 'Yes.'

'Did you watch the movie at home?'

'Yes, with Harry last Friday night. We got in pizza.'

'Did you have the lights down low?'

'Yeah.' This time Harry got in on things.

'You were awake, alert and comfortable?'

Mary Louise frowned. 'Yes, Harry and I were finished work for the week. We were relaxed and very comfortable.'

Harry nodded in agreement.

'During the time you were watching the film, were you conscious of each other at all times?'

'I knew Mary Louise was there, if that's what you mean,' Harry said.

'But you were thinking about the movie rather than her?'

'I suppose.' It was Harry's turn to frown.

'Harry, can you remember eating each slice of pizza?'

'No. I wasn't thinking about it, just eating it.'

'I can't remember either.' Mary Louise was quick to support her husband.

'After the two of you got settled into the movie, were you thinking about other things? What happened at work or anything like that?'

They looked at each other before giving a simultaneous 'No.'

'Were you concerned for the girl's welfare, the girl who was abducted in the movie?'

Again they answered together: 'Yes.'

'When Liam Neeson or, rather, the fictional character he was playing was running, driving fast or physically attacking the people he thought were involved with the abduction, did you feel his emotion?'

'I suppose so,' Mary Louise responded.

'I wanted to kill the bastards,' Harry emphatically declared.

'Was your heart racing, Mary Louise?'

She stared at Kate. 'At some points, yes.'

'Even though in reality Liam Neeson's daughter wasn't taken, the character that Liam Neeson played didn't exist, and all of them, including the actress in the role of his fictional daughter, were simply making a movie, you were nevertheless concerned for their safety?'

Neither Harry nor Mary Louise replied, so Kate continued: 'Both of you disassociated from reality. You don't remember eating each slice of pizza individually, yet you ate them. You forgot about your reality, lost your grasp on it, and for most of the period of watching the movie, you were no longer worried about work, or thought in any depth about each other.'

'I fail to understand, Kate, what this has to do with Imogen.'

'Mary Louise, when you and Harry watched the movie, you took the part of your consciousness that worries about work problems and other "real things" and separated it from your imaginative part. The imaginative part became dominant. You disassociated from one part of your consciousness for another.'

'But when the film was over, I got up. I put the kettle on. I came back to reality.'

'I know you did, Harry. But you acknowledge that for a period you left real events, even the simple act of eating a number of individual slices of pizza.'

'I suppose I did.'

'The same way you can't remember eating each individual slice, Imogen can't remember certain events. And it's not because she's watching movies, it's because at some point or points in the past, her mind opted out from the here and now. She disassociated herself from real events.'

'It still happens, Kate.' The concern was back in Mary Louise's voice.

'I know it does, but Imogen is making progress. She's beginning to remember. She won't always get it right. Memory is fragmented. Sometimes it will get mixed up with other things, but she is remembering, and that is what's important.' Kate paused again. 'There is one other thing I would like you all to think about.'

'What's that?' asked Jilly, keen to be involved.

'The example we just talked through is often described as escapism. We're all familiar with it. And the loss of huge chunks of memory where it involves things of little importance doesn't cause us any anxiety. It's different in Imogen's case. Let me explain it this way.

'Suppose one of you needs to pay a visit to the hospital to have a procedure done. You take time off work, arriving early at the hospital for your appointment. You receive a local anaesthetic. It all goes well. You get two stitches in your upper arm, because a wound hadn't repaired correctly. Going home, you're aware of a pain in your arm, but part of it still feels numb.' They all sit silently, listening to her. 'You get home. The anaesthetic is wearing off and, for some unknown reason, you've forgotten you've been to the hospital, or that you got two stitches in the arm. You're in a considerable amount of pain, a pain you cannot ignore. You check your arm in the mirror. You see a bandage. There's blood, and when you remove the bandage, you see the two large stitches. You're still bleeding, although not excessively.' Kate looked at them. 'What's the first thing you think?'

'You've lost your marbles.' Harry was the first to jump in.

'Don't say that, Harry.' Mary Louise, aware of the implications.

'It's okay, Mary Louise. Harry's point is valid. You'd be worried about more than the stitches. You might wonder if you'd lost your mind. Another couple of instances like that might cause you to really question your sanity. Not remembering, when the stakes are high, is frightening. It brings everything into question. Imogen may not remember things, but at least now she realises her loss of memory is simply that. Imogen has been through a great deal working her way to this point. None of us can underestimate what a difficult path it has been for her.'

Imogen, who had stayed quiet throughout, looked nervous when she asked, 'Kate, will I ever remember why this has happened to me? Why I can't remember large chunks of my past?'

'I hope so, Imogen. I really do.'

Clodagh

Turning the corner onto the strand, I see Dominic waiting for me. Despite the intervening years, my brother stands in the same way he did as a teenager, shoulders back, both hands held tight in the front pockets of his jeans. He leans against the front garden wall of our house like he doesn't belong there, or doesn't want to. I'm not surprised he's waiting outside. Whatever memories the house holds for him, they're no longer part of who he cares to be. Neither he nor Martin seems to see anything in the house other than financial gain.

When I'm within a few yards of him, he reluctantly stands upright, looking like he plans to assist but not lead. He says nothing about my bruises, although I know he has noticed them.

'Does Martin know you're here?'

'He's not my keeper.' I give him a look that says he should know better. 'Anyhow, he wouldn't care.'

'I don't know about that, Clodagh.'

'What's with you two buddying up? Has selling the house encouraged you on another business deal?'

'Nope. You forget, I know Martin well. He walks a line I'm not easy with.' His eyes shift to the side of my face where the bruises are now a murky purple and yellow mess. 'I may have grown up with him, Clodagh, but I'm not the one who married him.'

'You're the one who struck up the friendship, back in the day when Martin wouldn't have said boo to anyone, least of all you.'

'The guy changed.'

'Well, I guess I didn't see that coming either.'

'You thought you were marrying a softie.'

'Let's keep my marital affairs out of this.' I look at the house, hearing the waves crash behind me. I feel about twelve years old again, bickering with my brother when there are far most important things to talk about. 'Dominic, none of that matters now. Something strange is happening. With the regression bits keep coming back.' I hear the desperation in my voice. 'I'm remembering things from childhood, but I can't put all the pieces together.'

'Nothing strange is happening.' His voice is controlled.

I want to throttle him, as if we're kids. Instead I say, 'Let's go inside – it's cold.'

Before I open the front door, he asks, 'What are you looking for, Clodagh? What do you hope to achieve by coming back here?'

'I don't know. Some parts of my memory are coming back. Other parts are still missing. But I feel close to connecting with them. Does that ever happen to you, Dominic? Do you ever not remember and then get a sense that you're so close to something it's like an unlit fire waiting for a match to bring it to life?'

'None of us remembers everything, Clodagh.'

'No?'

'Nobody does.'

I close the front door behind us, leaning against it. 'Do you remember when Emmaline died?'

He doesn't flinch. 'Yes.'

'I don't.'

'You were only seven.'

'I should remember it, though. Mum and Dad must have been traumatised. I can't even remember the funeral. I thought I had, but then I realised it was Dad's funeral, not hers. Gerard thinks the memory loss could be connected to trauma, maybe even Dad's death.'

'Clodagh, you're making a big deal out of nothing.' His words are angry.

'But we never spoke about Emmaline. It was as if she was off limits.'

'You're being overdramatic.'

'No, I'm not.'

His tone changes again, becoming patronising. 'They say alcohol kills the brain cells.'

'That's a cheap shot. You're starting to sound like bloody Martin.' I can't hide the upset in my voice.

'Let's get this over and done with,' he says, walking up the stairs ahead of me.

Neither of us has mentioned Keith Jenkins or Uncle Jimmy since we arrived. I'm conscious that bringing up the subject of Emmaline has stressed him. I'd known it would. The same way I know he doesn't want to talk about Keith Jenkins either.

On the landing, he walks over to the window, looking out onto the strand. He has his back to me.

'Dominic, have you the key for the attic?'

'What? Oh, yeah.' He turns, reaching into his jeans pocket, taking out the small key, gesturing for me to take it.

'Aren't you coming up with me?'

'This is your wild-goose chase, not mine.'

'But don't you get it, Dominic? Two men are dead, and we knew both of them.'

'So?'

'You're unbelievable.'

'We knew them a long time ago, that's all. They're part of history, and not a pretty one at that.'

'Do you remember Mum being pregnant, Dominic?'

'Sort of.' He turns away again.

'What do you mean "sort of"?'

'What the fuck do you think I mean?' He turns as if his body is hitting out, his face angry. The same anger lines that appear on Martin's forehead when he reaches boiling point.

'Were Mum and Dad happy about the pregnancy?'

'How the hell should I know, Clodagh? I was a teenager. I had other things on my mind.'

'It's just …'

'What?'

'When I was hypnotised, I remembered something. It was about Mum being pregnant. Dad wanted to touch her, to feel the bump, but she pushed him away.'

'That guy is messing with your head.' The patronising tone is back.

But I keep on talking. 'Then I put Dad in the attic of the doll's house.'

'Christ, Clodagh – listen to yourself!'

'I know it doesn't make sense.'

He says nothing.

'Dominic, are you coming up or not?'

'I'll wait here.' There's something defeated about the way he says it.

'Suit yourself, but I need to go through your old bedroom.'

'It's only a room, Clodagh. Soon this house,' his eyes glancing around him, 'won't be part of either of us.'

I feel the warmth of the key in my hand, hot from him holding it. Once again I remember the heat on the back of my neck, that day on the strand with Mum, and the man I now know to have been Keith Jenkins lying beside her.

Ocean House, the Quays

Kate was pleased at how the session had gone with Imogen's family. They had all gained a better understanding of Imogen's memory loss and how it affected her. It gave Kate hope that good progress could be made. Imogen's close family was the structure by which she could rise or fall.

She checked the time. There would be another squad meeting at Harcourt Street in five minutes at three o'clock. O'Connor would be under pressure. There were still too many questions about the canal murders that didn't have answers, and he would soon be screaming for her report. Something had started to take hold in Kate's mind, and it went back to what she had said to O'Connor about there being more pieces to this jigsaw than they could see.

In most investigations you nearly always start with the victim. When you know the victim, you know more about the person who killed them. The connection of Jenkins and Gahan brought a whole other dimension. Jenkins being in the public eye meant the field of suspects was vast, but the frame of reference had shifted from concentration on Jenkins to how he and Gahan were linked. There was seldom only one reason for a crime taking place. More often than not, it was a combination of factors. Kate had no doubt that both killings had been emotionally charged, but was it the primary or only motivation? Could other rewards play their part? Financial gain? Or something else?

She thought again about Imogen Willis, how relaxed the girl had looked leaving with her family. Kate's own memory loss wasn't as extreme as Imogen's, but it often caused her to reflect.

She had speculated many times about her own attacker. Kate had barely turned twelve at the time. She could remember so much about that afternoon, the sense that someone was watching her, his breathing when he grabbed her from behind, her ultimate escape – individual images flashing forward, but when pieced together, there was still one image lost to her. She could never see his face. She remembered, moments before the attack, noticing him in the corner of her eye. Knowing something wasn't right.

She felt she must have seen him clearly at some point. She remembered turning back to look when she'd sensed him following her. But the face was a blank. It left another unanswered question: could she not remember his face because she already knew him? Had she blocked it out?

Picking up the photograph of herself, Declan and Charlie that stood on the desk, Kate saw her reflection in the glass. It caught only one side of her face. Even so, she saw enough to recognise anxiety. Whether she liked it or not, part of it involved the collapse of her relationship with Declan while another part involved her growing feelings for O'Connor.

Clodagh

Access to the attic is via a small staircase in Dominic's bedroom. It feels strange going into a room that has been dominated by my brother for so many years, him waiting on the landing, as if he's not connected with it any more, or doesn't want to be. It's stranger still when I open the door to a room that is empty but for a single bed in the corner. I smell fresh paint. There is freshly laid carpet, dark cream against the stark white walls. The wooden staircase to the attic is also white, as if the same colour makes the stairs almost invisible.

I close the bedroom door behind me, pulling across the old latch at the top. Again I visualise the room as it used to be, with a world map hanging on the wall beneath the attic staircase. I remember reaching up on tiptoe to touch Ireland. Russia was red, with orange Mongolia underneath, partly hidden by the underside of the attic stairs. In the same corner, Dominic had his drum kit, which he and Stevie McDaid loved to play, Martin sitting on the bed or lying on the floor, laughing and joking with the two of them. When was the last time I'd heard Martin laugh, really laugh, as if life was fun and worth living?

I don't feel like a trespasser, as I would have done years before, fearing Dominic would catch me in his room and give me what-for. Walking up the stairs, I hold tight to the narrow rail fixed to the wall. I take one step at a time, just as my mind had done with Gerard Hayden, counting each one. I stop at the top, pulling across another latch. I am hesitant about putting the key in the lock, reluctant to open the room that part of me hopes will be full of memories, and another part wants to be as empty as Dominic's bedroom.

I should expect the dark, but it jolts me. It's colder too, and I shiver. The attic is in complete contrast to the bright white walls I'm leaving behind. The door creaks on opening. I need light. My hand reaches for the old light switch, hoping it will still be there, even though it has been years since I stood in this room. The attic is not unlike the one in my doll's house, with its A-roof and slanted pitch at either end.

With the door closed, again I reach up, pulling over the latch on the opposite side, as if shutting out the rest of the world. I soak it all in, my eyes adjusting to the artificial light, a single bulb hanging from the centre at the highest point. It looks the worse for wear. I see the old rope ends where the boys hung hammocks from the wooden beams above. I'm sure they got up to plenty in this room, well away from adult supervision. There's an old dartboard hanging on the gable wall. At first, I can barely make it out, until I get close enough to see the rusted darts and metal divisions. I smell dust and rotting wood, my eyes scanning the low roof walls on either side. There are shelves packed with boxes, old sweet tins, bits of rubbish and a large wooden crate with Christmas decorations bulging out.

I'm looking for Emma, my doll with the cracked face. The one Dominic told me to throw away. To the right of the dartboard, the tall shelves don't look quite so tall any more. If I find her, I might start remembering more. I took her with me everywhere. I held her in the attic, that time I hid with the boys.

The shelves are full of dust. I have a sense of foreboding, running my fingers along the middle shelf, filled with open and closed boxes. I see my old spinning top and smile. It still has the blue plastic bottle-top stuck to the top. When the handle went missing, Dominic fixed it for me. There's an old paint set too, with Mickey Mouse, Pluto and Donald Duck on the front. Inside there is a mess of colours, bits of paint, hard and chalky, the underside of the lid like a grubby rainbow. I remember painting it. I can't understand why some memories are so clear and others not.

It's Emma's hair I notice first, even before I see her eyes. She's halfway down the box with the broken toys. Reaching in, I touch her porcelain face, running my fingers down the jagged crack. Again a sense of foreboding builds inside me. Her eyes look back at me. I see kindness. I sit below the old dartboard, trying to remember.

I'm trying to remember hiding in the attic, or the memory from the doll's house, when Mum and Dad were arguing and I heard the doorbell. I had felt fear, not understanding why the man I now know to have been Keith Jenkins was there. Uncle Jimmy was in the doll's house too.

I must look mad, a grown woman holding a doll.

I thought this room would have answers, but it doesn't. I listen for Dominic downstairs, but hear nothing. I'm about to give up when something comes back to me. It has nothing to do with Mum or Dad, or their arguments. It's the sound of boyhood whispers, Dominic, Martin and Stevie, talking in low voices. There are other voices too, adult ones. Suddenly I need to get out of this room. I jump up too fast from my hunkered position and feel woozy. I don't bother to dust myself down, running towards the door, the whispering getting louder, the voices more powerful. I reach for the latch. It's stuck. It doesn't want to budge. I feel like that scared little girl again, wanting to run away, to go somewhere to cry, somewhere she can be safe.

When the latch opens, I fall out into the bright walls of Dominic's old bedroom, pulling the door behind me. I rush down the stairs, not stopping until I reach the landing.

Dominic is waiting for me, leaning against the door of our parents' room. I can't read his face.

'Find what you were looking for?' His voice sounds uncaring.

'Not exactly,' I hear myself say. I realise I'm still holding Emma and feel embarrassed, but I regain eye contact with Dominic. 'You cleared out your bedroom, but you didn't do the attic.'

'Not yet.'

My next words surprise me, because it is as if someone else is doing the talking: 'Keith Jenkins.'

'What about him?'

'He loved Mum, didn't he?'

Dominic looks unperturbed. He waits the longest time before answering. 'Keith Jenkins wasn't the only man who liked our mother.'

I'm taken aback, but not because of his words: it's because of my reaction to them.

Incident Room, Harcourt Street Police Station

O'Connor knew he needed to be firing on all cylinders if Chief Superintendent Butler was to stay off his back. They now had two deaths on their hands, an established MO, both Jenkins's and Deborah Gahan's house under twenty-four-hour police protection, and still no clear idea as to who the killer was. Or why the hell he was doing it.

Kate talking about more players being involved, and different motivations overlapping each other, wasn't exactly cheering him up either. The likelihood of something else unforeseen going down was increasing. Which he didn't like one bloody bit.

The mood in the incident room was sombre. Every man and woman present knew Butler was about to unload his frustration. Nobody wanted to be in the firing line. O'Connor may have been the SIO, and more likely to get it head on, but Butler wasn't always selective in his choice of individual to suffer his wrath. The session at Harcourt Street kicked off with a general attack by Butler for the benefit of every single member of the force huddled in the packed room. Even Matthews, the bookman, was keeping his mouth shut as the chief superintendent let off steam.

'He's some bloody piece of work, putting a guy in the canal when he's already dead.' Butler stood up from the top table. The sound of his chair scraping backwards across the floor was the only noise other than his voice. He turned to look behind him at the large white incident-room board, while O'Connor, Matthews and Dr Martha Smyth, from the forensics team, remained seated. Everyone present knew to let Butler's last comment go unanswered. He would let them know when he was ready to hear them talk.

'I'm not happy, people, not one bit happy. The media love this blasted story, first Jenkins with his superstar status and now a bloody down-and-out. But I don't love it. I'm far from loving it. Jenkins took his dip in the early hours of Saturday morning, and I don't need to remind you all that it's now bloody Wednesday.' Butler paused, his silence an indicator that he was about to pounce again. 'Is Morrison sure Gahan was dead going into the water?' His question was directed at O'Connor.

'Completely sure, boss.' O'Connor hoped his positive affirmation of Butler's ranked superiority might ease the line of questioning. 'Heart failure brought on by the knife attack. There's no evidence of diatoms in the bloodstream, or pressure trauma in the sinuses or lungs, or any haemorrhaging in the sinuses as Morrison would have expected with a drowning. Nor is there debris from the water, which Jimmy Gahan would have sucked in, trying to breathe,' O'Connor coughed, 'had he been still alive.'

'What lines are you working on, O'Connor?'

'Lynch and CAB are looking into the running of a company called Hamilton Holdings, which was set up thirty-seven years ago. It was originally owned by the late Adrian Hamilton, and taken over by Jenkins after Hamilton committed suicide in 1978.'

'Suicide?'

'Or death by misadventure. At least, that's what the coroner believed.' O'Connor could see Butler was anything but convinced.

'Doubting inquest findings now, are we, O'Connor?'

'Keeping options open, boss, that's all. Jenkins started the company moving again about two years back. He got a shitload of investors. Most of them are low-key.'

'By low-key, O'Connor, I assume you mean they're keeping their identities under wraps.' The strain in Butler's voice was audible.

'That's right, boss. Investment in millionaire properties in Portugal type of thing, but Lynch, as I said, is working on it with the CAB guys.'

'Following the money trail is never fast, O'Connor.'

'I know that, boss, but—'

'No bloody buts.' Butler's face was reddening.

Matthews decided it was time to step in, turning to Martha Smyth. 'Martha, we understood from Sarah Walsh that you were examining fibres from the ledge on the canal.'

'That's correct. Hanley's team came up with a number of items for analysis.'

'What do you have so far?'

'We were able to identify some undyed white cotton strands with a twisted-ribbon pattern, too common to be of any real value. However, we also identified synthetic traces, a type of polypropylene often used in carpet manufacturing for cars. We're running further tests on diameter, shape, colour, curl and crimp to see if we can be more specific and match it to a particular model.'

'When will you have more?' Matthews was looking down into his case log rather than at Martha Smyth, ready to assign the next update to her.

'We're waiting on sample results from the UK. Hopefully, we'll have them tomorrow. In the meantime the tyre impressions taken, along with the witness testimony on the car type, have brought up a match with a couple of Volvo models manufactured in 2010. Again, we'll know more tomorrow once we have the fibre tests back.'

'If you or Hanley get any other information, let me and O'Connor be the ones to know about it first. I assume if we get a cross-match, it will be narrowed down to a particular vehicle type.'

'We're hoping the internal fibres match a model from the tyre impressions.'

Matthews hadn't finished yet, but this time O'Connor was back in the frame. 'O'Connor, did you get the visuals from the insurance company on the missing ring?'

O'Connor cleared his throat. 'Standard gold band, size nine, eighteen point nine millimetres, with roped edging top and bottom. The missing ring and the hotel receipt fire in a couple of other possibilities.'

'Go on, O'Connor.'

'Higgins and Clarke have given copy witness statements to Robinson, taken from the receptionist at the hotel in Blessington. She's confirmed it was Keith Jenkins who stayed at the hotel, although he and his female companion both used false names. We believe Gloria Sweetman was his companion.'

'What's the tie?' Matthews rapped.

'There's nothing conclusively linking that case to the Jenkins murder, but Gahan's drinking buddy, Ozzie Brennan, hinted that Gahan may have had something on Jenkins, putting pressure on him for cash. If that was the case, then Ms Sweetman's death via a drug overdose may have given Gahan what he needed on him.'

Butler couldn't keep quiet any longer. 'Have you found anyone else linked to Gahan and Jenkins?'

'We've spoken to Deborah Gahan. She and Isabel Blennerhasset confirmed a connection to Adrian Hamilton. They all knew each other, and Adrian Hamilton also drowned.'

'A death over thirty years ago. I don't know about that, O'Connor.' Butler was sceptical.

'Dr Pearson thinks the drowning is critical in this case. Our guy has displayed excessive aggression, and despite the minor variances in his MO, he's determined that his victims end up in water. She also thinks it may be some kind of personal vendetta. The taking of the wedding band from Jenkins and the hotel receipt being found close by could mean the killer is operating some kind of judgement on his victim or victims. I'm running background checks on Adrian Hamilton's surviving children, now adults. I'm also looking into the identity of the man who lent Hamilton the boat the day he died.'

Butler looked directly at O'Connor with raised eyebrows. 'Be careful. That old death could be immaterial.'

'I know that.' O'Connor kept his voice firm and assured.

Matthews spoke next. 'When will we have the report on the Gahan killing from Dr Pearson?'

'This evening or early tomorrow morning.'

'I'm assuming, O'Connor, that since Jimmy Gahan's body was found there's been more light shed on things?'

'As I said, Dr Pearson has a couple of theories. We'll know more once we have her report.'

Again Butler interjected, 'Matthews, mark that down as top priority on the assignments – and, O'Connor?'

'Yes, boss?'

'Make that sooner rather than later. If necessary, remind Dr Pearson we're dealing with a double murder.'

'She knows that, boss.'

'Good to hear it. Is there *anything* else, O'Connor?' Butler was forcing home how little they had, and seemed to lay the blame for the lack of evidence firmly at O'Connor's door.

'Dr Pearson thinks there could be more than one layer to this. Jenkins and Gahan are linked, that we know, but she thinks Gahan's immediate death wasn't the killer's intention. Assuming the same MO, the killer kept Jenkins alive for a period before death. She thinks it could have been to get or share information.'

Butler grunted. 'You said she thinks there's more than one layer going on here. What does she mean exactly?'

'We have the possible blackmail of Jenkins, the planting of the hotel receipt, the time delay between the attack on Keith Jenkins and his subsequent death. Dr Pearson thinks our guy is highly motivated and determined in his task, but she's not one hundred per cent sure that someone else isn't in the driver's seat.'

'And that's it?'

'Keeping our options open, boss.' O'Connor forced a smile.

'Good to hear it.' Butler remained stern-faced, turning to Matthews and Martha Smyth. 'As soon as we have something concrete on the fibre and the tyre markings, I want to run with everything we've got. Arrange a slot on *Crimecall*. I know it's short notice, but we need to get the public working for us. We don't know everything, so we want people talking.' He addressed the entire cast: 'Now, the rest of you, get out there and get some bloody answers. As O'Connor reminded you all at the start of this investigation, this is supposed to be an élite unit. Let's start bloody acting like one.'

The mumblings of the detectives forced Matthews to raise his voice above the din. 'The next full squad briefing will be ten a.m. tomorrow. You all heard the boss.'

Clodagh

As soon as the words were out of Dominic's mouth, telling me Keith Jenkins wasn't the only man who liked Mum, I knew he'd spoken the truth. I knew it because it felt like another building block had slipped into place, something solid and impossible to deny.

Gerard Hayden had told me this kind of thing could keep happening. Under regression I was seeing things from the past, even if my subconscious mind was trying to block out aspects of them. He was suspicious that this was happening with the dolls. According to him, when one truth is revealed, another could unlock itself.

Dominic's words were clear and equivocal. Without knowing why, I'd always known there was someone else in Mum's life. From the moment I'd remembered Keith Jenkins on the strand, and the two of them in the back room off the kitchen, something else had been pushing to the surface, there was another man, another face.

I asked Dominic for a name, but he wasn't talking. Maybe he thought he was giving away too many of Mum's secrets, especially when she wasn't there to defend herself. I guess I couldn't blame him for that. Considering his mood, it felt useless staying at the house any longer. Perhaps he has a point about leaving the past in the past. He was always the clear thinker, cutting through crap, saying it as it is, and absolute in his way with the world. How can old memories help anything? I'm a bit long in the tooth to change my life. At times, I don't even know if I bloody well want to.

It's raining now. I watch the drops slide down Ruby's bedroom window, relieved that Martin is still at work. I need more time to think things through. Dominic is right. There's no reason to believe we're connected to the murder of Keith Jenkins or Uncle Jimmy. I could go to the police, but what would I tell them? I remembered Keith Jenkins while I was under hypnosis. That Mum had never liked Jimmy Gahan. There isn't a whole lot of information in that. Dominic's accusation about me being overdramatic is ringing out loud and clear.

I text Martin and ask him what time he'll be back. He answers with his usual efficiency. He won't be home for another few hours. I feel relieved. I sit down on Ruby's bed, and pick up my old doll, Emma. I cradle her in my arms, like I did as a child. I can afford to be a little crazy, now that I'm alone.

Rocking her back and forth, I watch Emma's eyelids, with their long lashes, open and close. Each time I rock her, she looks up at me again. I stare into the crack running down the side of her face, remembering that old argument with Mum and Dad, how scared I felt, and once again, I feel like that child, the one who found escape with her dolls and her doll's house.

I'd thought about cancelling my next appointment with Gerard, but regardless of how stupid Dominic and everyone else may think I'm being, I want to find answers. A part of me needs to know more. I brush my hand across Emma's cold, cracked porcelain face, hoping she might unlock something. She stares back at me, giving nothing away.

I think about the happy little girl, the one held by my mother, the one I saw the first time I regressed. I don't know where she's gone. Can life change you so much, as if the first person never existed?

Emma is still staring at me, her eyelashes looking longer and more curled. I realise I'm still holding her like a baby, and it's then something else comes back. I see my mother. Her back is towards me, but I know she's been crying. She, too, holds a doll. She thinks she's alone, but she isn't, because I'm in the room. When she turns and looks at me, it isn't love I see in her eyes. It's hatred.

∞

I have no idea how long I've been sleeping, but when I wake, I'm still holding Emma. I put my doll on the bed, resting her head on the pillows. I walk across the corridor to the room Martin and I used to share as husband and wife. Looking around it, I'm hurt when I realise Martin has removed all the photographs of the two of us. I instantly wonder where he has put them. I start opening drawers in search of some proof that I once existed here. I feel like I'm in a maze, neither the past nor the present making any sense, but something is telling me to be afraid.

Outside, the October weather takes a turn, and the sound of hailstones feels like tiny hammers thumping away at my thoughts. With my back to the door, I decide, like some madwoman, that I need to toss the room. I won't be like that little girl and simply disappear.

I'm so engrossed in what I'm doing that I care little for the mess I'm creating, pulling clothes out of our wardrobe, flinging them onto the floor and emptying drawers. I find Martin's briefcase at the top of the wardrobe, but it's locked. I wonder why he didn't take it to work today. He could be home at any minute. I grab the stainless steel letter opener from the top of his desk in the corner, finally prising it open. It's practically empty, except for a couple of work letters in the leather flaps, so I unzip the centre pouch. I no longer hear the hailstones, losing all concept of time and anything else other than my desperate effort to find a small piece of me. When I pull the old photograph from the centre of Martin's briefcase, I feel as if my mind has finally cracked, that I'm like my doll Emma. It's only then that I hear him and know he is standing behind me.

Mervin Road

It was six o'clock by the time Kate arrived back at the apartment. O'Connor would be screaming for her report.

'Where have you been, Mum?'

'Work, honey, but I'm home now.'

Was she imagining it, or did she recognise the same sense of loss in Charlie's eyes that she'd seen earlier in her own?

When the phone rang, thankfully it was Declan. She'd hoped he would ring, not because she wanted to speak to him but because she knew Charlie needed to. Kate had avoided talking about him to Charlie, which had inadvertently told him something was wrong. Handing the phone to Charlie felt strange. Now it was as if every action, or inaction, needed to be viewed differently. Something to which before she wouldn't have given a second thought had become strained, different, questioned, front and back, inside and out.

She felt like an intruder in the room, hearing only one side of the conversation. At the same time, she was unsure if she wanted to know what Declan was saying. At the start of the conversation Charlie appeared guarded, and again she wondered if he was aware that something was wrong. She didn't need a degree in psychology to know children picked up the slightest change in mood or atmosphere, especially when that change went to the core of their emotional security.

Kate gave Charlie a reassuring look before turning away to look out of the living-room window. If he was feeling uncomfortable, the best thing to do was to give him space with his dad. It looked bitterly cold outside, with a dark, damp chill, as another shower of hailstones belted against the glass. Almost without thinking, she turned to her son. He looked so serious that she wanted to rush over and grab him, hold him so tight that no words were needed for him to understand the almost primal love she felt for him – a tiny tot stuck in the middle of it all.

'I'm okay, Daddy, honest,' she heard him say, and her heart broke some more. What the hell was Declan saying to him? So many times, adults dump their guilt on their children, looking for reassurance in whatever situation they've created, the younger and potentially more fragile person forced to help the adult, instead of the other way around.

Kate knew she couldn't interfere. She didn't want to make a scene in front of Charlie. She had to remain calm. For all she knew Declan wasn't unloading anything. But this was the beginning. The beginning of second-guessing what your partner, or ex-partner, was up to. Kate had seen these situations before. Trust blown apart because of doubt and disconnection. That was the thing about beginnings, even the beginning of an end: they might not dictate the final direction, but they set down a future pathway, one that either party in a broken relationship could encourage or pursue. She wrapped her arms tightly around her shoulders, staring at her reflection in the glass as, like her mood, the sky darkened.

'Will you, Dad?' Charlie's voice had an edge of excitement and adventure. 'I'd like that.'

Kate was almost in tears, and she wasn't sure why. All of a sudden the sense of loss, of division, made her feel nauseous. She kept her back to Charlie as he continued chatting with Declan, not wanting him to see the upset on her face. She continued to stare at her reflection in the glass, no longer sure who that woman was or what she wanted to do with her life. She thought about Imogen Willis, so much of her memory lost to her, Rachel Mooney's horrendous rape attack, before her mind drifted to the young girl called Susie sitting in Harcourt Street station with her mother.

Even though Kate had a ton of things on her mind, including the current investigation and the vulnerable five-year-old behind her, she made a mental note to contact Hennessy. O'Connor wouldn't be happy. He wanted her to concentrate on the main investigation, but O'Connor could go to Hell too. There was something about that young girl, her distant, lost eyes, which made her determined to find out more.

'Dad, do you want to talk to Mum?' Another silence. Declan was talking, no doubt. The realisation hit her again. Both she and Charlie were going through the biggest change in their family life and there wasn't a darn thing she could do about it.

'Okay, Dad, see you soon. Love you.' And with that Charlie hung up.

Kate turned to catch his expression: an old head on his young shoulders. She had to say something. 'Hey, Buster, what do you want to do now?' A wide smile forced itself across her face.

'Dunno.'

'Dunno? What kind of an answer is that?' She scooped him up and attempted to tickle him under the arm.

'Stop it, Mum!' His laughter broke the gloom both of them felt.

'What about painting? I know you love to make a mess.'

'I do not.' His stern but determined look this time brought a real smile to Kate's face.

'Or we could play Connect 4. Bet I win.'

'Bet you don't!'

Kate put him down. 'You get the game and I'll take out the ice-cream.'

'Can we have cones?'

'Sure.' Kate hoped there were cones in the kitchen cupboard.

As Charlie darted into his bedroom for the game, Kate shouted after him, 'What did your dad have to say?'

'Nothing.'

It was a very long nothing, thought Kate, but decided, all things considered, it was best to let it go. On opening the kitchen cupboard, she was relieved to find a box of cones at the back.

'Ice-cream on the way, Charlie.' As she turned towards his bedroom, she smiled again, watching her son carry the Connect 4 box to the coffee table. The last time they had played the game was a couple of months before. Both she and Declan had allowed Charlie to win every single time. She had every intention of applying the same rules, only this time, she knew, she was in it alone.

Clodagh

I brace myself for the brute force of Martin's aggression. I don't know how much more of it I can take. Almost without realising it, my mind shuts down, goes blank. I can't think what to do next. I have nowhere to run, no means of escape, and with that knowledge, my head and heart swell with such colossal fear that I can't breathe.

'What the hell are you at, Clodagh?' Martin's voice is edged with a mix of anger and disbelief.

I still haven't turned, unwilling to look at his face, to contemplate his mood.

'Nothing,' I say, for I can't think of anything else.

'Are you gone completely mad?' He slams the bedroom door behind him.

It is only then that I turn. He stands three metres away from me. The bedroom is completely tossed, and a part of me wants to kill him.

'What do you have in your hand, Clodagh?' He comes forward a metre.

'You know darn well.' My voice sounds like that of a madwoman because I'm screeching.

'Clodagh, give me the photograph.' Again he steps forward, reaching out his hand, almost touching me.

'What's going on, Martin?' I clutch the photograph, as if it's the only bargaining power I have, even though I know he could take it from me if he wanted to.

'You tell me, Clodagh.' His tone is gentler.

'I don't know, Martin. I don't know anything any more.' There is still anger in my voice, but also a note of pleading. I'm backing down out of fear because, right now, I'm more convinced than ever that I'll crack and my brain might simply cease to be.

'Sit down, Clodagh.' He gestures towards the bed.

I do as he asks, as if I'm on auto-pilot. He sits beside me, and I look up at him, my eyes taking him in, as if he's a stranger, not the man I married.

'You took the photograph, Martin,' I whisper. I place it on my lap, both my hands on top of it.

'I didn't take any photograph, Clodagh.'

'Didn't you?' I know he's lying. He's the master of lies when he wants to be.

He smiles, the kind of smile an adult would give to a child playing silly games. Martin could convince the world of anything if he set his mind to it. When he's angry or hurt, he hits out, blaming others for his own shortcomings. Another thing I discovered after we were married. He's doing it now. He's pretending he's kind, and that I've somehow imagined that the photograph of Dad and his old friends has made its own way into his briefcase.

'Of course not, Clodagh. Why would I want your photograph?'

'I don't know, Martin. Why would you?'

'You've been under a lot of strain lately, with rehab, Ruby leaving, your mother and all.' The back of his right hand gently strokes the bruised side of my face. 'You need to rest.' He stands up, pulls across the bedroom curtains, making the room darker. He takes off my shoes, placing them neatly together among the piles of clothes on the floor. He lifts my legs, his other arm around my shoulders, easing me to lie down, taking the large throw at the end of the double bed, covering me with it as I curl sideways, bringing my knees up to my chest, feeling my tears create a pool of damp on the pillow. 'You need to relax, my dearest Clodagh. Let me take care of everything. I'm going to get you something to help. I have some sleeping pills. Nothing too strong, just enough to help you get some sleep.'

My eyes stare back at him. The tears are taking his shape out of focus. His body looks large and looming. I feel afraid. It's a different kind of fear from before. It's not the terror of a wife worried about being battered by her husband. It goes far deeper, as if the world is caving in on me.

When Martin returns with the tablets and the water, I swallow both tablets together, unsure if my own husband is trying to kill me and unsure if I care.

'Martin.' My voice is faint – as light as a summer's breeze.

'Yes?'

I'm remembering the garden I visited with Gerard Hayden, and I want that peace more than anything else right now.

'Martin, why did you take away all the photographs of me?' I wait. There is nothing but silence, until I'm finally lost in sleep.

Harcourt Street Police Station

O'Connor's eyes were red and tired, as Mark Lynch knocked on his office door.

'I've got something on Keith Jenkins's buy-out of Hamilton Holdings.'

'I'm listening.'

'Jenkins was flash with money at the time – you know, expensive car, renting an apartment in Ballsbridge near to Montrose, eating out in expensive restaurants.'

'So?'

'He might have given the appearance of being financially sound, but in reality he was far from it.'

'So where did he get the money to buy Hamilton Holdings?'

'Precisely.'

'Lynch, would you quit playing bloody games? If you have something to say, just say it.'

'We have another player in the field, an Alister Becon.'

'That smarmy politician?'

'And also the owner of the boat that facilitated Adrian Hamilton's last journey out to sea.'

O'Connor stared at Lynch for a few seconds, as if the last piece of information was gliding through his brain. 'Have you spoken to Becon?'

'Briefly, sir. He said "the accident", as he called it, was a very long time ago, and he denies any involvement with the buy-out of Hamilton Holdings.'

'What makes you think he was involved?'

'I got talking to a contact in RTÉ.'

O'Connor raised his eyebrows. 'Mixing in famous circles, are we, Lynch?'

Lynch ignored O'Connor's comment. 'As Isabel Blennerhasset told you, Adrian Hamilton was influential in getting Jenkins his first break in television. Back then everyone who got to be anyone knew somebody. When Hamilton croaked it, there were questions asked about where Jenkins had got the money from to buy out Hamilton Holdings.'

'And?'

'Alister Becon was loaded and a close associate of both Jenkins and Hamilton, not to mention Jimmy Gahan.'

'Don't tell me, Lynch, another old college bud.'

'Indeed.'

'So why did Alister Becon do the deal via Jenkins? Why didn't he buy it himself?'

'My friend had a couple of theories on that too.'

O'Connor finally indicated that Lynch should sit down. 'I'm all ears, Lynch.'

'It seems the relationship between Becon and Hamilton's widow was strained. She would have been more inclined to take the money from Jenkins than Becon.'

'Sounds like this is going back to what Deborah Gahan said.'

'There were certainly rumours about Jenkins and Lavinia Hamilton being close.'

'So why did Becon want to play the hero?'

'I don't know, but three out of the four of them are now dead.'

'Which shines a very bright light on Alister Becon, even if it is only rumours.'

'He's not an easy man to get answers out of, sir.'

'Politicians rarely are, Lynch. But he won't be playing games with us. He's right in my firing line. It could also tie in with Kate's theory about there being other players in the field. Alister Becon would be an interesting addition to the mix.'

Standing up, O'Connor walked across the room to clear his thinking. 'We might not be the only ones with Becon in our sights.'

'The killer, you mean?'

'Yeah, the killer – or there's another possibility, getting back to Kate's theory.'

'The guy's description doesn't fit. He's a lot shorter than Jenkins, and I doubt he would be capable of bringing either Jenkins or Gahan down.'

'Lynch, his types rarely do their own dirty work. They have minions for that kind of thing. If Kate is right, and there is string-pulling going on, we need to get everything we can on him. I want to run his profile by Kate.'

'The guy has some Republican connections. He had a minor role in the gun-running scandal of the seventies.'

'Good friends with people in that circle?'

'You know the way it works. Once you're part of that crowd, you're never out of it.'

'That's all we need, Lynch, some Provo activity to get Butler hot under the collar.'

'I'm only telling you what I heard.'

'I know that, Lynch.'

'Do you think they could be involved?'

'I doubt it. It's not their style. A couple of bullets to the head would do it for them. These killings are far too messy for those boys to be part of it. No, Lynch, I think Kate's right. There's something more going on here than simply taking a couple of guys out of it.'

'The Republican connection does complicate the Becon situation.'

'You mean it might make him feel even more bloody protected in his ivory tower.'

'Probably.'

'Lynch, see what Undercover can tell us about Becon and his friends.'

'Will do.'

'Mind you, I still want to know more about why Hamilton Holdings collapsed in the first place. If this thing goes back to then, we need to have a complete handle on the ins and outs of it. Anything else from the CAB guys?'

'Hamilton invested high in some property company that went belly-up. Shoddy workmanship and a list of parties suing to strip Hamilton of everything he had. Becon's name came up there as well, as a part-owner, only he was better protected than Hamilton with a limited shareholding. Hamilton took most, if not all, of the risk. Gahan had a minor part in it too.'

'Right, Lynch, keep digging. In the meantime, I also want to find out why Alister Becon became so charitable.'

'Guilty conscience?'

'I doubt it, Lynch. His kind doesn't do guilt. No, there's more to this, I know it.'

'As I already said, sir, I'm not sure you'll get any answers out of him.'

'Plenty of professional tribunal training, has he?'

'I'm just saying.'

'Well, let's see how he feels about being the next potential victim. There's nothing like a life-threatening event tocconcentrate the mind. Right, Lynch, what's keeping you? We're off for a little chat with Mr Becon.'

'You're in charge.'

'Glad you understand that, Lynch,' he said, with friendly banter in his voice. 'Now get Becon on the phone. I don't want to waste my time on a house call if he isn't there.'

'He'll be there all right. I told him we might be paying him a visit.'

'A regular mind-reader you're turning into, Lynch. We'll need to let Butler know we're putting the squeeze on Becon. He won't be happy about us upsetting politicians. He'll probably want to keep in Becon's good books for his new career – whenever the hell he gets out of this place.'

'You heard those rumours too, sir?'

'I hear everything, Lynch, even if I let most of the crap slide on past me.'

'Right.'

'Oh, and, Lynch, we'll need to phone Kate Pearson along the way. See how she thinks this all fits in. Becon doesn't strike me as someone harbouring a sense of personal failure. Maybe he isn't our man, but that doesn't mean he isn't pressing someone else's buttons.'

Stepping out into the night chill, O'Connor looked at the cars parked on either side of the road. 'Did you happen to find out, Lynch, what type of car Becon drives in his spare time?'

'A 2010 black Mercedes.'

'And his wife, what about her?'

'A Land Cruiser.'

'Does a lot of mountain driving, does she?'

'I doubt it. Charity work mainly.'

'A right pair of do-gooders. I can't wait to meet them. You can do the driving, but don't break any green lights.'

'I won't.'

'What have we got back on Dominic Hamilton and Clodagh McKay?'

'He's clean, but she picked up a driving ban a few months back, drink-driving.'

'Right, we'll be chatting with them soon too.'

Getting into the car, O'Connor's mobile rang. Martha Smyth's call was brief. O'Connor turned to Lynch. 'Looks like the labs in the UK have brought in information earlier than expected. It seems our pal was driving a Volvo S60.'

'So the chief has his image for *Crimecall*.'

'Yeah, don't you love it when things start coming together?' The next call O'Connor made was to Matthews. 'I assume Martha Smyth has filled you in?' Lynch closed the driver's door as O'Connor continued, 'We'll need a list of owners. There can't be too many Volvo S60s bought in the middle of a bloody recession.' Then, looking at Lynch, 'What's keeping you? Get driving.'

Mervin Road

Kate could tell O'Connor was highly charged while discussing Alister Becon. Becon certainly sounded like a man who could do his fair share of string-pulling, and the financial connection with Hamilton, Jenkins and Gahan was a further tie. Money might be behind a lot of the events, but at the core, there was a strong emotional undercurrent. The level of aggression, the ancillary factors, including the missing ring, the hotel receipt and the overwhelming need on the killer's part for his victims to end up in the water, all pointed one way. This was personal.

After O'Connor's call, Kate decided to phone Hennessy. He wasn't happy to hear from her. Initially, she put his coolness down to her not being directly involved with the case. She had initiated the phone call on the basis of a connection with the Rachel Mooney attack, and the two other sexual assaults, though she knew it was unlikely that Susie Graham's case was connected. The perpetrator in the Mooney case liked successful career women, and Susie Graham didn't fit that profile.

Thankfully, Hennessy's mood shifted the more questions Kate asked, and he became a little more relaxed once she'd assured him O'Connor wasn't involved. She remembered O'Connor telling her that he and Hennessy weren't on the best of terms. In the interest of getting the information she wanted, she told Stuart Hennessy that O'Connor was unaware of her phone call, which was the truth. Once that was out of the way, he was happy enough to talk.

'Stuart, will you talk me through it from the beginning?'

'As you know, rules and structures are there for a reason. The regulation rape kit was used. It's our first point of evidence-gathering, and the initial link to identify the attacker. The tests were carried out at the Sexual Assault Treatment Unit in the Rotunda hospital. Susie Graham was examined there first. Medication was administered to help fight off any potential infection, and the standard follow-up appointments were made for blood-test results.'

'Who carried out the SATU evaluation?'

'Lucy Majors. She's one of the principal SATU nurses at the unit. We work very closely together. Once the bloods are back, the unit will take it from there, and monitor any need for further psychological care. We'll be keeping an eye on Susie to see how she's coping.'

'How is she now?'

'It's never easy, Dr Pearson, but as far as possible in these matters, our aim is to give the victim back a sense of control. SATU do an amazing job. Things have moved on from the old days. Nothing is done without explanation and permission. Susie Graham was under age, so the consent of the parent, the mother, was also sought.'

'What did you get?'

'The girl came to us within twenty-four hours. I know, Dr Pearson, you're involved in the Rachel Mooney case, so you'll be aware that up to seventy two hours after the attack, sperm is still alive and can be found for as long as seven days after the incident, even if the victim has washed.'

'Go on, Stuart.'

'The victim hadn't been licked or bitten but the bruising on her upper arms and the inside of her thighs was acute.'

'And psychologically?'

'It's hard to tell the extent of damage right now. The girl was subdued, very vulnerable and nervous. I know some people believe that reliving the event mentally is another trauma, but I've worked with SATU for some time now, and it's my firm belief that once a victim attends the unit, they've taken their first step, both physically and mentally, in the healing process.'

'I agree with you, but as you say, it's still early days for the girl. The body will recover, but the psychological trauma is different.' Kate hesitated before asking her next question. 'Did you interview Susie Graham?'

'Yes, I did. Only members of the force with specialist psychological training are permitted to interview victims. Currently, I'm the most senior in Harcourt Street.'

'When will you get the DNA results?'

'Do you really think this is connected to your case?'

'To be honest, I don't think so, but I'd still like to be kept in the picture.'

'We should get the results shortly. We'll run the usual checks, and I'll keep you posted.'

'I'd appreciate that.' Again Kate hesitated. 'Will you also keep me informed on how the girl is doing mentally? I have a full brief right now, but there's always room for another case if need be. I do a lot of work with Jigsaw, the voluntary group.'

'We do too, especially via SATU.'

'I know they're often brought in if a patient isn't coping and, like many psychologists involved, I offer my services *pro bono* in support.'

'Okay.'

After hanging up, Kate went to check on Charlie. He must have woken up without calling her because when she opened the bedroom door, although he was asleep, she saw an open *Tom and Jerry* colouring book on the bed, with crayons. She tidied them away, leaving his door ajar, as she headed to the living room to do her next report for O'Connor.

Clodagh

When I wake, the room is black. The only sound is my own breathing. The door to our bedroom is open. There are no lights on, not even in the hall. I have no idea if Martin is anywhere in the house.

My head feels as if it has done battle with a hammer. I push the heavy throw off my body. I don't know what time it is, or how long I've been knocked out. Even in the dark, I can see the room has been tidied.

My throat feels dry, and my mouth has an awful aftertaste. I sit on the side of the bed, then stand and walk into the bathroom. Switching on the light, I'm relieved to find I still have a toothbrush in the glass cabinet. Martin hasn't cleared everything away. I brush my teeth, leaning down to rinse my mouth. I stop. I have that fear again. The all-consuming terror that whatever happens next might be outside my control.

'Martin,' I say, low at first. My voice sounds weak. 'Martin.' This time it's a little louder. Still no answer.

I go out onto the landing, aware that my movements are causing further sounds, and pause before I switch on the landing light. I hear a creaking sound coming from Ruby's bedroom. As happened in the regression session with Keith Jenkins at the door, I'm unsure about opening another door. When I do, I see my old doll, Emma, where I left her, sitting in the middle of the bed, propped up on the pillows. The creaking sound must have been the house settling. I can hear the central heating kicking in. I walk over and pick her up, then lie down on the bed, facing the door, in case someone is there.

Out of nervous habit, I stroke her hair. I lower my hand to the coolness of her porcelain face, touching the crack, wondering if I've gone mad.

I check under the pillow for my mobile phone. It's still there. I realise it's gone eleven o'clock. Boston is five hours behind. If I contact Orla now, it would be six in the evening there, but the laptop is downstairs. I tell myself I'm acting crazy. I put Emma back on the bed and go down to the living room.

Orla answers straight away. Thankfully, she doesn't ask me to switch on the Skype camera and says nothing about the automatic female icon face. At first we talk about rubbish things. I can't believe I sound so calm. Maybe the sleeping tablets Martin gave me are still working.

'Clodagh,' she says, 'are you okay?' There is something in the way she says it. The same way Gerard Hayden sounded. As if they both care.

'I've been better.' I attempt a laugh.

'It's been tough on you. I know you and your mum didn't get on well, but she was still your mother.'

For a moment I can't think of anything else to say so I repeat her last words: 'Still my mother.'

'Clodagh?'

'Yes.'

'It's been a while since we talked properly, but friendship doesn't disappear. You do know I'm always here for you, don't you?'

'I do. It's just some things are a bit muddled right now.'

'That's only natural. Everyone grieves differently. When my mother died, I thought I'd never get over the heartbreak.'

It feels weird talking to the laptop screen. 'As you said, Orla, me and Mum weren't that close.'

There is a pause.

'Clodagh?' I can hear her sympathy.

'Yes?'

'Martin's worried about you.'

'What do you mean?'

'I know Martin and I didn't always see eye to eye, but he loves you very much.'

'What are you talking about?' The coldness in my voice runs through me.

'He emailed me to let me know you got my letter. He asked me to keep in touch.'

'He had no right. Neither of you have any right to be talking behind my back.'

'It wasn't like that. You're vulnerable right now. Martin explained everything to me.'

I remember him interfering with the letter. He must have taken down Orla's email address. 'Exactly what has he explained to you?'

'Clodagh, it doesn't matter.'

'It does to me.'

'Martin said you were going through …' She pauses.

'Through what, Orla?' I don't care if I sound harsh.

'A bit of a breakdown.'

'Go on.'

'He said you were recording messages to yourself. He's afraid you might hit the bottle again.'

'Orla, I can't talk to you any more.' I need to shut her off.

'Clodagh, please don't hang up.'

'You're on his side.'

'It isn't about taking sides, Clodagh. It's about your well-being.'

'Did he say anything else?'

'He said …'

'Orla, just say it.' I can't take much more of this.

'He said you were talking to …'

'Talking to whom?' I wonder if he's found out about Gerard Hayden.

'Clodagh, this is difficult to say.'

'Orla, please.'

'Dolls. He said you were talking to dolls. That you believed they could see and know things.'

I'm all out of words. I can hear Orla talking, but not what she's saying. I feel numb. I hang up, hearing the connection die, followed by a darkened screen, zapping it all out. I need to think. I go back to Ruby's room, unsure of what to do next. It's then that I hear him calling my name. The way he has done so many times in the past, old and familiar.

He climbs the stairs, and I wait. From the darkness of Ruby's bedroom, he looks like a large bear in the doorway. 'Clodagh,' he says, his tone soft and gentle. 'Are you okay?'

'I don't know, Dominic. I don't know anything, not any more.'

∞

As he walks into the room, Dominic's movements are slow. When he sits on the side of the bed, he notices Emma. 'I see you still have your doll.'

'In a way, Emma has always been with me.'

For a while he says nothing, giving me some space. Then he says, 'Do you remember the argument, Clodagh, the one where Emma's face split in two?'

'I remember Mum and Dad's voices. We were sitting on the stairs. You were trying to drag me away.'

'I didn't mean for your doll to fall, Clodagh. You believe me, don't you?'

'Yes.' His face is close to mine. It feels like we're kids again. Dominic, my older brother, looking out for me, protecting me, telling me everything will be okay, even when it isn't. 'What happened to us back then, Dominic? Why are there so many bits that I can't remember?'

'We had a shitty childhood, Clodagh. Only, for the most part, you were too young to understand a lot of it.' He looks pained.

'I couldn't help that.'

'Whatever. It was different for you. That's all I'm saying.'

'Just as well, considering what a fuck-up I've made of things.' I laugh out loud at myself, keeping my eyes on him. Dominic has had his fair share of crap to contend with too. I was always envious of his relationship with Mum. But after Dad died, she leaned on him. He became the functional man in her life, even if he was too young for the role.

'Dominic?'

'Yeah?'

'Yesterday, when I went up to the attic in Seacrest, I had another reason for going there other than looking for Emma.'

'What?'

'I remembered you and me and Martin and Stevie hiding up there. It had something to do with Emmaline.'

'You must have imagined it, Clodagh.'

'I don't know. Maybe I did, but I can't help feeling it's important.'

A zillion thoughts are rushing through my head now. If Dominic knew about Mum's infidelity, and the other shitty stuff, he wasn't like me. He didn't hate her for it, even though he was on the receiving end of her emotional baggage. My memory's a mess but I know that much. And, for the first time, I wonder if he had a sense of divided loyalty back then. If he knew about the affair and didn't betray her, had he betrayed Dad instead?

'Dominic, did Dad know Mum was having an affair, that there were other men?'

'Not at the beginning. He was too wrapped up in the business. He wouldn't have been able to see something sitting on the end of his nose.'

'So when did he find out? What happened then?'

'It was after the business collapsed.' Dominic draws a deep breath and lets it out slowly. 'One day he was this big success. Then everything started slipping away. His moods deteriorated. You don't remember it, Clodagh. At least, I don't think you do. He went to a very dark place.'

'How do you mean?'

'Angry outbursts, him wanting to punish the world, keeping his anger behind closed doors.'

'Like me and Martin,' I say. My next words are loaded with sarcasm: 'They say you always hurt the ones you love.'

Dominic doesn't respond. In the silence, something else comes hurtling back. More raised voices. I see bruises on Dominic's face. I thought he'd got into a fight with someone outside. But what if he hadn't? What if his injuries were caused by someone closer to home? I stare at him, remembering the whispers I'd heard in the attic on our last visit to the house – the whispers of young boys, as if they were scheming.

'Dominic, how did Dad find out?'

'He started looking for answers. Once that happened, it didn't take him long.'

'Do you remember the other day in the attic, when I found Emma?'

'What about it?'

'I thought I heard whispers, boys talking low. It must have been a memory. If it was a memory, it means I was part of it.'

'Clodagh, this isn't helping you.'

'Mum hated me. There has to be a reason she stopped loving me. She always loved you more than me.'

'She didn't. She found it difficult to show her love to you.'

'Why? What did I do wrong?'

'Nothing.'

And, for a moment, I'm not sure if he's going to touch me. I wonder if I'm doing exactly what Mum did for as long as I can remember: she'd loaded all her problems onto Dominic. But still I say, 'How hard can it be to show a child you love them?'

He takes my left hand in both of his. If Martin was to come in now, we would look ridiculous, a man, a woman and a doll with a cracked face.

'Dominic, there's something else.'

'What?'

'This evening when I came home, I went into that bedroom.' I point to the room Martin and I used to share.

'It's your house.' He sounds more like his clinical self.

'Martin had removed all traces of me, every single photograph.'

'Why would he do that?'

'I don't know.' I look down at Emma. 'When I married him, Dominic, I think I needed love too much. I thought he loved me. I don't think that now.'

'People change.'

'Dominic, do you ever see Stevie McDaid?'

'Why?'

'I was thinking about him today. When I went up to the attic, I remembered you all playing as boys, you, Stevie and Martin. The ropes are still there, you know, from your old hammocks.'

'Well, that was a long time ago, Clodagh. Let's mark it up as bad taste in friends.'

'I thought I saw him last week. I thought he might have been following me.'

'Don't be daft.'

'I can't be sure of anything any more.'

He says nothing.

'Dominic?'

'What?' He's closing up now. I know it. I need to push him.

'That photograph, the one with Dad, Jimmy and Keith Jenkins – the one from their college days.'

'What about it?'

'You know who the other man is, don't you?'

'Yes, I do.'

'What's his name?'

'Alister Becon.'

'It sounds familiar. He's that politician.'

'He and Martin have some business dealings.'

'What kind of business dealings?'

'You'd have to ask Martin about that.'

'He won't tell me.'

'Alister Becon has his fingers in any number of pies, including politics.'

I look around the room, as if searching for something.

'What are you looking for, Clodagh?'

'The photograph – Martin took it from my bag. He put it in his briefcase. I need to find it.'

'It's only a photograph.'

'Only a photograph,' I repeat my brother's words, more as if they're a question than an affirmation. Then I think of another question, one that unsettles me, realising my mind is still recovering from the sleeping pills. 'Dominic?'

'Yes.'

'How did you get inside the house without a key?'

38C Seville Place

As Stevie watched Wednesday's nine o'clock news, he thought long and hard about his next move. Being one of Alister Becon's minions wasn't a role he liked or cared to turn into a full-time career. He had no problem with following people around but he didn't take to being at someone else's beck and call.

Still, he knew Becon from before. Well enough to understand that, once you were caught within the fucker's circle, certain rules applied. He might have stumbled on some financially useful information regarding Ruby McKay, but Becon wanted his piece of flesh before he handed out any money – which was why Stevie had decided to do a little digging.

He'd been surprised to discover that Martin McKay was working with Becon. It brought a wry smile to Stevie's face: whatever business dealings Becon and McKay shared, he doubted that good old Martin had any bleedin' idea the old man had been screwing his daughter. That particular nugget might prove useful further down the line, but the first priority was getting the money out of Becon. All other nostalgic trips down Memory Lane had to wait.

Stevie poured himself a large Jack Daniel's, drank it in one go and immediately felt better for it. The next he left on the side of the armchair, to savour.

It was an awful long time ago, but he still remembered plenty about the good-old bad-old days, including how there'd been something between that fucker Becon and the ever-so-beautiful, up-herself Lavinia Hamilton. Even as a kid he'd seen it. The way Becon looked at her. Lavinia Hamilton had had no time for Stevie. Fuck her, had been his attitude. But that was the funny thing about people thinking you were lower than shit. They'd start forgetting you were there. Or even that you had a brain. One connected to your eyes and ears. Maybe Becon had been trying to regain his misspent youth with young Ruby. Turn back time by pretending he could start all over again with a newer model. He wouldn't be the first eejit to fall for that sad joke. Fucking ridiculous the way old farts think with their pricks.

Martin's involvement with Becon probably explained how he'd met little Ruby and thought, Presto, I'll have a bit of that. Stevie didn't really blame him.

He smiled, thinking about the first time he had kissed Clodagh Hamilton. A crowd of them had gone off with some cans to the old railway tracks. Pissed out of their heads, most of them. He hadn't known any of the girls at first but recognised Clodagh as soon as she arrived. She was all glammed up, looking gorgeous and shiny, glitter on her arms, and that fucking amazing red hair of hers. To this day, he can't be sure she knew it was him when they met. She'd had a good few on her. She went for it all the same. In the dark, the two of them eating the face off one another, while the others laughed and messed around in the background. Muck under both their arses. She wore white jeans, as tight as anything. They didn't look very pretty when she stood up. He'd thought she knew who he was, especially when he was feeling those lovely pert breasts of hers.

It was when he'd called her by name, his face buried in the warmth of her neck, smelling that red hair and wanting more, that he'd detected the first signs of withdrawal. Then had come the turn of the head, the arching of her body, the quick double-take as she'd tried to work out how he knew her. She got out of there like it was the only option in town.

He ran after her, and caught her. He grabbed her into a laneway. Tried it on again, but it had lost its beauty. She didn't think he was good enough, and he wanted to give her a good lash there and then, take some of that prettiness off her face. Teach her not to be mixing with the big boys, playing fucking dress-up in her tight jeans, far too much sex-on-legs not to be fucked. Christ, she couldn't have been more than thirteen. Four years younger than her daughter was now and already pissed out of her head, ending up in the wrong place with the wrong company. Stevie took a swig of his whiskey. Boozed up or not, she'd still tasted beautiful.

A quarter of a lifetime on, part of Stevie still bore a gnawing thought. The reason he hadn't taken her that night didn't sit easy with him. It was because a fucking huge slice of his brain knew that, where Clodagh Hamilton was concerned, he could never be good enough – in her eyes or his own.

He poured another whiskey, smirking to himself. Here they were, all these years on, and a bit like that fucker Becon clapping eyes on Ruby McKay, wanting to rekindle some kind of fucked-up happiness, he'd been contemplating the bleedin' same. Not for the first time in his life he damned ever hooking up with the Hamiltons, and all the other fuckers that frequented their miserable fucking world.

Stevie made up his mind. His time playing fucking detective for Alister Becon would be short-lived. He had no intention of being strung along as a fool. No matter what nasty fucked-up logic Becon lived by.

Clodagh

It takes Dominic an age to answer. The room is in semi-darkness, the only light trickling in from the landing.

'Clodagh, I was worried about you. I asked Martin for a set of keys, just in case.'

'In case of what?'

'In case you needed me.' He keeps his eyes fixed on me. 'I told Martin I was worried you weren't coping, that I needed the keys in case ...'

'In case I decided to top myself, or drink myself into some drunken stupor? Is that what you're saying?' Again I want to throttle him.

'It was a precaution, and it wasn't only that.'

'I can't wait to hear the rest.'

'Less of the dramatics, Clodagh. I'm only thinking of you.'

'The whole world seems to be thinking of me. You, Martin, Orla —even Val's expressed her concerns. But do you know what the laughable thing is, Dominic?'

'What?' He stands up, barely able to contain his own anger.

'Despite everyone's bloody concern, I've never felt so shagging lonely in my whole bloody life.'

'I know that, Clodagh.'

'So what was the other reason for you needing keys?'

'I don't trust Martin.'

'Well, why didn't you ask me?'

'I wanted him to know I had them.'

'Why?'

'In case he got any ideas.'

'Do you mean his temper?'

'Yes, but not just that. I don't want to be worrying you, Clodagh.'

'But you are worrying me, Dominic.' My words are more fearful than angry now.

'Martin's got involved with some nasty people.'

'What people?'

'You don't need to worry. It's just an added protection.'

'Dominic, you would tell me if this is connected to either of those killings?'

'I'm not saying that, Clodagh …' he paused as if lost in his own thoughts '… but it doesn't do any harm to be careful.'

'Who is Martin involved with?'

'Alister Becon for one. You don't remember him, do you, Clodagh?'

'No, I don't.' I can hear the frustration in my voice. 'I remember there was someone else, a man's face in the shadows.'

'He gave Dad the boat.'

'On the day of the accident?'

'Yes, on the day of the accident. Becon said he had no idea what was on Dad's mind.'

'You've spoken to him?' I'm unable to hide the shock in my voice.

'Yes – after Mum passed away.'

I think about my row with Dominic after she died. How the two of them had made me feel so left out, whispering to each other on her deathbed. This was more of it. More bloody secret conversations. 'What did he say?' I ask, with more venom than I intend. Losing it with Dominic will get me nowhere.

'Nothing of any importance. His kind always plays it cagey. He wasn't going to share any secrets.'

'Dominic, do you ever think Dad's still around?'

'No,' his answer bitter and defiant.

'Sometimes, I feel him close.'

'I wish I could hear or see him.'

'You'd better go. Val will be worried about you.'

'I'll stay another little while. You get some sleep. You look tired.'

'Martin gave me some sleeping pills.'

'Right then, get some rest. You have your mobile?'

'It's under the pillow.'

'Keep it there.'

Sandymount Strand

Once I knew Clodagh was out for the count, I checked that her car was still safely under wraps in the garage. After that, I made my way to the strand. I needed to think straight, pull all the bits together. I can't afford to let others see that I might be unravelling.

My mind keeps skipping. There are so many things I need to get right to reach the end game. Some say solitude and walking can clear the mind. I walk alone, but my thoughts aren't clear. At some point this is all going to be over. Then everything will be done, and that will be the end of the whole sorry mess.

It's good that I have Jenkins and Gahan behind me. But only part of the job is done. It makes carrying on all the more intense. I had my doubts at the beginning that I would get this far. Planning is one thing. Making it happen can be very different.

I hear the seagulls squawking overhead. Even the stupid birds seem to be mocking me. Clodagh is on the brink, as fragile as that cracked doll of hers. She thinks she's working things out, getting to grips with the truth. She doesn't know yet that the truth isn't all it's cracked up to be. She'll know it soon enough because I'll be taking her out of her misery. She won't have anything to worry her any more. If I'm careful, and keep her sweet, she won't see it coming.

I've felt the pressure over the last few days, my mind buried in so much bloody shit. Walking away from Gahan, his body floating in the canal, I thought I heard the sound of drums, loud, absurd and deafening. I stopped to listen. But there were no drums, or drummer, nobody other than me.

I hear myself laugh out loud. Again no one else is listening. I feel like two men, the exterior and the interior, as if a slice of my brain thinks I'm not doing this. If someone other than me is doing it, I hope one of us stupid mother-fuckers knows what we're at because it's far too late to stop things now.

Another thought slithers through my mind. It crawls into corners, feeling comfortably at home. And once it does, there's no way of stopping it. I think of Jenkins and Gahan spread out like the brown eagle in the attic at Sandymount, the piercing black of its eyes and how the death of the bird failed to kill its soul. It looks down on all that has happened, knowing evil has its own path to follow.

Ocean House, the Quays

When Kate arrived at Ocean House on Thursday morning, she rang O'Connor before sending through her report. He hadn't been in touch after his meeting with Alister Becon. That wasn't a good sign. She had thought again about both murders being a form of spree killing, with the killer having a final destination, or last victim, in mind.

When victims are chosen, rather than taken at random, the deaths sometimes occur in a particular sequence, more often than not the killer saving the most important killing until last.

O'Connor answered the phone briskly. 'Kate, I don't have long. Butler wants to meet me before the ten o'clock session.'

'I won't delay you. I was wondering if you'd talked to either of Adrian Hamilton's surviving children.'

'Not yet, but hopefully today.'

'I'd like to be there, O'Connor.'

'What's tweaked your interest?'

'What do you know about either of them?'

'Dominic Hamilton has no priors. Clodagh McKay had her driving licence taken from her – she was drunk, well over the limit. I understand she's on the wagon now, but other than that, not a whole lot. I should have more information later on.'

'You have the DNA results from the deposits under Keith Jenkins's nails. I assume you'll be using them.'

'Only if we have reason to demand a comparison or people are in an obliging mood. So far this case isn't oozing with friendliness.'

'How did you get on with Alister Becon?'

'Slick bastard.'

'Not good, then.'

'He gave us nothing, and he didn't seem particularly concerned about his own safety either.'

'What was your impression of him?'

'As you know, he comes from a privileged background. I'd say he enjoys power and control. He probably gets off on being a well-known public figure. Most likely doesn't give a shit about anyone other than himself.'

Kate laughed. 'Maybe you're the one who should have studied psychology, O'Connor. You've just described typical psychopathic traits – power, control, needing sensation, and a blatant disregard for others.'

'Anything you'd like to add to that list, Kate, seeing as how we're enjoying this psychology lesson?'

'Well, the most intelligent psychopaths, especially those coming from privileged backgrounds, tend to avoid violence. They know it will get them into trouble. They prefer to use safer means of exploitation at their disposal.'

'You mean they don't get their own hands dirty?'

'Exactly – you said he didn't seem concerned about his own safety.'

'That's the impression I got. But Becon would be well used to saying one thing and meaning another. The guy is either putting up a great front, unwilling to show weakness, or he knows something and doesn't want to share it.'

'Or both.'

'His hands are dirty too. I'd lay money on it.'

'What do you mean?'

'There's been more than a few rumours about his finances. The guy is no saint, but right now, it's all bloody rumour.'

'I see.'

'Kate, I've got to go. Myself and Butler are about to have our little chat, but he'll be looking for your report.'

'I'm sending an interim one over now. And good luck with Butler.'

'Hopefully, I won't need it.'

'And, O'Connor …'

'What?'

'Let me know what more you find out about Dominic and Clodagh Hamilton.'

'It's Clodagh McKay. She's married.'

'What does her husband do?'

'Financial adviser. He has an office in town. I'm looking at him too. Kate, I gotta go. Butler's smiling at me, and I fucking hate when he does that.'

Clodagh

It was late when Martin arrived home last night. Thankfully he left me alone. This morning I thought about phoning Ruby after he'd left for work, then thought again. Every time we speak, we have another row. It's as if the same bloody chasm that existed between me and Mum is destined to infest another generation.

In a few minutes I'll see Gerard Hayden again. I walk down the now familiar street, with its small houses on either side of the road, and click down the handle of the gate. I remember that sound from a previous regression session. When I ring the bell, it's as if Gerard Hayden has been expecting me for some time because he opens the door within seconds. He must sense my mood because straight away he tries to put me at my ease, speaking to me about all kinds of things that are of no importance. But they relax me, taking my mind off how strange this process feels.

As we walk through the door with 'Office' stuck on it in black letters, Gerard asks, 'Are you okay, Clodagh?'

Without meaning to, I give him the automatic response: 'Yes.'

Soon I'm lying back on the bed, the room now lit by vanilla-scented candles. Gerard is asking me to count backwards from two hundred. I can smell the wax burning, the light in the room softening. More than anything, I want to release my mind of all thoughts. This time I feel different. It's as if some sort of soft cloud is gathering, telling me to really let go. I count down the numbers, my voice getting lower with each one, as if it, too, wants to give way to this release.

The numbers start to get mixed up. I'm finding it harder to remember the next one. I raise my index finger to tell Gerard that I have lost track. He is asking me to visualise the garden, the one with the flowers smelling so rich that their scent is stronger than any other I have experienced. I can feel the grass beneath my feet, as the relaxation touches some safe layer below my consciousness. I almost look for the staircase, even before Gerard mentions it. The steps that will take me down deeper, to a place beyond the wild flowers and the beautiful garden I can now see.

This time the stairs are different too. They are the stairs of Seacrest. Gerard is telling me the staircase can look however I want it to look. It can be made of any material I want it to be made of, marble, stone, wood, but no matter how hard I try, the stairs remain unchanged. He is asking me to count again, and when the numbers get muddled, he tells me to raise my index finger. I'm counting backwards from one thousand. The staircase feels as if it goes an awful long way down. Gerard tells me there is no limit to the number of steps in it. The more I go down, the deeper my hypnotic state will be. I begin to wonder if I've lost track of the numbers, but my conscious mind keeps jumping in. It tells me to keep counting. As if it needs more time, as if it has decided that it doesn't want my subconscious to take over.

Gerard asks me if I want to raise my index finger, and I reply, 'Not yet.' I keep walking down the stairs, and all the time I feel as if there may be nothing more than an abyss below me, one I'm not yet ready for. I hear Gerard's voice once more. He's saying, 'Clodagh, your conscious mind is putting up resistance. We're going to try something else. Is that okay?'

I hear myself say, 'Yes.'

'Clodagh, I want you to continue with the counting, but I also want you to move your eyes from right to left, then back again. I want you to keep doing this, and while your eyes are moving back and forth, you will also count backwards from thirty-seven. At some point, Clodagh, I'm going to tap you on the forehead, and when I do, it will aid your journey into your subconscious. At no point will this cause you any pain. Do you understand me, Clodagh?'

'Yes.'

Gerard has spoken to me about this before, in case we ever get into difficulty in attempting to regress. He told me that the physical act of him touching my forehead, while my conscious mind is trying to count, will confuse it – a form of shock treatment allowing the subconscious part of my brain to step in, jerking it back into memory. When this happens, it can cause a sudden change to my physical condition. It's not unusual to feel a huge swell of emotion. The sheer shock of snapping from my conscious to my subconscious mind might even bring me back to the trauma, or past event, that I may be least prepared for. If this happens, and he feels I'm at any risk, he will pull me out of my regression.

I have no idea at what point he will tap my forehead. I'm finding it harder to count down the stairs, while moving my eyes from right to left, and back again. I'm still counting backwards from thirty-seven. I can feel those soft, dark clouds all around me, as Gerard's hand taps my forehead twice, and I know I'm going back.

Ocean House, the Quays

Kate put the framed photograph of herself, Declan and Charlie face down in her desk drawer. Soon she would replace it with a different one, with only her and Charlie in it.

Her next appointment wasn't for another half-hour. She looked at her case notes. Keith Jenkins's body had been discovered in the early hours of Saturday morning. It was now Thursday. O'Connor would need all the luck he could get when he was talking to Butler.

She knew all changes in pattern meant something. The killer had changed his *modus operandi* with Jimmy Gahan: the attack and drowning had happened in the same area. Altering behaviour wasn't unusual, and familiarity with the victim might have initiated the change. Repetition of a similar location could well connect him personally to the area, choosing it because of some attachment, irrespective of its suitability. The creation of mental shortcuts, whether during repetitive tasks, like making breakfast or sitting behind the wheel of a car to drive to work, is perfectly normal. In this regard, killers were no different. In general, people's activities are mainly confined to familiar neighbourhoods, which are often connected to their home or work, acting as mental anchor points.

Kate looked at the photographs of Jenkins's body spreadeagled in the water, and Gahan's the same – carbon copies of each other. Gahan was single, but Jenkins was married. If the killer had removed the wedding ring, it constituted an act of rebuttal. If he was making a moral judgement on his victim, the killing could be tied to anyone with whom Jenkins had had an affair.

She flicked to her notes on the hotel receipt. Assuming it was a plant, apart from being proof of Jenkins's infidelity it meant the killer had been tracking him for some time. He might have taken the receipt months before, especially if he was the one who had given the information to Gahan.

Whoever the killer was, he'd been planning this for a protracted period. O'Connor needed to dig deeper on his background checks. Whoever the perpetrator turns out to be, he wouldn't be capable of maintaining a normal existence. Someone close to him must have seen the signs.

Clodagh

'Clodagh, I want you to try to open your eyes. Can you do that?'

Again my eyelids feel like they've been stuck down with the strongest glue, and again I cannot open them. 'No,' I hear myself say, but this time my voice sounds different, as if it belongs to someone else.

'Good,' says Gerard. 'At the count of three, you'll be able to open your eyes again. One, two, three ...'

I open my eyes.

'Clodagh, can you hear me?'

'Yes.'

'Where are you?'

'I'm inside the doll's house.'

'How do you know that?'

'I can see the small sash windows. There are floral curtains on each of the windows.'

'Who else is in the doll's house with you?'

'I don't know. There are sounds coming from everywhere.'

'What kind of sounds?'

'Whispers, muffled voices – adult voices, I think.'

'What are you doing, Clodagh?'

'I'm looking around the room.'

'Which room?'

'My old bedroom.'

'Your bedroom looking out on the strand?'

'Yes, but it's inside the doll's house. I know it doesn't make sense, but that's what I see. The girl is there too.'

'Your younger self?'

'Yes.'

'What age is she, Clodagh?'

'Seven.'

'Does she know you're there?'

'I think so, but she's busy playing.'

'What is she playing, Clodagh?'

'She has my old blackboard standing up in the corner. She's writing words on it in yellow chalk.'

'Can you read the words?'

'It says, HAPPY FAMILIES.'

'What are you doing now, Clodagh?'

'I'm walking over to her. She has her back to me.'

'Is she saying anything?'

'No.' I stop talking.

'Are you okay, Clodagh?'

'I'm kneeling down beside her. I think …'

'What do you think?'

'I think if I kneel down I can make myself smaller. She mightn't feel afraid.'

'Do you think she is afraid?'

'I don't know. I can hear her singing. It's an old nursery song.'

'What song is it?'

"Rock-a-bye Baby'.' I hear myself singing it out loud, but again it doesn't seem like my voice. I can't be sure, but I think it's the voice of the little girl:

'Rock-a-bye baby,

On the treetop,

When the wind blows,

The cradle will rock,

When the bough breaks,

The cradle will fall,

Down will come baby, cradle and all.'

'She keeps singing it over and over.' I let out a gasp.

'What's wrong, Clodagh?'

'She's turned around. She's looking straight at me. She's known I was there the whole time and ...'

'And what?'

'She's crying. I want to help her, but ...'

'Keep going, Clodagh, you're doing great.'

'I'm reaching out my hand. Her face is changing. It isn't her face any more. It's Emma's face.'

'Who's Emma?'

'She's one of my dolls.' I can hear hysteria in my voice. 'Her face is cracked. She's talking to me, but it's not her voice.'

'Relax, Clodagh. If it's not her voice, whose voice is it?'

'Debbie's.'

'Your other doll?'

'Debbie says, all smart, "CLODAGH, THERE'S NO POINT HIDING IN YOUR ROOM. WE NEED TO GO ON AN ADVENTURE."'

'Are you okay, Clodagh?' I hear Gerard ask.

'I think so. I need to go on an adventure.'

'Where?'

'I don't know. I'm leaving the room. Now I'm on the landing – the landing of the doll's house. The whispers are getting louder. I'm following my little-girl self. When she smiles back at me, she looks like Debbie, all smug. She knows the way. She keeps turning around, making sure I'm following her.'

'Clodagh, I'm going to bring you back. Do you understand me?'

'Yes.'

'I want you to remember this point, the landing and your doll called Debbie. I want you to fix on this moment, following your little-girl self. Can you do that?'

'Yes.'

'We'll return to this tomorrow, but for now, I want you to come back. I want you to look for the staircase. Can you see it?'

'It's very far away.'

'Keep walking towards it. Is it getting any closer?'

'I think so.'

'Good. Now start counting.'

I do as Gerard asks, and soon I can smell the candle wax. He's sitting on the chair as he did before. 'Why did you bring me back, Gerard? I was going on an adventure.' Even as I say the word 'adventure', it sounds ridiculous. 'It felt important.'

'Clodagh, I want you to tell me about Emma.'

'She was my doll. She fell. Her face cracked. Did I not tell you this before?'

'When she fell, what age were you?'

'Seven.'

'The year your dad died?'

'Yes, the same year as Emmaline.'

Mervin Road

It was after nine o'clock by the time O'Connor got back to his flat. After putting in a fourteen-hour shift he should have been exhausted, but he felt as far away from sleep as anyone could feel. The day had been a fiasco. They'd had a lead about an ex-boyfriend of Siobhan King with a nasty temper. He fitted the physical description of the killer, and also had a vague connection to Gahan through family ties. It had come to nothing in the end because the man's lawyer had spent the day wasting everyone's time. It didn't take O'Connor long to down half a bottle of whiskey. Surprising how easily it can disappear.

It was on a whim that he'd phoned Kate. He should have rung her earlier, but so far they hadn't unearthed a whole lot more on either Dominic Hamilton or Clodagh McKay. O'Connor knew he had taken his eye off the ball, and wasn't keen on being reminded of it. Tomorrow he would invite them all down to the station, including Clodagh McKay's husband, Martin, who it seemed had done business with Alister Becon. If any of them played awkward, the mountain would have to go to Muhammad.

After phoning Kate, he got a taxi to her apartment, but decided to give it a few minutes before going up. He really wanted another drink, but he lit a cigarette instead. He knew he'd been burying his head in the sand. It was partly the reason he'd got into this mess in the first place. He could trust Kate, and he needed to talk to goddamn someone.

The yellow streetlights on Mervin Road blurred his eyes. Leaning back against the lamppost, he asked himself for the hundredth time how he of all people had managed to fuck it up so much. Maybe that was why he'd never married: he hadn't wanted to get dragged into a complicated compromise with anyone. Like everyone else, he had a past and his own demons. He looked up at Kate's apartment. She could test his resolve.

O'Connor sucked in some air in an attempt to clear the smell of nicotine and booze. He thought again about Alister Becon. That bastard had got under his skin too, with his larger-than-life self-belief. He had treated O'Connor's warning about potential danger with the kind of disdain that only his kind of self-opinionated, egotistical, rich bastard could perfect. O'Connor had been left in no doubt about the man's character. All that fine talk and good education didn't fool a seasoned detective like him. Maybe this was the drink talking. He didn't really care. In his eyes the man was capable of murder, but whenever the shit hit the fan, Alister Becon would be well protected.

Misjudging his footing, O'Connor roared, 'Shite!' to the empty street. Straightening, he reminded himself that tomorrow was another day. He glanced at his watch. It was already Friday morning.

Mervin Road

Kate was so engrossed in work that she'd lost all track of time. When O'Connor phoned, she hadn't realised it was already past midnight or she would never have agreed to him calling to the apartment. She thought she'd detected a slight slur in his voice.

After checking on Charlie to make sure he was fast asleep, she tidied herself up, brushing her hair, cleaning her teeth, applying some blusher so she wouldn't look half dead, making herself presentable to the world. Taking one last look in the bathroom mirror, she added some lipstick.

Much to Kate's annoyance, O'Connor kept his finger pressed on the intercom buzzer although she'd told him Charlie was asleep. It was only when she opened the apartment door, and got the whiff of whiskey, that she realised why there had been a slur in his voice. When he stepped into the hall, she saw that his eyes were glazed. He wasn't out and out drunk, but he had a good few on him.

'I have the kettle boiled, O'Connor. Strong coffee is looking like a good option right now.' If he'd noticed the sarcasm in her tone he kept it to himself, happy to follow her down the hall into the kitchen. As they passed Charlie's bedroom door, she warned him, 'Keep your voice down. Charlie's asleep.'

O'Connor put his index figure up to his lips like a guilty but obedient child. She must be a complete lunatic allowing him to call at this ungodly hour. He'd better sober up fast, or this meeting would be a waste of time for both of them.

Kate made a large pot of coffee, placing it on the kitchen table with two mugs. 'I tried to get you earlier.'

'Sorry, Kate. It was a mental day.'

Kate didn't know if the coffee would do the trick, but as O'Connor was taking up a chair in her kitchen, she decided to continue. 'I've been going over my case notes and a number of things have cropped up, although nothing's conclusive.'

'Very little ever is …' He took a large gulp of coffee.

'We've already talked about the stabbing being frenzied,' Kate wondered if O'Connor was drifting, 'and the drowning as a form of cleansing.'

'A religious nut?'

'Not necessarily.'

'So what is he getting out of it?'

Kate topped up O'Connor's mug. 'He could be trying to purge himself of something rooted in his psyche, an earlier emotional trauma, and takes risks for it.'

'Meaning?'

'As I said before, that the fear of being caught is not uppermost in his mind. We know we're not dealing with a young guy, yet despite his maturity, his emotional drive is the overriding force.'

'The CCTV footage showed Jenkins talking to a perceived stranger.'

Kate was relieved that O'Connor's brain was beginning to function. 'But there's something else.' She hesitated. 'There are important issues around location. I don't think our killer is travelling far, or if he is, he has some previous connection in the area, either through work or home life. Listen, O'Connor, I'll be honest with you. I've been under a bit of pressure with personal stuff, which might explain why I missed this, but we all take mental shortcuts, and something is bringing the killer there. The taking of the ring ties him strongly to Jenkins's life.'

'You're not the only one who's been distracted. Any more thoughts on why the drowning is floating his boat?' O'Connor let out a snigger.

'You need more coffee, O'Connor, if you're starting to think you're funny.'

'I need a cigarette.'

'Not here. This is a no-smoking zone.'

'Right. Keep pouring,' he gestures towards the coffee pot.

'If it's a cleansing ritual, it tells us the wounds go deep. People seldom commit murder unless the stakes are high.' Kate poured the dregs from the coffee pot. 'Whoever it is, O'Connor, as I said in my last report, they'll have shown clues to others, probably the person closest to them. You haven't mentioned how you got on looking into Dominic Hamilton and Clodagh McKay.'

'I'll be chatting with them tomorrow, along with Martin McKay, her husband.'

Kate swallowed the last of her coffee. It tasted bitter. 'What's the delay?'

'Fucking cul-de-sacs going nowhere. Do you think this is all connected to Adrian Hamilton's death?'

'If it's some form of emotional revenge, the killer has kept his hatred at bay for a prolonged period of time. It's a difficult one. It means he waited until after Lavinia Hamilton died to take action. That's a long wait. Emotions don't work in isolation from our behaviour. Much and all as we try to control them, O'Connor, our emotional selves, especially where deep wounds are concerned, are hard to keep at bay.'

'So?'

'It's not my role to play detective, but if Lavinia Hamilton's death was the stressor, it could be because she or someone else revealed something before she died. It might even be something she needed to purge herself of.'

'The physical description fits Dominic Hamilton, but it also fits a few hundred thousand others.'

'I'm not pointing the finger at anyone. Any number of other connections are possible. It would be dangerous to latch onto one suspect. I don't need to tell you, others who knew the Hamiltons or, for that matter, either of the victims could still come forward as potential suspects. We're aware of certain factors, but we also need to acknowledge that there's a hell of a lot we're unaware of.'

'Maybe.'

'As I said in my report, whoever's doing this, O'Connor, they'll be showing cracks. That's why we need to look at Dominic Hamilton, Martin McKay and any other important links very closely.'

'First thing tomorrow, Kate, I'll be looking at them all.'

Kate stood up, hoping O'Connor would take it as his cue to leave, but O'Connor didn't look in any particular hurry to go anywhere.

'I hear you've been talking with Stuart Hennessy about the Susie Graham rape,' he said, still sitting down.

'Who told you that?'

'Never mind.' He slumped back in the chair, spreading his bulky frame as if he had no intention of moving.

'I was interested in the case, that's all. The girl had looked vulnerable, and I thought it might be connected with the Rachel Mooney rape.'

'That bastard Hennessy, he fucking hates me.'

'He struck me as a fair-minded individual,' she said, but she knew

O'Connor was building up to something. The sooner she got it out of him, the sooner she could get him out of her kitchen.

'Can I be honest with you, Kate?'

'I would hate for you to be any other way.' She attempted a laugh. 'I'm all ears.'

'You'd better put that kettle on again so.'

'And you'd better have good reason for keeping me up at this hour of the morning, and turning me into your housemaid.' Kate hoped her lighter tone would encourage him to get off his chest whatever was eating away at him.

'They say it's good to talk.'

'This thing you want to talk about, has it been bothering you for a while?'

'Months.'

'Is it to do with work?'

'Yeah … well, kind of.' O'Connor fidgeted in the chair. 'I've done something stupid. I've made a mistake.'

'None of us is perfect. Making mistakes is part of what makes us human.'

'Someone paid the price for my stupidity, Kate, a big price.'

'Have you spoken to anyone about this before?' Kate could tell by his manner that they were dealing with something big. And a part of her wasn't sure if she wanted to hear it.

'It's been keeping me awake at night. The only way I seem to be able to get any sleep is if I drink myself out of my head and then some.'

'Drink doesn't change anything, O'Connor. Whatever troubles you have, they'll still be there in the morning.'

'I know that only too well.'

'For what it's worth,' Kate sat down opposite him again, 'anything you tell me will be in the strictest confidence.'

'Am I one of your clients now?' And for the first time since he'd arrived, he smiled.

'No, not quite, but I am a friend.'

'Are you, Kate?' He was staring at her now. 'It's just that sometimes, with work and all, it's hard to tell where professionalism ends and friendship begins.'

His words made her uneasy. She knew it wouldn't take a lot for them to cross the line. She wasn't ready for that, not yet. 'Look, O'Connor, why don't you tell me what's been bothering you? No matter how long the two of us sit here, it's not going to feel like the right time.'

'I covered up for a guy.'

The awkward moment had passed. Kate thought about what he had just said. 'What guy?'

'A young fella. He was brought into the station a few months back.'

'Arrested?'

'No, brought in for questioning. He had no priors.'

'How did you cover up for him exactly?'

'Do you remember Donoghue?'

'The bookman on the Devine and Spain case?'

'That's the one.'

'What about him?'

'It was his son. He managed to get himself into a bit of trouble.'

'What kind of trouble?'

'He fell for some young one.'

'O'Connor, I'm not quite following you. What has the love life of Donoghue's son got to do with you?'

'It should have nothing to do with me, but Donoghue got me involved. The girl wanted to press charges.' O'Connor looked down at his feet. 'Donoghue said there had been a misunderstanding. Both kids got drunk at a house party, the inevitable happened, the girl, he said, must have regretted it afterwards … and his son was a good kid, never in trouble with the law.' O'Connor looked up at Kate. 'He said he knew it would shake him up – if the charges went anywhere. An innocent teenager marked for life.'

'The girl said he raped her. Is that what you're telling me, O'Connor?'

'Donoghue said it was consensual. It just got a bit out of hand. Donoghue thinks both of them were given, or had taken, something at the party. The boy knocked the girl about a bit.'

'It doesn't sound consensual to me, O'Connor.'

'I know it fucking doesn't. The point is, Kate, when Donoghue approached me, he said I was the only one he could trust with it. He needed it sorted. All I had to do was apply a bit of pressure on the girl, point out the complications involved, how hard it would be for anything to be proven – you know, her word against his kind of thing.'

Kate purposely kept her voice calm, knowing that if she came over top heavy with O'Connor now, he would close up shop completely. 'Why did you cover it up, O'Connor? Why didn't you tell Donoghue that there wasn't anything you could do?'

'I met the boy.'

'And?'

'And he was a mess, nervous as hell. He looked like a good kid, exactly as Donoghue had described him, quiet, nerdy and bright. He had his whole life ahead of him, and these things can fuck up a guy's head.'

'Not to mention a girl's.' Kate's voice was low. 'So what happened next? Something tells me this isn't the end of the story.'

'No, Kate. It's not the bloody end.' O'Connor stood up. 'I made a fucking wrong call.'

'How do you mean?'

'Two months later the kid was pulled in again.'

'Another accusation of rape?' Kate couldn't keep the shock out of her voice.

'Yeah.' O'Connor looked straight at her, his voice strained. 'This time the girl was badly beaten up. You should have seen her, Kate. Only an animal could have done it to her.'

'Did you approach Donoghue?'

'What would have been the point? We both knew we'd got it wrong. It was his son charged, not mine.'

'When is the case up?'

'Not for another month. Hennessy was assigned to the second case. He has his suspicions, I know. Someone told him I interviewed the boy earlier on.'

'Did he ask you about it?'

'Yeah.'

'And what did you say?'

'I shrugged it off as nothing. With no official charges pressed, there's nothing on record.'

'You're going to come clean now?'

'I haven't made my mind up.'

'You don't have a choice, O'Connor.' Kate could hear anger seeping into her voice.

'Look, Kate, I totally fucked up, I know that. Why do you think I've been killing myself over the bloody thing?' His anger was bursting out of him, and she could see he'd been bottling it up for some time. 'Kate, if I hadn't leaned on the first girl, the second attack wouldn't have happened.'

'Glad you can see that, O'Connor.' It was her turn to stand up. 'You have to come clean. You have to go to Butler, tell him what happened.' All she could think of was the two girls. No matter how fucked up O'Connor's head was at that moment, it was nothing to what those girls were going through.

'You think I've been a prick, don't you, Kate?'

'Yes, if you want me to be honest.'

'Honesty is overrated.' There was a reluctant sarcasm in his reply.

'You don't get it, O'Connor, do you?'

'Get what?'

'What either of those girls must have gone through.'

'I guess that would be impossible for me, Kate, being a man. It's played on my mind. Jesus Christ, has it played on my mind.'

'So what stopped you going straight to Butler the moment you discovered your mistake?'

'I don't know.'

'Weak answer. I'm not buying it.'

'I could lose everything.'

'Your career, you mean.'

'I suppose you could call it that. It's what I do. It's the reason I get out of bed in the morning, to catch the bad guys.'

'And now you're one of them.' Her tone was judgemental.

'Thanks for not sugar-coating your answer.'

She could tell he was hurting, but hurt came with that kind of territory. 'O'Connor, I know you're not a bad person. This was out of character for you. You thought you were helping a friend, but a girl has been raped, and your actions were partly responsible for it happening again. No matter how you try to dress this up, there's no getting away from that.'

Kate was so wrapped up in their conversation that she didn't hear

Charlie's bedroom door opening or his footsteps as he entered the kitchen.

'Mum?' He looked as if he was about to cry, and he seemed tiny beside O'Connor. Kate needed to get O'Connor out and fast.

'It's all right, darling. Detective O'Connor is just leaving.'

'Kate?'

Kate lifted Charlie into her arms. 'Listen, you're not stupid. You know the right thing to do.'

'It doesn't make it any easier.'

'Get a good night's sleep. We can talk tomorrow.'

'I'll let myself out. You put this chap back to bed.' O'Connor attempted a smile at Charlie.

Charlie buried his face in his mother's neck.

Kate was relieved to hear O'Connor pull the front door of the apartment closed behind him. Charlie wasn't happy about being put back into bed. Nor, Kate reflected, would he have been happy to find his mother talking to a man other than his father in the early hours of the morning.

Clodagh

Unless Martin locked me into the house with chains across all the doors and windows, I wouldn't let him, Dominic or anyone else stop me seeing Gerard Hayden this morning. My mind is shifting. I feel close to something.

Martin was suspicious before he left for work – I could see it in his eyes. He was watching my every move. Again last night he didn't come home until very late, and he's yet to explain why he took the photograph, or why our bedroom was cleared of all traces of me, other than an old toothbrush. After I've seen Gerard today, I'm going to take a taxi to Ruby's flat. She doesn't have lectures on Fridays, and if I have to wait there all bloody day to see her, I will. Whatever existed between Martin and me is well and truly over. We'll all need to start working on a future with the two of us apart.

Dominic also rang last night. He, too, is playing it cool. In one way, I don't give a damn about either of them. I care about the frightened little girl who once was me. I need to fight for her, even if I haven't always been capable of it.

Thanks to Orla, I know Martin has listened to the recordings on my phone. Before I leave for Gerard's, I listen to them again, pleased, at least, that he hasn't deleted them.

On the way over to Gerard's in the taxi, Ruby calls. There's something different about her too. She seems less angry. When she asks if I want to meet her tomorrow, I can't wipe the smile off my face. I say, 'That would be great.' It gives me a real boost. Maybe things can be different. Maybe we can start afresh.

The phone call also makes me feel more assured. I even chat to the taxi driver about how cold the weather has turned. I feel like a normal person. But that will soon change.

When I reach Gerard's, I will go back to that point from yesterday. Gerard isn't one to give opinions. He says he needs to be beyond reproach. He can't manipulate my thought processes. But he does more than listen, even if his words are carefully chosen. And I know he believes this is all connected to some trauma, and the darkness I feel exists in my past.

As I get out of the taxi, a sharp breeze nearly knocks me over, pulling me from my thoughts. The same apprehension I felt on that first day gathers inside me, a form of nervous panic. What if this time it doesn't work? I want to go back to that little girl more than anything, but will my conscious mind let me?

Again Gerard answers the door as if he has been waiting for me beside it. Neither of us says anything beyond a simple 'Hello', but I realise I'm walking down the hallway faster than before. He makes no comment, but begins the ritual as he has done on other days, closing the blinds, lighting the candles, asking me if I'm ready to start. Today there is no need for any elongated delivery. It is as if, within seconds of listening to his voice, I'm back where we left off the day before.

'Clodagh, you say you're walking across the landing.'

'I'm following my little-girl self. When she talks, she sounds like Debbie. We're going on an adventure. We're standing at the door to Mum and Dad's bedroom. It's dark, but I can see streetlights coming in from outside.'

'Do you feel safe, Clodagh?'

'Safe?'

'Yes, safe. Are you afraid?'

'I don't know. It's strange.'

'What's strange?'

'Even though I don't know what's going to happen, I know I need to open this door, the one to my parents' bedroom.'

'Remember, Clodagh, the past cannot hurt you. It has all happened before. All we are doing is visiting it. Do you understand me, Clodagh?'

'Yes.' My little-girl self opens the door for me. She struggles with the handle at first, but then it opens, not completely, but enough to see into the room. The slit is narrow, making it hard at first to distinguish who is in there. But then I see both of them. 'I can see my parents,' I hear myself saying.

'Are you inside the room, Clodagh?'

'Not yet, but I'm pushing the door further over. My dad is sitting in the darkest corner of the bedroom. His head is in his hands. He's wearing his favourite pinstripe navy suit, the one with the long straight lines that travel for ever and ever.' I pause. 'He's crying, Gerard.'

'And where is your mother, Clodagh? Where is she?'

'She's standing by the window. She looks tall. She's wearing really high heels. There is a cigarette in her mouth. I can see the mark of her red lipstick on the tip when she takes it out, blowing smoke clouds. Her face is angry, but it's more than angry.'

'You're doing great, Clodagh. Now think hard. What other emotion do you think your mother is feeling?'

I look at her then, really look at her. Past the cigarette smoke, past her beauty, her long neck and lovely hair, tied neatly in a bun. I'm drawn to her eyes, and when I am, my first thought is to look away, for I see what is hiding beyond the anger. It's a form of madness. I've seen it before, when I looked at myself in the mirror, at those times when I felt the most lost, and instead of my own reflection, I saw the warped face of ugliness inside of me.

'My mother is …'

'What is your mother, Clodagh?'

'She looks like she's on the edge.' It's only then that I glance at my little-girl self. She doesn't sound like Debbie any more. She is singing that lullaby again, and when she does, without knowing why, I stare at the cradle in the corner, the one opposite where Dad is crying. I walk over to it, unsure of what I'm going to do or see.

'I need to look into the cradle,' I hear myself saying to Gerard, and all the while, my little-girl self is singing, swinging her arms back and forth as if she's holding a baby doll.

'Do you want to look in the cradle, Clodagh?' Gerard Hayden's voice is my only link with the present.

'I don't have a choice.' My little-girl self takes me by the hand but now she's humming as we walk over to it. She stands back when we're within touching distance, and I step forward. I can hear Dad sobbing. My mother is still standing by the window. Before I look inside the cradle, with its white lace and tiny pink bow at the top, somewhere in my mind I acknowledge a silence that isn't right, but, without looking inside, I know the crib isn't empty.

'She's dead,' I hear my mother hiss. 'Killed.'

'It was an accident, Lavinia. You have to believe that,' my father pleads.

I pull back the pale pink blanket on the top. There is a cool cotton sheet underneath. When I take back the sheet, deep in the shadows from the canopy, I see her.

'Touch her,' my little-girl self says. 'She's still warm.'

I lean inwards, rubbing the back of my hand down the side of her warm cheek. It feels like nothing I've ever touched before, until I remember how I used to do the same thing with Ruby when she was small, over and over again, amazed every time I felt her tiny life,

real, close, intimate and so fragile. But this is different because now
I can feel the life fading. It is drifting to some place from which it
can never come back. It is then that I feel tears filling my eyes. The
first of them trickles down and drops on to her mattress. More than
anything, I want to stop time.

'She's beautiful,' I hear my little-girl self saying, as if my parents
are not there. As if we are the only ones in the room.

'Is she …' I can barely breathe, 'dead?'

'Yes. There was a fight.'

I stare at my little-girl self, wondering why she sounds so calm,
relieved her voice doesn't sound like Desperate Debbie's any more,
and her face is normal.

'Did you see it?' I ask her, the tears now streaming down my face.

Gerard asks if I'm okay. I can't answer him. He belongs to a
different place. He isn't in this room. He isn't inside the doll's house.
He doesn't count, not any more.

'I hid,' she says, 'Debbie knows the truth, but she's not saying.'

'Where did you hide?'

'In my room – the one Sandy and Debbie like to play happy
families in. They told me everything would be okay.'

I hear myself scream inside my head. The scream won't go
away. I try to speak, but no words will come out. Questions repeat
themselves over and over in my mind, as if I'm in a dream and can't
find the answers. But the questions are simple. *Why did she have to
die? Why do I feel I'm to blame?* I can feel my body shaking.

'Clodagh, try to remain calm,' I hear Gerard say. 'Who is dead?'
But again, I don't answer him. Not at first. I'm looking at my little-
girl self, because I know she has something more to say.

'There could only be one Daddy's little girl.'

Mervin Road

Kate hadn't slept well, tossing and turning throughout the night. It was almost a relief to see glimpses of daylight creep into her bedroom on Friday morning. This was beginning to feel like the longest week of her life. Getting out of bed to shower, she couldn't stop thinking about O'Connor from the night before. It was a mess in more ways than one. Charlie waking up was also playing on her mind. What if he told Declan? Did it bloody matter? She knew it did. Just as she knew that she wouldn't have let O'Connor into the apartment at that late hour if Declan had been around. She was already behaving like a single woman, but she was also a mother, and no matter what she felt about O'Connor, or whatever mess he had got himself into, she was that first and foremost.

She switched on the small television in the kitchen. The headlines were still dominated by the canal murders so she changed to a channel showing cartoons. After setting the breakfast table, she checked her watch: seven forty-five, time to wake Charlie. Walking towards his bedroom, Kate felt uneasy. Was it because the temporary adjustment of the two of them alone had turned into a permanent one, or was it the aftermath of the conversation with O'Connor? Of all the people to break the rules, she would never have guessed it would be him. He had always struck her as solid, but he wouldn't be the first, when a personal connection came into play, for whom the rules became guidelines, landing him in a whole lot of trouble. When Kate opened Charlie's bedroom door, she smelt urine, her guilt about O'Connor slapping her in the face. What the hell was she at? She knelt down beside Charlie's bed.

'Come on, Buster. It's time to get up.'

He gave a tiny moan, then turned away from her. Kate pulled together his clothes – clean socks, pants, vest, his school uniform – and fresh sheets for the bed before waking him again. After she'd removed his wet pyjamas, she wrapped him in a large towel. There was barely a peep out of him as she carried him to the bathroom.

With the shower going full throttle, she put the wet bedding and dirty clothes on to wash. She would say nothing to Charlie about it, not when he slurped his cereal or at any other time.

Her mobile rang as she and Charlie were about to head out of the door. It was Hennessy.

'Dr Pearson, we've found a match for the Susie Graham assault.'

'Really? That was fast. Is he known to you?' Kate continued, as she buttoned Charlie's coat.

'It's a guy called Steve McDaid. He's a mechanic, works local. The match is against a suspected assault in Liverpool a few years back. He was over there on a stag weekend.'

'That's good news.'

'I'm pulling him in for questioning today. If I see any connection with your case, I'll let you know.'

'That would be great, Stuart. I have to go, but do call me.'

On the drive to school, Kate caught a glimpse of Charlie yawning in the back seat. She smiled to herself, thinking about his teacher, young Ms Nolan, and what she had in store for her, with twenty-nine other five-year-olds to contend with on this wet and murky morning.

Looking at the other mothers and fathers at the school gates, all getting ready to pick up their work and home lives once their children were safely deposited at school, Kate decided to use her time driving to Ocean House wisely. She made numerous phone calls, including setting up another follow-up meeting with Imogen Willis, then finally she dialled O'Connor.

He was on the back foot from the beginning. 'Kate, look, about last night.'

'Last night was last night, O'Connor. You know my feelings on the matter.'

'I'm sorry for waking Charlie.'

'I know you are. Now, listen, I'm heading into Ocean House. When is your next full squad meeting?'

'The usual, ten o'clock.'

'Good. Ring me with anything you have. I've a crazy schedule today, but I want you to get in touch as soon as you make contact with Dominic Hamilton, and Martin and Clodagh McKay.'

'Lynch is setting up the meetings now. I'm sorry again about last night.'

'No need to be. Look, O'Connor, I don't mean to sound harsh, but do the right bloody thing.'

'I'm working on it.'

'I'd better go.'

'Talk later, Kate.'

'By the way, I've emailed you my follow-up report based on our conversation last night.'

'I appreciate that, Kate.'

'No problem. It's what I do.'

Parking outside Ocean House, she thought about their conversation, and how much she needed O'Connor to do the right thing, regardless of the repercussions. She also knew she was giving him time to make up his mind. Would she report the incident, if he didn't? A part of her wasn't sure. She'd said he could talk to her in confidence, but that was before she'd known what she was agreeing to. If she had to, she would report it. She had no other choice. Certain lessons in life were hard learned. They had a habit of staying with you, no matter how many years passed. She had been younger than the latest victims when she was attacked. She also thought about her conversation with Stuart Hennessy. It would help Susie Graham to know the identity of her attacker if only because it would be one less unanswered question – a question to which, after all these years, Kate still had no answer. It led her to look into every sea of strangers, knowing one of them could be him.

Clodagh

Tears are blocking my vision and I'm stammering, 'But – but – I would have loved her, I know I would.'

'It's not your fault, Clodagh.' She sounds as if she is the adult and I am the child. 'Emmaline wasn't Daddy's little girl. She belonged to somebody else. She wouldn't have been right here. Not with us.'

I can hear Gerard's voice. He's asking me again, 'Clodagh, who is dead?'

'Emmaline,' I say.

'How did she die?' he asks, as if it is the most normal question in the world.

I look around the room. My mother stands rigid by the window. My father sits, with his head bent, in the corner. Then I look back to the crib. My little-girl self is swinging the cradle, singing the lullaby again.

'It's okay, Clodagh,' I hear her say. 'She likes me to sing to her. It helps her to sleep.' I hear Gerard's voice. Again he is asking how the baby died.

How did Emmaline die? I find it hard to get the words out. If I say them my whole world may tumble. Instead I scream, 'I don't know, I don't know.'

'Do you want to come back, Clodagh?'

I look to where my mother is standing. I hear her voice, low, stern and without pity: 'I will never forgive you,' she says, and I'm not sure who she is talking to, me or my father.

'Clodagh, can you hear me? Do you want to come back?'

I stare at my father. His face is no longer in his hands. He is looking at me, then at my mother. He is trying to say something, but his words are stuck. I see the frown lines on his forehead, regret in his eyes, his stooped, beaten frame, and I feel his pain. It is weighing me down too. It is like a giant albatross across our shoulders.

'Clodagh, I am taking you back, do you hear me?'

'Yes.'

'I'll start counting backwards from ten, and when I do, you will leave the bedroom. You will leave the doll's house. You will find the staircase that led you there, coming back into the garden.'

Incident Room, Harcourt Street Police Station

O'Connor, followed by Lynch, entered the incident room with more on his mind than the current investigation. He'd taken certain things for granted, until he'd risked losing them. Butler, regardless of hostile outbursts, had an underlying admiration for O'Connor. How you earned your stripes within the force meant more than your position. It was a reflection of years of hard graft and accomplishment. It could easily go down the tubes once O'Connor came clean.

But the height of an investigation wasn't the time for guilty reflection. Despite his thumping headache, O'Connor had a job to do and, no matter how this whole saga turned out, he was damned if he wasn't going to be up to the task in hand. Whatever repercussions came afterwards, he would have to deal with them. Kate was right in practically everything she had said. But he had never expected her to be any other way.

Matthews got the proceedings under way. 'Right, O'Connor, fill us in.'

'We should have a list of owners of the Volvo model in the next hour.'

'Anything more from Dr Pearson?' Again the question came from Matthews.

'She's sent an updated report, which includes observations about the perpetrator, and potential geographical area.'

'Seeing as I don't have a copy in front of me,' Butler, keen to get his spoke in, 'perhaps you'd be good enough to fill us all in.'

'Considering both men knew each other, the probability of

them knowing their attacker is rated by Dr Pearson as high. This has given us a sub-set within the wider circle. The relationship between Gahan and Jenkins went back a long way. We'll be talking to Dominic Hamilton, Clodagh McKay and her husband, Martin McKay, today. As you know, we've already spoken to Gahan's sister, Deborah, all immediate members of Jenkins's family and Alister Becon. Alister Becon was the last person to see Adrian Hamilton alive.'

'You still think this is all connected, do you, O'Connor?'

'Yes, boss, I do. We still have security in place on Jenkins's house and Deborah Gahan's.'

'Bloody logistical nightmare.' Butler's words required no response. 'Get back to what Dr Pearson has given you.'

'She believes the drowning is critical, and could be a form of cleansing.'

Matthews sat up straighter in his chair. 'Anything else from her?'

'Our killer is older and therefore more calculating. Despite this, he's willing to take risks. His fear of being caught is outweighed by his needs.'

'What does she mean by "his needs"?'

'She thinks he could be rating his victims in order of importance, keeping his most significant victim until last. Of course, there's every possibility that Gahan was the final victim, but we can't be sure.'

'I see.' Butler sounded deadpan now.

'Dr Pearson has also narrowed down the geographical location. She believes the perpetrator is operating in a physical area with which he is both familiar and comfortable. It could be the area where he is currently living or working, or one he has been connected to in the past. Based on this, I'm intensifying the house-to-house enquiries around the stretch of the canal three bridges back and three forward.

Once we get the list of possible vehicle registrations and owners, we can start picking up other connections.'

'I want to know how you get on with Hamilton and the McKays.' Butler looked across at Matthews to log the follow-up. 'Where do they all live, O'Connor?'

'The outskirts of Sandymount, boss.'

'What? All of them?'

'That's right.'

'It's not far from either crime scene.'

'No, boss, it isn't.'

'Car models? I assume you'd tell us if there were any matches.'

'Dominic Hamilton's doesn't match. We're checking the others.'

'It doesn't rule him out, though.'

'No.'

'Anything else, O'Connor?'

'Considering what Dr Pearson has said, the house-to-house enquiries will be extended to the area around the Hamilton and McKay homes. Both, as I said, in Sandymount.'

'Right. Hold back nothing on the house-to-house.' Butler turned to Matthews. 'We have the model of vehicle for *Crimecall*. Has that been set up?'

'It's scheduled for this evening.'

'O'Connor, keep us posted during the day. Where's Stapleton?'

'Here, boss.' Stapleton waved from the back of the room.

'You're in charge of the press. Feed those guys exactly what we want them to hear. Officially we're following some definite lines of enquiry. Acknowledge that Gahan and Jenkins knew each other. The link should calm public anxiety, at least the jitters of anyone who didn't know the men. It might shake some others.' Butler looked around the room. 'We need to get some more answers. Good ones.

That means asking the right questions. Get out there and do what you do.'

If the rumours about Butler seeking a future career in journalism were true, O'Connor couldn't help but wonder if his attitude would change once he was on the other side of the fence. Right now, the only news Butler wanted was good news, and faster than he'd been getting it.

Ringsend

The police pulled Stevie in this morning. I know because I followed him to work. He didn't look so pretty in the face. Even if getting the shit beaten out of him is nothing unusual for Lover Boy.

He seemed shocked at first but he composed himself quickly. He'll play it cool. Stevie was always the one with the cool head, streetwise, crap-wise, and capable of reading folks, especially their weaknesses.

Stevie doesn't know that I know about his little run-in with Clodagh all those years back. I make it my business to know these things. Just as I made it my business to keep my eye on him. Some things are best handled by you alone.

McDaid being dragged in isn't going to cause any change to my plans. He's another pawn in this game of chess. The next marker feels safe right now. He thinks he's off-limits. But no one is. It won't be long now, and then it will be Clodagh's turn. One should always keep the best till last.

They'll have to be taken down close to one another. Anything else is too risky. I can't take the chance of anyone working out my game plan. Not until everything is sorted exactly as it should be and precisely as I planned it. Destiny is funny, the way it has a whole momentum of its own.

Clodagh

When I come back from my regression, the first words out of my mouth are 'The dolls know the killer.'

'You're talking about Emmaline?' Gerard puts his thumb and index finger into his eyes, as if he is trying to think clearer.

'Yes. Who else would I be talking about?'

'What makes you think someone killed her, Clodagh?'

'My mother said so, when I was inside the doll's house. Only I don't know who she was blaming.'

'Explain to me how you felt when I was bringing you back.'

'I felt like I was being pulled out of the room, sucked out of the darkness. I thought about the people I was leaving behind, my father, my mother, my little-girl self and the baby, that they were all trapped inside the doll's house.'

'And when you reached the staircase, the one leading to the garden, how did you feel then, Clodagh?'

'The emotion felt enormous. I could barely hear you. When I got back to the garden, I could smell the sweet scent of summer flowers, then the faintest smell of vanilla candle wax. And then …'

'And then what, Clodagh?'

'I heard sounds coming from outside. A car passing by and the click of the gate.'

'The gate outside?'

'Yes.'

Gerard stood up. 'But I'm not expecting anyone.'

'Maybe I was mistaken.' I start to shake. Gerard puts a blanket around me. He tells me this often happens. That my body is coming to terms with the emotions involved.

I say again, 'Gerard, the dolls know,' calm and clear.

'Clodagh, the dolls are an extension of you. You do understand that?'

'Yes, I suppose so.'

'If there are answers, you already know them. You simply can't remember them. It's as straightforward as that.'

The shaking has stopped, but he asks me to remain lying down.

'Gerard, is it possible I'm mistaken? Could I have imagined it all?'

'It's possible.'

'But you said memories are stored completely intact in our subconscious. They're more reliable than actual recall because our conscious mind alters memory over time. It adds in layers.'

'I did say that, Clodagh, and it's true, but the mind is fragile.'

'Meaning?'

'As I explained before, in hypnosis one has to be careful not to manipulate.'

'Do you think you've manipulated me?'

'Perhaps I've influenced you, inadvertently used the power of suggestion. I make a point of avoiding asking leading questions but outside influences can play their role too.'

I think about finding that old photograph, the one with my father and his old college friends. How, after Keith Jenkins's murder, I'd seen his face at the door of my doll's house.

'Could I have superimposed images or ideas on my memory?'

'Perhaps. It happens, especially if a client is under duress.'

'I see.'

'Clodagh, do you want to talk about the things you remember from the regression?'

'I'm not sure.' He waits, not wanting to rush me. The fear I felt is still close. It was all-consuming. The world of the doll's house was more real than the here and now. 'Gerard, it didn't feel imagined.'

'You have to realise, Clodagh, in your case, when you regress, your adult mind is there but so, too, it seems, is the mind of your younger self. In part, you're looking at things through the eyes of a seven-year-old. Any number of influences could be brought to bear in how childhood perception comes to be. Whatever your younger self believes she witnessed may not be true. When you're a child, some things are hard to grasp. Your mind can force a solution, or an understanding, a shortcut of the truth.'

'So it can't be trusted, this truth?'

'It's a different kind of truth. But it's all you have right now. Ultimately, the hope is that, with your adult self being present during the regression, the true picture will unravel.'

'When I regressed, Gerard, did I regress to an actual memory or an imaginary one?'

'What you experienced most likely did happen. It wasn't a dream but, as I've already said, it seems to be coming from a child's point of view. It has to be taken in the context of a seven-year-old mind.'

'But what my mother said, about the baby being killed, why would I remember that if it wasn't true?'

'I wish I could help you, Clodagh, tell you which parts can be relied upon and which cannot, but within your regression, there is a form of truth. We simply need to find the correct roadmap to it.'

'Can I tell you something else, Gerard?'

'What?'

'It's hard to explain.'

'I'm a good listener.' He smiles. 'Helps with the territory.'

'I keep thinking about why I came here in the first place.'

'Go on.'

'I thought it was to understand why the relationship between my mother and me was so difficult, to explain the barrier between us, and why I turned to alcohol for escape.'

'I know that.'

'The death of my sister could explain it. Perhaps my mother wasn't able to love me because she'd suffered such a huge loss.'

'It certainly sounds reasonable, Clodagh.'

'But I don't feel that's all of it. You see, there have been times over the last while, during my regression and in part through memory recall, that I ...'

'You what, Clodagh?'

I stare past Gerard, concentrating on the candle still burning by the window, the tiny flame swaying, changing colour and shape. 'That I think about the way she looked at me.'

'Your mother?'

'Yes.' I continue looking at the flame. 'It's as if everything that happened is somehow my fault. And that's not all.'

'What?'

'It's to do with the boys.'

'The boys?'

'Yes.' I sit up. 'Martin, Dominic and a boy called Stevie McDaid.'

'What about them?'

'I heard them whispering. We were all in the attic.'

'This is from memory, Clodagh?'

'Yes. It was when I went to our old house with Dominic.'

'Go on.'

'I felt frightened. I can't remember any more, but it feels connected.'

'Clodagh?'

'Yes?'

'There is something else we could try.'

'What?'

'During the previous session, not the one today but before, your conscious mind resisted the regression. It forced me to use an alternative method. I had to endeavour to overload it, tire the conscious mind, before the use of tapping on the forehead to shock it into subconscious regression.'

'So?'

'We could try to regress again but this time use the format from our previous session. We could attempt to pinpoint the regression in a very specific way.'

'How do you mean?'

'Direct you to the root cause of your childhood distress.'

'Around the death of my sister?'

'Perhaps, or it could turn out to be something else entirely. It's a risk, Clodagh, and one you must be fully sure you want to try. The truth could turn out to be extremely difficult. We're entering this blind.'

'Not knowing, Gerard, can be a whole lot worse.'

'I appreciate that, Clodagh. It's up to you.'

'Can we attempt it now?'

'Yes, if you want to. As I said, I'm not expecting anyone else today.'

'Okay, then. Let's try it.'

'Clodagh, can I ask you something else?'

'Of course.'

'How did you get here today? Did you come alone?'

'Yes. Why do you ask?'

Ocean House, the Quays

Kate hadn't heard back from O'Connor after the incident-room briefing. She thought about phoning him but decided against it. If he had something to tell her, he would have called.

The black-and-white photograph of her and Charlie stared at her from the desk. It spoke volumes. She checked the time. Imogen Willis was due shortly. She reviewed her case notes on the Jenkins and Gahan killings again, knowing the specific area she wanted to concentrate on: the sense of reward that the drowning offered the killer.

If the method of killing far outweighed the risks, was this a one-way trip? One that the killer had no intention of ever coming back from? If so, the possibility only pointed one way: personal destruction.

Kate considered O'Connor's interpretation of Becon. He wasn't a man to get his own hands dirty. He was capable of using others. If he had been involved with Jenkins's shaky financial dealings, the prospect of proving it, considering his level of power and protection, would be difficult, but there was more at stake here than money.

She had started to question the possibility of psychosis in the murders. In the public domain, there was often confusion between psychopathic and psychotic behaviour. In reality, they were poles apart. At extreme levels of psychosis, there were serious mental disorders, like schizophrenia, but as with all mental illnesses, it could take varying forms. It was often brought on by severe depression, disintegration of personality, and sometimes resulted in grossly distorted thoughts, perceptions and heightened levels of anxiety. All these factors could be bubbling over in the killer, including how and why he arrived at this juncture.

Kate heard a low tap on the door: Imogen. 'Come in,' she called from her desk. When the door opened, Kate saw instantly that she was distressed. 'Close the door, Imogen. Come and sit down.'

'Thanks.'

'Are you okay? Can I get you a drink of water? You look a little pale.'

'No, I'm fine. Actually, no, I'm not fine.'

'Let's start nice and easy. Take your time. When you're ready, you can tell me what happened.'

Imogen wasn't in the mood for waiting. 'When I woke up this morning, I thought it was two days ago.'

'You mean you got the days mixed up?'

'No. I lost two days. Forty-eight hours gone.'

'You can't remember any of it?'

'Nothing.' Panic rising in her voice. 'I went down to the kitchen, and Jilly started to ask me stuff, and I had no idea what she was talking about. Kate, I can't even remember coming in here with my parents and sister. Jilly told me we did, but I don't remember it.'

'Don't worry, Imogen. Calm down. We'll work this out.'

'Okay.'

'What is the last thing you remember, before you lost the two days?'

'I was with my friend Alicia.'

'Where?'

'At her house. We were using her laptop, chatting on Facebook.'

'Were you relaxed?'

'Yeah, I was grand. Alicia was in great form too.'

'What were you talking about?'

'Different things.'

'Give me an example.'

'How cute Harry from One Direction is.' Imogen managed a smile.

'What else?'

'Alicia talked about her sister. She's away in London, but she's coming home. They're very close.'

'When is her sister due back from London?'

'I don't know. I can't remember. I remember her saying her sister was coming home, and after that I remember nothing.'

'Imogen, do you recall what we spoke about before, about how disassociating yourself from events can happen?'

'Yes.'

'I think it's possible that when Alicia was talking about her sister, you lost yourself for a while. Something triggered it, but we can't be sure what.'

'Do you think it has anything to do with me and Jilly? I mean we're close, like Alicia and her sister.'

'It could be. The important thing, Imogen, is not to let this upset you.'

'It's hard, Kate.'

'I know it is, but you're on the right track.'

'Do you think so?' Imogen sounded unsure.

'Yes, you'll have to trust me. It will come back. It's just a matter of time.'

∞

Shortly after Imogen had left, Kate phoned O'Connor. The more she thought about the killings, the more the influence of psychosis made sense. If Becon was a driving force, considering what O'Connor had told her about their conversation, it was unlikely that he was the one in any kind of psychotic state.

If psychosis was involved, it tied in with the killer not functioning within his normal routine. It would be practically impossible for him to do so. The signs should be obvious to those near to him.

O'Connor was quick to answer. 'Kate, I was about to phone you.'

'I need you to examine the behaviour patterns of the key players we know of, starting with Dominic Hamilton and Martin McKay.'

'Kate?'

'What?' Kate didn't like the sound of O'Connor's response.

'Hamilton's missing.'

'How do you mean, missing?'

'He didn't go home last night. Lynch spoke to his wife, Valerie, about ten minutes ago. It seems he's been taking a lot of time off work. His wife felt he had been originally working too hard, but she was also worried that he might be depressed.'

'And she has no idea where he is?'

'They've barely talked the last number of days. She's been trying to convince him to get help.'

'Did his wife say anything else, mention any signs of pent-up aggression, self-harming?'

'Not that Lynch said.'

'Can I talk to her, O'Connor?'

'I'll get Lynch to give you her number, but there's something else.'

'What?'

'It seems Hamilton and you have something in common.'

'What's that?'

'You both enjoy the occasional run.'

'Pushing his body hard?'

'It's where he does his occasional running that's important.'

'Don't tell me – the canal?'

'That's right.'

'Damn it, O'Connor, maybe we should have connected all this before now.'

'He's matching the profile. Strong links to the area, outward signs of life falling apart. He knew both victims.'

'O'Connor.'

'Yeah?'

'If it is Hamilton, and he's been pushed over the line, it could have been his mother's death, but it feels like more than that. As I said before, she might have said something before she died or perhaps someone else did.'

'Whatever, Kate, either way, he's in my sights.'

'What about Martin McKay?'

'I've sent a car to his office in town.'

'You need to tread carefully.'

'I always do.'

'Listen to me for a second. There's a strong possibility that, whoever the killer is, he's suffering from some form of psychosis.'

'You mean he's nuts?'

'Let's stick to the medical term, shall we? If the killer is psychotic, he's most likely only heading one way at this point.'

'What's that?'

'Self-destruction.'

'You're talking suicide?'

'If Dominic Hamilton is unaccounted for, and he turns out to be the killer, you need to remember he hasn't an awful lot left to lose. He's risked it all already. But that isn't the thing that's worrying me most.'

'What is?'

'If he hasn't already attempted suicide, as I said the other night, there's every chance he has another victim in mind, and he won't be capable of waiting a protracted interval either.'

Clodagh

Gerard Hayden's face looks troubled. The longer he takes to answer me, the more apprehensive I feel. 'What is it, Gerard?'

'Someone called to see me the other day, a man. He told me he was your brother.'

'Dominic?'

'Yes. He expressed concern for your welfare, advised me to treat you carefully, that you were—'

'That I was what?' My voice is suddenly louder, angry.

'He said that you are somewhat delicate. He used the word "disturbed".'

'And what did you say?'

'Well, naturally, Clodagh, I needed to take his concerns on board.'

'What did you tell him?'

'Not a lot. Nothing he didn't already know. My primary responsibility is to you, which is why I'm telling you this now. If we're to continue, I don't want any side issues getting in the way.'

'I see.' The thought that Dominic had been meddling, talking to Gerard behind my back, feels like he's taken something without my permission. The same way Martin has in the past. Did Dominic follow me here? Otherwise how would he have found Gerard Hayden's house? Perhaps Valerie gave him the address. 'I need your word, Gerard, that if we're to continue, anything I reveal to you is kept between ourselves.' I'm surprised by the strength in my voice.

'You have it, Clodagh. It's important that you trust me.'

'I don't know that I can trust anyone, Gerard. Not any more. But it doesn't matter. The only thing that matters is going back, finding out what happened, and if I had anything to do with it.'

'Clodagh, do you want to continue?'

I can still see the concern on Gerard's face. 'I don't have any choice.'

'Right then, Clodagh. Let's start.'

I look at the first candle Gerard lit, and as I count backwards, I can't get the image of the flame out of my mind. I feel the same resistance by my conscious mind. A part of me doesn't want to let go. Is it because I don't trust Gerard now, or is it because I'm afraid?

'Clodagh, can you still hear me?'

'Gerard, it's not working.'

'It will, don't worry. Relax as much as you can. Keep your eyes closed. Clodagh, I'm going to talk you through complete physical relaxation from the tips of your toes to the top of your head. Each step along the way, another part of you will relax, until your body is ready to let your mind follow.'

It's a relief to physically let go. To feel my body become limp and loose, willing my mind to do the same. Again Gerard needs to change the game plan, first by asking me to count backwards, then counting forward to thirty-seven, moving my eyes from right to left, and back again. It's harder to let go, now I know what to expect. Gerard asks me to open my eyes, to concentrate on a point on the ceiling above me. When I do, I realise he's doing the counting, mixing up the numbers, skipping forward and then backwards again. When I least expect it he taps me twice on the forehead, and on the second contact, I feel my mind racing. Almost instinctually, I close my eyes, unsure of where I will end up.

'Can you still hear me, Clodagh?'

'Yes.' My voice is so low I can barely hear it.

'Where are you?'

'I'm falling, down, down. It's dark, black. I'm so afraid. I don't like this feeling. I don't want to be here.'

'Where are you?'

'At home in Seacrest. The dolls are here.'

'Which dolls?'

'Sandy and Debbie. They're sitting under the blackboard.'

'Can you see your younger self?'

'Yes, but it feels wrong.'

'How is it wrong?'

'Nobody is talking. I have scissors, small hand scissors. I'm cutting off my dolls' hair.'

'Why are you doing that, Clodagh?'

'I don't want them to be pretty any more. Their hair is scattered beneath them, like falling leaves. Sandy looks so sad. Her lips are drooping. But Debbie's different.'

'How is she different?'

'Her eyes are angry, wild. "You'll be sorry," I hear her say.'

'Clodagh, what are you feeling?'

'I still feel frightened. I don't understand what's happening. It's like a bad dream I can't wake up from.'

'I want you to go further back, Clodagh. Go back to the first time you felt frightened.'

I have a sense of falling again, tumbling through time and memory.

'Where are you now, Clodagh?'

'I'm with my father.'

'Are the two of you alone?'

'No, there are others here.'

'And where is here?'

'We're on the strand at Sandymount. The tide is coming in. My seven-year-old legs wobble, feet sinking into the sand, seaweed between my toes. In my arms I hold a doll, with curly blonde hair and sea-blue eyes.'

'Breathe easy, Clodagh.'

'It is neither night nor day; the light is white, sparse, as if, like memory, it can be whisked away …'

'Keep going, Clodagh.'

'A cold breeze batters my face, exploding into my ears. I see my father. Against the sea and the sky he stands, trouser legs rolled up, chalk-white skin. He is smiling at me, the centre of my canvas. I wonder about his voice. I try to hear him, even a whisper, but I hear nothing. I scream, the wind cutting out the sound, swallowing my sobs.'

'Try to slow down. Why are you screaming, Clodagh?' Gerard's voice remains calm.

'I'm afraid I'm going to lose him.'

'How?'

'I don't know. That he'll leave us, my mother, Dominic and me. I want to run out to him, but someone's stopping me. They're holding me back.'

'Can you look up, Clodagh? Can you see who's holding you back?'

'My father turns away from me, looking into the ocean. He has his back to me as the ice-cold water eats his feet …'

'Clodagh, listen to me. You need to look up. You need to tell me who is holding you back.'

Harcourt Street Police Station

'Kate, when you say he isn't capable of waiting a protracted interval, what kind of time frame are you talking about – days, hours?'

'The gap between the Jenkins and Gahan murders was less than three days. The first murder took place in the early hours of Saturday morning, with Gahan's killing late Monday night. He's already allowed a lengthier timeframe to elapse. My guess is he won't wait much longer. If it's a form of psychosis, the progression will be gaining momentum as each day passes. He might have been capable of managing the second murder with reasonable efficiency, but as time moves on, the level of his anxiety will heighten, and the disintegration of his personality will continue, as will his grossly distorted thoughts. Once the first killing occurred, everything would have changed for him. Things will have accelerated. It's impossible to say how long, other than that the time will be short, within days, I would imagine, and maybe even hours.'

'Kate, can you hold on? I've a call coming in. Don't go away.'

Kate bit her lip as she waited.

O'Connor was soon back. 'Something's come in on the house-to-house.'

'What?'

'Once you narrowed down the geographical reference, we extended the parameters to include the neighbourhood around the Hamilton and McKay households. One of Martin McKay's neighbours mentioned a car arriving home at unusual hours of the morning.'

'When?'

'Over the last few days. Martin McKay's name is also on the list of the 2010 Volvo S60 owners.'

'Do you have enough to get a search warrant?'

'I think so, but the concept of reasonable grounds depends on which judge is sitting. Matthews has it in train.'

'What about a search warrant for Dominic Hamilton's house?'

'You know how these things work, Kate. If we get anything useful back from the first location, it will help us move the search further out.'

'Where are Clodagh and Martin McKay now?'

'I've sent a reconnaissance team to the McKay and Hamilton houses along with the one I've sent to McKay's office. Right now, McKay isn't in either location, but that's not unusual. He often has business meetings outside the office. Neighbours say they saw him leave the house earlier today. Clodagh McKay also went out this morning, some time after the husband. With the recon team in place, if either of the McKays or Dominic Hamilton shows up, we'll know about it.'

'O'Connor, it's imperative that I talk to Valerie Hamilton and Clodagh McKay. I need to assess the mental state of both men, and there's no better way than talking to those closest to them.'

'As I promised, Kate, as soon as I hang up, I'll get Lynch to ring you with Valerie Hamilton's number. Clodagh McKay isn't answering her phone, but you'll get that number too. If there are any issues with them agreeing to talk to you, let me know.'

'Okay.'

'Right now my priority is pulling both men in. You can do all the psychoanalysis you want on them. I doubt you'll have any problem with Valerie Hamilton, now that her husband has gone AWOL. Having said that, I don't want you making private visits to any of the locations, not until the recon teams have established all the risks involved.'

'O'Connor, I want to be kept in the loop.'

'You will be.'

Clodagh

I know Gerard wants me to look up, but my younger self is resisting. She's frightened. Her feet are sinking further into the sand, as if they're being swallowed by the seaweed. The smell of the sea is getting stronger, the sound of seagulls squawking overhead. I'm not sure if she will look up, but then she does, and I can see with her eyes.

There's no denying the face or her expression. It's a look of accusation. 'Gerard, I can see who's holding me back.'

'Who is it, Clodagh?'

'It's my mother.'

'Are you sure?'

'Yes. She's looking down at me. It isn't a nice look, or a loving one. I think she hates me. Her eyes move from me to my father, as he walks further away. The further he walks, the smaller he becomes, just like a figure from my doll's house.'

'Clodagh, you're crying. Remember, at all times you're safe. This is simply a memory.'

I feel my mind drifting, as if it's trying hard to stop me staying on the strand. As if I need to get as far away from there as soon as I can. It is then I begin to fall again, and a part of me is wondering – Will I ever stop?

'Clodagh, are you okay?'

'No.'

'What's wrong?'

'I'm falling. My mind is falling but …'

'But what, Clodagh?'

'I think I'm back at home.'

'At the house in Sandymount?'

'Yes. I'm with my father.'

'What are you doing, Clodagh?'

'I'm looking outside my bedroom. My eyes are fixed on the landing light. I see my reflection in the landing mirror. My eyes look like dolls' eyes, as if they're made of glass, rolling inside my head. My father is standing in the darkness at the back of their bedroom.'

'Your mum and dad's room?'

'Yes. My little-girl self is there. She's walking over to him, slowly, but with determination. She looks older than her years. He bends down, allows my little-girl self to whisper something in his ear.'

'What did she whisper?' Again Gerard's voice is calm.

'I don't know.' I feel agitated. 'I can't hear what she's saying. Gerard, I can't hear her.' My voice is rising. More than anything I want to know what she's telling him. I can see his face change, anger replacing softness. My little-girl self pulls away from him as he stands upright again, leaving the room.

'What's happening, Clodagh?'

'We're alone, my little-girl self and I.'

'You can ask her what she told him. The answer is there, Clodagh.'

I walk closer to her. Her eyes are now like the glass eyes of a doll. 'What did you tell him? What did you whisper in his ear?'

At first I think she isn't going to say anything, as if she's trying to make up her mind whether she should trust me. It's then that my voice changes again, to her voice, and I hear my younger self saying, 'I told you, the dolls know. Go ask Debbie.'

I look around the room for her.

'What's happening, Clodagh?' I hear Gerard ask.

'I'm looking for Debbie.'

'Is she there?'

'I see her now. She's standing at the door, blocking my way out. She's laughing, and her hair is cropped.'

'ARE YOU CURIOUS, CLODAGH?' She laughs again.

'What did I tell him?'

'You told him Dominic knows a big secret about Mummy.'

My body starts convulsing in the chair. I feel as if I'm caught in a nightmare. My mind is going around in circles, so many questions without answers.

'Clodagh, breathe deeply. I want you to concentrate on your breathing. Slow it down. As you notice it slowing, you will begin to relax. Can you try that?' Gerard's steady voice feels calming.

'I think so.' I can still sense my anxiety, but when I do as Gerard asks, it seems as though I'm putting a wall between me and the fear of not knowing what will happen next.

'Clodagh, do you want me to bring you back?' Gerard's voice is a constant, a safety net, my tentative link to the present.

'No. I think I'm okay. I need to keep going.' This time it's my voice I hear, not that of my younger self. She is drifting, moving further away from me, but then she turns again, looking at me. She's waving, telling me to follow her.

'Clodagh, what's happening now?'

'We're going somewhere else, and there are loud voices, adult voices, noise coming from downstairs, and all the lights are on. It's late. I'm not supposed to be up. There are lots of people in the house.' I'm talking fast, as if I need to get all the words out quickly. 'The little girl is taking me across the landing, to Dominic's bedroom. Somebody's in there. I'm holding Emma under my arm. I mean, my little-girl self is holding her. She's my doll with the cracked face. Emma's hair is dangling upside down.'

'Who is in Dominic's room, Clodagh?'

'It's dark. It's hard to make them out, but there are things falling to the floor. The drum set in the corner is making a loud clanging noise – something's crashed against it. I can hear a man's voice. He's saying, 'For fuck sake.' My little-girl self is crying – low whimpers, like she's in pain. They don't see her.'

'Who doesn't see her, Clodagh?'

'My mother and a man, but I can't see his face. It's in the shadows.'

'Try, Clodagh, keep looking. Who do you see?'

'I don't know. I told you, I can't make him out.'

'Do you know his name?'

'He's hurting her. He's hurting my mother. She's trying to fight him off, but it's no use. He's too strong for her. My little-girl self is screaming, her mouth opening wide, but there's no sound coming out, as if she's lost her voice, and she can't move away.'

'Clodagh.' Gerard's voice is raised for the first time.

I don't answer him.

'Clodagh, you must answer me, or I'll have to bring you back.'

'He's …'

'He's what?'

'He's attacking my mother. I can't help her. I can't do anything. The little girl …'

'What about the little girl, Clodagh?'

'She can't stay, she's too frightened, but she has no one to run to. She doesn't know where Dominic is. He's the only one she can talk to. She can't tell Daddy – he isn't there. He and Mum had a big fight.'

'Look around you, Clodagh. I want you to take in as much as you can about what you see.'

I do as he asks. Then I say, 'There's something else.'

'What is it?'

'There's a tiny strip of light. It's coming from the attic room, up the stairs from Dominic's bedroom. The light is coming from under the door. It's like a torchbeam the way it moves. He must be up there.'

'Who is up there?'

'Dominic. He hides up there when he wants to be away from everybody. The same way I do when I play with my dolls.'

'Clodagh, do you recognise the man in the room with your mother?'

'I think so, but it's very dark. I can't be sure. He has the face that always stays in the shadows, but …'

'But what?'

'I can't explain it.' I sound scared. I breathe in deeply.

'You're doing great, Clodagh. Keep your breathing steady. None of what you see can harm you. Remember, it all happened in the past. Try to tell me what your younger self is afraid of.'

'It's not only what I'm seeing, Gerard.'

'What is it, then?'

'It's the way he makes me feel.'

'I don't understand.'

'He frightened me before. He has scared my little-girl self. He isn't a nice man.'

'How do you know this, Clodagh?'

'I just do.'

'Clodagh, I want you to go back to when he first scared you.'

I say nothing, my mind caught between the memories.

'Clodagh, can you hear me?'

'Yes.'

'Where are you now?'

'I'm at my friend's birthday party, the one where I wore the purple taffeta dress, with the silver beads on the collar.'

'Is your mother there?'

'Yes, she is, and so is he.'

'Why does he scare you?'

'I don't like him.'

'Why don't you like him, Clodagh?'

'His voice is creepy. Sometimes it's loud and …'

'And what, Clodagh?'

'It's as if I know he can get angry at any moment. His hands are ugly, chunky, like hairy-bear hands. He's talking to Mum, but I don't look up at him. I stay close to my mother. Sometimes he clenches his hands tight into fists. Other times, his hands touch her. I don't like him touching her.' My voice is loud and angry. I roar, 'And–I–don't–like–the–way–he–makes–me–feel.'

'How does he make you feel, Clodagh?'

'Horrible. He makes me feel dirty.'

'Are you ready to come back, Clodagh?'

'I don't know.'

'Clodagh, I'm bringing you back. I want you to close your eyes. I'll start counting backwards from two hundred, and you will walk towards the staircase, the one that will bring you back to the garden, a place that is peaceful and safe, and soon you will be in this room.'

When I open my eyes again, I can see Gerard. Tears are streaming down my face.

'Are you okay, Clodagh?'

I don't answer. My mind is still caught between the present and the past. I can still remember the man. How he made me feel afraid. And that night, in the dark, in Dominic's old bedroom, not being able to help my mother.

'Clodagh, it's over now. You're back. You're safe.'

'Gerard.' I can taste my tears, salty on my tongue. 'I remember being in the bedroom,' my voice sounds desperate, 'the one where my mother was attacked.'

'What about it, Clodagh?' His voice is soft.

'Dominic was there too. He was upstairs in the attic room. He knows about these things. I know he does.'

'Will he tell you? Will he talk to you?'

'I don't know.' And I'm thinking about the image of the iceberg, the one Gerard described at the beginning of all this. How my conscious mind is at the tip of it, above the waterline, while below there is a giant dark mass, one that is now filled with more doubts and fears than I'd thought possible.

Harcourt Street Police Station

O'Connor could almost taste this point in an investigation, when things were moving so fast that absolutely nothing outside it mattered. But with that came the knowledge that one slip-up now might mean the whole bloody thing could come crashing down around him.

He was uneasy about Dominic Hamilton being missing. They had the fibre results from the lab, and the analysis of the deposits under Jenkins's fingernails. Once he had Hamilton and McKay in for questioning, it should only be a matter of time before all the building blocks slotted into place. If they were lucky, they'd get the domino effect, each piece of information connecting, giving the required momentum towards the truth.

But one thing was still niggling at him, apart from having to wait for the bloody search warrant, and his inability to pull either McKay or Hamilton in. It was the reference Kate had made to there being another potential victim or victims, and the acceleration in the killer's mind.

The perpetrator was a risk-taker seemingly with little to lose. His task more important to him than anything else. According to Kate, he could be psychotic and unable to contemplate any protracted waiting period. It meant that whoever had killed Jenkins and Gahan was capable of thinking outside a logical framework. Desperate men do desperate things. The last thing O'Connor wanted was another dead body or an injured party on his hands.

When his desk phone rang with an in-house call, O'Connor

assumed it would be a detective from his team. When he heard Hennessy's voice, he adjusted his tone, unsure as to what the detective sergeant was about to say to him.

'O'Connor, I know you're the SIO on the canal murders.'

'That's right.'

'I may have something for you.'

O'Connor wasn't sure if it was the relief that Hennessy's phone call had nothing to do with the rape charge or his keenness to get another angle on the case. Either way, a part of him relaxed. 'Let me hear what you have.'

'We pulled in a pal this morning in connection with an alleged rape.' O'Connor felt himself tensing again. 'The guy's name is Steve McDaid. He's denying the whole thing, of course, saying it was consensual, but when we started talking to him, he had no idea why we'd dragged him in. He began spouting on about how he knew nothing about nothing, that he wasn't anywhere near the canal.'

'He thought you were pulling him in over the murders?'

'It would seem so. It turns out he knew both victims, but he got his bearings fairly fast. Anyhow, one way or another, the rape allegation will be a long haul, but he's here in the station now. I thought you might like to have a few words with him.'

'I can't think of anything I'd like more. Which interview room is he in?'

'22A.'

'I'm on my way.'

Clodagh

When I leave Gerard's and see Dominic's car parked outside, in a strange way I'm not one bit surprised. Despite all the upset, it's anger I feel towards him. He knows so much more than me and, like Mum, he keeps shutting me out.

As I get closer to the car, I realise he's slumped over in the driver's seat, as if he's sleeping. My legs feel shaky after the session with Gerard. I take my time walking towards him, unsure of the best way to handle things. There are gaps in my memory that I might never be able to fill, but Dominic knows more than he's saying. The hard part will be getting the information out of him.

Knocking on the driver's window, I feel somewhat energised again. The truth is within my grasp, if I can reach out in the right direction.

Dominic smiles at me, his hair tossed, his eyes sleepy. I sit in beside him. 'When was the last time you got a good night's sleep?'

'I don't need sleep.' He yawns.

'Dominic, did you follow me here?'

'Yes.'

'Why?'

'Because I was worried about you.'

'You haven't been telling me the truth, Dominic.'

'Haven't I?' A chill enters his voice.

'You need to stop treating me like a child. Martin does it all the time. It drives me mad.'

'Don't compare me to him.'

'Then stop acting like him. I need you to tell me everything.'

'What do you want to know?'

I blurt, 'The lot — what you know about Emmaline, how she died, how Dad died, why Mum stopped loving me.'

'She never stopped loving you.'

'She had a funny way of showing it.'

'You want to know about Dad?' Dominic almost spitting out the words. I can't believe how quickly his mood has turned.

'Yes.' Even as I say it, I worry about what is coming next.

'The boating accident.' He looks straight ahead of him.

'What about it?'

'It wasn't an accident.'

'How can you be so sure?' My head wants to explode.

'Dad was under pressure, the business, everything.'

'Jesus, how long have you known?'

'I think, in a way, I've always known. But sometimes, Clodagh, you don't want to face the truth. I learned some things while Mum was sick.'

A part of me feels angry all over again. 'She confided in you?' I don't attempt to hide the hurt.

'It wasn't like that.'

'And Emmaline, Dominic? Did she tell you what happened to the baby?'

'What about the baby?'

'How she died.'

'You know how she died. It was a cot death.'

'I don't believe you.' I keep my eyes fixed on him.

'Believe what you want.' He turns his head away from me, looking out of the driver's window.

'I went back, Dominic. During my regression, I saw things.'

'What kind of things?'

'There were arguments, fights between Mum and Dad. She blamed him, or me, or someone for the baby dying. She …'

'What?'

'She said the baby was killed.' The words sound unbelievable.

'Christ, Clodagh!' His voice is shaky, his eyes fixed on me.

'Stop playing games, Dominic.'

'I'm not playing games. Games are for children.'

'You went to see Gerard Hayden. He told me.'

'It wasn't me who went to see him, Clodagh.'

'What do you mean? You're not talking sense. I want the truth, Dominic. I want the truth!'

'It was Martin, if you must know.'

My mind is racing again. 'Why would he do that? How do you know?'

'Because I followed him too.'

'You what?'

He turns the key in the ignition, then pulls the car out from the kerb.

'Where are we going? I don't want to go home, Dominic. I want to talk this out.'

'We will, but first we need to go somewhere.'

'Where?'

'Somewhere you'll be safe.'

'I don't understand.'

'You will, Clodagh. You just need to trust me.'

Interview Room 22A, Harcourt Street Police Station

The first thing O'Connor did on entering Interview Room 22A was give Steve McDaid a great big smile. The second thing he did was press the record button for their session. Then he sat down, facing McDaid across a narrow but adequate chrome table.

∞

Time - 11.45 a.m. Incident Room 22A, Harcourt Street Station.

Interview with Mr Steve McDaid, of 38C Seville Place, Ringsend, Dublin.

Interview to be carried out by myself, Detective Inspector O'Connor, SIO in charge of the Jenkins and Gahan murders.

Also present for the duration of interview, Detective Sergeant Stuart Hennessy.

∞

Hennessy remained standing by the door, more an observer than a participant.

'Steve, I understand from Detective Sergeant Hennessy that you knew the two men who were killed – Keith Jenkins and Jimmy Gahan.'

'There's no law broken in knowing them.'

'Of course not.' O'Connor leaned back on the hard wooden chair, stretching out and folding his legs to the side of the table. 'I'd be keen to hear what you have to say about them.'

'It's been years since I spoke to either of them.'

'So you all go back a long way?'

'Long enough.'

'To when exactly?'

'My teens, I guess.'

'That's a long time ago.' O'Connor smiled again, but McDaid didn't look impressed. 'How did you get to know them, Steve?'

'They hung out at the Hamiltons'. I used to be friendly with Dominic Hamilton.'

O'Connor was giving nothing away, although there were plenty of questions running around in his head. He was finding it harder to keep his anger under wraps too. McDaid had been pulled in for the Susie Graham rape, and somehow the thing that had fucked with his head over the last few months seemed to be represented by the lowlife in front of him. 'Have you seen him recently? Dominic Hamilton, that is.'

'Look, I don't know anything about any of this.'

'Nobody is saying you do, but I'd like you to answer my question. When was the last time you saw Dominic Hamilton?'

'Recently.'

'How recently?'

'The last few days.' McDaid also leaned back in his chair, as if wanting to put further distance between him and O'Connor.

O'Connor sat forward. 'Listen, you fucking lump of shit, we can do this the hard way or the easy way.' Standing up, O'Connor grabbed him by the shirt collar. Pulling McDaid up, he pushed him back against the wall, saying, 'You don't want to be here all fucking day, and neither do I. So why don't you save us all a whole lot of time and tell us what you fucking do know?'

Hennessy took a couple of steps forward from the door. 'Take it easy, O'Connor.'

O'Connor let go, but not before he gave McDaid a look that didn't need any words.

It didn't take him long to compose himself. 'Okay, Detective, I don't mind talking.'

'And I'm listening. Now don't fuck me about.'

'I used to hang around with Dominic Hamilton. It wasn't a match made in Heaven, me and him. Let's just say we came from different backgrounds. That's how I got to know Keith Jenkins and Jimmy Gahan.'

'Did you know them well?'

'Not particularly. They were just men in suits who visited the Hamilton house.'

'Keep going, Steve, you're doing great.' Anger was still seeping into O'Connor's words.

'I saw the sister too, about a week ago. She didn't see me, but I recognised her straight away. She's a bit of a looker even now.'

'Clodagh McKay?'

'That's right.'

'You have a soft spot for her, do you, Steve?'

'She was only a kid when I met her. We got reacquainted a few years later. I doubt she remembers it, though. Out of her head, she was. Her daughter's the same. Must be a family weakness.' He smiled.

'Let's get back to you and Dominic Hamilton. How come you two had this recent reunion?'

'I got a bit of a job.'

'What kind of a job?'

'Someone wanted me to keep an eye on him.'

'Who?'

'I'd rather not say.'

'Don't fuck with me, Steve.'

'Just a guy. I think he might have been put out by Jenkins and Gahan taking a swim.'

'I'm going to ask you again, and this time I want an answer. Who wanted you to keep an eye on Dominic Hamilton?'

'He said he had some trust issues with him. I wasn't keen on doing it, but sometimes a guy doesn't have a lot of choice.'

'A bit like now, Steve. A name, please.'

'Alister Becon, if you must know, but that's all I can tell you. Mr Becon isn't one for sharing a lot of information. He wants you to do something, you do it.'

O'Connor knew he was getting only part of the story. He needed to keep pushing. He stood up again. McDaid braced himself for another attack, but O'Connor kept his anger in check. 'And when you were keeping an eye on Dominic Hamilton, what did you discover?'

'Not a lot.'

'No?' O'Connor was sceptical.

'He liked going for long drives.'

'Long drives?'

'Yeah, out to Malahide, down by the estuary. He would sit in the car for hours on end. That's where his father croaked it, wasn't it?'

O'Connor wasn't about to allow him to take over the questioning. 'Did he fancy driving anywhere else, Steve?'

'Sometimes he'd park down by Sandymount Strand, a regular water lover he was.'

'Sandymount?'

'Yeah. The Hamiltons had a house on the strand, a fine big one. Not everyone grows up with a view of the sea, do they?' A note of bitterness had crept into McDaid's voice.

'No, they don't, Steve. Would you care to share an address?'

'Sure. It's no skin off my nose.'

'Lovely.' O'Connor smiled at him, then heard a double tap on the door.

Lynch opened it. 'A word, sir.'

'Hennessy, will you wrap up the interview?' O'Connor got up from the table.

'No problem.' Hennessy walked over to take O'Connor's place.

Before leaving the room, O'Connor leaned down and whispered in Steve McDaid's ear, 'Don't go anywhere, Steve. I'm not finished with you yet.'

Outside the room, Lynch was the first to speak. 'We have the search warrant.'

'About time. Anything on Dominic Hamilton or Martin McKay?'

'That's the bad news, sir.'

'What?' O'Connor was waiting to hear that one of them had croaked it.

'The unmarked car picked McKay up when he returned home. He didn't stay long, but shortly after he left the house, they lost him again.'

'Shit.' O'Connor paced the corridor. 'Right. I want you to take a team over to the McKay house. You're in charge, Lynch. But keep me posted. I'll need to set up another recon.'

'Where?'

'The Hamiltons' old family home in Sandymount. It's on the strand. No doubt it's been lying empty since the mother's death. I'll need to talk to Robinson too, get some more house-to-house done and fast. Find out if the neighbours have seen anything out of place over the last while.'

'Okay, sir. I'll check back with you.'

'And, Lynch …'

'Yes, sir?'

'Make sure you have Hanley's crew on standby too, should anything ugly raise its head at the McKay house, especially on that motor of his.'

'Okay, will do.'

Clodagh

I have no idea where I am. It's dark, and my body hurts from lying on a hard surface. I reach out, spreading my fingertips along what feels like a wooden floor. It's dusty, and I sneeze.

My head hurts too. I reach up, touching the wall beside me. Parts of the plasterboard come away in my hands, half rotten. I use my eyes next, scanning the room from the floor upwards. I see boxes on shelves, and an old rope hanging from the roof beams, thick and dirty with age, the ends separated into loose strands. Twisting, I turn around, looking above me. I see the outer ring of the old dartboard, and above it, the dark feathered wings of an eagle. I'm in the attic at Seacrest.

I think I'm alone. There are no sounds other than those coming in from outside, the faint hint of the world beyond this attic room. I crawl towards the door. I listen for noises from downstairs, but I hear nothing. When I look through the gap under the door, I can see no movement. It's still daylight, for there is light coming in from the landing.

I have no bag, coat or mobile phone. My shoes are in the corner. They must have fallen off my feet. I can't remember how I got here. The last thing I remember is being in the car with Dominic. Where is he? The pain in my head is getting worse. I reach up again and tentatively touch the back of my head. I must have fallen, or was I knocked unconscious?

The only way out of here is through the door into Dominic's old bedroom. The latch is off at the top, so I drag myself upright.

I reach for the upper handle and hold it for a couple of seconds before I attempt to open the door, hoping I won't make a sound. Even though I have no idea what is going on, I know something is wrong.

I turn the small handle as far as it can go and pull the door towards me. It doesn't budge. The latch is closed over on the other side.

'Hello,' I call. 'Hello! Is anybody there? Dominic, are you out there? What's going on?'

I wait, not knowing what else to do, until I realise I'm banging the door hard. I need to think. I need to work out why the hell I'm here. Just for a moment I wonder if I've gone completely mad, if I'm imagining all of this. Until I hear a noise downstairs. It's the sound of the front door opening, and then, seconds later, closing again.

I hold my breath and wait, looking around the room for something to defend myself with. I pick up an old baseball bat that belonged to Dominic, sitting on one of the boxes on the low shelves. I can hear the creaking of the floorboards on the hall staircase, and count them one at a time, the way I counted them with Gerard Hayden, each step bringing me closer to the unknown. At the top of the landing, the footsteps stop. I think about shouting again, but realise my only hope is that whoever is out there may think I'm still unconscious on the floor.

Then I hear the footsteps on the attic staircase, the person on the other side of the door getting closer to me all the time. When the door edges open, it hardly makes a sound. I can hear my own breathing, loud and deep. As the door opens further, I lunge forward with the baseball bat, hitting out as hard as I can, as the man, whose face I cannot see, sniggers in response, overcoming me and my futile attempts at defence.

'Clodagh, dearest, gentle, delicate Clodagh. There's no need for such melodrama, is there?'

I pull away from him but he keeps a firm grip on both my arms. His hands hurt, closing tight around me, hurting me like Martin does. Using his foot, he slams the door shut behind him, before shoving me to the floor. Then I look up and see his face.

Ocean House, the Quays

Kate tried Clodagh McKay's mobile phone for the third time and still had no luck. Then she rang Valerie Hamilton's landline. This time, she was answered.

'Mrs Hamilton, my name is Dr Kate Pearson. I'm assisting the police, and I was wondering if I could have a quick chat with you about your husband, Dominic. I know this is difficult, talking over the phone, but—'

'What's going on? I can see a squad car outside.' The woman was panicking.

'There's no need to be alarmed, Mrs Hamilton. Try to keep calm. It's just a precaution. The police would like to talk to your husband. I'm sure everything is fine, but if you could let me know a couple of things, it might speed up finding Dominic.'

Kate waited, hoping Valerie Hamilton would decide to talk.

Finally she did. 'What do you want to know?' she asked, her voice shaking.

'Valerie, I understand you were concerned about Dominic, about him being depressed. Can you tell me how his low moods affected him? Did he have any problems sleeping?'

'Yes, and he's been worse over the last couple of weeks.'

'In what way?'

'He's been getting barely any sleep, walking around the house at all hours of the night. It's been impossible for him to go to work.'

'How long has he been out of work?'

'He took time off when his mother died, but it was difficult for him when he went back. I told him he was working too hard. He needed to take a break.'

'How long, Valerie?'

'About a month, I guess. We didn't tell anyone other than his office. Dominic didn't want attention drawn to it. He said he'd handle it in his own way.'

'In what way was it difficult when he went back?'

'It's hard to talk about.'

'I understand, Valerie. I'm a doctor. I know how hard the grieving process can be.'

'At first I didn't pay any attention to it, hoping it would pass.'

'Hoping what would pass, Valerie?'

'He hasn't been himself.'

'Valerie, are you okay?'

'I don't know, Dr Pearson. Will you tell me what's going on?' Her voice was becoming shakier by the second.

Kate softened her tone. 'Kate, please call me Kate.'

'Is Dominic in some kind of trouble?'

'You say he hasn't been himself, Valerie. Can you tell me how?'

'The last couple of days he thought people were watching him, following him.'

'What makes you say that?'

'He kept looking out of the window, checking the front and back of the house.'

'Was there any other behaviour that worried you?'

'He's been distant.' Valerie Hamilton drew in her breath.

'How has he been distant?'

'Leaving the house, not telling me where he's going, shutting me out every time I try to talk to him.'

'Apart from thinking someone was watching him, were there any other feelings of paranoia, thinking people might be out to get him, or any delusional behaviour?'

'He's been finding it hard to concentrate on things.'

'What kind of things?'

'He stopped reading, not even a newspaper. He couldn't bear to watch television or listen to the radio. He kept making excuses, saying he had a headache, or that he was too tired, or that his mind was …' she stalled.

'His mind was what, Valerie?'

'Skipping. He was finding it hard to think.'

'Valerie, I want you to try very hard to remember. Was there any point at which Dominic mentioned hearing voices?'

'Do you mean inside his head?'

'Yes.'

'No, not that he told me. But he hasn't been telling me very much. Kate, I'm very worried about him.'

'I know you are, Valerie. Now, I'm sure the police have asked you about his movements over the last few days. What did you say to them?'

'I told them he wasn't sleeping well, which he wasn't. Sometimes he'd go out to clear his head in the hope that when he came back he'd feel better.'

'Did he ever take the car?'

'A few times.'

'Have you spoken to anyone else about Dominic, members of his family, his sister, perhaps?'

'Clodagh?'

'Yes, Clodagh.'

'Dominic doesn't like me bothering her. She has always been a bit …'

'A bit what?'

'A bit delicate, edgy, over-sensitive, if you get me.'

'Dominic and Clodagh, are they close?'

'I suppose.'

'You say Dominic hasn't been the same since his mother's death. How did Clodagh take it?'

'Hard, I guess. Clodagh and Lavinia were never that fond of each other.'

'Clodagh and her mother?'

'They had a somewhat strained relationship. Dominic was always caught in the middle.'

'Valerie, have you spoken to Clodagh today?'

'No.'

'When was the last time you spoke to her?'

'Not for a few days.'

'When exactly?'

'She rang me, I don't know, late last week. We were out for dinner the night before. She wanted to know if I could recommend someone to her.'

'What kind of someone?'

'Look, I don't think this means anything.'

'Tell me anyway, Valerie.'

'It sounds daft.'

'It's okay. Go on.'

'Well, if you must know, she wanted me to recommend a hypnotist.'

'A hypnotist?' Kate kept her tone controlled.

'Yes, she'd heard about regression through hypnosis. I think she wanted to try and go back to her childhood.'

'I see.'

'She made me swear not to tell anyone, not even Dominic. I think she felt a little silly.'

'And the hypnotist you recommended, you trusted him?'

'Of course I did. Otherwise I would have never given Clodagh his details.'

'Can I have them?'

'Hold on. I'll see if I can find his card. He's very nice, I understand.'

'I'm sure he is.' The phone was clattered down. Kate wasn't sure how this was fitting into things, but it didn't sound as if either sibling had been coping well with their mother's death.

'Dr Pearson, Kate …'

'I'm still here.'

'It's fifty-one Tycon Avenue. His name is Gerard Hayden.'

'That's great, Valerie, and don't worry, I'm sure everything will turn out fine.'

'I hope so.' And with that Valerie Hamilton hung up.

Kate's next call was to O'Connor. 'It's Kate, I've just been talking to Valerie Hamilton.'

'There's still no sign of Dominic Hamilton, and Martin McKay is also conveniently missing.'

'That's not good, O'Connor. Did you have any luck with Clodagh McKay? I've tried to get her by phone, but there's no answer. Do you have a landline?'

'There's no one at the McKay house. We got the search warrant. Lynch and the team have just arrived.'

'According to Valerie Hamilton, her husband has been under a lot of duress. I've asked her a number of questions around psychosis, and although there wasn't anything definitive, other than him feeling someone was following him, she told me enough about his behaviour patterns to trouble me.'

'I've been chatting with a guy called Steve McDaid.'

'The guy Hennessy pulled in for the Susie Graham attack?'

'I don't even want to know how you know that. According to McDaid, Becon had him keep an eye on Dominic Hamilton and, believe me, there's plenty going on to trouble me.' His voice had a hardened edge. 'I'll be talking with Alister Becon again.'

'Look, O'Connor, I'm going to head over to an address Valerie Hamilton gave me. It's not far from here. It seems Clodagh McKay has been seeing a hypnotist.'

'Jesus bloody Christ, what next?'

'He may give us an insight into what's going on.'

'Okay, fine.' Although he sounded anything but. 'If he happens to have a crystal ball, Kate, the way things are looking right now, it might come in bloody handy.'

Clodagh

I recoil into the corner of the attic, the one furthest away from the door, wanting to put as much distance between us as possible. If he's aware of my deep-rooted fear, he's ignoring it.

'I can see you're surprised, Clodagh. Didn't expect me, did you?'

He stares at me as if I'm something to be pitied. It's not his face that frightens me the most, it's how his body moves, his sharp tone, and his hands, chunky, the hair on the backs now grey.

'Why did you bring me here, Alister? Where's my brother?' I pull my knees close to my chest. 'That's who you are, isn't it?' I know I sound nervous, despite my attempt to hide it.

'Always curious, aren't we, Clodagh? You were the same as a child, sneaking around as quiet as a mouse, happy to stay in the background while you took it all in.'

'I don't know what you mean.'

'Don't you? I doubt that, Clodagh. Your mother thought you were a bit scatterbrained, more into make-believe and playing doll's house than real life. But you see, Clodagh, I'm a good judge of people. It's partly why I've been so successful in life, seeing how everyone operates, knowing which buttons to press and when.'

'Martin works with you. Dominic told me. Has Martin put you up to this?'

'He's a fool.' He hesitates, as if considering his next sentence. 'Ambition can get in the way of vision. Martin doesn't know any more than he needs to know, and your brother, Dominic, is much the same. You forget, Clodagh, I knew both of them as young boys.

You can observe a lot about a person when you're the adult and they're the child, an awful lot.'

'What else did you observe about me?' I sense I'm buying time.

'You were interesting.' He takes a step closer.

'Interesting?'

'A beautiful child, intelligent, and with the wildest imagination.' He reaches down, taking some strands of my hair into his hand, running his finger through my tangled curls. 'Your mother thought you were like your hair, wild and fancy-free. But behind it all, you were more of a rebel.'

'I never felt like one.'

'Didn't you? All those wild nights out as a teenager, hitting the bottle hard. You became quite the handful for Martin. You tested his intelligence in the early days, and even now. He never liked that. A man doesn't like to be undermined.'

'How do you know so much about me? I haven't seen you since I was a child.'

'I like to keep track of people. It makes it less likely that they can do you any harm. It's always good to be more educated about others than they are about you.'

'You still haven't told me why you have me here.' I tell myself that the longer I can keep him talking, the better chance I have of working out how to get out of there.

'Clodagh, Clodagh,' he smiles, 'if you keep asking the wrong questions, you will keep getting the wrong answers.'

'What do you want with me?'

'You look a bit like her at times.'

'Who?'

'Lavinia, of course.'

'My mother?'

'Yes, your mother. You do know I loved her? Some might say I was obsessed with her.'

I stare back at him, seeing little in the dark, feeling the dusty wooden floor beneath me.

'Don't be shocked, Clodagh. I may be an old goat now, but inside I'm still the man who remembers falling for an exciting woman, the kind who comes into your life and never leaves you, at least, not completely. It was meeting Ruby that rekindled the memory.'

'Ruby? My daughter?' I can hear the panic in my voice. 'What has she to do with all this?'

'A carbon copy of your mother looks-wise, you must agree.' Despite the near blackness, I see him smile in reflective admiration. 'Yes, Clodagh, your lovely daughter. We met recently. Martin introduced us.'

'When?'

'I was the main speaker at a function. Some drivel about supporting suicide victims. Funny now, all things considered.'

'What do you mean?'

'It doesn't matter. What matters, Clodagh, is that your beautiful, intelligent mind has managed to get you into a whole lot of trouble.'

'I don't understand.'

'Don't you?' He pauses, as if wondering whether he should confide in me. 'I went to see your mother a couple of months before she died. It was meeting Ruby that spurred the whole thing on. I guess I realised I'd never stopped loving her, your mother, that is.'

'When she was dying? You went to see her when she was sick.'

'Yes.' He kicks the baseball bat to the other corner of the room, the noise vibrating long after it lands on the floor. My body tenses. His voice lowers. 'I could still see her beauty. I'm not a fool. I knew she didn't have long left, which made it all the more poignant for us to reconcile.' He let out a low, malicious laugh. 'But she didn't want me around. She was having none of it.' He moves closer, the tips of his fingers touching my hair again, his voice bitter. 'Even though I helped her more than any other man in her life.'

'How did you help her?' I'm sputtering my words.

He pulls back his hand, clenching his fist, the way I had remembered him doing from before. 'I covered up for your pathetic father and the baby, that's how.'

'You know about the baby?'

51 Tycon Avenue

Kate drove along Tycon Avenue twice, all potential parking spots on either side of the narrow street taken. She found a space in a side-street, turned off the engine and phoned Ocean House, checking they had successfully rearranged her next two appointments. Her next call was to Sophie.

'Hi, Sophie, I'm glad I caught you.'

'Is everything all right, Kate?'

'Something's come up and I've had to reschedule some of my afternoon appointments. I may not get back until after six.'

'Don't worry about it. I've no plans for this evening.'

'There's mince in the fridge, Bolognese sauce and pasta, if either you or Charlie gets peckish.'

'No bother.'

'You're a star. Tell Charlie I'll be there before seven at the latest.'

Kate disconnected and put her mobile in her briefcase, wondering again about her visit to Gerard Hayden. Turning into Tycon Avenue, she took in the small red-brick cottages with tiny front gardens. She soon found number fifty-one and stopped at the low gate. It gave ample notice of her visit, creaking noisily when she opened it. A brass plaque with Gerard Hayden's qualifications hung beside a panelled black front door. Kate coughed before she pressed the brass bell button, then waited for a response. She could hear carpeted footsteps before the door opened and a small, middle-aged man, with short dishevelled grey hair, looked at her in mild surprise.

'Can I help you?'

'I hope so.' Kate was endeavouring to sound encouraging. 'I understand Clodagh McKay is a client of yours.'

'May I ask who you are?'

'Sorry, of course. My name is Dr Kate Pearson. I'm a psychologist. I work with the police.'

'I see.'

Kate tried again. 'Gerard, I understand Clodagh has been seeing you about regression into childhood.' She hoped her friendly, even tone would help.

'I don't like to discuss my clients, Dr Pearson, with anyone other than themselves, and certainly not on a doorstep.'

'I understand completely, and normally I would have phoned and talked to you beforehand. Unfortunately there have been some developments, and I've been unable to contact Clodagh myself.'

'Is she in some kind of danger? You say you work with the police.'

'Would it be possible to come in, Gerard? I won't take up too much of your time.'

Gerard Hayden hesitated, then stood back and held open the door as Kate walked in. Closing it behind her, he said, 'Follow me,' and led her down a dark, carpeted hallway to a room with 'Office' in black stickers on a faded cream door. Once inside, she smelt candle wax. He beckoned her to sit down on the first of two comfy chairs at either side of a desk, then took the one opposite.

Kate decided to waste no time. 'Gerard, how successful have you been with Clodagh's regression?'

'You say you haven't been able to contact her?'

'That's right. The police do have some concerns. I completely understand your reluctance to break client confidentiality, but any help you can give me may make a difference.'

'We've been reasonably successful, but I can't tell you anything directly about the regression.'

'I understand that, Gerard. I should probably explain a bit about why I'm here.' She could see he was used to the role of listener, sitting back in his chair to hear what she had to say. 'Gerard, the reason I'm helping the police is because two men have been killed. Both men, it appears, were known to Clodagh.'

'I see.' His face contradicted his words.

Kate decided to persevere. 'Her brother, Dominic Hamilton …' She waited for a reaction. The slight rising of Gerard Hayden's eyebrows confirmed he was familiar with the name, so Kate continued, 'Dominic is also missing, as is her husband, Martin McKay.'

'Missing?'

'Perhaps that's too strong a word, but right now, the police are keen to talk to all three.'

'I don't really see how I can help.'

'Perhaps you could tell me how Clodagh was on her last visit.'

'She was here earlier today. It was a difficult session – regression can be traumatic.'

'I understand that.'

'As you said, Clodagh came to me to regress into childhood. I'm not breaking any confidence when I tell you that normally this is because clients have issues they need to address from that particular time. Very often their memories are suppressed. Have you experience in this area, Dr Pearson?'

'Quite a lot, actually.'

'Then you'll understand that these things are not always straightforward and, as I've already said, can bring up difficulties.'

'Would you say Clodagh was stable, Gerard?'

'The word is subjective, but yes. I think she's more stable than even she might believe.'

'These childhood difficulties, do they concern her brother?'

'There may be some trust issues. He came to see me a short while back, but without wanting to say anything out of turn, Clodagh's concerns are not restricted to her brother.'

'He came to see you?'

'He wanted to know what was happening during the regression.'

'And did you tell him?'

'No, I certainly did not.'

'And you're positive it was her brother, Dominic?'

'No, but why would he lie?'

'Indeed.' Kate tried to remain expressionless. 'Gerard, these childhood regressions?'

'Yes?'

'I know this is difficult for you, but it would be a great help if you could tell me whether or not there was a particular age Clodagh regressed to or, indeed, any recurring location.'

'I'm not sure I should.'

'Gerard, I know Clodagh and Dominic lost their father at a young age. These early traumatic childhood events have a habit of following you into adulthood. Clodagh lost her mother recently, isn't that correct?'

'Yes, she did.'

'So I'm guessing that's partly why she came to see you.'

'I believe so.'

'Would I be right in thinking that a lot of Clodagh's regression focused around the loss of her father?'

'It was part of it.'

'And at the time she would have been what age?'

'Seven, I believe.'

'Did Clodagh discover anything during her regression that she had previously shut out?'

'Yes, she did, but I can't—'

'And would this put her life at risk in any way?'

'I don't think so. I'm not really sure.'

Kate could tell the conversation was unsettling him. 'Gerard, if you were looking for Clodagh now, where would be the first place you would go?'

'Other than her own home?'

'Yes.'

'I would probably go to her old house. The one she grew up in. It's on Sandymount Strand somewhere.'

'Thanks, Gerard. That may be useful.'

'There's an attic room. I think you can access it through one of the upstairs bedrooms. Clodagh went there a couple of days ago, with her brother, I understand.' Gerard Hayden's expression was both puzzled and concerned now. 'Clodagh said she felt frightened.'

Kate stood up. 'Okay. You've been most helpful.' She put her hand out to shake his, and he responded more firmly than she had expected. 'I'll let myself out, Gerard. I've already taken up enough of your time.'

'Dr Pearson?' He stood up.

'Yes?'

'You will let me know if anything is …'

'I will, Gerard, and thanks again.'

Clodagh

Alister Becon doesn't answer my question straight away. But, despite my fear, his silence doesn't unnerve me. It's as if, within this strange and somewhat surreal communication between us, my need to listen far outweighs everything else.

He moves away from the door, walking easily in the attic space, his short height an advantage, with the low ceiling. I'm not sure if I'm imagining it but as he contemplates answering me he keeps looking back to the door, as if he's expecting someone. His hands are again clenched into tight fists. My mind is torn between wanting him to tell me about the baby, wondering about Dominic, and my need to know who, if anyone, he is waiting for.

'Your mother came to me after the child died. She was distraught, angry, frightened out of her wits.'

'Why you?' I try to keep my voice steady.

'For once in her life, she needed me.'

'Do you know how the baby died?'

'Yes.'

'Then you know who. Was it my father?' It sounds crazy. I can't trust this man, and I have no confidence in my own memory. A part of me wants him to say yes to my second question, because if it wasn't my father, I'm not sure I can take the reply that I'm frightened he will give.

Alister Becon looks down at me, huddled in the corner, with hatred. And, for the first time, I wonder if perhaps he had been Emmaline's father.

'Your mother was in shock. At one point she even considered telling the authorities what had happened.'

'So it's true?' I sit upright, with my back against the attic wall, the large brown eagle with his soulful black eyes above me. 'Why didn't she go to the authorities? Who was she protecting?'

'She knew your father was weak,' Alister Becon says, as if it gives him some form of pleasure and inner satisfaction. 'He wouldn't have been able to survive prison, but she also knew it was partly her own fault for screwing around with pretty-boy Keith.'

He isn't Emmaline's father, and a part of me feels relieved. 'Was Emmaline Keith Jenkins's baby?'

'Who can tell? Your mother treated your father like an idiot.' He's enjoying himself.

'I still don't understand what happened.' My sentence is a mix of statement and question. I look away from him to the boxes on the low shelves. I see my rusty spinning top on top of a torn cardboard box with 'Blow Football' printed on the side. Dominic used to play that game all the time. Then I notice her, and I can't fathom why I didn't see her before. Now her blue eyes are looking straight at me. It's as if Sandy is telling me everything will be fine. Her hair is cropped short. I remember cutting her and Debbie's hair. I look back at Alister Becon, knowing the madness in seeking answers from a man I fear and despise.

'Let me spell it out for you, Clodagh, since we're getting on so well together.'

I'm silent, hoping he will keep talking.

'After the baby died, your mother had no choice but to come to me. She knew I had the connections to get it hushed up, brushed under the carpet as another mysterious cot death. No great issue there. These things happen all the time. All you need is some medical expertise. That, like everything else in life, can be bought.'

'Go on.' My voice is crackly, unsure.

'Afterwards I figured it would be a matter of time before your mother dumped your father, leaving the way open for me. But that wasn't her style. She liked to keep up appearances, no matter what. She had no intention of leaving your father, or their sham of a marriage.' I can hear the hate rising in his voice. 'I'm a man who expects to get what he wants.'

'She didn't love you,' I say quietly. He doesn't hear me, hell bent on continuing with his rant.

'I like to control outcomes, Clodagh. With control you gain success. I needed to adjust my tactics. Apply more pressure on the weakest link, convince your father that he couldn't live with himself after what he'd done. He didn't need much persuasion. Alcohol can deepen the darkest mood, don't you agree, Clodagh?'

I remain silent.

'Of course, everyone thought it was the collapse of the business, that and the rumours of his wife's infidelity. Either way, it didn't matter. He was out of the picture. I waited, knowing financial pressure and the prospect of raising two children alone would be difficult for your mother.'

'And then what?'

He smirks. 'I underestimated her or, rather, I underestimated how abhorrent I was to her. It's a strong word, "abhorrent".'

'I guess so.'

'That's what she said to me. That she found me abhorrent. She didn't want me or my money. After all I'd done for her. Can you believe that?'

'Things are often said in the heat of the moment. Things we don't always mean.' I can't believe I'm speaking to him like this, pretending everything is okay.

'Perhaps you're right. She was ill, I became aware of that. Postnatal depression in your mother's case was severe.'

'I can't imagine what it must have been like for her.' Again Alister seems to ignore me.

'You are quite beautiful.' Once more he runs his fingers through my hair, and I want to scream. He pulls them away swiftly. 'It seems, Clodagh, that I was both abhorrent and foolish. Maybe it was because I knew how sick she was, but in the end I gave in. I arranged for that idiot Jenkins to convince her to take the money, to say it was from him. Her knight in bloody shining armour ...' his voice is filled with hate again '... with money I gave him. She took it then, of course, even though she wanted nothing more to do with him either.' His voice changes, sounding sarcastic. 'She wanted to look after her darling children, yourself and Dominic. Start afresh.'

'And you simply walked away?'

'At the time, I had no other choice. The money was nothing, a drop in the ocean. Maybe I thought time would change things. I don't know. As the years went by, I let it go. But then I met Ruby and was drawn back to my own ghosts.'

I cringe at hearing Ruby's name coming from his mouth. 'You can let the past go, you know,' I say. 'It's not always good to look back.'

'From you, Clodagh, that's a little trite. Isn't that what the hypnosis is about? Looking back, trying to find the truth?'

'How do you know about that?'

'The same way I know most things. A friend helped me out.'

'Well, the truth isn't all it's cracked up to be.' It's my turn for anger to bubble over. 'What friend?'

He laughs. 'It doesn't matter. Not now. Perhaps, Clodagh, I chose the wrong Hamilton to fall for. Do you believe in karma?'

'Not particularly.'

'Well, neither did I, until I met your mother again. You see, Clodagh, sometimes what goes around comes around, and all that.'

'What do you mean?'

'I told you, I'm a man who expects to get what he wants.'

'So?'

'Some things had started to get tricky over the last year. My reputation, my territory were being threatened. When that happens, I have to go on the attack.'

None of this is making any sense to me. 'I still don't understand.'

'Your father's bankrupt company, the one Jenkins used a fistful of my money to take off your mother's hands, started to get messy. Maybe it was jinxed all along.' Again he looks to the door. 'You see, Clodagh, the lovely Keith Jenkins got greedy. He decided to get some heavy hitters to invest in the company again. Do a bit of money-laundering. Turn dirty money all nice and clean. Sooner or later the trail would have led back to me, and I couldn't have that.'

'So you figured it was time to get rid of him?' Again I wonder at the madness of my question.

'Dead men don't talk, Clodagh.'

'But what has that to do with me?'

'Karma.' He smiles. 'What goes around comes around.' He stops talking, as if again he's wondering should he share something. It doesn't take him long to make up his mind. 'When I went to see your mother, Clodagh, I realised it was payback time.'

Harcourt Street Police Station

Lynch's call from outside the McKay house came shortly before four o'clock. 'Sir, we have the car.'

'What have you got exactly?' O'Connor's question sounded both strained and impatient.

'Hanley and the crew are here.' O'Connor was finding it hard to hear, with the external noise coming over the line from the street. 'I've secured the area.'

'You haven't told me what you have.'

'Enough blood deposits in the car to keep the techies busy for some time.'

'Good. Are there any photos of Martin McKay in that house?'

'There's one with his daughter.'

'Get the clearest you can find. Contact Matthews and have him alert all transport links in case this guy does a runner.'

'Will do.'

'I'm going to set up checkpoints, using the triangle of the McKay, Hamilton and old Hamilton houses. I expect to hear back from the recon crew at the strand shortly. Shit, I have a call coming in from Robinson. I'll phone you back.'

'Okay.'

'Lynch, before you go, I want nothing left unturned in the McKay house.' He hung up to take Robinson's call.

'I hope you and your guys doing the house-to-house haven't been spending your time sightseeing on the strand.'

'We have something for you.'

'What?'

'One of the elderly neighbours said she noticed lights going on and off in the old house at odd hours of the night and morning. Her husband spoke to Dominic Hamilton about it.'

'And what did he say?'

'Not a lot. He told the neighbour not to worry about it, but that's not all.'

'What else?'

'A few others saw a Volvo recently in the vicinity. One of them reckons it belonged to the McKays.'

'I've just had Lynch on the phone. The car is connected all right, enough blood deposits to keep them plenty busy. Hanley's working on it now. Listen, Robinson, good work. By the way, I've sent a recon down there.'

'We've already crossed paths.'

'Hopefully we can piece together enough to get a warrant issued on the house. Will you fill Matthews in on what we have?'

'Sure.'

'I've got to go. I have a call coming in from Kate Pearson. Talk later.'

He took Kate's call. 'Talk fast, unless that guy's crystal ball has worked.'

'I'll talk as fast as I can.' Kate hated O'Connor giving her short shrift, but this wasn't the time for side issues. 'Clodagh McKay has done a number of regression sessions. She seems to have memory gaps from childhood, most probably related to some form of trauma. It ties in with her father's death, but I think there's something else.'

'What do you mean?'

'It was more in what Gerard Hayden didn't say than what he did. The regression sessions were difficult. Sometimes these things can recover memory in a very disjointed way. If you throw in possible psychotic behaviour on the part of her brother, there's a troubled family history, nothing surer.'

'Anything else?'

'It struck me when I was talking to Gerard Hayden that he might be the only person Clodagh McKay has openly talked to lately. She spoke about being afraid the last time she visited the old family home in Sandymount. When I asked Gerard where he thought she might be, the old house on the strand came up again. The house is some form of common denominator.'

'You must have used that fella's crystal ball. I have reconnissance in place at seventy-four Strand Road. Depending on what the guys get in, I'm hoping for a warrant on the house. It looks like we have the car, by the way. Lynch rang in from the McKays' house a couple of minutes ago. Did that fortune-teller tell you anything else?'

'He's a hypnotist, O'Connor.'

'Whatever.'

'He didn't give a lot away, but it looks like neither of the siblings is handling the mother's death well. And, according to Valerie Hamilton, Clodagh's relationship with her mother was strained.'

'So both siblings were under a lot of stress?'

'Yes, but according to Gerard Hayden, although Clodagh experienced a high level of emotional turmoil during the regression, she is mentally quite strong.'

'Right. Kate, I don't mean to rush you but I have to go.'

'Okay. Let me know how it goes with the house on the strand. The roots of most adult problems begin in childhood. The old house as a tie-in could be exactly the place to look.'

'Talk soon.'

'Take it easy, O'Connor.'

'Will do.'

Clodagh

'What do you mean payback time?' The wall behind me creaks. I look up at the old dartboard with the rusty darts still *in situ*. I think about getting them without Becon seeing me.

'Jimmy Gahan – you do remember him, Clodagh?'

'Yes. What about him?'

'Like Jenkins, he knew too much. Jimmy was always one to have some scheme or another on the go. Unfortunately, Clodagh, the friends you make in younger life tend to hang around for a long time. If either Gahan or Jenkins had started to open their big mouths under pressure, with questions about me and my success, especially my connection with Hamilton Holdings, they wouldn't have been questions I would have wanted answered. That couldn't be allowed to happen. I've worked hard to keep my reputation clean. I wasn't going to risk it now, not because of some sloppy business deals done by bloody Keith Jenkins.'

'I still don't see what this has to do with me.'

'The truth, the twisted truth, is that nothing ever happens in isolation, Clodagh.' He takes a deep breath. 'Shortly after I called to see your mother, I realised she hadn't told either you or Dominic the whole truth. She'd allowed both of you to believe your father's death was an accident, not suicide.' His voice starts to rise again, the bitterness returning. 'She didn't want to tell you he took his own life, that he hadn't given a damn about any of you.'

'What difference did it make to you? You said yourself you helped persuade him.' I want to pull this man's eyes out. 'You always knew it was suicide, you encouraged it.'

He turns away again, looking to the door once more. It's then I hear the sounds downstairs. Someone is moving around. I wonder about shouting, but think the better of it. For as Alister Becon looks from the attic door to me and then back again, he calls a name, one I don't want to hear.

'Martin, is that you?' And another part of me dies inside.

74 Strand Road, Sandymount, Dublin

The knife in my hand feels like an extension of me, cold, sharp and capable of great harm.

It's the strangest thing waiting for something to happen for a long time. When the moment finally arrives, it feels almost imagined. As if thinking about it over time has made its reality strangely unbelievable.

I don't answer Alister when he calls – at least, not at first. Let him sweat. I enjoy the thought of keeping him on his toes, even if he doesn't realise it yet.

Clodagh is with him. She was completely out of it before I left. I gave Alister plenty of time to arrive, for the two of them to get acquainted. Alister, the master planner: his arrogance will be his ultimate downfall.

I wonder what version of the truth he has shared with her. It won't take a lot to bring him down. He doesn't have the strength he used to have. And then it will be Clodagh and me – exactly as it should be.

It's been difficult. There's no denying that. Knowing I'm near the end of this whole bloody thing offers some relief. There can be no backing away now. The pathway is clear, although the end game was never in doubt. Alister might have had other ideas. He hadn't been happy when I dragged my heels with things. All the time I spent following Jenkins and Gahan around, getting to know their latest dirty little secrets. I enjoyed setting one up against the other, a rare pleasure in the shitstorm of events. Playtime before getting rid of them. And now it's Alister's turn. He'll be surprised, taking me for a fool along the way, his pawn to be manipulated – exactly what I wanted him to believe.

He calls again. I ignore him. He's so used to getting other people to do his dirty work that he still sounds smug – but not for long.

The stairs creak under my feet, my hand sliding up the banister. The closer I get to the top, the more assured I feel. I'll need to be fast, take him unawares. And then he, too, can feel his lungs fill with water, the survival instinct kicking in, the will to live strong, but not strong enough to save him.

Clodagh

Deep inside me, I'd known Martin was a part of this. Maybe that's what happens when your past is clouded in mystery: you live in a half-light, tinged with denial of the things you don't want to admit.

Denial or not, neither Alister nor Martin has me here for any good reason. However I'm connected to this, there's no easy way of getting back from this place.

Alister calls to Martin again, and when he does, so many questions flood into my head. Had my father felt betrayed by my mother? Did she make him feel a failure because of it? Why the hell did I stay with this man, other than for Ruby's sake? Like one train wreck following another. For the briefest moment, I see my father trying to place his hand on my mother's tummy. Her pushing him away, as if he must not touch the life inside her. I can forgive my father his rage, but I can't forgive him choosing to die. *You deserted us too!* I scream inside. *What about me? What about Dominic?*

I hear Martin walking up the staircase from the hall. The one Dominic and I played on as children. The one where I sat at the top and he covered my ears against the angry shouting coming from below. I think about my brother, how much he suffered with the loss of our father, how he became the man my mother leaned on most, even though he was only a boy. I envied their relationship, Dominic being the recipient of her love. She didn't have enough left for me. I hold my breath, not knowing what will happen next. My regression has left so many unanswered questions, so many unfilled gaps. I look across at Sandy, as if a doll is going to help me. When I do, I hear another question. Was I the one who initiated my father's suspicions while Dominic remained her confidant? The son who didn't betray her and therefore more deserving of her love?

The closer Martin's footsteps come, the more I worry about Dominic. He's the last person I remember talking to. Has Martin or Alister done something to him? I have to think. I don't care so much about dying, but I don't want to leave Ruby behind. Not with a man capable of this. I won't leave her like my father did, not without a fight. My body and mind contract, tight and full of resolution, until the door opens, and my life falls apart all over again.

74 Strand Road, Sandymount

O'Connor's conversation with the recon team was brief but effective. He knew he had enough to get the search warrant for 74 Strand Road. Apart from the neighbours spotting activity in the deserted house in the early hours of the morning, the team had given him plenty of reason to be suspicious, specifically the two black Mercedes parked a couple of streets away. One registered to Martin McKay, the other to Alister Becon.

The surveillance unit, led by DI Merriman, had first checked the exterior of the building on Strand Road. Initially everything looked as it should. It was only when they called into the houses to the immediate right and left that more had come to light. A woman in number 75 believed she had heard loud voices coming from next door. Her husband told her she must have imagined it, but she was adamant.

Finding Martin McKay's abandoned car, on top of what Lynch and the team had uncovered at the McKay house, would have been enough on its own to establish reasonable grounds for the warrant. Either way, O'Connor made good time getting to Sandymount, having left instructions with Matthews to call him as soon as the warrant came through. Turning his car onto Strand Road, O'Connor, who wasn't feeling particularly patient, phoned Matthews again. 'What's happening with the bloody warrant?'

'It won't be long.'

'I hope the judiciary aren't messing us about.'

'Justice Langham is taking care of it now.'

'Good.' O'Connor could see Merriman giving instructions to

the recon crew ahead of him, and their unmarked cars parked a few houses back from number 74.

'Matthews, has Hennessy got anything more out of that McDaid fella?'

'Not yet.'

'Tell him to keep pushing.'

'I will. By the way, all the checkpoints are in place within the triangle of the three houses, and we've alerted both airport and port options. Hanley and the tech guys are still working at the McKays' house. Lynch is handling the logistics there.'

'Phone me as soon as you have the warrant.'

The next call O'Connor made was to Kate. 'I'm at the house in Sandymount.'

'What's happening?'

'The recon team have a report of raised voices coming from inside the premises. We also have McKay's and Alister Becon's Mercedes in the area. I should have the warrant in the next couple of minutes. We're keeping a close eye on things here. Is there anything more you'd like to add before we go inside?'

'That depends on who the killer is, O'Connor. I assume Dominic Hamilton is still unaccounted for.'

'Correct.'

'I don't know enough about either McKay or Becon to give you any concrete advice other than the obvious. But if Dominic Hamilton's pulling the strings, his state of mind is volatile, especially if we're working with psychosis. The killer has already demonstrated on two occasions that he's capable of extreme levels of violence. If the killer is psychotic, we're dealing with a serious mental disorder, disintegration of personality, someone with grossly distorted thoughts and perceptions.'

'Like imaginary voices?'

'Not necessarily, O'Connor, but his internal messages cannot be relied upon. He could be experiencing heightened levels of anxiety. As I said to you the other night, his whole mind-set will be bubbling over with emotion, none of which can be trusted.'

'You're saying he's out of control.'

'Whoever we're dealing with, he's not thinking like you or me. His views are entrenched. And there's another issue, O'Connor.'

'What?'

'It's about Clodagh McKay.'

'What about her?'

'I don't like the fact that she hasn't returned home.'

'I don't like that a number of people, including Clodagh McKay, are unaccounted for.'

'Do you remember what I said, O'Connor, when I spoke to you about spree killings?'

'We're back to the list.'

'I said this case didn't have all the characteristics of spree killings, but the murders had some similarities. Depending on how much pressure the killer is under, and if his mind is fully contracted, he hasn't finished yet. Clodagh McKay is missing. We know she's not the killer. In cases like this where the victims are not random but specific, as I said before, the killer could have a last victim in mind.'

'You're thinking Clodagh McKay?'

'Like I said, there is nothing to say the killings will remain gender specific.'

Having parked the car, O'Connor looked at the front façade of 74 Strand Road. 'Did that Gerard Hayden guy tell you anything about the house?'

'He said he believed Clodagh visited with her brother a couple of days ago. She went alone into an attic room above one of the bedrooms.'

'Right, Kate. I've got to go.' O'Connor rang Matthews for the second time. 'Where's that fucking warrant, Matthews?'

'There's a bike on its way to you.'

'Matthews, get Hennessy to find out from McDaid anything he can about this house in Sandymount, specifically access to the attic. Something tells me we're running out of time, so make sure McDaid is a fast talker. And, Matthews …'

'Yeah?'

'I want the Emergency Response Unit on alert. If I get a whiff of anything shaky going down here, ringing front doorbells may not be the best option.'

Clodagh

When the attic door opened, I discovered that seconds could last for hours.

Recognition and relief came first, before the onslaught, the almost crazed look in his eyes, the glint of the knife in his right hand – once seen, impossible to deny.

My gasps came next, when words failed me, him lunging forward and Alister Becon fighting back. My body instinctively retracted. Shock and panic set in. And then my futile attempts at stopping him.

The smack across my jaw was delivered with the strength of someone twice his size, followed by my disbelief, rushing to make sense of it all.

Then the longest silence of all, as Alister Becon slid to the floor, still breathing, face down, blood pooling, spreading out across the floorboards, like the wings of the eagle above me. His blood seeping between cracks, my brother's eyes locking onto mine, as our past dangled, like skin caught on barbed wire – torn, trapped, the pain immeasurable, before the next blow and the dark.

∞

I'm unsure how long I've been out. Not very long, as I can still see daylight beneath the door. I look across the attic, and even before his shape becomes clear to me, I know it's him. My voice is croaky, my body pulling itself up, then once more leaning against the wall, my legs in front of me, bent at the knees, like they belong to a rag doll.

I say his name, deep and resolute, 'Dominic.' An affirmation, and so many goddamn questions rolled into one.

'Hello, Clodagh.' His voice is calmer than I expect it to be.

He waits for me to sit up straighter. 'I didn't want to hurt you, but it was necessary. I couldn't have you getting in the way.' He looks pained. 'I'm sorry about hitting you. I'm not like that bastard husband of yours.'

'Dominic, have you gone mad?'

'Mad?' He smiles. 'I don't know, Clodagh.' I sense his eyes boring into me. His voice, when he next speaks, is low. 'Maybe I am mad, but what's done is done.' He takes a gold wedding ring out of his trouser pocket.

'Whose ring is that?'

'Keith Jenkins's. Do you know what he said before he died?'

'No.'

'He said he never loved her.' Putting the ring back inside his pocket, he says, 'Don't worry, Clodagh. I made sure he suffered.'

'Dominic, where's Alister? What have you done with him? My desperation and disbelief rage side by side. I roar, 'Jesus Christ, Dominic, what the hell is going on?'

'We still have time.'

'We still have time for what, Dominic?' I can't believe the calmness in his voice.

'Time for the truth, Clodagh. Isn't that what you wanted all along?'

I stare at him as he continues to talk.

'I warn you, Clodagh, don't try to make a run for it. You're not going anywhere. We're in this together now.'

'What do you mean?'

'I suppose Alister told you he went to see Mum before she died.'

His words are filled with anger. 'He thought he was manipulating me,' he smirks, 'but I've seen too much for that.'

'I don't understand. You're not talking sense.'

'He wanted Gahan and Jenkins out of the way. He saw me as his way of achieving it.'

'WHAT?' I can't believe what I'm hearing.

'He thought by telling me about Dad's suicide, he could manipulate me, telling me how Jenkins and Gahan put Dad under financial pressure, and about Jenkins and Mum. That he would understand me wanting to take revenge. That if I wanted to, he would help me. He made the mistake of thinking I knew very little, but I knew a lot more than anyone.'

'You killed them?' Even saying the words sounds crazy. But now, it's like Dominic has stopped listening to me. As if I don't exist. Because he continues talking as if he's thinking out loud. As if his words confirm his own logic. And all the while he has that horrible knife in his hand.

'I've always suspected it was suicide,' again the anger, 'but suspecting and knowing are two different things.' He looks at the pool of blood on the attic floor. 'Alister thought he could fool me, like he fooled Dad. That I was there for the taking to do his dirty work for him.'

'And you let him think that?'

'He said he owed me an education,' another smirk, 'that he owed me the truth. None of that matters, Clodagh. Don't you get it? They had to die.'

'Dominic, what have you done with Alister?' My voice is finding a new form of fear as I look at this man, my brother, who has become a crazed stranger.

'It doesn't matter. What's done is done.'

'Will you stop saying that?' I realise I'm pleading. I stop talking. I stare at him again, the brother I have known my entire life, before I finally ask, 'Is this all about her? Is this all about Mum? You covered up for her all those years ago, didn't you?'

'I envied you, Clodagh. You do know that? You were a child. You couldn't see or understand the things that I could see.'

'I saw more than you think, Dominic.'

He shrugs off my last words. 'Maybe you did.'

I remember the light in the attic that night in Dominic's bedroom. 'You were here in this attic, Dominic, when Mum was attacked?'

I can see the pain on his face, etched across his brow.

'Weren't you? Answer me, goddamn it.'

'I wanted to help her. I really did.' Now it's Dominic who sounds desperate, pained. 'I was too afraid. I was a coward back then.'

'You were only a kid.' My mind feels like a seesaw.

'No, I wasn't, Clodagh,' he roars. 'I was old enough to see, to know, to stop it.' Then he lowers his voice: 'I was old enough to tell.'

'Why didn't you?'

'You wouldn't understand.'

'You said we had time, Dominic. Give me the chance to understand.' Again I'm pleading. And for what feels like eternity, there is a silence between us, Dominic staring at me, then looking away. Finally he says, 'I didn't want Dad to think any less of her. I thought if I kept my mouth shut, it would all pass, but none of it passed.'

'What happened, Dominic?' I sound unsure and nervous.

The crazed look I saw when he opened the door shrouds his face. I look at the knife, as he leans down and asks coldly, 'Don't you remember, Clodagh?'

'Remember what?'

'Daddy's little girl,' he says, mocking.

'What about me? What are you saying?'

'You were the one who told him.'

'How could I have known? I was too young to understand.'

'Do you remember when Emma, your doll, fell and her face cracked in two?'

'Yes.'

'After the row, the house was horrible. The anger caught up in every wall, every room, roaring even in the silence.'

'Go on.' Although I'm terrified of what is coming next.

74 Strand Road, Sandymount

The two men stood with their backs to the sea, while Merriman brought O'Connor up to date.

Despite the neighbour's observation, the house initially appeared empty. But one of Merriman's crew had picked up something on the last check. With the wind dying down on the strand, they thought they'd heard something inside: raised voices in line with what had been reported from the house-to-house.

Crossing from the strand, O'Connor and Merriman went to the back of the building, knowing that if either of them confirmed what the officer had reported, O'Connor would have no choice but to call in the Emergency Response Unit.

Within seconds, they heard a woman screeching from high in the house. Both men backed away. Once O'Connor was at a sufficient distance, he put in his call to ERU at Harcourt Street. An on-scene commander was immediately briefed. James Maloney was the same rank as O'Connor, but he would call the shots once the marksmen were deployed. If what O'Connor's gut was telling him was true, Maloney would also be the ultimate decider in any potential hostage negotiation.

Knowing the ERU boys would be going in, O'Connor made a final call to Hennessy. McDaid had been very willing to talk about the old house, coming through with decent information that O'Connor passed on to Maloney, who had arrived within moments of the alert being received at ERU.

He was accompanied by two sharp-shooters, Morgan and Quinn.

Their first job was to get inside and report back. It was an old house and, according to McDaid, had an out-of-operation food shaft, with access from the kitchen. McDaid had said they used to mess about in it as kids.

There was no guarantee that it was still in place, but it was a chance, and probably the only way of getting the two marksmen to the top of the building without being seen. Maloney decided that they would gain access to the premises from the rear. There was a back window which could easily be prised open, even if they needed to create some kind of a decoy sound for it to go unnoticed. O'Connor instructed Merriman's reconnaissance squad to clear the occupants of the nearby houses, closing off the street, while Maloney set up the decoy, a group of police dogs barking like blazes.

As the two officers gained access to the building, O'Connor picked up his mobile phone, which he had put on silent. Matthews had news.

'We have one of your missing amigos.'

'Which one?'

'Martin McKay. They picked him up on the outskirts of the city. He might have been heading to the airport for all we know. He took a company car. Apparently his Mercedes went missing earlier on.'

'And he decided not to report it?'

'Claims he was going to, but hadn't the time.'

'Where is he now, Matthews?'

'He's here. He's also claiming he has no idea where his wife or brother-in-law could be. Neither does he know why the Volvo is covered with blood. According to him, he never drove the car, it belonged to his wife, and, O'Connor …'

'Yeah?'

'He's asked to have his lawyer present.'

'I already dislike the fucker. Listen, Matthews, I have to go, but don't take any shit off that lawyer of his. The bottom line is, we have the car, we have the blood. If he wants to come up smelling of roses we'll need a DNA sample.'

'What's happening there?'

'The ERU boys are going into the house now. Maloney's in charge. It's impossible to know who exactly is in there, but one thing's for sure. It isn't Martin McKay.'

'What do you think is going down?'

'I don't know, Matthews, at least not yet, but if it is Dominic Hamilton, and he has his sister or anyone else there under force, they're in danger.'

'I hear you.'

'Listen, Matthews, depending on what the shooters report back, we're probably in hostage negotiator territory. I'm going to phone Kate Pearson. I've already spoken to Maloney about it. If our man is psychotic, as Kate suspects, it might be an idea to set up audio communications between Kate and the negotiator. We're going to need all the help we can get if we want to avoid this turning bloody nasty.'

'Right. I'll keep the pressure on McKay.'

'And, Matthews, make sure Butler's up to date on all of this. You know how he needs to be kept in the loop. I'm ringing Kate Pearson next.'

Dominic, please tell me.' He can't stop talking now.

'You went to your room to play with your doll's house. I hid up here, out of the way, trying to shut it all out.' Again he looks away, as if the more we talk, the harder he finds it to work things out.

His face looks as if it's shifting from rage to confusion. He's breathing deeply, tightening his grip on the knife. When he does speak, it's almost in a whisper. 'Dad came to look for me. He said you told him I knew a secret about Mum. He wanted me to tell him.'

'What did you say?'

'I told him to go to Hell.' His voice is angry.

'And then what?'

'He hit me hard. He'd never hit me before. And do you know what, Clodagh?'

I look at my brother, not understanding why some warped happiness is lifting his mood. 'What, Dominic?'

'It felt good. It felt good to feel the pain on my face, a form of release, my jaw throbbing. The punishment felt sweet.' For the first time, Dominic turns his back to me, and even though I know it's my chance to get out of there, I do nothing, only listen.

'After he'd hit me, he went back downstairs. Not to Mum, but to you.' Dominic turns to me again. 'I followed him, Clodagh. I stood outside your bedroom like a lowlife spy, and listened while Daddy's little girl told him everything.'

'But I couldn't have known, not fully.'

'You knew enough for him to work it out. Jenkins and Mum

being together, how you thought she loved him more than she loved Dad and …'

'What else did I tell him?'

'You told him Jenkins came to the house to visit Mum and the baby. I wasn't there and neither was he.'

'I don't remember it.'

'You saw Mum give Emmaline to Jenkins to hold in his arms, saying she was theirs.'

'I can't have.'

'You said she wasn't Daddy's little girl, that she couldn't be. You were Daddy's little girl.'

I feel sick. I don't want to believe him, but then I hear myself say, clear and low, 'Dominic, what happened then?'

He puts his head in his hands, as if he's in pain, and I'm afraid he won't tell me what he has to say. I plead with him again, 'Dominic, please tell me what happened next.' I can't hide the nervousness in my voice.

He looks up at me, and then his words are spoken in slow motion. 'He had already been drinking. That was why he hit me so hard. He and Mum started roaring at each other again, and he stormed out. Mum was crying. You were too. Then Martin and Stevie called. I brought them up here to the attic. They started slanging the state of me, my face bloated from his fist. I ignored them. I went back downstairs. I took you up to the attic too. I told the boys to stay quiet. We had torches and we were whispering. It felt exciting. You were playing with Sandy. I thought everything would be okay, it would blow over. But then I heard him come home.' Dominic stops talking. He looks like he's in some kind of trance.

'Dominic, what happened when Dad came home?'

My words jolt him back. 'I heard doors slamming, glass smashing.
You started crying. I told you to stay here. Martin and Stevie were
sniggering. They didn't know. None of us could have.'

'Know what, Dominic? Jesus Christ, tell me.'

'I told you to stay with the boys. I went downstairs, and that was
when … I stopped in front of their bedroom door.'

'Why?'

'I was scared. He was so angry. I stood in the doorway, doing
nothing. The same way I had when Alister Becon attacked her. But
this time it wasn't her under attack, it was Emmaline.'

'What are you saying?'

'I saw him. I saw him kill her. He lashed out blindly. The crib fell
over. She hit her head. Mum was screaming, "She's dead! She's dead!
You've killed her!"'

'Oh, God.' I put my hand to my mouth, hardly able to take it in,
but he keeps talking, like I'm not there any more.

'Emmaline looked perfect,' his words are soft, 'there wasn't even a
mark, not at first, but then her eyes rolled into the back of her head,
and then came the …'

'Dominic!' Again I'm screaming. 'What came next?'

'The silence, Clodagh, the long, agonising silence that said
nothing could ever be the same again.'

I stare at him.

'Then I walked away, Clodagh. I came up here. I told the boys
that the baby wasn't well, that they had to go home. You started to
cry because you were scared. I took you to your room, told you to
stay there.' Dominic's eyes lock onto mine.

Everything feels shattered, savaged by memory, shredded, torn
and soiled. My mouth is wide open. I'm finding it hard to breathe,
but Dominic keeps talking. 'I saw him kill her, Clodagh, and I did

nothing.' With that, his tears come, years of guilt heaving with ever
one of them.

'I didn't stay in my room,' I say.

My words surprise him. He stares at me.

'I crossed the landing and opened their bedroom door. Mum wa
standing by the window. Dad had his face in his hands. He was s
upset, but she was angry, and full of hate.' I realise my hands ar
shaking. I hold them together tightly. 'I cut my dolls' hair.'

'What?' He looks confused.

'Afterwards, I cut off Debbie and Sandy's hair with a scissors
I didn't want them to be pretty any more. Mum was pretty, reall
pretty. That was why Keith Jenkins loved her.' I wait before finall
saying, 'Dominic, it wasn't your fault. It wasn't either of our fault.
But even as I say the words, a part of me doubts that they are true
What if I hadn't said what I did? What if I had said nothing?

I feel rage, fear and then uncertainty, until a form of exhaustio
takes hold, as if our past has become bigger than both of us.

'Dominic, you're not well. You can't be, to have done what you'v
done. Now, you need to tell me everything, including why Aliste
Becon expected Martin to come through that door.'

Instead of answering me, he turns the knife in his hand, the blad
glinting, and I wonder for the first time if I will be the next to die.

4 Strand Road, Sandymount

Listen, Maloney, I'm going to phone Kate Pearson now, just in case.'

'Okay, but I'll be giving the instructions.'

O'Connor's voice was sombre as Kate answered his call. 'Kate, how long will it take you to get over here?'

'To Sandymount?'

'We have a possible hostage situation on our hands. I'm working with Maloney from ERU. He's heading this thing up. We already have two sharp-shooters in the premises. We're waiting for them to report back. Once they do, we could be calling in a hostage negotiator. Considering we could be dealing with someone psychotic, it could make a difference if you are on board.'

'But, O'Connor—'

'We're not going to put you at any risk. I know how your involvement in the Devine and Spain murders went badly wrong. We'll set you up with detectives in one of the adjoining buildings. If you're happy to work with the negotiator, your communication will be by audio link. The only people going into seventy-four Strand Road will be the two sharp-shooters already deployed, and the hostage negotiator.'

Kate hesitated. O'Connor kept his silence, not wanting to force her.

'Okay, I'll do it. What else can you tell me?'

'Give me a minute, Kate. Our men are exiting the premises. We'll know more once we talk to them.'

'I'll head over there.'

'No, I'll get an unmarked car to pick you up. You'll make bett
time. The road is closed off at both ends. I'll get a couple of the guy
to meet you at the Ringsend side.'

'Okay.'

∞

Morgan and Quinn exited the premises with the ease and controlle
silence that had been trained into their every muscle. Dressed i
dark navy, with narrow yellow stripes on their upper jacket and low
er sleeves, they held their armed rifles high and tight to the ches
Their expressions gave nothing away. Their task now was to repo
to Maloney on what they had found inside number 74. It was Mo
gan, the older and more experienced of the two, who did most o
the talking.

'We have a man down. Multiple stab wounds to the upper ches
possible drowning. The body is submerged in a bathtub on the secon
floor. The food hatch entry point is still in the kitchen. Intern;
examination shows the shaft reaches up to the top of the building
All areas are clear except for the attic – we heard a minimum of tw
voices from inside, male and female. Main access to the attic is via a
upstairs bedroom at the rear of the building.'

O'Connor asked the first question. 'The man down, Morgar
can you describe him?'

'Victim is short in stature, mid-sixties, moderately overweight
black-grey hair.'

'Becon,' O'Connor muttered, below his breath, more to himsel
than Maloney, or the two men in front of him.

Maloney didn't hesitate with his instructions. 'Morgan, I nee
you both to go back in there. I want you to assume a position at th

eight of the shaft, near the attic joists. Hopefully you'll get a visual
to the attic space from there.'

'We won't need much of an opening, sir.' Again Morgan did the
talking.

Maloney looked at both his men. 'It's an old building. I'm hoping
we'll get lucky.' Morgan and Quinn nodded in acknowledgement,
Maloney continued, 'Quinn, I want you to be the first to take
position up above. When you're *in situ*, and have a clear view and
'm within the upper space of the house, give Morgan the signal. I'll
end the negotiator in once I know you're both in position. The aim
to get out of here with no more loss of life, but if things take a turn,
ring the male down. Is that clear?'

Again they nodded, then turned their backs on Maloney and
O'Connor to re-enter the building.

'Maloney, who are you getting to do the negotiations?'

'Anne Holt. She's already on her way, and she's one hell of a
negotiator. I don't need to tell you, O'Connor, if the guy up there is
psychotic, the odds are stacked against this having a happy ending.'

'Will the sharp-shooters aim to kill?'

'They're armed with SSG69 sniper rifles, and SIG pistols. There's
floating corpse inside, and based on what you've told me, it's not his
rst killing. In such close proximity to the hostage, an injured killer
s dangerous, but we do have options.'

'Exactly what are they?'

'Things changed a couple of years back, when we had a siege,
ot unlike this one.' Maloney paused, but kept his gaze firmly on
umber 74. 'It went badly wrong. There were mental difficulties
nvolved there too. Ever since, our shooters are also armed with non-
ethal weapons, Taser, both close and distant. The cartridges can
each a target twenty feet away. They've twelve-gauge shotguns too,

again non-lethal, but they will take a target down, and keep hir
down long enough for us to get inside and render him harmless. Bu
make no mistake, O'Connor, I'll be making the judgement call, an
I won't be sitting on the fence waiting for any sideshow.'

'Right, I'm going to update Kate Pearson. If anyone can get thi
bloody mess to a safe conclusion, hopefully she and Anne Holt car
I'm going to ring Matthews too. I want to let him know it looks lik
Alister Becon has taken a hit.'

'Okay, let's get this show on the road.' Maloney walked awa
from O'Connor to brief the remainder of his team, including Ann
Holt, who was now waiting at the ERU van, parked further up th
street.

'Matthews, O'Connor here. Are you doing the McKay interview
'No, Quigley and Patterson are.'

'Alister Becon looks to have taken a hit.'

'Shit.'

'I know it's not good news, but tell Quigley and Patterson t
let McKay know the score. It might make him more talkative.
O'Connor hung up and phoned Kate. Everything now depende
on ERU, including Anne Holt, and whatever Kate could bring t
the table.

Clodagh

Dominic tells me to be quiet. He says he needs to work something out. Part of me thinks he wants to talk more, but another part is wondering if even now it's too late for both of us.

Even within this madness, at times I feel it's just him and me, the same way as we have been our whole lives. At others, I feel I'm here with a stranger, someone out of control. He's quiet and still now, but I know he could turn back into the monster I saw earlier, the one who stabbed Alister Becon, the one I'm most afraid of.

I need my brother, and to get him back, I need him to talk. On my hunkers, I move until I'm flat against the attic wall, beneath the eagle, saying, more calmly than I feel, 'Dominic, you were going to tell me why Alister Becon expected Martin.'

'Was I?' He sounds as if he can't remember what happened a few moments earlier, his anger again replaced by confusion.

'Yes, you were.' I try to sound reassuring.

'Your husband is a fool.'

'Please tell me, Dominic.'

He pulls his fingers through his hair, looking down to the floor, a chilled edge returning to his voice as he says, 'Alister had Martin keep an eye on you. He was never fully sure what you'd seen or heard back then, even if you were only a child. People were less guarded around you. You had gaps in memory, and he preferred it that way. This hypnosis business had him spooked. He wasn't worried about either of us witnessing the attack on Mum, that was immaterial to him, but he had played his role in covering up the death of the baby. He couldn't afford to take that risk. Alister Becon doesn't like people or things he can't control.'

'When did you find out Becon had covered it up?' But I can already guess the answer.

'Mum told me before she died. She swore to Becon she would never tell anyone, especially Keith Jenkins. But Becon had come to see her at the hospital. She said she needed me to know.'

'What has Martin to do with it?'

'Money – he was feeling squeezed. Martin was Alister's backup plan.'

'How do you know all this?'

He stares at me, and I'm not sure but I think there are more tears in his eyes.

'I've been watching everyone for months, since Mum became ill, you, Martin, Becon, Jenkins, Gahan, *everyone*.' Again he runs his fingers through his hair, as if to calm himself. 'I haven't been able to sleep. I haven't been able to do anything much, except …'

'Except what, Dominic?

'Sort things out, Clodagh. Mum might have shared some secrets with me, but she never said Dad's death was suicide. Finding that out changed everything. I no longer had any other choice.' He looks at Becon's blood drying into the floorboards. 'That arsehole thought he was using me, telling me how he was the good guy, blaming Jenkins for the affair, and Gahan for the rest of it. He figured I was like the old man, easy pickings. But he didn't know I'd recognised him for the sick fucker he was.'

'But he used you, Dominic.' I know my words are dangerous.

'No, Clodagh, you're wrong. I used him. All along I was using him. One by one, each of them needed to pay the price.'

'But I still don't understand. He expected Martin today? This doesn't make any sense.' Again I know I am walking some kind of treacherous tightrope.

'I made Martin send a text to Alister,' Dominic says slowly. 'He told him you'd worked something out. Alister would have known that meant something dangerous for him. The plan was that if you got too close to something, Martin would make it look like suicide.'

'I don't believe you.'

'Believe what you like. It didn't take much to get Martin talking. He was always a snivelling baby at heart. Clodagh, you were an easy target. It wouldn't have been difficult for him. Goddamn it, you don't think he loved you?'

'No, not any more.' I take a deep breath and exhale.

'Money makes people do lots of things.' The harshness is back in his voice. 'Alister would have found Martin easier than most. I'd have killed him too, only Alister had to be next, then ...' He turns the bloodied knife in his hand.

'Dominic, this is crazy. You need help, do you hear me?' I move closer to him, pulling myself across the floor. 'You're not thinking right – you're distraught.' I'm pleading again.

'I chose her over him, Clodagh. I kept her secrets.'

'But you didn't kill him, Dominic. You weren't the reason Dad died. He killed himself. We were only children.'

'Only children,' he repeats, as if the words are alien to him. 'Everyone killed him, Clodagh.' The crazed look is back in his eyes. 'Mum, Jenkins, Gahan, Becon and finally ...' He stops, as if he has already said too much.

'Dominic, don't shut me out.' My voice is filled with the hurt of being excluded for years, the truth hidden from me for as long as I can remember.

'Don't you see, Clodagh? There is no other way.' He tilts the knife again.

'There is another way, Dominic. There has to be.'

'Clodagh, I have to right the wrong, make amends for it all. I turned my back on him too. I also have to pay the price.' He then points the knife at me. 'I have to cleanse the sins of the past, Clodagh. There is no other way. Our lives have been built on lies and secrets.'

'That's not a reason to die.'

'Isn't it?' He smirks, and again I sense him drifting.

'Afterwards, Clodagh, I became the man she leaned on most.' He looks away from me, again almost in a trance. 'Her trusted ally. I nailed my colours to the mast, taking her side over his. You have no idea, Clodagh, how suffocating it was. Her constantly over-compensating for what had gone before, almost as if keeping our relationship sweet held everything else at bay.'

I can almost taste the anger rising inside me. 'And what about me, Dominic? What did that make me? The fucking traitor?'

He stares at me.

I can hear dogs barking outside.

'She always loved you.' His voice rises above the noise.

'She didn't!' I roar, wanting to hit out at him.

'She loved you. She just couldn't show it.' He lowers the knife. 'She wasn't well after the baby, and then every time she looked at you, she saw …'

'Saw what, Dominic? What did she see?' And again I'm screaming at him.

Our eyes lock.

'She saw her own failings, Clodagh. How one day you might work it all out and know everything.'

'I don't understand. Why would that matter?'

'Don't you see? Mum knew she had me, lock, stock and every fucking smoking barrel, but *you* – she never knew when you would remember. She thought by keeping you at a distance, in a strange way, she was keeping you with her. Better to have a distant daughter than none at all.'

'And the baby, Dominic? Did she blame me for that too – did she?' For the first time since this crazy conversation has begun, my body is shaking uncontrollably, the urge to heave so strong that I don't know if I can keep on talking. 'Tell me!' I roar, 'DID SHE?'

His anger gives way to softness. 'I don't think so.'

But I can't let it go. 'Do you know what I think, Dominic? I think when Emmaline died, I died for her too.' At this, my body gets a new form of stillness. 'It's a funny thing, the truth. When you hear it, really hear it, it's as if a bloody loud silence slots everything into place.'

'It ends here, Clodagh. It ends with the two of us.'

I don't doubt him, and I know what he means, with him looking down at the knife, as if it's an extension of his arm.

'We're damaged goods, Clodagh, both of us.' I see him tense, determination returning to his face. 'Don't worry, it'll be fast. I know you've already suffered enough.'

Whatever anger I had collapses inside me. I'm finding it hard to think, but I latch on to one single thought: I won't abandon my daughter. I won't abandon Ruby. And as Dominic drifts into another half-trance, my eyes are drawn to the narrow strip of daylight beneath the attic door, as I watch it go from light to dark, then light again. The dogs have stopped barking.

Ringsend

Kate sat in the back of the unmarked police car as it sped from the city centre towards Ringsend. Although the siren was blaring for most of the journey, she did her best to keep focused.

On reaching the outskirts of Ringsend, she got the call from O'Connor.

'Kate, it looks like Alister Becon is down. McKay is being questioned by Quigley and Patterson at Harcourt Street. We have a male and a female in the attic space, presumably Dominic Hamilton and Clodagh McKay. The sharp-shooters are resuming a position inside the house, hopefully with a decent view of Hamilton.'

'How was Becon killed?'

'Stabbed. Same MO as the others, so we know our man is armed with a knife. We're not sure of what else. The sharp-shooters reported hearing a male and female voice inside.'

'Assuming it's Clodagh and Dominic Hamilton, considering what Valerie Hamilton said about her husband's state of mind, and what we already know about the killings, he may be at the point of advanced psychosis.'

'Anne Holt will be doing the negotiations. She's here already with the rest of the ERU. Once Maloney gets the all-clear from the sharp-shooter inside the house, we'll be good to go.'

'How long have you been there, O'Connor?'

'Here in Sandymount?'

'Yeah.'

'Three-quarters of an hour. What are you getting at?'

'If he hasn't killed Clodagh yet, it tells us something. Even in a heightened level of psychosis, moods can swing back and forth, one side of the brain looking to dominate. But if he was clear about wanting Clodagh dead, she would be dead by now. Something's stopping him. He may not even be aware of it but he's looking for something.'

'Most hostage-takers usually are, Kate. At the basic level, it's all a form of bloody bargaining.'

'This isn't your standard hostage situation, but no action means something, and that is what we have to work on.'

Kate could see the barriers that closed off Strand Road. Within moments she would be in the thick of it. 'We're just there, O'Connor. I'll see you shortly.'

∞

Kate met Anne Holt and Maloney upstairs at number 75, the adjoining house. The first thing that surprised her was how young Anne Holt was – but she soon realised the young woman beneath the anti-ballistic vest was well able for the job in hand.

'I understand we could be dealing with someone suffering from psychosis.'

'That's correct, Anne. His mental state would be both desperate and volatile.'

'Have you ever been in a hostage situation before, Kate?'

'Not from this standpoint, no.' Kate didn't care to elaborate, and Anne Holt didn't press her on it.

'Kate, all hostage situations are desperate acts. It's the last chance for the taker to gain power. I don't know the exact reasons why Dominic Hamilton is holding his sister, but his objective is important, even if he is psychotic. Once he knows we're here, and he continues with the hostage situation, he will also know that one of the possible outcomes is his own death. He knows he's taking a huge risk, but he feels that he has no choice. In many ways, he's already helpless.'

'I know that, Anne, but as I said to O'Connor and Maloney, his inaction over the short term is positive. Something is holding him back.'

'We apply the Schlossberg theory as the general rule. When the heightened-arousal state of the hostage situation subsides, if the hostage-taker goes past half an hour without killing a hostage, they probably won't kill them.'

'But he's still unaware of anyone else's presence.'

'That's true, Kate, and we do have a man down.'

'Nevertheless, if Clodagh McKay is still alive, we need to find out what's holding him back.'

'I agree.'

'I'm hoping, Anne, that after the attack on Alister Becon, his heightened-arousal state has passed. And if so, mentally, Dominic Hamilton is coming down. He is probably experiencing levels of exhaustion – psychosis and sleep deprivation going hand in hand. The surge of adrenalin he experienced from killing Becon will have depleted his sugar levels. That combined with fatigue will make him more vulnerable. If the negotiations coincide with a more calm and lucid state of mind, we can work with that.'

'Okay, let's get this going.'

∞

With the audio link in place, Kate remained in number 75 as Anne Holt took her position with Maloney and the rest of the ERU team outside. Anne Holt, as the trained hostage negotiator, mentally prepared herself to enter the premises once the sharp-shooters and the on-scene commander gave her the all-clear.

Soon after Anne Holt left number 75 Strand Road, O'Connor joined Kate and the other detectives positioned there. No one spoke, everyone waiting for ERU to make the next move.

Clodagh

Someone is here. Nothing else would explain the change of light at the bottom of the door. Perhaps the neighbours alerted the police, having heard the shouting.

Dominic hasn't said anything for ages, and I'm not sure if this is a good or bad sign. I know that if I make any sudden movements he'll respond. It's as if, in his silence, he's trying to find the energy to make his next move, and I have no idea when or what that will be.

The darts in the old dartboard are too high for me to reach without alerting him, but the more I look at my brother, the torment on his face, the more I wonder if maybe, just maybe, I can pull him back from the brink. If there are others in the house, they're bound to make their presence known soon. That has its own risks. I have no choice but to try to talk to him again. Get him to see some kind of sense.

'Dominic,' I say, as gently as I can. He doesn't look up so I repeat his name, 'Dominic.' This time it registers, although I'm not sure that he knows it's me. His eyes are frantically shifting around the room as if others are here. 'Dominic, it's me, Clodagh.' He stares at me blankly. 'Dominic, you look tired.'

'I am tired.' He looks down at the knife again.

'Dominic, you do know that I love you.'

Again he stares ahead of him.

'You've always taken care of me, Dominic, my big brother.' I keep my tone soft, hoping that somewhere in his mind he can hear me.

'None of that matters, Clodagh, not now.' His voice is chilling.

Again, I hear the dogs barking outside. Although I can't be sure, I think I hear movement beyond the attic walls, as if the noise is coming from the old shaft. I look at Dominic to see if he's noticed it, and as I do, a woman's voice calls from outside the attic door.

'Dominic, my name is Anne Holt. I'm here to help you.'

Her voice isn't threatening, but Dominic panics, jumping up from his resting position.

'Dominic, can you hear me? My name is Anne. I'm here to help you.'

I'm not sure what to do next, so I do nothing.

'Dominic, it's Anne. I can hear movement in there. What's going on? Are you okay?' She sounds sympathetic.

Dominic roars, 'GO TO HELL whoever you are. Keep away from us.'

'Don't worry, Dominic. I'm not coming any closer. I'm sorry if I gave you a fright.'

'FUCK OFF.'

'Dominic, I don't mean to upset you. I'm here to help. You're the one who's in charge here.'

75 Strand Road, Sandymount

Kate could hear Anne Holt's first tentative interactions with Dominic Hamilton, and was imagining how hard it must be to walk willingly into a dangerous situation as Anne had just done. She knew that the first thing she and Anne had to accomplish was to calm the situation. Kate spoke to her through the audio link.

'Anne, right now Dominic Hamilton will be experiencing a high level of panic. It's a time of chaos in his mind. We've shifted the goalposts and he isn't sure where he fits into all this. Well done on the reassurance. Keep the conversation going, one-sided if necessary, repeating a similar mantra.'

Anne's voice remained calm. 'Do you hear me, Dominic? You're the one in charge. I won't come any closer unless you want me to.'

Kate heard a loud thud at what she assumed was the attic door, then a male voice shouting at Anne, 'I'll kill her if you come any closer, I fucking will.'

'Dominic, you have my word that I won't.' Anne's tone was unchanged.

'Anne, keep talking to him, but allow short intervals in between, even if it remains a one-sided conversation. He's still listening. Slowly we'll move it forward to finding out what he really wants.'

'Kate, can you hear me?' Anne murmured, to avoid being heard on the other side of the attic door.

'Yes.'

'I'm going to keep the concentration on Dominic Hamilton. He's the one I'll be empathising with. Right now, the less focus I place on the hostage, the better her chance of survival.'

'Okay, but take it carefully.'

'Dominic, can you hear me? It's Anne again.' This time, there was no response. 'Dominic, I know you've been through a tough time. I can help you if you let me.'

'I don't want your fucking help.'

'You've had to do some difficult things.'

'I did what I had to do. I'm no coward.'

'Of course you're not.' Anne allowed an interval, as Kate suggested. 'Dominic, none of this is your fault. You are not to blame. Nobody is blaming you.'

'Who the fuck are you?' His voice rose again.

'My name is Anne. I'm here with the police. Can we talk face to face?'

'I don't want to talk to you.' This time his tone was less aggressive.

'I understand that, Dominic.' Another interval. 'I appreciate that you're listening to me.' Pause. 'I'm sorry if I took you by surprise.'

'What do you want?'

'I want to help. Are you thirsty, Dominic? If you are, I could try and get you some water.'

'I'm not thirsty.'

'Thanks, Dominic. Thanks for answering me.'

Kate kept silent, allowing Anne to get on with the job she was trained to do. Part of it was the necessity to appear non-hostile, appreciative, and build a rapport to develop trust. Kate also knew Anne was endeavouring to distract Dominic Hamilton, taking the conversation in unrelated directions, asking him if he was thirsty, shaping their interaction, forcing him to think and also to answer.

'You sound tired, Dominic.'

No response.

Kate spoke through the audio link: 'Anne, we both know we're dealing with a Pandora's Box here, but you're doing great. He's starting to calm down. I can hear it in his voice. Don't worry about him not answering you. He's listening, and that's critical right now.'

'Dominic, are you okay?' Anne's voice sounded as calm as her original introduction.

'I don't know.' This time Dominic Hamilton's response was less hostile.

Kate spoke through the audio link again: 'Anne, keep up the empathy. Let him know his wife, Valerie, has been worrying about him.'

'Dominic, it's been tough on you, I know that. Valerie's been worried about you.'

'You spoke to her?'

'She wants you home, Dominic.'

'This has nothing to do with her.' His voice rose.

'I know that. I don't mean to upset you. Valerie cares about you. If you come out, you can talk to her.'

'I'm not coming out …'

Kate spoke again: 'Anne, can you hear me?'

'Yes, Kate.'

'Take your time. He's talking to you now. Speak to him about his not being able to sleep, how much strain that must be placing on him. The longer we keep the conversation going, the better.'

'Dominic, it's Anne again. I know you haven't been well. Not sleeping can put a huge strain on a person.' Again she allowed an interval. 'You must be tired.'

'That doesn't matter. I'm not looking for your sympathy.'

'I know that.' Another interval. 'Dominic, it's going to be okay. I'm here to help.'

'Nobody can help.'

Kate spoke: 'Anne, he's opening up. Even his negative response could be his way of acknowledging your willingness, at the very least, to help. Keep your sentences short, and continue to allow the intervals. If nothing else, maintaining a conversation will tire him more, but we're still on shaky ground. With the pressure he's under and the psychosis, this is hard to call. Focus more on his needs. He's the older sibling in this relationship. Everything about the killings suggests he's been on some kind of mission, taking down people who have hurt his family. We can only assume, with the drowning, that this is all tied into his father's death, but his mother's death is still raw.'

'Okay, Kate. I get you.'

Kate continued: 'He'll feel like he's been carrying a heavy burden. His feelings of isolation must be enormous. You need to acknowledge both those things.'

'Dominic, can you hear me?' Anne's voice was clear and steady.

'What do you want?' A slight tension in his voice.

'I want to help, Dominic.' Another pause. 'You've been carrying a heavy burden on your own. I understand that. You've had to do things that others didn't have to do.'

'What would you know?' He sounded drained.

'I know you're the eldest in the family. That can be tough at times.' Again there was no response, but Anne Holt pushed forward. 'You lost your mother too.'

'Death is part of life.'

'That doesn't mean it isn't hard.' Anne Holt moved closer to the

staircase. 'Dominic, I know you've felt isolated for a long time.' She
let him absorb the affirmation, then said, 'What is it you need? I'll
try and help you.'

'I don't want to feel burdened, not any more.'

'That's okay, Dominic. I understand that.'

'I've been fucking responsible my whole fucking life.'

'I know that too, Dominic, but you don't have to be responsible
now. You can let go. It's okay to let go.'

'You don't understand. Nobody does.'

'I know you don't want to hurt Clodagh, Dominic.' Another
interval. 'You're not a bad man. I know that.'

'Things had to be done. I had no choice …' His voice lowered.

'I know, Dominic,' Anne said softly.

'Anne, it's Kate again. With his psychosis, he could turn at any
point. You need to get him to put down the knife if he still has it.'

'Dominic?'

'What?'

'Do you still have the knife?'

'Yes.'

'Would you put it down for me?'

'I don't know.'

'I want you to get well, Dominic. I want you to get help. If you
could put the knife down on the floor that would be a good thing.'

'I've put it down.'

'Thanks, Dominic. I appreciate that.' Another pause. 'Is Clodagh
okay?'

'She's okay.'

'That's good. Thanks for that, Dominic. I know deep down you
really don't want to hurt her. As I said, I know you're a good person.'

'I've killed people.'

'Dominic, you've been through a lot. You haven't been well. None of this is your fault.' Anne waited, hearing nothing from behind the door.

'Anne, it's Kate – it's a huge thing that he's put the knife down. See if you can get him to talk to you face to face. Keep emphasising that you want to find ways to help him. Remember what he said about being tired of feeling responsible? Work on that. It's the key. We need to take some of the burden off his shoulders. It'll buy us time, and reduce the risk to Clodagh's life.'

Maloney, who had been listening down the audio link, intervened: 'Anne, do as Kate says, continue the empathy. If he does open the door, we'll have made real progress. We're close at hand if you need us.'

'Dominic, are you okay? I'm sorry you've felt so burdened. It must have been hard on you. Sometimes we all have to let go, take the responsibility off our shoulders. You need to get better. You've been unwell. I know that, and everyone who loves you, including Valerie and Clodagh, knows that too. Why don't you open the door, and we can talk face to face?'

'I don't know. I don't know what to do any more.'

'It's difficult, I know, but thanks for answering me, Dominic. You're doing really well. Do you think we could talk face to face? It might be easier that way. You don't have to take all the responsibility. You can let go of it.'

There was no response.

'Dominic, can you hear me?'

Although Kate was in a different house, she might as well have been standing right beside Anne Holt, both of them knowing that there were only two possible outcomes: surrender and arrest, or a tactical assault by the sharp-shooters. 'Anne, can you still hear me?'

'Yes, Kate.'

'You need to become more direct. He still hasn't harmed the hostage, but with his psychosis, he won't remain lucid for much longer. Another large interval, and this could turn bad on us.'

Maloney, who was still listening through the audio link, spoke again. 'Anne, you've heard what Kate has just said. We need to move now. This will go one of two ways, and it's always been something of a long shot. I'm going to put the shooters on alert. If you push it, and his response is not what we're looking for, we'll be going for plan B. Do you hear what I'm saying?'

'I hear you, sir.'

Anne backed away from the staircase, taking up position safely below potential range of gunfire. 'Dominic, you do want me to help you, don't you?' Again she received no response. 'I will help you, Dominic. The two of us will sort through this together. Why don't you send Clodagh out, and the two of us can talk properly?'

'I'm no coward.' His voice was raised and angry.

'I know that, Dominic. Now, send Clodagh to me and we can work things out.'

'Anne?' Maloney's voice both low and stern was on the line. 'The shooters say the knife is still on the ground. Give it one last go. If it doesn't work, we're taking him down.'

Kate spoke next. 'Anne, the last surge of panic, when he realised your presence, will have depleted his sugar levels further. Fatigue and mental exhaustion with the psychosis are also taking their toll. I'm not saying the situation isn't dangerous. But it won't take a lot to weaken him.'

'Sir, did you hear Dr Pearson?'

'I heard her. As I said, give it one last go.'

'Right, sir.'

The next couple of seconds would be critical. It would be either surrender, or Morgan and Quinn would be instructed to fire. Anne Holt continued, 'Dominic, can you hear me? If you send Clodagh out, we can talk.'

'I CAN'T.' Both panic and anger in his voice.

'Dominic, calm down.' Anne had raised her voice marginally for the first time.

'You don't understand. Nobody does. I never wanted any of this, but I had to undo all the wrongs, especially mine.' He was near hysteria.

Anne heard heavy movement from behind the attic door. She guessed he was going for the knife. 'Dominic, it's Anne. What's going on in there?'

Maloney wasted no time. 'We're going less lethal. Take him with the Taser, NOW.'

Anne's question was followed by the roar of multiple shots, reverberating through the building, echoing down the audio link.

It was Anne's voice that Kate heard next. 'Kate, I think he's down. I can hear Clodagh McKay screaming.'

'I can hear her too.'

O'Connor instructed Detective Monroe to remain with Kate, while he and the other detectives stormed out of number 75 to join the ERU team.

Clodagh

When I scream, it sounds like it's coming from a wild and desolate place, the kind of place that brings Hell on earth with it. Anne Holt' voice, from the other side of the attic door, had been my only tentative link to ending this madness, a madness that in its wake brings our whole life, Dominic's and mine, sliding through every part of my mind.

I curl up in the corner, seeing his body fall onto the dried pool that is Alister Becon's blood. I scream again, unsure if he's alive or dead. I crawl over to him and grab hold of his body. He's still breathing. I hear a low, painful moan leave his lips.

There are loud, fast movements coming from behind the attic wall. I can hear people running through the house, strangers. The seconds are fleeting past, but inside this room, it feels as if everything has stopped. I lie beside him, placing my hand on his chest, feeling his heart beat fast, his body like a tightened knot.

As the outside sounds become louder, they seem to become more distant. My voice is barely a whisper as I lean close to his ear, my dry lips feeling the heat from his body. My words sound like the whispers of sea shells. 'Dominic, you don't have to worry any more.'

He tries to speak, but I can barely hear him, his broken words escaping in low gasps, like my memory of the strand, when I tried to hear my father's voice, my feet sinking into the sand, caught in tangled seaweed. I say again, 'Dominic, you're going to be okay.'

When the door bursts open, I don't take my eyes off him. I can feel somebody beside me, a woman bending down. She's telling me ne's going to pull through. I want to believe her more than anything in the whole world.

'We need to get him help, Clodagh. You're going to have to pull back.' I feel her grab my shoulders, tugging me away. Strangers are leaning over his body, shouting at each other. Another of them turns to me, a man. He, too, tells me Dominic will be okay. But none of it is okay. None of it can ever be okay, not ever.

74 Strand Road, Sandymount

The smell of the sea rose up through Kate's nostrils, as a sharp breeze came in from the strand, spattering her face with misty rain. She turned her back to it, and faced O'Connor.

'What now?'

'We'll tidy up here. All in all, things could have turned out a lot worse. It looks like Dominic Hamilton is going to pull through.'

'And what about Clodagh McKay? Is she still inside?'

'Yes. The medics are giving her something to calm her down.'

'Can I talk to her?'

'I don't know, Kate.'

'O'Connor, I'll take it easy. You owe me.'

'All right, but give it a little longer, until ERU are finished. Once I know everything's settled, you can talk to her then.'

'What about you, O'Connor? What next for you?'

He shrugged. 'What has a guy to complain about, standing here by the sea, listening to the sound of the waves in such great company?'

'I never took you for an old romantic.'

'There are lots of things you don't know about me, Kate.'

'O'Connor?'

'Yeah?'

'The other night. I'm glad you told me about what happened. What I mean is, I'm glad you felt you could tell me.'

'It's immaterial now.'

'Will you be talking to Butler?'

'He's next on my to-do list.'

'I see. Well, if there's …'

O'Connor spotted Maloney, who was beckoning to him from the front of the house. As he walked away, he turned back to Kate and said, almost as an afterthought, 'Declan still away, is he?'

'Declan won't be coming back, O'Connor – at least, not to me.'

'I'm sorry, Kate.' A look of awkwardness on O'Connor's face.

'It's all right. It's not your concern.'

He gave her a reassuring smile. 'I doubt that, Kate. You and me, we've been through a lot together.'

'I guess we have.'

Kate waited while he talked to Maloney. It didn't take him long to return.

'Are you ready to talk to Clodagh McKay?'

'As ready as I'll ever be.' With that, the two of them entered number 74 Strand Road.

Harcourt Street Police Station

O'Connor closed the door of Chief Superintendent Butler's office behind him. Martin McKay wouldn't be going anywhere for a while. A heap of fraud and tax evasion charges were mounting by the hour. They'd get the bastard on something. But that was no longer his worry. Walking through the corridors of Harcourt Street station, the closer O'Connor got to the front entrance, the more he felt his past and his present give way to an unknown future.

He hadn't been surprised by the suspension: it was standard – removal from active duties for an unlimited period, pending an internal investigation. But despite knowing this, he had been taken aback by how empty he felt inside. The force had been his whole life. Walking away from it was harder than even he had thought possible.

Out in the daylight, his survival instincts kicked in. He braced himself for the hard path ahead. He drew in a long, deep breath, feeling the cold air of the city hit his lungs, sharp, chilling, amid the noise of heavy traffic and throngs of people. All of which now felt alien to his stationary frame.

'Sometimes you have to stop before you can move forward,' Kate had said to him. Maybe she was right, but that would also require looking back. Not a thought he felt comfortable with. Nor was he looking forward to his empty flat, which he did his level best to get the hell out of most of the time. It held the remnants of what used to be.

If it was only the mess of the cover-up, a one-off bad judgement call, it wouldn't have been so difficult, but O'Connor knew it was more than that. It went right back to the old demons he would now ultimately have to face: the reason he had let that boy off the hook in the first place. He had looked so much like Adam, his son, reminding O'Connor of what a lousy father he had been.

As he walked away from Harcourt Street station, and the life he had known for so long, the prospect of picking up those old pieces filled him with more trepidation than the emptiness.

Clodagh

Sometimes there can be calm after a storm, when your thoughts go to a melancholy place that is not unlike the garden Gerard Hayden brought me to, a safe oasis in the centre of the madness.

That is partly why I find myself back in my old bedroom at Seacrest; my adult body hunkered down as I stare into the small rooms of my old doll's house. Part of me wants to shed tears, but it's too soon for that. Yet another part of me wants to let go. Right now, I am content to be still.

When they took Dominic away, they said I could stay here for a while. I pulled my old doll Sandy with her cropped hair from the wooden crate in the attic. Her sea-blue eyes stared back at me as if to say, it's all over now.

The woman they sent to talk to me was called Kate. I asked her if she had any brothers or sisters, but she said, no, she didn't. It's funny the way all our lives are so different, none of us walking in the same shoes as others.

She asked me about my doll's house and my doll. I told her I had called her Sandy after the strand because of her sea-blue eyes. I had forgotten about that. I told her about Debbie too. How I thought I remembered somebody by that name, someone who was beautiful on the outside but ugly within. It got me thinking about all the other bits I'd forgotten, and how much more will surface over time.

The past cannot hurt you, Gerard Hayden had said, because it has already happened. I now know that isn't true. The past forms you. It can reach out like a giant claw and drag you back into it. I had asked Kate about that too, whether she thought the secrets of the past, the memories locked within our minds, were best left in peace. Her answer surprised me.

'Not knowing can be equally hard,' she said. She looked pensive. I felt she had her own story to tell. Perhaps we all do. She told me she has a patient, a girl close to Ruby in age. She too has memory gaps. Over time Kate hopes all the missing bits will come back. I hope so too. The truth might be harsh, but it is your truth. Without it, like Emma's cracked face, the pieces are all there but so too is the dark.

I talked about the doll's house, and how I remembered calling my doll with the porcelain face after my sister Emmaline, when I knew Mum was bringing her home.

I explained that after the regression I felt I had left my little-girl self behind. That I knew she still needed me. She needed someone to tell her everything would be okay.

'She's still inside you,' Kate had said, 'waiting for you to be okay too.'

I pick up the doll called Sebastian, the one that looked so much like Dominic as a boy. My brother is getting help now, but it's a long road ahead.

I place my hands in every room of the doll's house, touching Ben the brown terrier with the black-and-white-spotted ball in his mouth, the intricate pieces of furniture, the miniature plates and cups, the tiny dressing table with the pretend powder and lipstick, and all the while I'm remembering that little girl. The one who ran away to be alone, away from the loud voices and fear, the one who sought refuge with her dolls, and a life inside the world of a doll's house.

Acknowledgements

Writing a novel is a journey, one that is filled with many hopes and questions. It takes time and the path isn't always clear, but if your story is worth telling, it's worth writing. *The Doll's House* was such a journey, and it wouldn't have happened without the help and encouragement of a great many people.

The first people I want to thank are my family, especially my ever patient husband, Robert, my children, Jennifer, Lorraine and Graham, to whom this book is dedicated, and my granddaughter, Caitriona, who has brought so much joy into all our lives.

I owe a huge debt to everyone directly involved with the creation of this novel, starting with my agent Ger Nichol, of The Book Bureau, who has been there for me every step of the way, the great team at Hachette Books Ireland, especially Ciara Doorley, commissioning editor, who believed so enthusiastically in this story from the beginning, and also thanks to Hazel Orme, copy editor, for her wonderful work on the manuscript.

My research for this novel has taken me to unusual places, from my initial curiosity about hypnosis, to a fascination with memory and how it is created, to finally finding myself sitting having cups of coffee with a hostage negotiator. I want to thank all members of the police who assisted with my research, especially Tom Doyle of Rathfarnham Garda Station and Mary Fitzsimons of the Emergency

Response Unit, who were so generous with their knowledge and experience. Thanks also to Niamh Bonner of SATU, who is part of the first step back for survivors of sexual assaults. I also want to thank Dave Gogan for his keen psychological insight, for lending me even more books on criminal psychology, and for giving me confidence that I was on the right track with some of the facets of this story. I couldn't have written this novel except for all I discovered about hypnosis along the way, and I want to give particular thanks to hypnotherapist, Michael O'Brien, for the many long conversations we had in this regard. I confirm here that any errors or factual deviations made in the writing of this novel are mine and are not attributable to the professionals who assisted in my research.

I would also like to thank my friends, old and new, who have been so encouraging and supportive of me, and to again give thanks to Mary Lavelle, who read the full manuscript at first draft stage. My thanks also to Vanessa O'Loughlin of Inkwell and Writing.ie for her on-going support and energy, the great team at the Irish Writers' Centre, especially Carrie King, June Caldwell and Fergal O'Reilly, South Dublin Libraries, Domitilla Fagan, Patricia Fitzgerald, Caroline Higgins, and Una Phelan, and Emer Cleary of Emu Ink.

A special thanks to the many other groups I've had the pleasure to be part of, Lucan Writers' Group, Platform One, especially Eileen Casey, Irish Crime Writers' Group, the amazing people at the Tyrone Guthrie Artist Retreat, The People's College, with Valerie Sirr, Carousel Creates, with Carolann Copeland, and Seven Towers writing group.

I would also like to thank Gerry Gilvary of ITT, media students, Luke Ryan, Clark Wickstone, Elizabeth Wilson, Dave Barnaville, Colm O Searcoid, Sinead Kelly, Martin Kennedy, Shauna Ryan, and Gemma Butterly for their help during the year. A special thanks to

Danka Lochowicz, for her absolutely brilliant web design, and to my daughter Jennifer Phillips for her wonderful photography over the last twelve months.

Finally, I would like to thank you, my friends, family, colleagues, and readers, who are not mentioned here individually, but who are of the upmost importance to me. I feel privileged to have been gifted with so many wonderful people in my life, and I have been especially moved by the amount of readers making contact to tell me how much they enjoyed *Red Ribbons*. I hope you enjoy this story too.

Reading is so much more than the act of moving from page to page. It's the exploration of new worlds; the pursuit of adventure; the forging of friendships; the breaking of hearts; and the chance to begin to live through a new story each time the first sentence is devoured.

We at Hachette Ireland are very passionate about what we read and what we publish. And we'd love to hear what you think about our books.

If you'd like to let us know, or to find out more about us and our titles, please visit www.hachette.ie or our Facebook page www.facebook.com/hachetteireland or follow us on Twitter @ HachetteIre.